Nichole Severn writes explosi
strong heroines, heroes who d
hell of a lot of guns. She resides with her very supportive and patient husband, as well as her demon spawn, in Utah. When she's not writing, she's constantly injuring herself running, rock climbing, practising yoga and snowboarding. She loves hearing from readers through her website, nicholesevern.com, and on Facebook at nicholesevern

Juno Rushdan is a veteran US Air Force intelligence officer and award-winning author. Her books are action-packed and fast-paced. Critics from *Kirkus Reviews* and *Library Journal* have called her work 'heart-pounding James Bond–ian adventure' that 'will captivate lovers of romantic thrillers.' For a free book, visit her website: junorushdan.com

Also by Nichole Severn

New Mexico Guard Dogs

K-9 Security
K-9 Detection
K-9 Shield

Defenders of Battle Mountain

Dead Giveaway
Dead on Arrival
Presumed Dead
Over Her Dead Body
Dead Again

Also by Juno Rushdan

Cowboy State Lawmen: Duty and Honor

Wyoming Mountain Investigation
Wyoming Ranch Justice
Wyoming Undercover Escape
Wyoming Christmas Conspiracy

Cowboy State Lawmen

Wyoming Mountain Hostage
Wyoming Mountain Murder
Wyoming Cowboy Undercover
Wyoming Mountain Cold Case

K-9 GUARDIANS

NICHOLE SEVERN

WYOMING DOUBLE JEOPARDY

JUNO RUSHDAN

MILLS & BOON

First Published in Great Britain 2025
by Mills & Boon, an imprint of HarperCollins*Publishers* Ltd
1 London Bridge Street, London, SE1 9GF

www.harpercollins.co.uk

HarperCollins*Publishers*
Macken House, 39/40 Mayor Street Upper,
Dublin 1, D01 C9W8, Ireland

ISBN: 978-0-263-39703-1

0325

This book contains FSC™ certified paper and other controlled sources to ensure responsible forest management.

For more information visit: www.harpercollins.co.uk/green

Printed and Bound in the UK using 100% Renewable Electricity at
CPI Group (UK) Ltd, Croydon, CR0 4YY

K-9 GUARDIANS

NICHOLE SEVERN

To all the pups out there. You will be mine.

Chapter One

They were coming.

Scarlett Beam stared at the security feed longer than she should have. Seconds ticked off one by one, putting everyone in this building in more danger the longer she refused to move. She had to be sure. To confirm she wasn't seeing things coming off a twenty-four-hour shift.

Dust kicked up in front of the perimeter cameras and blocked out early morning sun coming up over the cliffs to the west. "Don't make me do this," she said to herself.

She couldn't make the call until she had visual confirmation. Her hand hovered over the alarm she'd hand-wired throughout the building. One press. That was all it would take to start an outright war. She licked at dry lips.

The dust cleared.

Revealing four fully loaded—and most likely bulletproof—SUVs. Coming straight at Socorro's headquarters. Every cell in her body spiked with battle-ready tension.

Sangre por Sangre had crossed the line.

Scarlett slammed her hand down on the alarm. Ear-piercing shrieks urged operatives into action. She backed away from the security console built with her own two hands and reached for her sidearm. Compressing the release, she caught the magazine and inventoried the rounds stacked inside as she headed into the corridor. Low shouts echoed off black walls, tile, artwork and ceilings and drove her toward the armory.

It shouldn't have come to this. She thought they'd have more time.

Socorro Security's orders to dismantle the most bloodthirsty drug cartel in New Mexico had come straight from the Pentagon. A year of intelligence gathering, close calls and surveillance hadn't come close to an attack like this. Each organization knew the danger of provoking the other until the time was right. Seemed Sangre por Sangre had gotten tired of waiting.

Movement registered ahead as Socorro's counterterrorism agent dashed ahead of her. Two other operatives followed after as she rounded into the armory. They were private military contractors. Trained in war, weapons, strategy, combat and intelligence gathering throughout their military careers. Each of them moved with efficiency as they pulled high-powered rifles from mounts and stashed extra ammunition in their vests.

"What do we got, Scarlett?" Granger Morais holstered a backup pistol at his ankle. The former counterterrorism agent knew all about surprise attacks, having worked the investigation of 9/11 and the ambush on the American consulate in Benghazi. If they were going to get out of this alive, it would be because of him.

"Four vehicles, upgraded, one mile out. I'm not sure how many hostiles inside. Assume your rounds won't pierce the bodies or windows given Jones's run-in a couple weeks ago." Socorro's combat coordinator had barely survived the encounter as he'd tried to protect a war correspondent who'd gotten herself in the cartel's crosshairs. Scarlett strapped into her Kevlar as the tick of nails grew in intensity from the corridor. She really needed to trim those.

Competing *growls* told her the vet had sent out Hans and

Gruber to back Scarlett up. The Dobermans charged into the armory, most likely having sniffed out her scent, and circled in tight rotations around her legs. The K9s had come from the same litter—brother and sister—and had learned to stick to Scarlett's every order since she signed on with the company. There wasn't anyone else she'd want at her side once they headed out into this mess.

"Damn it. They're getting ballsy. I'll give them that." Granger sheathed an oversize blade into the holster along his thigh. No matter the situation, he'd be prepared. That was what made him one of the best. What made them all the best. "All right. Cash, you and Jocelyn take the high ground. I want as many targets in your scopes as you can manage in case this goes sideways. Scarlett, you're with me in the welcome party. Bring the twins. They look like they haven't bit anyone in a while."

Cash Meyers—the operative charged with predicting the cartel's moves before Sangre por Sangre made them—dragged two heavy-duty cases from the steel shelf at the back of the room and handed one off to his equally experienced partner, Jocelyn Carville. "We need to alert Chief Halsey and the rest of Alpine Valley the cartel is in the area. Make sure all civilians shelter in place until the threat has passed."

"The alert was sent out the moment I hit the alarm. I'm sure Alpine Valley PD is already issuing the order." Because that was their job. To protect those who couldn't protect themselves. It was why Scarlett had signed on with Socorro in the first place. She secured her sidearm, hand pressed along the grip. It'd been a long time since she'd had to unholster her weapon, and that same dread that accompanied the last time infiltrated her focus.

"Good. Then let's move." Granger took the lead, with Cash

and Jocelyn splitting off with their rifles slung over their backs into a separate corridor.

Hans and Gruber kept on her heels as they weaved through the maze meant to confuse and disorient unwelcome visitors. Though Scarlett had done everything in her power as Socorro's security expert to ensure that never happened. Her gaze cut to the space where the ceiling met the wall, where she'd hidden the backup plan that would even any score should her team find themselves cornered.

Speckles of dust glittered in front of her face as she and Granger cut through the building's front lobby and toward the double glass doors. Socorro's headquarters had been set into the side of a mountain range in the middle of the New Mexico desert. Why the structure had a lobby at all—as though they were expecting visitors or potential clients—had never made sense to her. But gratitude shifted through her at the added space between her and the outside world.

Granger paused before hitting the door release, that unkempt swatch of facial hair hiding any tell around his mouth. "You good?"

No. She wasn't. Injuries from two weeks ago still pulsed, suffered from taking on a cartel member much stronger and much bigger than her in an attempt to save Jones's journalist. But she wasn't about to back down. She hadn't before. She wouldn't start now. "I have one of Jocelyn's oatmeal bakes in the microwave. Let's get this over with so I can eat."

Granger's laugh took a bit of the uncertainty out of her nerves. He pushed through the doors and out into the open.

They moved as one, weapons raised as four SUVs skidded to a stop a mere twenty yards from the building. Sangre por Sangre had never before attempted to get this close.

Which meant something was very, very wrong.

Scarlett clocked Cash and Jocelyn taking up position on

the roof, each tucked into their own corner for the best advantage. She and Granger were covered. No matter what happened next, her team had her back. And the Dobermans would eat anyone alive who tried to take her down. Sweat secreted around her grip and threatened to loosen her calm.

"Steady." Granger leveled his chin parallel to the ground with all the confidence and authority she didn't have. "We're not going to be the ones to shoot first. Understand? Anything that happens today, we want them to make the first move. That way, any retaliation is sanctioned by the Pentagon."

"Understood." Her voice shook on that single word, giving away the earthquake shuddering inside. This was her job. What she'd trained for. She was good at this, yet there was still a small part of her that wished she was stronger. More in control. Made better choices. Coming to Socorro—supporting her team, taking responsibility for others—was supposed to be her way to make up for the past, but she still couldn't shake the tremor in her hand.

Granger pulled up short. Waiting. The message was clear. One wrong move, and Socorro would do whatever it took to defend their territory.

Only the cartel didn't make that move.

Seconds split into minutes, into what felt like an hour, as the rising sun glinted off the SUV windshields.

Impatience undermined her forced calm. She really did have an oatmeal bake in the microwave, and her stomach wasn't too proud to admit its desperation for calories. "What are they waiting for?"

"I don't know." That wasn't like Granger. Certainty had always been one of the qualities she most admired the few times they'd been partnered on an assignment together, but this was something neither of them had experienced. Sangre por Sangre had always moved with compulsion rather than strategy. This…this was something else.

The hatch of one SUV raised behind the lead SUV. A dark, heavy tarp rolled out of the cargo area and hit the ground. Dust exploded from the impact and punctured Scarlett's resolve. She took a step forward. The Dobermans were ready to follow, but one throaty warning from Granger pulled them all up short. "What is that?" she asked.

The answer was already shoving to the front of her mind. Cartels like Sangre por Sangre lived for theatrics. Tires filled with accelerant and set on fire draped around victims' necks, raids on innocent towns, underage recruits, bombings of high-level law enforcement officers, soccer balls packed with nitroglycerin that exploded on impact in civilian parks. More recently, the abduction and torture of a war correspondent who'd seen too much.

The cartel's MO was bloody and violent and usually followed by weeks of media coverage. Sangre por Sangre's leadership wanted their name to be known, to be feared. It was domination, manipulation and control in the purest form. Because as long as the general public feared them, there was no one brave enough to stand up to fight them.

But Scarlett was. She had to be.

Engines caught, one after the other. Daytime headlights lit up as the SUVs backed away from the package and retreated. Billows of dirt scattered into the air, surely making it hard for Cash and Jocelyn to keep the targets in their sights.

Scarlett stared at the tarp. Willed it to move.

"Wait." Granger hugged his rifle close to his chest. The wear in his face was more evident than it'd ever been before. It was as though he'd aged a decade in the span of ten minutes.

This job… It was getting to him. To all of them. The constant threats, the need to be in the center of the action, the physical and mental scars that came with fighting an enemy a whole hell of a lot stronger and more violent than you. Who gained pleasure from hurting the very people you swore to protect. All she and Socorro had done was wait. And now the cartel had the upper hand.

"No. I'm tired of waiting." Scarlett took that first step, breaking Granger's order. Then another. She picked up the pace to a jog, then a flat-out sprint as she closed the distance between her and the elongated shape under the tarp. Her muscles ached as she pulled to a stop a few feet away.

Hans and Gruber dashed ahead, circling the package. A corner lifted on a dry breeze and gave her the first glimpse of what was inside.

A human hand.

She captured the tarp on the next gust and ripped it back as Granger stepped into her peripheral vision. But all Scarlett had attention for was the blade stabbed through a law enforcement shield and into the body's chest. Her stomach knotted tight. "He's a DEA agent."

HIS PARTNER WAS DEAD.

King Elsher stared down at the body, not really seeing the man unmoving on the examination table. Adam had gone missing three days ago. No activity on his credit cards. No outgoing calls from his cell phone. It was as though his best friend and partner of three years had up and vanished.

Only that wasn't true, was it?

Sangre por Sangre had finally found a way to get their message to King. Though why they'd delivered it to a private military contractor's doorstep, he had no idea.

The DNA, dental records and fingerprints all lined up. There was no denying his partner was the one lying here in the middle of the Alpine Valley morgue.

Cold air tightened the tendons in King's hand, making them ache. A blue papery sheet hid the stab wound centered in Adam's chest. Two inches in length, a few centimeters wide. Photos taken from the scene where his partner's body had been dumped showed the blade had gone through Adam's badge. Something that would've taken a lot more force than your average stabbing. This had been methodical. Purposeful, even.

"Do you have any questions, Agent Elsher?" The medical examiner—a guy who looked on the verge of retirement if it weren't for the fact he probably didn't have a cent to his name—stuffed thin hands into his white lab coat. Round wire-framed glasses slid down a beak-like nose, and the examiner scrunched up his face to put them back in place. Practiced. This was a guy used to multitasking when his hands were busy.

"Who found him?" That wasn't what he meant to ask. King had wanted to know if his partner had suffered. If he bled out in a slow crawl or if the blade did the job quickly.

But he already had the answer. Cartels like Sangre por Sangre—viruses that had no care for their hosts and fought against every vaccine in its path—didn't believe in mercy. They would've ensured Adam knew what was happening, felt it. For as long as possible.

The pathologist broke his statue-like observation and reached for a clipboard off to the side of the examination table. He flipped through a few pages. "There's a Scarlett Beam listed in the report. One of those private military contractors up at Socorro Security. I don't see any contact information, but I imagine you and the DEA know how to get in touch with her."

The DEA. Right. Because this was now an official investigation. Everything King had done to find a way into the cartel would come to light. There was no more hiding. No more unofficial requests or surveillance. No more covering his personal mission to dismantle the cartel on his own. Adam's case was about to expose him in every way. Had that been Sangre por Sangre's plan? To find a way to take King off the board? Hell. It would work. Unless…

Socorro and private military contractors like them had their own set of rules. They didn't answer to anyone but the Pentagon. The past few weeks had proven that with coverage of a New Mexico state senator accused of using his own resources to render Socorro's federal contract void, claiming the company was intentionally letting Sangre por Sangre increase in size and strength for the sole purpose of keeping operatives employed. The accusation lost its merit when a journalist widely exposed the senator for working with the cartel to achieve his goals.

If King played his cards right, Socorro could legitimize his investigation. Assuming Ivy Bardot and her operatives wanted to know who'd ordered the murder of a DEA agent as much as he did. Which, based off the reports he'd read on the company's dealings with the cartel, collaboration between their agencies was looking like a good option.

King scrubbed a hand down his face, taking in the dry skin around Adam's eyes, the darker coloring of a bruise settling along his partner's jaw. No. Sangre por Sangre didn't get to slink back into the shadows and use his partner as an example. Adam deserved better. His family deserved better. And King was going to make the people who'd done this paid. Starting with finding Scarlett Beam. "Thanks, Doc. I'll be in touch."

He shoved through the double freezer-like doors separating the morgue from the rest of the building and hit something solid on the other side. Red hair and a whole lot of tactical gear consumed his attention as the woman fell back from the impact.

King shot his hand out, catching hers to soften the blow. But the weight of her gear dragged him down with her. They landed on the tile floor with a smack. Pain ignited into his palm and through his wrist as he ended up pinning her against the floor. His breath shot free from his chest. "Oh, hell. I'm sorry. I didn't realize there was anyone of the other side of the door."

"You certainly know how to make an exit." She grabbed for the back of her head, pulling her hand back as though looking for blood. Three lines cut across the bridge of her nose in a wince. Right before she set intensely clear eyes on him. "You're welcome to get off of me anytime."

"Oh, right." King shoved to stand. Heat flared into his neck as he replayed the past few seconds over in his head. Nope. There was no rewriting this. No matter how many different ways he imagined it. Offering his hand to help her stand, he threaded the other through his hair. "Didn't realize the zombie apocalypse was already here. I should've come more prepared."

She didn't bother taking his hand as she got to her feet. Recentering her vest, she checked to ensure her sidearm was still holstered. A SIG Sauer. Preferred military issue. Instinct had him filling in the blanks. Without any military bases this far into the desert, there was only one conclusion to come to. She worked for Socorro Security.

Wide almond-shaped eyes lined with black and framed by perfectly shaped eyebrows landed on him. "Sorry?"

"Your gear. The morgue." King hiked a thumb over his shoulder toward the swinging doors he'd effectively used to ruin her day. "This is as good a place as any to make sure there aren't any walking dead wandering around." Another wave of embarrassment undermined his social skills. King offered his hand. "Agent King Elsher. DEA."

She took his hand. Not at all as soft as he'd expected. As though she spent every day in the field rather than protected by shiny glass bulletproof windows. "Scarlett Beam. Socorro. And I figure it's better to be constantly alert for the zombie apocalypse rather than find myself in the middle of an ambush."

His laugh took him by surprise. A woman after his own heart.

"I take it you're here about the agent the cartel dropped off at my doorstep this morning," she said.

Tightness he'd always associated with the excitement of a lead knotted behind his sternum. Followed quickly by the dread pooling at the base of his spine. King released her hand as the latter won out. Reality punctured through the ignorance of the past few minutes. Hell. What was he going to tell his son Julien about today? How was a ten-year-old supposed to deal with the fact Adam wasn't going to be there anymore? "He was my partner. His name was Adam. Adam Dunkeld."

"I'm sorry, Agent Elsher." Sincerity laced the low register of her voice, and King suddenly had the thought of what his name would sound like on her lips. Which letter she would enunciate over all the others. "I'm sure you've read my statement Alpine Valley PD took at the scene. I'm here to check in with the medical examiner about any developments, but I'm happy to take a few minutes to answer any questions you might have."

"You're working the investigation." This was what he needed. What would save him in the end. Partnering with Scarlett could exonerate him in more ways than one. Could help him keep his job. And, hell, he needed this job. Suddenly finding himself a father of a ten-year-old kid he hadn't even known existed until two months ago came with a weight he hadn't expected. Financially, mentally, emotionally. He was still sorting through the responsibilities of being a father and how to balance his job with the first taste of a personal life. Working cases for the DEA—working to bring down the evil that threatened people's futures, like his son's—drove him to be the man he was. The kind of man Adam had been.

"No. There is no investigation. At least, not from my end. Socorro is a lot of things, but murder falls to local police and federal agencies." A shift in her weight told him how uncomfortable she was one-on-one. The kind of steel it took to be in the middle of the action—one that couldn't ever be forged on the sidelines—didn't like to stand still.

They were similar in that respect. He'd always been more inclined to get his hands dirty rather than push paperwork. Though now that he was approaching forty, past fractures and aches he'd acquired in the field took a bit longer to shake off.

"I just wanted…" She paused. "I wanted to know who he was. See how I could help the case."

She was right about the investigation. The DEA would partner with local police to stay up to date on Adam's murder, but ultimately, Alpine Valley PD would make every call and run every lead. Didn't matter that it was a federal agent who'd landed on the other side of these double doors. Seemed King had jumped the gun assuming Socorro would want in on the action. "I appreciate it."

"Did he have a family? Anyone waiting for him to come home?" Scarlett asked.

King had the urge to run for the door. To put as much distance between him and this place as he could. But running had never solved anything. And damn it, he was the reason Adam had been abducted and murdered in the first place. He owed his partner this. "Yeah. A wife, couple of kids, another one on the way."

"The medical examiner usually contacts next of kin." Scarlett nodded toward the big doors that'd taken her down. "But that's why you're here, isn't it? You want to be the one to tell them what happened. So you asked the ME to hold off on the notification."

How had she read him so easily? As though they'd known each other longer than a tackle to the floor and a potential concussion. "I was his partner," he said again.

"I understand," she said. "I've been where you are. Lost people I cared about."

He had to do this. For Adam. For himself. Hell, for his son's future where the cartel didn't haunt their dreams. And there was only one way to do it. Through Socorro.

King closed the distance between them, lowering his voice. "Then you know I'm going to do whatever it takes to find the person who stabbed him. Official or not."

She held her ground. Not the least bit intimidated by his intentions. A hint of curiosity filtered into her eyes. "All right, Agent Elsher. In that case, what can Socorro do for you?"

Chapter Two

She was going to catch hell for this.

Socorro was under scrutiny. Not only because of the past few weeks of media coverage that exposed a senator with a personal vendetta against her and her team but from the towns impacted by a military contractor's presence. Seemed every move Socorro made to save lives put others in more danger by antagonizing the cartel.

But Scarlett believed in the work. In keeping Sangre por Sangre and organizations like it from swallowing this state whole. It was because of her and her team that the fire hadn't burned out of control.

Picketers had set up beneath pop-up canopies of varying colors outside of Socorro's headquarters. She spotted them even this far out, and her grip tightened on the steering wheel as they carved along the one-lane dirt road leading straight home. Protestors wanted Socorro out of New Mexico. Convinced Socorro had brought the cartel straight to their doorstep, but the truth was, Sangre por Sangre had been there all along. Waiting. Preying on the innocent. Biding their time to make their moves from the dark. Socorro had only exposed them for what they really were. A sleeping disease no one could diagnose until it was too late.

Headquarters itself looked as though it'd come from space.

All sharp corners, dark windows and mystery. At any moment, a large metal ramp could descend to reveal the alien occupants inside.

"Didn't realize you guys liked to throw parties." Agent Elsher—King—leaned forward in the front seat. She'd confirmed his credentials by cloning his phone to hers. Not exactly legal, considering he was a federal agent of the highest order, but she wasn't going to use the data against him. King Elsher, thirty-eight, served with the DEA for the past six years. Former cop from Seattle. Not a whole lot of activity in recent calls, but there'd been quite a change in his expenses over the past few months. A large increase in spending without anything to show for it. At least, not yet.

Something she'd have to dig into deeper when she had a few minutes to herself. Because that was where it started. Where the cartel liked to add pressure. It'd happened too many times than she wanted to count. Financials were the easiest way to corrupt even the best officers and agents. She once fought to give most people the benefit of the doubt, but she'd been burned one too many times.

"And here I'm just now finding out I wasn't invited," he said.

She tried to stop her mouth from hiking at one corner into a smile, but there was no stopping it. Despite her personal suspicions and need to unearth every small detail of a person's life before she trusted them, King was easy to talk to. Didn't hurt that they shared that same sarcastic and detached sense of humor, either. Like seeking like, and all that brain science. "Oh, yeah. It's a rager. Been going for weeks with no end in sight. I'm sure they wouldn't mind if you joined. They've been recruiting as many as they can into the We Hate Socorro fan club."

"The people here are really pissed, aren't they?" King distanced himself away from the window as Scarlett slowed to break through the growing crowd.

"They're scared. And with good reason. Seems every mission we carry out against Sangre por Sangre is returned tenfold," she said. "Only we're not the only ones who reap the consequences."

The herd had moved to stop her from entering the parking garage. Two operatives—she recognized Jones and Granger—took positions on either side of the entrance to ensure trespassers couldn't slip in unnoticed. Her teammates faced off with the verbal assaults without so much as responding.

Someone hit their hand against the back window of Scarlett's SUV. Then another. Each punctured deep through her nervous system and spiked her heart rate.

Posters with crude writing demanded Socorro leave while others threatened individual agents. Since the senator's accusations two weeks ago, every one of these people had taken up the mantle to protect themselves the best way they could. No matter how illogical their strategy.

"But fear can be far more dangerous than any perceived threat," Scarlett said.

King didn't have an answer to that.

Scarlett heaved a sigh of relief as she maneuvered the SUV down into the belly of the garage. Darkness slipped over the windshield, suddenly making the cabin that much more intimate. Without her full vision, her senses picked up on other things. Like how King had set his arm on the center console dividing their seats. Even the slight hint of dirt and cologne she'd gotten a lungful of when he'd fallen on top of her in the morgue seemed more intense. Not entirely unpleasant.

No. Wait. That might be coming from her vest after he tackled her.

"You sure you still want to get involved with Socorro?"

She pulled the vehicle in front of the elevators and cut the engine. Shouldering out of the SUV, she hit the pavement and strode to the keypad she had personally upgraded as soon as the picketers set up shop outside. The garage door rolled to a close at the head of the ramp, both of her teammates now inside. "We're not exactly popular right now. Could kick back onto you and the DEA."

King met her at the keypad, the tendons linked between his neck and shoulders strung tight. She'd talked with him long enough to understand he was in unknown territory, putting his career on the line. Why else would he turn to Socorro rather than the DEA? "I don't have any other choice."

This wasn't about competing with local law enforcement for jurisdiction over his partner's investigation. There was something more he wasn't telling her. Something only she could give him. Hesitation closed in around her throat. She'd been used once before. She wasn't eager to experience it a second time. Scarlett pressed her hand onto the print reader. The elevators engaged, their polished shiny silver doors parting down the middle. She motioned him inside the car. "After you."

They took the elevator to the fourth floor and stepped out into a cavern of black. The cameras she'd installed in every corner catalogued more than their faces. Her top-of-the-line security analyzed body heat, a person's walk and homed in on any weapons they might be carrying. Which, around her, was usually a lot. Ivy Bardot would know they were coming. There wasn't a single detail that woman missed inside this building or out.

"You have to give me the number of your decorator." King seemed to be taking everything in but most especially the locations of each of her cameras and which turns they made away from the elevators. Planning for an escape. Just as she would. "I never thought black on black could be so…"

"Absurd? Yeah, me neither. At least not until I moved in here." Scarlett guided him around one corner and toward the penthouse office at the end of the corridor.

It was odd, having someone to talk to while she walked these halls. Like she'd invited King into her personal space. Every inch of these walls had felt her touch as she ensured nothing could hurt her and her team. She was the only one who preferred to stay in the building, out of sight. It was where she did her best work.

"Operatives live here." A hint of disbelief crept into his voice, and it was under these too-bright florescent lights that Scarlett finally got a good look at King Elsher. Not encumbered by a possible concussion or the limited view in the SUV.

Lean muscle banded around his neck and sprawled down into his chest. He took care of himself, that much was clear. His T-shirt—far more worn than she would have expected—kept the last few remnants of a design over his heart. But whether he wore it for its personal connection or because he couldn't afford anything newer, she didn't know. That was where an audit of his finances would come in handy. Light-colored hair had been closely shaved up the sides of his head, leaving a mop of controlled curls at the top. He'd retained a sense of boyishness in his features, soft in some areas. Around his mouth, for example. But experience had hardened the skin and shape of his eyes.

"Voluntarily?" he asked.

"Makes the most sense for us. My team takes shifts where we're on call twenty-four-seven. So we each have a bedroom with a connected bathroom, we share a communal kitchen. Though one of my teammates will gut you with a whisk if you try to mess anything up in there and probably smile while doing it. We have a theater room for downtime, an on-call physician in case of emergency, a gym with every machine known to man and a food delivery service. Even a vet who takes care of our K9s. We have everything we need." Scarlett heard the pride in her own voice. Out of all the places she could've ended up after her last tour, Socorro was the only one that'd thrown her a lifeline. For her, this was more than she deserved. "We're all former military. We like to be ready when we're needed."

"So what you're saying is, you live inside your own end-of-the-world bunker, and you're preparing to take over the world without ever having to leave." King nodded in appreciation. "I like it."

"Stick around long enough, I'll introduce you to Hans and Gruber." She shoved through the conference room door, holding it open for him over the threshold.

Confusion warped those handsome features. He lowered his voice. "Is that code for…you know." He nodded to her chest. "Because I should tell you I'm not really in a position for a relationship right now. My partner was just found murdered, and—"

"Agent Elsher." Ivy Bardot stepped out from behind the conference room table. "As interesting as your relationship status is, I think there are more important topics we should discuss."

Granger's failed attempt to keep his laugh to himself filled the room.

Scarlett couldn't stop the appreciation for this moment or the deep flush of embarrassment coloring King's neck and face as he dared a step into the conference room. She was going to remember him. For a long time. She let the door automatically close behind them. "King, meet the founder and

CEO of Socorro. Ivy Bardot. And this is Granger Morais, our resident counterterrorism expert."

"Why do I suddenly feel like I'm being brought into the principal's office?" King nodded at each in turn instead of extending his hand. He seemed to memorize everything about this room and the people in it.

"Because you know as well as we do, you're not supposed to be here, are you, Agent Elsher?" Ivy took her position at the head of the table and motioned for King to take a seat. An offer he didn't accept. "You and your team work cartel cases from a drug standpoint. You don't get involved in homicide investigations, even those of your agents. Which means the DEA doesn't know you're here."

Scarlett battled the dread pooling at the base of her spine.

"You're right. My superiors have no idea I'm here," King said. "I came because I've been investigating a Sangre por Sangre lieutenant for the past eight months. Off the record and with DEA resources. Now that investigation has gotten my partner killed."

HIS CAREER—his whole life and that of his son's—was suddenly in someone else's hands. King didn't like the idea of not being able to choose his own path.

The pressure of those seconds as Socorro's founder stared back at him, unblinking, felt as though he were right back in the moment when a social worker had showed up on his doorstep and dropped off a ten-year-old kid King hadn't known existed.

Then again, he'd been the one to bring himself to this point. In both scenarios.

He'd been the one to go home with a woman he barely knew for more than a couple hours a little over a decade ago. It'd been mutual, a way for him and a visiting ATF agent he'd been partnered with during an investigation to blow off some steam, and he hadn't regretted that choice for a single moment. Until two months ago. Now he had Julien, and he didn't know how to take care of a kid, but they were trying to make it work. Little by little. Day by day. Fruit snack by fruit snack.

"Will you help me?" Because Socorro was the only thing that could save him now. This group of military contractors who seemed to trust each other more than King even trusted himself. He had nowhere else to go. No one who could justify his actions of the past eight months of looking into Sangre por Sangre unsanctioned. And the minute he was exposed, he'd lose everything. He'd be arrested and charged. His career would be over. The state would take his son.

A burning lodged in his chest at the mere thought. King wasn't going to let that happen.

Awareness spiked as Scarlett's warmth seeped into his arm. A trick. Experience told him it was just a game his mind was trying to play on him, a way to connect with the very people who could dismantle his life. But a part of him wanted that sincerity she seemed to put into every word and every expression to be true.

"You want Socorro to corroborate your unsanctioned investigation into the cartel." Ivy Bardot lived up to her reputation. Smarter than those bureaucrats on Capitol Hill wanted her to be and definitely out of their league. She wasn't just playing the game. She was calling the shots, and the federal government would only take so many commands before turning to bite the hand that fed them cartels like Sangre por Sangre. "Who is your target?"

Hope jumped in his chest where it had no right to land. "Hernando Muñoz."

"We know the name. Intel says he took a hard leap to the top of the cartel's hierarchy once the Big Guy's only son was found with a bullet between the eyes. Making quite a name for himself, too. Violently." Morais—the counterterrorism agent—set his elbows on the conference table, a quiet intensity churning in the space between them. As though waiting for the perfect time to ambush. "Guy's a thug. Hangs out with a trusted group of cartel members, but we've never been able to link him to any of the drug activity in the area. Any business we suspect he's involved in is divided between his crew. Totally hands-off. Our team's got surveillance, but all we've managed to gather is he likes takeout almost every night of the week, and he buys his wife a lot of flowers. So I'm curious. What do you have on him?"

"Nothing." King smothered the hope he'd stupidly allowed himself to feel. "All I've got is rumors Muñoz is stirring up trouble from within. Getting ready for a takeover. And you're right. He's careful, and none of his crew is willing to talk. He makes sure he never touches the money that comes his way from his guys working corners, but I don't care about the drugs or what kind of pies he's got his fingers in on the cartel's behalf. I have reason to believe he ordered the murder of an ATF agent who was getting too close to his operation two months ago. The investigators couldn't come up with anything conclusive, but I know Muñoz is involved. Just like I know he's responsible for Adam's murder." His tongue felt too big for his mouth as his personal life bled into his professional. "She was a good agent. And a good mom."

"You knew her." Scarlett's voice eased through him as slick as chocolate syrup.

There it was again. That uncanny ability she had to practically read his mind. King didn't have the guts to face her head-on, not trusting his ability to keep his emotions capped right then. "When it comes to Sangre por Sangre, we all know someone who's been hurt."

That was starting to look like his own personal motto.

The knot in his gut tightened as Ivy Bardot studied him for a series of breaths. Leaning back in her chair, Socorro's founder shoved to stand. "Send me your investigation notes. I want to know every detail of your operation, what resources you've used and what you have on Muñoz. We can't step on law enforcement's toes during your partner's homicide investigation, but if you're right about the lieutenant's intentions and what he's done, we'll need to put together a strategy. One that makes it look like you've been working with Socorro these past two months."

King barely had the sense to take his next breath.

"Scarlett, get with Agent Elsher and familiarize yourself with the ATF agent's murder. The case is closed, so you shouldn't have any pushback from police. Reach out to Chief Halsey from Alpine Valley PD, if needed, and bring me something concrete we can use to reopen the case and connect it with Adam Dunkeld's," Ivy said. "Granger, I want up-to-date information from the surveillance team. Patterns, logs, movements, identities of Muñoz's crew and everything you have on the wife. All of it."

Time seemed to speed up.

"You're going to corroborate my investigation," King said. "Why?"

The question seemed to slow down Socorro's founder. Something he was sure she wasn't used to. "Because I don't want it to be true, Agent Elsher. I don't want to believe that when it comes to Sangre por Sangre and cartels like it that we all know someone who's been hurt. Because if that's the case, then Socorro hasn't been doing its job, and innocent lives have been sacrificed for nothing."

He didn't know what to say to that. What to think. To the point, King didn't even bother getting out of Ivy Bardot's way as she maneuvered around him and shoved through the conference room doors. "She takes her job seriously, doesn't she?"

"Operatives like us don't have a choice, Agent Elsher. There are too many good people counting on us to come through for them. I'm sure you and the DEA know that better than anyone." Granger Morais got to his feet with a bent manila file folder in one hand. He headed for the door, smacking the file into King's shoulder on the way out. "Bring us something solid. We'll have your back."

"I appreciate that." It took longer than it should have for the past few minutes to sink in, but King couldn't let the time slip away too easily. He'd already wasted two months of hard work trying to do this on his own. Now he had an entire team willing to help him bring Muñoz to justice. He turned to face Scarlett. "Looks like we're going to be working together."

"That ATF agent. The one whose murder you suspect Muñoz ordered. Were you partners?" she asked.

King had to swallow the urge to shut down this line of questioning. He'd gotten what he wanted: support in pinning two murders on the son of a bitch who'd ordered the deaths of an ATF agent and now a DEA agent and an entire security firm to corroborate his personal investigation to do so. Scarlett wasn't asking to dig into his life. She needed the facts of the investigation to connect it all back to Muñoz. "We worked a case together a little over ten years ago. She was called in from DC to help my team analyze a device we picked up during a raid on one of the cartel's safe houses. Before everything got complicated."

"Complicated." That single word seemed to answer everything she needed to know, but Scarlett didn't push it. "Can I assume you believe these two murders are connected based off of MO?"

"Muñoz has a pension for making an example out of anyone who gets in his way. A knife through a law enforcement badge gets the point across, don't you think?" he asked.

"Even so, I'm going to need her name and the complete investigation file." Scarlett seemed to produce a tablet out of nowhere.

"Her name was Eva Roday." That last syllable caught in the back of this throat. It'd been months since he'd had the guts to say her name out loud. Especially around Julien. "As for the file, you'll have it within the hour. Washington DC detectives closed the case three weeks ago. We shouldn't have any problem getting access."

Scarlett countered the added distance between them. "I'm sorry. That you've had to go through this more than once. Doesn't seem fair."

"Fair's got nothing to do with it." His response came harder, more bitter, than he meant it to. Because she was right. It wasn't fair. It wasn't fair that the cartel got away with murder—literally—and left kids and families and partners and wives holding the grief all to themselves. Sangre por Sangre had taken the most important person his son had in the world, and even having known about him for only a short amount of time, there wasn't anything King wouldn't do to try to fix it. That was what fathers did, didn't they? Fix things. "All the cartel has done is make me fight harder. They're the ones who are going to wish I played fair in the end."

"I'm going to have to be careful then." Scarlett brushed past him, wrenching the swinging glass door wide open. Long hair caught against the shoulder of her vest, and King suddenly found himself wanting to untangle it. She leveraged her foot against the bottom and held the door open for him.

One step. One leap of faith was all it would take to bring him into her world. The DEA didn't play small, but Socorro?

Private military contractors like Scarlett operated on a whole new level. And she wanted him to come along. “Why’s that?”

Her mouth flattened into a thin line. “Seems anyone who partners up with you ends up dead.”

Chapter Three

There wasn't anything she could do to take the pain out of his eyes.

But the internal drive she fed more often than not—the one that'd led her to Socorro—told her this was how she bought back her right to be here instead of a dark hole where she was referred to as a number instead of by her name. How she got rid of the guilt slowly eating away at her from the inside.

Scarlett dragged her finger from the bottom of her tablet screen up to review the file that hit her inbox a few minutes ago. Eva Roday's murder file.

Reaching for a steady breath, she tried to take in the overwhelming amount of information stuffed into one document. The detective who'd investigated the ATF agent's death had done a good job interviewing everyone in her life. Every detail seemed to jump out. Including the fact her ten-year-old son, Julien, had been left behind after her death. Her mouth dried. "Give me the basics."

"Agent Roday—Eva—was found with a blade similar to the one the ME pulled out of Adam this morning in the morgue." King settled that lean frame against the counter across from her in the too-small galley kitchen, a mug of fresh coffee in hand.

He needed it from the look of him. Dark circles had deepened past exhaustion and straight into night of the living dead. He'd run his hands through his hair one too many times, breaking up the careful sections of curls. The DEA agent with the eyes of steel turned out to be human after all.

"Six inches, serrated, with a patterned carbon fiber handle. No fingerprints left on the blade or the handle, but the medical examiner did manage to pull DNA off one of the blade's teeth. Problem is, they have nothing to compare it to."

Scarlett lost her grip on composure as the first crime scene photo filled her tablet screen. The spike in her heart rate could've been heard from across the room, she was sure of it, and she couldn't help but look up at King for confirmation. She tightened her hands around the edge of the screen. Pressure led to nausea, and a surge of acid tried choking her from within.

Patterned tile—new from the looks of it—supported the body as a pool of blood slipped out from the wound in the woman's chest. Cotton pajamas soaked up a lot of it. Not a suit. Nothing to suggest Eva Roday had been in the field during her murder. No. Whoever had done this came into her home. Located her badge, positioned it over the agent's chest and plunged the blade straight through. "She was found in her own home. Who called it in?"

"Her son. Julien," King said. "He's ten."

His voice did that. Caught on names. She'd noticed it earlier, and Scarlett couldn't help but imagine him doing the same with hers. Not with her last name as everyone addressed her. As Scarlett.

King crossed one ankle over the other. So relaxed in this place, somewhere he'd never even stepped before. That confidence bled off of him and settled deep in her bones. "The detective who caught the case didn't get a whole lot out of him that night. Medics couldn't find anything physically wrong with him, but…"

"You think he was there. That he saw what the killer did to his mother." Her heart constricted at the thought. There were some things in this world no one should ever have to see. Least of all the person you loved most in the world taken from you so brutally.

"Police found him beneath a pile of towels on the couch not five feet from where they found Eva's body. The killer would've done his research before stepping foot inside an ATF agent's house. He would've known she had a kid, and the son of a bitch went there anyway." King stared down into his coffee mug. The drop in his voice told her he was trying for detached—same as she was—but there was no amount of distance that could calm the rage boiling in that tone. "They thought Julien might've been injured, given the amount of blood on him, but none of it came back as his."

"He tried to save his mother?" Scarlett kept scrolling. To drain the dread growing in the pit of her stomach. To give herself something to do. A distraction. It didn't help. Because beside the agent's body was a too-small handprint. Made with blood.

"Yeah. He did." King set down the mug. There was no point trying to force it down when you couldn't physically stomach the aftermath of a case like this. Something he had to live with every day working for the DEA, she imagined. "Julien has been nonverbal ever since that night. He can't or won't tell police what he saw, if he noticed anything specific about the killer or the order of events. He's been seeing a child psychologist for the past two months, speech therapists, you name it. They all say the same thing. He understands his mom isn't coming back. He knows he can help police find her killer, but there isn't anyone in this world who can make him speak up until he's ready."

"Trauma-induced mutism." Scarlett made a note straight into the investigation file to read up on the symptom. Because it was something to do. A possible way she could help should she have to sit down with Julien. "It says here Agent Roday wasn't married. I don't see any beneficiaries for her life insurance or bank accounts listed other than Julien. Do you know anything about his father? Where he might be or if there were any hard feelings between him and the victim?"

King's expression hardened in an instant. "They hadn't had any contact in over a decade. He didn't even know Julien existed until Eva was killed and he was questioned by DC police. The detective cleared him of any involvement seeing as how the father was on assignment two hundred miles away. I'd say he's not pertinent to this investigation."

"Okay. Well, it's been two months." Scarlett mapped out a quick order of to-dos. "If he got custody of Julien, there's a chance we might be able to reinterview the boy—"

"No." That single word was a bark from across the kitchen. Aimed directly for her. King seemed to catch himself. The tendons along his neck and shoulders dropped away from his ears, but there was no hiding the truth. Protectiveness. He cared about Agent Roday's son. "I already told you Julien isn't talking. He's in a better place now. He's made friends at schools. His nightmares are becoming less frequent. Bringing all of this up might undo that, and I don't want to take that chance."

Her chin wobbled slightly, out of her control. It wasn't the aggression that'd caught her off guard. She lived and operated with an entire team of testosterone on the brink of blowing up in her face. She was trained to neutralize any threat—physical or digital—but King's intensity felt personal. As though she'd hit some kind of button he'd tried to hide away. "I understand."

"Good." He dumped his still-hot coffee into the sink and headed for the corridor that ran parallel to the kitchen. "I have copies of Eva's files. The last few cases she was working right before she died. I've been through them a thousand times, but there might be something in there you can pick up on."

"I wasn't finished." Scarlett lowered her tablet to her side as King slowed to a halt. The intensity she'd witnessed had simmered. Still there, but not burning out of control as before. Replaced with a kind of isolation, a loneliness she recognized every time she caught a reflection of herself in the bathroom mirror. "I understand why you wouldn't want to retraumatize a ten-year-old boy by interviewing him about his mother's murder, but if you want me to help you find whoever killed Agent Roday and who killed your partner, you're going to have to be honest with me. Otherwise, your deal with Socorro ends here."

King didn't look at her, didn't even seem to breathe.

"Every time you talk about Agent Roday, you call her by her first name. Which means you knew her as more than a colleague you were teamed up with ten years ago." The pieces were starting to fit together. His personal investigation into the cartel that started two months ago, why he wanted to see his partner's body at the morgue for himself. Why he wouldn't want Scarlett or anyone else stepping foot near Julien. "And based off of your defensiveness about her son, how old he is and how well you seem to know him, I'm guessing there's a good reason for that."

The fight seeped from King's arms and shoulders. "I didn't lie before. Eva was called into analyze a device we found during one of the DEA's cartel raids on Sangre por Sangre. We worked well together in the field. She was smart as hell, to the point I tried to recruit her to work for us. Told her the cartel would roll over the second we brought her on, but she was happy in DC with the ATF. Had a whole life there, but the truth was there was something about her I wanted more of."

Scarlett braced herself against the obvious grief he'd held on to after all these years. Not just from Agent Roday's death, but from losing her in the first place ten years ago.

"Once our case was finished, we went out to celebrate with a couple drinks. One thing led to another, and in the morning, she was gone. Back to DC." A scoff escaped up his throat. "No goodbyes. No note. Nothing. I reached out a couple times but never heard anything from her again. Until two months ago when a ten-year-old boy who looks exactly like her shows up on my doorstep with a social worker in tow. She tells me Eva is dead and that I'm responsible for Julien now. That I'm his father."

Her blood pressure spiked. "You had no idea?"

"None at all." Life breathed into his rigid frame as King turned to face her. Devastation—so familiar and gutting—carved into his handsome face. "Listen, I know you're just trying to do the thing that makes the most sense. Talking to the only witness who was there the night of Eva's murder is standard protocol, but that little boy is finally coming to terms with having his entire world ripped away from him."

He took a step toward her. "And I won't let you or anyone else mess with that. He's my son, and I'm going to do whatever it takes to protect him."

HIS SON.

He wasn't sure he'd ever said the words out loud. Not in passing. Not even to Julien. Pathetic, wasn't it? His entire world had shifted in the course of weeks, but he hadn't even been able to put a name as to why. Until today.

King checked his smartwatch for the dozenth time. They weren't getting anywhere with Eva's investigation file. They sure as hell couldn't prove Muñoz was even remotely connected to her murder or to Adam's today. And now he had mere minutes before he had to be back in Albuquerque for school pickup.

This was his life now. He'd gone from pulling all-nighters and chasing every lead until he had nothing left, to cutting his days short in time to make sure Julien would see a familiar face when he got home. It was an adjustment. One King was still trying to get used to. It wasn't about him anymore. Hell, none of this was. It was about giving his son a future free of fear, of suffering and maybe a little bit of justice in the process.

He scanned through Eva's file for the thousandth time. Nothing had changed. No light bulb moments or new leads. He wasn't sure what he'd been hoping to uncover with Scarlett's help. Just…something.

King scrubbed his face. They were out of time. He checked his watch again.

"You keep doing that," she said.

Scarlett was everything he'd expected from a Socorro operative, but at the same time nothing like he'd imagined. She'd read through the investigation file without so much as a change in expression, which made King wonder what horrors she'd seen to make this case seem like basic training. The woman hadn't slowed down for a minute, charging through page after page. Photo after photo. Hadn't even stopped to eat. She was dedicated. He'd give her that. Either that, or a straight up workaholic.

"Checking your watch," she went on. "Either you've got some place to be, or I'm not living up to your ideals of a good partner."

"School pickup." He shoved to stand.

The conference room they'd taken over looked like the aftermath of a back to school warehouse sale. Note cards, highlighters, reports discarded across the oversize table. Felt like he was back in college cramming for an exam in a class he hadn't shown up to all semester.

Drug cases were simple. The crap they pulled off of street corners could be traced. Find the exact combination of poison and trace it back to a dealer. Force the dealer to flip on the supplier, then do it over and over again until there wasn't anyone left. The cartel would fall the same way, but homicide?

Ivy Bardot had been right. He didn't know how to do this.

King grabbed his jacket from the back of his chair. "If I leave now, I'll only be five minutes late. Which is better than my fifteen to thirty minutes late most days."

Scarlett shoved straight out of her chair and stretched. Her shirt slipped free from the front of her cargo pants as she reached overhead. A dark line cut across her abdomen. Jagged. As wide as a pencil eraser, but before King had a chance to follow it to the end, she was pushing her chair back under the table. "I'll drive you."

"Not sure if you know this, but DEA agents are trained and licensed to operate motor vehicles," he said.

"Did you forget I'm the one who brought you out here?" Scarlett gathered the file spread across the table back into a single stack, crisscrossed in sections for easy access.

Oh, hell. He'd left his SUV back at the morgue. And he didn't have time to get it. King threaded his arms into his jacket. "Yes. Yes, I did."

"Then let's go. I just have to make a quick stop." Her smile flashed wide, and an instant jolt shifted in his gut. There was something light and genuine about that smile that didn't make sense in their line of work. Something she should've lost a long time ago.

She took the lead through the maze until they landed at a nondescript door. “Brace yourself. Meeting the twins for the first time can be a little overwhelming.”

“The twins?” King didn’t get an answer before Scarlett shoved through the door. A low howl jogged his nerves as all hell broke loose. Two dark-haired Dobermans sprinted straight at him, teeth bared.

“Sit.” One word from Scarlett, and the dogs pulled up short, planting their butts on the tile. Bright pink tongues licked at sharp teeth ready to sink into whatever could fit in their mouths, and King had no trouble imagining his arm made a good chew toy in their eyes.

King eased his hand over his sidearm, keeping an eye on the devils. “What is happening? Are these monsters yours?”

“This is Gruber and his sister Hans.” Scarlett crouched, putting her face between theirs, but King couldn’t help but notice while the Dobermans kissed at her face and neck, they kept their gazes solely on him. She scratched behind their ears. “They’re defensive K9s. Any hint of a threat to me or the people in this building, they respond with force.”

“What you’re saying is, it’s their job to eat people.” King suddenly had the urge to unholster his weapon, but doing so might be seen as an act of aggression.

“Yeah.” Scarlett stood, and the Dobermans fell in line on either side of her. “I’m their trainer, so don’t piss me off.”

His throat dried. A minute later, they wound their way to the elevator after a series of lefts and rights King lost track of halfway, all the while keeping his distance from Jekyll and Hyde. Truth be told, he couldn’t tell which way was up in this place.

“How does anyone manage to navigate through the building? It all looks the same,” he asked.

“I designed it that way in case of a breach.” They stepped

into the elevator car and faced off with their reflections as the doors closed. "Disorienting the enemy can be useful in times of war. That, and a few other security measures I built in."

His stomach launched higher in his chest as gravity lost its hold during their descent into the garage. King had the instinct to reach out for Scarlett's shoulder to steady himself, but grabbing a coworker—in any field—could land him facedown with a knee in his back. Not to mention a couple flesh wounds. He closed his eyes and breathed through the disorientation. He needed a distraction. "I take it you served."

"Army. Security specialist." Her voice echoed off the walls of the elevator car. Steady, reassuring. If something were to happen right now, she'd be the one to know what to do. "Twelve years, three tours and partridge in a pear tree."

Impressive. Twelve years, though. Meant she hadn't served a full twenty and gotten her retirement like most of the vets he worked with in the DEA.

The nausea receded as the elevator landed in the garage. He pried his eyes open before taking that first step from the car after Scarlett. The scent of gasoline infiltrated his lungs and hauled him back into the moment. He'd gone all day without eating. Any longer and his blood sugar would get the best of him. "Is that where you got the scar?"

Scarlett pulled up short, and the Dobermans followed suit. A hint of betrayal contorted her expression. Just for a moment before she wiped her face of emotion. "Don't ask me about the scar, Agent Elsher. Not ever."

She didn't wait for an answer, heading for the nearest SUV. The alarm chirped as they approached, and she got behind the steering wheel without waiting for him to catch up. The dogs climbed over her lap and went straight for the cargo area at the back. As though they'd done it a thousand times before.

Every interaction they'd had since he tackled her in the

morgue opposed her reaction a few seconds ago. King made his way to the passenger seat and buckled in as she navigated through the garage.

Picketers rushed to his side of the vehicle. Neon signs written with barely legible handwriting and exclamation points. Yells filtered through the tinted glass. Blinding desert sun enveloped them as they left the safety of Socorro's headquarters, and suddenly he felt as though he'd screwed it all up. Just as he had those first couple weeks after Julien came to live with him. "I'm sorry. It was none of my business. It won't happen again."

The seconds ticked off one after another as they carved through the dry landscape, and King couldn't help but wish they could go back to how it'd been before he opened his mouth. "So does this mean we're going to be all awkward and standoffish with each other from now on?"

A whisper of that smile he'd witnessed in the conference room made an appearance and released the pressure strangling his insides. "Probably. Guess it's a good thing this arrangement is temporary."

He'd missed this over the past few days. Having someone to bicker with. When it came right down to it, working drug cases and chasing down leads took a toll. The things he'd seen in the field would stay with him forever, but being able to joke and laugh systematically released the darkness that accrued inside. Something he never wanted his son to see.

Adam had given him that for a while. Now King wasn't sure what would happen.

"Why Socorro?" he asked.

Scarlett checked the rearview mirror. "What do you mean?"

"The cartel dumped my partner's remains outside of your headquarters. Why not at his home or the DEA?" He pried his phone from his jacket pocket. Sixteen missed calls. A handful from his superior, the rest from Adam's wife.

She deserved answers. She deserved to know the truth. He'd convinced the medical examiner he should be the one to notify Adam's family of his death, but he'd been so caught up in going back through Eva's case looking for a connection, he'd managed to put it off as long as possible. King wasn't sure if the same applied to the DEA. If the media got hold of the story and broke the news first, he'd never be able to face Adam's wife and kids again.

His thumb hovered over the screen. One tap. That was all it would take to give her the relief she needed.

"I've been wondering that myself," Scarlett said. "You haven't told the family your partner was murdered."

"I've tried at least a dozen times, but there's not really a Hallmark card for that, is there? Nothing I could say that would make this any better." King pocketed his phone. He would do it. He'd make the call. But now wasn't the time. Not until he could assure her he'd gotten justice for Adam. Though he was sure his wasn't the only number she'd dialed the past few hours after not getting an answer from her husband. "'Sorry, I got your husband killed. My thoughts are with you.'"

"Just keep it simple. And mean what you say. It makes all the difference." Scarlett turned that intense green gaze on him.

"You have to deliver a lot of bad news in your line of work?" It was a stupid question and completely on the line of procrastination. He couldn't avoid the call forever. At this point, he was just making excuses.

"No, but I've been on the receiving end more times than I can count." Scarlett maneuvered through the neighborhood surrounding his son's elementary school as though she'd been here before. "We're here. Where is your son waiting?"

King sat up straighter in his seat, all thoughts of his partner's family draining as he searched for his own. Checking the time, he confirmed they weren't much later than his normal arrival. There were still a couple kids hanging around on the playground equipment soaking up a few more minutes with friends. Parents waiting in vehicles too. "He's supposed to be at the corner. Probably went into the office to wait. I'll be right back."

He shouldered out of the vehicle and jogged to the double glass doors beside the kindergarten area. The first layer of doors opened without issue, but he had to be buzzed into the office. He waited until the administrator unlocked the barrier. "Hi, I'm here to pick up Julien Roday. I'm his dad, King Elsher."

"Oh. There must've been some kind of mix-up on your end," she said. "Julien was checked out a couple hours ago."

No. That wasn't right. "Checked out? By who?"

The administrator collected the clipboard from her desk and handed it off. "By his mother."

Chapter Four

The water bottle exploded on impact mere inches from her face as she and King waited in a conference room off the school's main office.

Droplets sprayed out from the impact zone against the wall and attached to her skin, but she wouldn't wipe them away. They were evidence of a man's descent into desperation. She needed them to keep her focused.

King's son had been kidnapped.

Her heart rate hit a high point as he turned to face whoever had come through the door. Ready to unleash all that burning rage on the nearest unsuspecting witness. His shoulders hiked with tension, almost painful to look at, but in a split second, the anger drained.

King sank into one of the chairs around the too-small conference room. Nothing like Socorro's. Not in size, at least, but the work done in this space was just as important to the families that needed this school. "They took my son, Scarlett."

"We're going to find him." It was easy to match his tone. Her chest felt too tight at the thought of someone coming in here, claiming to be Julien's mother and walking away with King's son in order to punish a man for doing his job. Hadn't he been through enough? "The administrator at the front desk checked the woman's ID when she requested to check him out. She remembers the name matched Eva's. But it looks as though when the school in Washington, DC, transferred his records, there was no note about Eva's death. Her name is still attached to his records. I sent the district the death certificate to have that information changed."

That was all she could think to do while King raged. The principal had contacted the police. Officers were searching the school property and the surrounding neighborhood, but whoever took Julien wouldn't stick around. They wanted him for something, and it would be hell to get him back.

"He's ten years old." The strangled words sounded practically forced from his throat.

And she understood that. The amount of effort it took to confront your greatest fear. To realize that despite your training, you were absolutely powerless when the people you loved were in danger.

"He deserves to have a ten-year-old life," King said. "Obsessing about every sport known to man, begging me to stay up late, losing brain cells on his tablet, hanging out with friends. Not this."

Scarlett moved to close the distance between them. Slower than she wanted to. Heat climbed into her neck as she pulled out the chair next to his and took a seat. A tremor shook through one hand as she reached out for his, enfolding it in her palms.

His skin was warmer—hot even—and rough with dryness from spending most of his days in the desert with a gun in his grip. But soft in other places, like the webbing between his fingers. She latched on, mostly for her own stability as this entire partnership threatened to fall apart. "Is there a chance the cartel knows Julien was there the night his mother was killed?"

"I asked the investigating detective to keep Julien out of

all the reports because he was a minor." King stared down at his hand, as though he couldn't comprehend how he'd ended up here in this elementary school conference room with her when he was supposed to be out there looking for a connection between two past partners' murders. "You read the file. There's no mention of his name."

"Then we need to assume taking Julien is meant to be a warning to you." Air stalled in her chest as she internally braced for what came next. "Just as Adam Dunkeld was."

Surprise mixed with a hint of that anger as King leaned back in the chair. His hand went with him, leaving a streak of heat in her palms. "Muñoz. That son of a bitch. He's got to be the one behind this." Another shift wrecked the determination that flared in his eyes, gutting Scarlett in an instant. "Adam was missing for three days before he turned up dead at your doorstep."

And yet Eva Roday was murdered in her own home. There hadn't been an abduction. No grace period for law enforcement to play catch-up.

"King, if you're right about Muñoz being behind Eva's death, I think it's safe to say if the cartel learns Julien witnessed his mother's murder that night, he doesn't have that kind of time." She didn't want to put a countdown clock on this case, but they had no other choice.

"He's all I've got left, Scarlett. He's the only thing that matters. All of this—working for the DEA, running that investigation on the side—I was doing it for him. To protect him."

The defensiveness she'd come to expect from King since he'd inserted himself into her life this morning wasn't there anymore. He'd been stripped of his armor by a ten-year-old, and there was nothing she could do about it. No security patch could fix this. She had no backup plan in place.

He brought his gaze to hers, the whites of his eyes reflecting the harsh fluorescent lights overhead. "And now they have him."

"We're going to get him back. Alive," she said. "I give you my word."

"Don't do that." The fire she'd witnessed behind all that devastation exploded. He shoved out of his chair, letting the wheels crash into the table leg. "Don't promise me something you have no intention of following through on, Scarlett. Because this is my son. This is my life, and if I lose him because your word isn't good enough, I will spend the rest of my life making you pay. You understand? So think very carefully about what you're promising me."

She pushed to her feet, meeting him on his level. "You asked about the scar across my stomach. You want to know how I got it? By keeping my word. I don't give it casually, King, and I don't give it to anyone who I don't believe deserves it. But once I do, I won't give up until I'm finished. Now, we can debate about the worth of my promises all day with examples and my résumé, but your son is out there. He doesn't have as much time as we need, and I'm one of the only people in this country who knows what we're dealing with. So are you going to trust me?"

He held his own, seemingly taking it all in one word at a time. "Yeah. I trust you."

"Good. The principal has queued the security footage taken during the time Julien was checked out. I suggest we start there." Pent-up energy flooded into the streak of scar tissue across her abdomen as she headed for the door. Most days she could pretend it didn't exist. That her closest friend hadn't tried to kill her while they'd been stationed overseas. Today wasn't one of those days. Scarlett wrenched open the door and stepped into the main office.

Formica-coated, two-tiered desks separated two administrators from the parents and students meant to stay on one side. Cabinets stacked high on one another behind each station and showed off motivational posters like the kind she used to hang in her room as a kid. An entire wall of glass gave school staff a view into the long corridors making up the industrial-carpeted school. Two doors provided access into the main school once entrants were allowed past the auto-locking doors.

Scarlett bypassed the officers taking statements from teachers and staff and headed down the hallway into the back of the main office. She clocked each and every camera installed throughout the space as she moved. Not enough. Not nearly enough to keep these tiny souls safe. Cutting to the principal's office at the very end of the hallway, she didn't bother to confirm whether King had kept up. "Principal Doleac. This is King Elsher. Julien's father."

"Yes, of course." A trim woman who looked as though she lived off of long miles, few carbs and a tanning bed got up from behind her desk and offered her manicured hand. "I wanted to express how sorry I am about all of this, Mr. Elsher. We haven't had anything like this happen before. We will be working closely with Socorro and law enforcement to bring Julien home as quickly as possible. Anything you need, please don't hesitate to ask."

"You have the security footage of when my son was taken?" King didn't bother extending his own hand to shake.

The principal retracted into herself as she took a seat in front of an old monitor from the Stone Age. "Yes. I have it pulled up here. It's not the most sophisticated system, but as I said, we've never had anything like this happen before."

"Could you give us a few minutes?" Scarlett asked.

Hesitation deepened the lines around Doleac's eyes and mouth. Midforties, Scarlett would guess. Though she imagined the stress of the woman's job and the political pressure she handled on a day-to-day basis had added a few unkind years. "I'm sorry. I can't just leave you alone with the district's system. These computers contain students' private information and internal information about our teachers. I'm happy to navigate through whatever footage you need."

King set his badge on the principal's desk. "I'm not interested in teacher or student information, Principal Doleac. I'm here for my son. Anything we come across not pertaining to this case will remain confidential."

She studied the badge for a moment before climbing back onto impossibly high heels that accentuated how short Doleac really was. "Please let me know if I can be of any further assistance."

Scarlett slid into the principal's chair as the administrator made her way out of the office. A zing of anticipation crackled through her fingers as she scanned through the thumbnails of footage. "Their system could use an upgrade, but it seems simple enough to navigate. Let me pull up the camera and time Julien was checked out."

King shifted into her peripheral vision, then closer. Right up against her right side. Leveraging one hand against the desk and the other against the back of her chair, he pressed in. He pointed at the screen. "That's Julien."

The window expanded to the full width of the monitor and automatically started playing the footage. The angle looked as though it'd come from one of the cameras directly outside the office, recording students in the corridor leading up to the front of the building. The boy's face was pixelated, but there was no mistaking the similarity between him and the man beside her.

Scarlett studied King for a moment, taking in the softening of his jaw as he studied his son in the footage. "He has his backpack. So this must be after he was already called down to the office to get checked out. Which means we should be able to see who's waiting for him."

She sorted through the other frames recorded at the same time. And pulled up the image of a woman with her back to the camera. Thick curly hair pinned back away from the suspect's face, but there wasn't a good angle to get an ID. "She's avoiding the cameras. Let me see if I can follow them out to the parking lot."

Which meant whoever'd checked Julien out had been in that school before. Had cased it. Knew the ins and outs. Most likely had a security blueprint or a map of the building. Julien's abduction hadn't been a one-off reaction to punish King for sticking his nose where it didn't belong. This was a coordinated effort.

"Do you recognize her?" Scarlett asked.

"Hard to tell without a shot of her face, but I've been through all the surveillance we have on Muñoz multiple times over. The only woman in his crew was killed a few months ago." King straightened, getting closer to the screen. "Wait. Look. Julien stops when he sees her."

He was right. Scarlett saw it then. The terror in the boy's face. A fawn response. She intensified the frame of Julien's face. "Like he's seen her before."

THERE WAS ONLY one reason for a ten-year-old boy to act like Julien had in that footage.

Fear.

A pressure King couldn't seem to get rid of followed him as he shoved through the elementary school's doors and out into the open. He scanned every car, every window from the houses facing the school. His son had been right here. Alone. Scared. Forced to follow the orders of a stranger or get hurt. King scrubbed a hand down his face. Damn it. He should've been here. Not chasing some dead end of a case he shouldn't have his nose in in the first place.

The school's exterior surveillance hadn't caught the vehicle Julien had been forced into, but King didn't need it. He knew who was behind this. And he knew exactly what he had to do to get his son back. He took his cell from his pocket.

"You're going to regret making that call." Scarlett's voice battled the loss and rage spiking through him. Which was impossible. He knew that, but there was something about her that argued with the natural man inside him that wanted to tear through this entire city to find Julien. And, hell, he wanted to give in to her. To feel some sense of peace for himself. For his family.

King let his thumb hesitate over the phone's screen. "What call is that?"

"The one where you call up the team you have sitting on Muñoz and give the order for them to breach the compound." Scarlett moved into his peripheral vision with far more grace than should be possible with all that gear she carried. Like she'd made it part of her over the years. Based on what she'd told him of her experience, he guessed that was true. "You're not in the right frame of mind to think about this logically. You're too close to it. The second your team crosses Muñoz's property line, you'll be declaring war with Sangre por Sangre."

"And you don't think kidnapping a DEA agent's son is an act of war?" His grip tightened around the phone as he turned to her. She was right. There was no logic behind this, but life wasn't always logical. It was the connections that made the difference between the ordinary and the meaningful, and the only one he cared about right now was Julien. "How about stabbing an agent through the chest?"

"Whoever did this is baiting you, King. They want you

running off emotion instead of common sense. That's how they win, and if you make that call, you'll be playing directly into their hands," she said.

"Why?" That was the question. The one that'd been constantly ticking at the back of mind after he'd gotten the call about Adam's murder this morning. It churned until he swore his blood started to boil. "First Adam, now Julien. My investigation into Muñoz didn't turn up anything significant. I have nothing. He's made sure to keep his hands off cartel business, so why make an example out of me? Why go after the people I care about?"

"I don't know." Scarlett stared out over the parking lot, seemingly memorizing the quickest exits and any vehicles that might get in her way. Like the good soldier she was supposed to be.

His gaze dropped to the hem of her T-shirt and the scar hiding beneath the fabric. She'd told him she'd gotten it by keeping her word. If that was true, she might be the only one who could help him now.

"According to our intel Muñoz is making a move for leadership," she said. "He wants the old regime out. You or your surveillance team must've stumbled across something that could put a stop to that. Killing your partner—abducting Julien—they're warnings."

The truth of it resonated through him, but no single piece of evidence came to mind. The pressure behind his sternum strangled the remaining air in his lungs. Helplessness threatened to erode the last of his strength. It took everything he had right then to stay on his feet as his mind replaced Eva's crime scene photos with ones featuring the boy he'd come to love more than life itself. "I'm all he has left, Scarlett. I promised I would take care of him. That as long as we were together, nothing could hurt him, and now..."

"I know." She stepped close to him. Tendrils of hair escaped the ponytail tied at the nape of her neck and tickled across his face. That simple focus conquered the downward spiral tearing through him. "I need you to listen to me. Sangre por Sangre doesn't play by the rules. They don't stick to MOs unless they're sending a message. There's no telling how much time Julien has, but if we can prove Muñoz was behind Eva and Adam's murders, we'll have the leverage to use against him. You know Muñoz's current operation better than anyone. Do you have any idea where the cartel might've held your partner during the three days he was missing?"

"I've been through Muñoz's holdings a hundred times." Addresses, bank accounts, phone records—all of it had been aboveboard to an outsider looking in. None of it useful. "He owns a couple car dealerships in town, a restaurant that's under investigation by the state health department and a couple McMansions outside the city."

Scarlett's face lit up. "The restaurant. The health department would've shut it down until Muñoz addressed the problems they found, right? No one would be allowed in or out, and restaurants usually come with those locking freezers. If Muñoz worked it right, he could've stashed Adam Dunkeld without anyone knowing."

He loved the way her brain worked. Electricity shot through him at the idea of their first real lead. King swiped through his phone and brought up the address, moving toward the SUV. "The restaurant is only a couple miles from here. I'll put in the request for the search warrant."

They moved as though they'd been partnered for more than a few hours. In step with each other. Scarlett rounded the SUV to the driver seat as King hauled himself into the other side. Both Dobermans paced back and forth across the cargo area. As though they sensed what was coming.

War.

He would go to war with the cartel for his son.

King submitted the warrant request up the DEA chain. He'd worked his own personal investigation into Muñoz up to this point, but stepping foot inside the restaurant without a warrant would throw anything they found into question. Or dismiss it altogether. And he couldn't take that risk. Not with Julien's life on the line.

The Dobermans stuck both of their heads over the center console with low groans.

"They don't look too pleased you left them in the car." King found himself leaning away from the duo. His instincts told him this breed could turn on him at any moment. One wrong move, and they'd turn him into their next meal.

"A lot of people hold grudges against Dobermans." Scarlett angled out of the elementary school's parking lot, bringing up the GPS on the SUV's navigation screen. "They believe the aggression is innate. That it can't be bred or trained out of them, so I try to keep the twins away from the general public. But in the year I've worked with Hans and Gruber since coming to Socorro, they've only grown more attached to me and the team, including the other K9s."

Attached enough to kill anything that threatened their handler? "I'll be sure to stay on your good side then."

Her laugh filled the cabin of the SUV and physically attacked the tension along his spine. Which shouldn't have been possible. Not when they were on their way to search a building where his partner could have been tortured and killed. Where Julien might be held now. But he was quickly learning what he saw of Scarlett wasn't exactly what he got. A security consultant for the country's most well-funded private military contractor would have to be controlled, perfectionistic and critical of everything and everyone she encountered, but at the same time there was a hint of softness in the way she spoke. A passion to help that he couldn't ignore.

"Only if you want to stay alive," she said.

They settled into a few minutes of silence as they got closer to the restaurant.

"This is it." Scarlett shoved the SUV into Park. She leaned over the console to get a better look through his window at the stucco building across the street.

Hints of her body soap—something like eucalyptus and lavender—filled his space and dove into his lungs. Soothing and exciting at the same time.

Unholstering her sidearm, she released the magazine and checked the ammunition before reassembling her weapon. Efficient. Quick. The woman knew her way around a gun. "Catalina's?" she asked.

"It's named after his wife." He'd never been here in person, but King felt as though he knew every inch of the place from the amount of surveillance he and his team had done over the past two months. He noted the pillars holding up the overhang protecting the double glass doors, intricate designs carved into the wood. Sharp corners and a flat roof complemented the look and feel of the surrounding buildings and homes with benches and plants funneling customers inside from the heat. "One entrance at the front, an exit at the back that leads into the alley between all these other buildings."

"How do you want to play this?" she asked.

King checked his phone. "We've got the search warrant." Unholstering his own weapon, he ensured his badge and credentials were visible to anyone who might want to intervene during their search. "That means we can knock on the front door."

"Great. I love Mexican food." She shouldered free of the vehicle and wrenched open the back door to let Hans and Gruber out. King followed suit. The Dobermans immediately rounded the SUV in playful leaps. *"Fuss."*

Each dog took to Scarlett's side as she holstered her weapon and headed for the restaurant's front door. "After you."

He'd waited a long time for this. King forced the knot in his gut out of his mind as he approached the building. No movement from the windows. A seal plastered over the double doors warned customers of the potential dangers of stepping foot inside, but he wasn't worried about E. coli or contracting food poisoning. King was here for his son. He pounded his fist against the thick wood. "Hernando Muñoz. DEA. We have a search warrant. Open up."

One minute. Two.

There was no answer from inside, and his heart rate notched higher.

"Let me help." Scarlett pulled a blade from one of her cargo pant pockets and slit the seal down the center. The Dobermans sniffed at the crack between the doors before she pulled at the handle. The doors parted with a frigid burst of air from inside. "Pretty sure these are supposed to be locked."

Warning flared in King's gut. He took to one side, Scarlett doing the same. "Go."

She stepped over the threshold, and the K9s followed close on her heels.

Swinging around the door, King swept his attention over a ghost town of chairs and tables. Dark walls and flooring made it hard to see without overhead lighting as they moved section by section. Blinds had been drawn to keep outsiders from looking in, but the edges lit up with bright sunlight that reflected off stacks of glasses.

He nodded toward a swinging door at the back of the building. "The kitchen."

"Right behind you," she said.

King took the lead. No matter what waited on the other side, he wanted to be the first through the door. Wanted Julien to see his father hadn't given up on him. Hinges protested as he shoved into the back room. Clean stainless steel glimmered as King hit the light switch to the right.

The K9s jogged ahead, spreading out. Before meeting in front of the oversize freezer doors.

"They've got something." Scarlett lowered her weapon but didn't move to put it away. Sidestepping to the freezer's handle, she glanced back at King. Silently waiting for his go-ahead.

He gave it.

She wrenched the door back, exposing what waited for them inside.

King held his breath as he moved into the too-small space but kept his distance so as not to disturb the blood patterns arcing across the floor and walls. Fresh. Recent. He lowered his weapon. "Adam was here."

Chapter Five

DNA didn't lie.

And right now it was telling them that Adam Dunkeld had suffered for a very long time before his killer or killers put him out of his misery.

Albuquerque PD's forensic unit moved in a chaotic dance. It'd taken less than an hour to confirm the blood's owner against the federal agent's file, and the entire DEA was on alert. A flash burst from the tech photographing every square inch of the refrigerator.

Scarlett wouldn't need to study these resulting photos. She couldn't unsee the patterns the blood spatter had made across the tile every time she closed her eyes. Couldn't help but wonder if routinely torturing people in the restaurant's fridge was what led to the county shutting the place down in the first place.

"I take it this is your first crime scene." King penetrated her peripheral vision as she watched the team move almost like a hive mind. Each knowing what to do and under orders to get it done.

The muscles down her back urged her to stand straighter, to be more prepared for the shot of heat darting through her. To be good enough to even stand next to an agent like King. "How can you tell?"

"You still have a little bit of throw-up on your vest." He nodded to her right shoulder, handing over a bottled water soaked in condensation. Sympathy softened the cut of his jaw and the lines around his eyes.

Scarlett took the bottle faster than she'd ever drawn her sidearm and chugged. Liquid leaked at the corners of her mouth as she attempted to wash the sick taste from her mouth, but there was no point.

"You're going to want to slow down." He settled into the worn cushioning of the other side of the booth, a thick wood table dividing them. "The faster you drink, the faster it comes up. Believe me."

"From experience?" she asked.

"Back when I was a rookie agent with the DEA, Sangre por Sangre was just getting its legs. They came in fast and hard by trying to knock out their competition. First time I set foot in a crime scene, the prosecutor assigned to the case had to convince the judge I wasn't a member of the cartel." His mouth hiked into a half smile that had the ability to freeze time if Scarlett allowed herself such small pleasures in life. "I left so much of my DNA all over that scene, the techs refused to work with me for a year. Any time Adam and I came up on a scene that required a crime scene unit, he had to be the one to put in the request or the techs would give us the runaround."

There was no way a knowledgeable, committed, responsible agent like King would ever contaminate or compromise a scene like that. "You're just trying to make me feel better."

"I'm really not." He took a slug of his own water. "Adam got the entire incident on video. Lucky for me, I get to experience that moment all over again every team Christmas party." The smile drained slowly, as though he just realized he wouldn't have to go through the embarrassment this year.

"He was a good agent. A good friend. Deserved a hell of a lot better than I gave him."

She studied the pattern the photographer followed as he circled closer to the single chair with every compression of the shutter button. King was losing everyone he ever cared about. Methodically. "How long were you and Adam partnered together?"

"Since the beginning. We came up together. Recommended each other for promotions, knew each other better than anyone else. Right down to our allergies." He stared across the solid wood bar, through the propped-open kitchen door and into the refrigerator at the back. "I had Sunday dinner at his house every week with his wife and his kids, and I paid for lunch whenever we were out in the field. We'd spend hours driving across the state working cases in absolute silence. He was the kind of person who was fine not trying to fill every second with conversation but always knew when I needed a distraction. The fact people can do this kind of thing to each other never sat right with me, and Adam always knew what to say to make it a little more tolerable. Even right now, I'm expecting him to walk through those doors and make me feel better. We had a good thing going."

Her heart leaped at the opportunity to be that person for him. A replacement for his partner who could inject a small amount of good in the middle of so much bad. But being that source had nearly gotten her killed in the past. Her need to make up for all the terrible things she'd done would put her right back where she didn't want to be. And she'd worked too hard to take a step back now. "I'm sorry."

It was all she could think to say. And she meant it. With every cell in her body, she was sorry she couldn't make the hurt controlling him go away. But they weren't partners. They weren't friends. They were barely acquaintances. He was using her and Socorro to legitimize an off-the-books operation that'd led to the death of his partner and the kidnapping of his son. That was all she was. A resource.

Just as she'd been to the man who almost killed her.

But there was something about King that wanted to convince her she was more. In the way he thought about her needs in the middle of a scene where his partner and best friend had been murdered. The way he made every conversation lighter and pulled out the laugh she'd forgotten the sound of with sarcasm and banter. It'd been a long time since she'd felt this comfortable with a partner. And she almost wished she could hold on to that a little longer.

But she couldn't. This investigation would end. Sooner or later, they'd find Julien. King would go back to the DEA, and she'd return to Socorro. They couldn't make time stop. No matter how much she wanted to live in quiet moments like this. There was no point in trying.

Scarlett thumbed water beads off the bottle gripped between both hands. "What did Agent Roday have on the cartel?"

"What?" He cut his gaze to her.

"You said your partner was targeted to send you a message, and from what I'm seeing here, I'm inclined to believe Sangre por Sangre was using Adam to get to you or at least to learn what you had on them." Her brain frantically scrambled to connect the dots. When a piece of circuitry failed in the security system she'd hardwired into Socorro's headquarters, the whole system was compromised. It was her job to make sure her team was safe. She couldn't do that with gaping holes. "But Julien's mother was killed two months ago. You hadn't spoken in years. You didn't even know about your son, and it was her murder that triggered your investigation into Muñoz. There must've been a reason the cartel considered her a threat."

"I reached out to the supervisory special agent over Eva's unit a couple days after the social worker brought me Julien." King directed his attention back to the officers working the scene, taking any prints that might've been left behind and marking areas safe to walk through the restaurant. "He claimed whatever Eva was working on before she died was above my pay grade. Classified. He couldn't or wouldn't tell me if the job was what got her killed, but I know for a fact Eva had looked into Muñoz in the past."

"How can you be so sure?" she asked.

"That case we worked together, the one before we..."

The idea of him and the mother of his child together shouldn't hit her nervous system as hard as it did.

King leveraged one arm against the shiny, lacquered table. "The DEA asked her to consult on a device we uncovered during one of our operations. We'd gotten intel from an informant that Sangre por Sangre and the head of the Marquez cartel out of Mexico were meeting in a warehouse outside the city. But by the time my team got there, we were just recovering pieces of the device after it did its job tearing through a good chunk of the Marquez cartel. Turned out, Sangre por Sangre was on a mission to consolidate power."

"You said Adam had been with you from the beginning," she said. "Was he there for that operation?"

"Of course. We..." King sat up a bit straighter. "We've been partners for over ten years. That was one of the first assignments we took on together."

The answer was right there in front of them. A time and place where both victims had come together against the Sangre por Sangre cartel. A connection. The first real lead they'd had so far. "Then they knew each other, at least peripherally.

Is there any chance Agent Dunkeld and Agent Roday have been in contact since that operation?"

King scrubbed a hand down his face. "I don't know. Adam never said anything if he was, and police didn't find anything in Eva's phone records or emails to come to that conclusion."

There was another explanation. Because the odds of two federal agents being stabbed to death in the span of two months—both of which landed in King's orbit—were too great to ignore. "Unless your partner didn't want you to know."

"What are you saying?" He turned that internal intensity that could start a wild fire given enough space on her, and Scarlett's defenses spiked. He shoved free of the booth and circled until he cut off her view of his face. "You think Adam and Eva were working on something together? There's no way. He was my partner. We told each other everything, and he was a shit liar. Did everything by the book. I would've known if he was keeping something from me."

"What if he couldn't tell you?" Scarlett got to her feet, closing the distance between them. "Think about it. If Eva was investigating Sangre por Sangre and Muñoz after all these years, she would've needed a contact in the DEA. Someone who was there during that operation, but she couldn't come to you. Not without telling you about Julien, and she obviously didn't want that seeing as how she kept his existence a secret from you for ten years. So is it possible she reached out to Adam to get what she needed?"

His shoulders slowly relaxed away from his ears as King faced her. "It's possible, but I don't see how going through a ten-year-old operation gets her Muñoz or helps bring my son home now."

Scarlett latched on to his forearm as the potential for answers heated through her. "Then let's go find out."

HE COULD STILL feel her.

That single touch that had somehow released the pressure valve behind his sternum.

The scene at the restaurant would take hours, if not days, to process. Time he and Scarlett didn't have. Because if she was right, if a decade-old DEA operation was the reason Adam and Eva had been killed all these years later, and was why his son had been taken, they couldn't wait for answers.

But he hadn't wanted to find them here.

"You sure you want to start here?" Scarlett met him at the end of the driveway as Hans and Gruber sniffed their way down the sidewalk.

It probably didn't seem like much from her end, but having her here meant something. It meant she was going to keep her word, that in a world where he couldn't even trust the man he'd partnered with all these years, she was going to come through.

"I've been putting it off long enough." Well-maintained bushes hid the initial view of the house he'd been to every morning for the past ten years. It wasn't anything spectacular, but the clean rockscaping punctuated with bright purple cactus flowers told him the place was loved.

King hiked up the oil-spotted driveway toward the two-car garage hiding the view of the front door. A large bay window on the other side provided the homeowner with a view that guaranteed she saw them coming, and nervous energy shocked through him.

It wasn't every day you had to tell your partner's wife he wasn't coming home.

Hinges protested from the metal screen installed over the front door before he had a chance to ring the doorbell. The woman folding her arms over her chest in the doorframe barely had anything left to grab on to. She wasn't taking care of herself, that much was clear in the thinness of her skin and the oil overtaking her blond hair. She was close to six months pregnant, but from her current size, he might've assumed three. Four max. She'd pulled it back into a ponytail. He wasn't sure he'd ever seen her without those signature waves, a couple layers of makeup or the leggings she liked to wear despite the heat.

No echoes of kids yelling or something being thrown down the hallway after Adam had told them for the thousandth time their mother was going to kill them for playing soccer in the house.

King pulled up short at the base of the walkway and just… stopped. Too heavy to get the words out. He hadn't wanted this. Ever. He didn't want to be the one standing here. In his mind, he always pictured it the other way around. Adam followed the book. Never took a risk unless King was the one to push him. King should've been the one the cartel had dragged into that refrigerator. Not his partner.

Warmth prickled at his arm where Scarlett had touched him, as though she were still touching him. Giving him the courage he needed right then. "Hi, Jen."

"He's dead, isn't he?" Chipped fingernails dug into Jen's arms as she ducked her chin to her chest, and King's entire world threatened to split open.

"Yeah. Adam's dead." There wasn't any more to say. Nothing he could do to take on her pain, even for just a few seconds. He was powerless in this moment, and he hated the feeling with every fiber of his being. King crossed the distance to the front door, prying his partner's wife away from the doorframe and into his arms. "I'm so sorry. I wasn't there. I couldn't protect him."

Jen pressed her face into his chest. Sobs tremored through her body until all he heard was great big gasps for breath. Digging those usually manicured nails into his arms, she cried until there was nothing left.

King didn't know how long they stood there with Scarlett watching. He didn't care. Because he owed this to Jen. Owed Adam.

"Tell me how. How did this happen?" she asked.

"The cartel." It was all he would give her. His partner's family deserved to remember him as he was. Not as the corpse he'd ended up.

Life bled into Jen's face and replaced the paleness there. She shoved at him with one hand, though she didn't come close to knocking him off balance. "You came into my home every day, King. I welcomed you at our breakfast table. I let you near my children because you promised. You promised me every morning before you and Adam left that you would back him up."

She shoved him again. This time with both palms, and King took a big step back as she advanced. The metal screen door snapped closed.

"Why weren't you there, King? Why weren't you the one…" Another wave of emotion cut her short as she brought her hands to her face. Jen doubled over as her strength failed.

"I wanted to be." And he had. A thousand times over in the hours since he'd gotten the call about his partner. He'd wanted to be the one on the slab. To save Jen and the kids from the black well of grief. But that wasn't how life had played out. King raised his gaze to Scarlett. She was good at fixing things, but she couldn't fix this. No matter how much he wanted her to. "Jen, I need to know. Was Adam working on anything off the books? Did he say anything about an operation the DEA ran ten years ago or mention the name Eva Roday in the past few days?"

The sobs quieted to a low moan. Jen pushed back the tendrils of hair that escaped her crude ponytail. The fire that'd held Adam captive for years exploded in her eyes. She straightened, facing off with him as the roller coaster of pain and loss vanished.

"You son of a bitch. Really? You tell me Adam isn't coming home, that the cartel killed him, and you're asking me if there's anything my husband said about a case he was working five seconds later." She poked a finger into his chest. "You're always chasing answers, King, but you know what the sad thing is? You're never going to be happy with what you've got. Adam felt bad for you, you know. Said this job was all you had, even after you learned about Julien. That's why he thought it was so important to stay your partner and turn down all those promotions that came his way. And he was right. You're always going to be looking for that next lead. Letting the things that matter pass you by."

The words stabbed through him, one at a time, until King couldn't take his next breath.

Scarlett took a step forward, and he knew right then she would always be the one to take that first step. Into the fight, to stand up for those who couldn't stand up for themselves. It was just the kind of person she was, and he admired the hell out of that. "Hey, that's—"

He held Scarlett off as the pull of something desperate and illogical took control. Jen was right. He'd built his entire life around this job. It'd gotten him through, given him purpose. It'd kept him focused when he suddenly found himself taking care of a kid who wouldn't talk to him and missing the woman he'd let slip through his fingers. But it wasn't what was driving him now. "They took my son, Jen."

Shock stole the anger in Jen's expression. Her finger drifted from his chest as she lost the will to keep him in his place. She blinked those big doe eyes filled with tears. "What?"

"They took Julien." And King lost the will to keep years of classified intel, secrets and emotions to himself as the truth bled into existence. "I know I failed you. I know there's nothing I can do to bring Adam home, and you're more than welcome to hate me for the rest of your life, if that's what you need to do. But there is a little boy out there in the hands of the very people who murdered your husband. And he's scared, Jen. He doesn't know what's going to happen to him or if anyone's coming for him. Help me get to him. Please."

One second. Two.

Jen stared at him, and hell, King didn't know what she saw. He just hoped it was enough. "Adam never said anything about his cases. I didn't want to know after…" She didn't have to finish that sentence. He knew about her family, about how she was raised by an addict who frequently beat her and her brother when her stepdad was coming down from a high. It was a life she worked hard to leave behind. "But I knew he was working on something that wasn't for the DEA. I have a strict rule about bringing work home from the field, and he never broke that rule. But I caught him two weeks ago in the middle of the night. In his office. He was unscrewing the cover on the air return vent and putting something inside."

Anticipation shot through him. "Did you see what it was?"

"No. And I didn't ask." Jen leveled that gaze at him, a hardness taking over that he'd only ever seen when Adam and the kids were in trouble. It only lasted a moment before the grief moved back in. She folded in on herself all over again, and right then, Jen suddenly seemed so much smaller than he remembered.

Adam's life insurance would cover hers and the kids' cost of living, most likely pay off this house, but there were some things money couldn't take on, and King would be the one to step up. To make sure they got through this.

"But I haven't touched anything in there since he went missing," Jen said. "I figured…he would want it to stay as he left in when he came home. And if not, then the DEA might need to go through it first."

She moved aside, giving him and Scarlett a clear shot to the front door. "Find the bastards who did this and get your son back, King. Make them wish they hadn't come after your family."

"I intend to." King didn't wait as he pried the metal screen door open and crossed the threshold, Scarlett and her Dobermans close behind.

The front door deposited them straight into a tidy living room with worn carpet and oversize leather couches. The dining room that'd hosted a thousand family breakfasts every morning King had showed up to collect his partner stared back at him with a grudge. There wouldn't be any more breakfasts at that table. Not for him.

"The office is this way." He moved down the hall on instinct until they found the room they were looking for. The house wasn't all that big, but there were enough rooms to give the kids their own and provide an office for Adam with a view out the back window.

Hesitation gripped the small muscles in the bottom of King's feet as he set eyes on the air return vent Jen had mentioned. Three steps. That was all it took to set himself beneath it. The screws popped out easier than he expected, and King jammed his hand into the vent.

Something was stuffed inside the return.

"What is it?" Scarlett held on to each of the dogs' collars as he brought down a manila file folder.

"Some kind of file. I've never seen it before." King flipped open the cover. And froze at the notepaper clipped inside the front cover.

Scarlett moved in to get a better look, raising her gaze to his. She took the folder from him and scanned through his partner's handwritten notes. "Looks like Adam was running his own off-the-books investigation into the cartel. With Eva Roday, from what I can see of these notes."

"Yeah." A million thoughts were going through his head, but King only had attention for one. He pointed to a section of notes Adam had circled over and over. "And figured out Sangre por Sangre is far more dangerous than we gave them credit for."

Chapter Six

It was all there.

Scarlett had read the file they'd recovered from Adam's office so many times the words were starting to blur together. Every detail accounted for. Every move Muñoz had made over the past decade. It all made sense.

Sangre por Sangre hadn't just started consolidating power by taking out the heads of the other cartels during that DEA operation ten years ago. They'd been absorbing the orphaned soldiers left behind. And accepting funds from an outside source.

Overseas funds.

The kind that never ran out. The kind that came from organizations that had outlived the fall of governments and were impossible to dismantle because of their sheer size. Sangre por Sangre had always been in the drug business, but the partnership that Agents Dunkeld and Roday theorized was slowly taking place revealed something so much worse.

The drugs confiscated at the borders every day were a mere fraction of what actually got through. Cartels were willing to take the risk, knowing the payoff was worth a small sacrifice of product, but with this? Sangre por Sangre would have unfettered access. Humans. Drugs. Weapons. There was no limit if this intel was right.

"Ten years of operations." King pressed his thumb and index finger into his eyes. He checked his phone again. She'd lost count of how many times, but there was no word about Julien. The tension in his shoulders relayed nothing but concern and impatience. Albuquerque PD had nothing. "Neither of them said a word."

She and King had been at this for an hour, trying to absorb as much of Adam's notes as possible. The sun had dipped behind the half-moon ring of mountains to the west. All of this… It was too much for any one person. Or maybe the information was meant to be shared by a team. Designed to ensure one person didn't have to take it all on themselves.

Scarlett closed the file on her lap. Sweat built along the collar of her shirt as Hans and Gruber kicked in their sleep from the corner of the room.

Turned out the vent in this office wasn't actually functional for anything other than a poor man's safe. Adam Dunkeld purposefully put himself in misery every time he sat down at this desk to work the investigation. As though he were punishing himself.

But he had company every single time. Scarlett's gaze turned to the family photo facing off with her from the corner of the desk. Of smiling faces and happier times. The chair protested as she leaned forward. Her joints screamed for release. "I imagine Eva wanted it that way. In case something happened to her. That way Julien had somewhere to go. Somewhere he'd be safe."

"Maybe you're right." King tossed his section of the file onto the desk and pushed to stand. "Doesn't make it any easier to swallow, though. Because now my son is right where Eva didn't want him, and there's not a damn thing I can do to help him."

Not until they figured out Muñoz's involvement in all this.

Adam Dunkeld and Eva Roday had stumbled onto something Socorro hadn't even considered possible for the enemy they'd been fighting, but the intel fit. The increase in soldiers, the upgrade in weapons and armored vehicles. The escalation in violence, abductions and raids. Sangre por Sangre wasn't the same small-time cartel Socorro had been contracted to dismantle. This was a new threat altogether. One they didn't know.

"You haven't heard anything?" Scarlett asked.

"No. No ransom call. No request for money." King did that thing where he scrubbed a hand down his face before checking his phone. "Which means they're not interested in negotiating."

He didn't need to finish that sentence. It was already burned into the front of her mind. Julien's abductors weren't interested in negotiating because they had no intention of letting the ten-year-old come home alive. It'd taken all her persuasive powers to get him to slow down enough to uncover some kind of lead from these files. But was it enough?

Scarlett couldn't take the thought of watching King lose someone else. This man who'd already sacrificed so much for the innocent lives he protected from the cartel, who'd already lost everything and everyone. She needed to contact Socorro and hand over the intel they'd uncovered. Ivy had to know what they were up against. Every second Sangre por Sangre was connected to whoever was funding them overseas, the less chance she and her team had of winning this war.

But there was something she had to do first. Something only she could fix. "What if we don't wait for Julien's kidnappers to contact you? What if we go get Julien ourselves?"

A mirrored ache to do *something* carved into King's expression. "We don't have proof Lieutenant Muñoz is behind my son's abduction. If we go in there without a solid lead, we could be putting Julien in more danger."

"You're right. But what if we find him?" And Scarlett wanted to find that boy. More than anything. For King. "We might not have hard evidence, but there's enough in these files to support a real DEA investigation into Muñoz. And it all started with that operation ten years ago. That can't be a coincidence. What if your suspicion hasn't been for nothing? What if Muñoz is at the center of all of this? That he had Eva Roday and your partner killed. That he's the one who sent his crew after Julien."

King's left hand fisted and released. "I can't walk into DEA headquarters with a theory and authorize a raid team, even with Adam's proof that there's something more going on inside the cartel. And I know Ivy Bardot well enough to know she's going to want solid evidence that Sangre por Sangre has my son before she signs off on any operation Socorro will be linked to." His shoulders hiked on a deep inhale. "So how would we do this?"

Scarlett dragged out a photo from a decade's worth of surveillance. "We start here. As for backup, you have me and the twins. That's all you'll need."

"You certainly think highly of yourself, don't you?" King studied the photo of a warehouse. Ten years ago, the DEA had found the *hefe* of the Marquez cartel handless with a bullet between his eyes. This was where it had all started for Adam Dunkeld and Eva Roday. Investigators had needed to scrape the body of the former Marquez cartel leader off the floor to collect his remains that day, and King had been there. Was everything that'd happened since then punishment?

"With good reason." Scarlett tapped the photo.

"What makes you think Muñoz stashed Julien here?" he asked.

"Because he knows you were there that day during the DEA operation." Her brain had settled into strategy mode. Where she took apart the problem in front of her and figured out a way to go around it. Or through it. It was one of the skills her instructors and the army had taken advantage of more often than not. "Muñoz is smart. He's managed to gather support for overthrowing the head of Sangre por Sangre while keeping himself alive these past few months. He doesn't leave anything to chance, because one wrong move could take him out. Which means he'll have studied you. Your habits, routines, the people you surround yourself with. He'll want to know everything about you, including your operation history, which cases you seem to take a particular interest in, how you approach an investigation. He would've known Adam was your partner and started looking into him, too."

"Doesn't explain why Adam's body was dropped outside Socorro headquarters. But you think he's been watching me?" His voice hitched on that last word. "Watching Julien?"

"And anyone else in your life. It's what I would do." The plan was already taking shape in her mind. Where she would be, how she'd breach. All from a single photo. Though a decade-old surveillance picture wasn't enough to make a move on. She needed up-to-date intel. "But I'd bet Muñoz's fascination with you started when he suspected Eva Roday was closing in. She most likely led the cartel to Adam, then to you."

"And now Julien." King seemed to break free of the stiffness in his body. "Do you think… Do you think they know Julien was there the night Eva was killed? That he saw the person who killed his mother?"

Scarlett lost her train of thought, taken aback by his concern for a little boy he hadn't even known existed up until a couple months ago. And remembering the utter look of sheer terror on Julien's face from that surveillance footage. King had stepped into the role of father despite not knowing how the hell to take care of anyone but himself, and it looked good on him. All that intensity, all that defensiveness and lack of trust he applied to saving lives through his work was nothing compared to the obvious love burning through him. That was what would bring his son back now. “No. I don’t think the cartel is aware Julien was there that night. If they were, he would already be dead.”

There would be nothing left for them to save.

“Okay. What now?” He nodded, seemingly convincing himself this was the best course of action, that at the end of this, he’d have his son back. No matter the consequences.

She gathered the file together in one pile and whistled low to call the Dobermans from sleep. Each snapped to attention and got to their feet. “We need to get eyes on the warehouse. Photos help, but they don’t tell me everything I need to know.”

“All right. Let me tell Jen we’re leaving.” King stepped free of the hot, too-small office and headed down the lengthy hall to the back of the house.

Investigation file in hand, Scarlett caught sight of the interaction that seemed to stretch mere seconds into full minutes. Of King’s hand on the widow’s arm, of how he’d lowered his voice as another sob shook through the woman.

A knot twisted in Scarlett’s stomach, reminding her of a time when she’d needed someone like King there when her entire world had fallen apart. But she’d had no one. Too ashamed to tell her parents the truth, outcast by the rest of her unit. Dishonorably discharged with nothing and no one to fall back on. If it hadn’t been for Granger Moraise and Ivy Bardot, Scarlett would hate to think of where she’d have ended up. Who would’ve come for her if she hadn’t had Socorro’s protection.

Her throat dried as King secured his partner’s wife in his arms, and Scarlett didn’t have the guts to watch anymore.

Jealousy had the ability to do that. To take a heartfelt moment and twist it into something ugly and lacking, and she hated herself for it. That no one had been there to do the same for her when the person she'd cared about the most had betrayed her and everything he'd believed in.

Didn't matter. Rescuing a ten-year-old boy from his abductors mattered. It was the *only* thing that mattered, and the only way Scarlett could redeem herself.

King broke away from the grieving widow and headed toward her. "I'm ready. Just tell me what you need me to do."

There was a level of trust in that statement. It dug beneath the shame and guilt of her past life and burrowed deep in her chest, annihilating any lingering layer of jealousy and resentment for not getting the care she deserved all those months ago. King was willing to give up the ego built over years of DEA operations for the slightest chance of recovering his son.

She had a plan. They could do this as long as they worked together. Scarlett headed for the door. "Have you ever handled C-4 before?"

HE HADN'T EVER planned on coming back here.

Old yellow external spotlights peppered the building and chased back the closing darkness. Didn't help. No matter what Scarlett had planned for them to get inside, they would be working in the dark. And King hoped like hell he'd be enough to get Julien through what came next.

"Place is registered under a shell company. It'll take a while to untangle who really owns it, but that's not the purpose of today's field trip." Scarlett swiped her finger across the tablet, casting a white-blue glow across her face and chest from the driver seat. "Doesn't look like it has any active permits. At least not from what I can see, which means there's a chance we could be walking into an empty building. It's got a great security system, though."

He ran his gaze over the harsh corners and along the rooftop. No cameras. "How can you tell?"

"The keypads on the doors." She nodded through the windshield to the nearest side door, an outline that nearly bled into the rest of the building. "That brand is one of two Socorro installs for our clients. I've already checked. We weren't the ones who put it in, but no one installs that kind of system on an empty building. They're trying to keep people out for a good reason. Oh, they have Wi-Fi. That helps."

"Or they're trying to keep somebody in." The words didn't quite make it across the center console. King memorized the outlines of rows and rows of orange cable he usually saw on the side of the road during the summer lined up behind the warehouse. Construction crews always seemed to be closing lanes to lay it down somewhere, but it was hard to imagine Sangre por Sangre creating a utility business and benefiting the infrastructure of the state they were trying to take control of. Which could mean they were in the wrong place.

Dead flat landscape stretched out into a sea of nothingness. The other warehouses in the area had gone dark a long time ago. Years of threats and instability in the area had driven out a good chunk of businesses as the cartel grew. If King remembered right, there was a dried-up canal just on the other side of the single construction trailer to the right.

The warehouse itself wasn't anything special—a rectangle with gray-white panels for walls. The bright blue rolltop door stood out, though. Julien's favorite color of the week. His son could be behind that door. Scared. Calling for help and not getting a single answer back. The thought heated King's palms. "Are we doing this or what?"

"I've piggybacked off their W-Fi and accessed the security

system." Scarlett's fingers moved across the screen as though she were playing the most complicated piano concerto. Pure magic. "I can take it down from here."

King tried to get a good look at her tablet screen, seeing nothing but a mess of code he didn't understand. "Wait. You can do that?"

"Ride with me long enough, and you'll see that's not the only thing I can do." Scarlett reached into the back seat, rousing the Dobermans as she pulled a heavy Kevlar vest forward. One for her, then one for him. "We have about ten minutes before the security company realizes the system isn't reporting back and brings the system back online. You ready?"

He slipped his head through the opening in the vest and strapped it tight. Nervous energy prickled at the back of his neck, almost as if in warning, but there was no way in hell King was going to turn around now. Not with the possibility his son was in there. "Let's do this."

They shouldered out of the vehicle at the same time, keeping low and to the shadows. Hans's and Gruber's nails tapped against the asphalt but not loud enough to illicit a security response. King slid through the long line of cement parking space barriers. No vehicles in the lot, and half of the pine tree rooted at the corner of the building had succumbed to dry rot. They should have a straight shot inside, but his gut was telling him it wouldn't be that easy.

It never was with Sangre por Sangre.

Unholstering his sidearm, King crossed the crumbling parking lot to where the tree provided cover. And waited. His breath lodged in his throat. The night was thick with heat, and he couldn't swallow past the doubt. This didn't feel right. Of all the raids he'd executed over the years, this one felt uncomfortable.

King didn't have time to dig into that now. Julien needed him.

He scanned the surrounding desert as Scarlett reached for the pocket door nearest their location. Ten minutes wasn't enough time. Not for a place this size, but he'd do whatever it took to recover his son before those seconds ran out. He gave the okay to breach as he had a dozen times before.

Scarlett wrenched the door back on its hinges and stepped into the blackness waiting to consume them, weapon raised. The Dobermans followed without hesitation. Just before King was swallowed by a vast emptiness on the other side.

His heart rate doubled, thudding hard behind his ears as his senses tried to make up for the complete lack of stimulus. He pressed his feet down harder into the cement floor. He was grounded. As for everything else, he was at a loss.

A click registered in his ears, and a beam cut across the floor in front of him. Holding up one hand, he tried to block the onslaught of light, but it was no use. His senses couldn't adapt that fast.

"You look like you've seen a ghost." Scarlett directed the beam toward the floor and the K9s at her feet. "Come on. We don't have much time before the security company alerts whoever owns this place we're here."

He followed Scarlett's outline. Both hands gripped around his weapon, he took in as much as their limited light source provided.

The layout had changed in the last ten years. Now it was designed as a completely open space with exposed girders stretching across the ceiling. Some kind of inventory created a maze with pallets of crates stacked four or five high. Each box sported red-and-yellow stripes along one side, as if Scarlett and King had been thrown into some kind of messed-up circus he didn't want to get lost in. Two forklifts were wedged under pallets ahead. But it was the unending rows of product that had him picking up the pace.

There was no evidence a bomb had gone off in here ten years ago that'd required the ATF to consult. No sign of the past infiltrating into the present. It was as though that operation had never happened, and yet Adam and Eva couldn't seem to let this place go during their investigation into the cartel.

It didn't matter. King was here for one reason. "They wouldn't leave Julien out in the open. There's got to be offices or something around here."

"Follow me." Scarlett pressed forward with all that confidence King wished he could siphon for himself. She was every bit the military operator she was supposed to be, and there wasn't a single cell in his body that wasn't grateful for her at a time like this. A time when his training had seemingly gone out the window in search of the only person he had left.

She carved a path to the right, weapon held high as though the weight wasn't getting to her like it was to him, and heel-toed it forward like she'd already memorized the layout. Which, she probably had. They passed a steel support running straight up to the ceiling with another row of the red-and-yellow-striped boxes to his left, and that obsessed part of himself that'd pushed him from case to case all these years King prodded him from inside.

He slowed, trying to keep an eye on Scarlett and the Dobermans as he studied the nearest box.

"What are you doing?" The flashlight beam landed at his feet. Scarlett retraced her steps to him. "We have to keep moving. We have about two minutes before the security system pings."

"The photos in Adam's file. He and Eva were watching this place." King holstered his weapon, punctuated by one of the Doberman's low groans. He wasn't sure which. "I need to know why my partner and Julien's mother were killed. I need to know what the cartel is trying to hide."

He pulled a switchblade from his pocket and sliced the packing tape straight down the middle. Grabbing on to Scarlett's wrist, he forced her to angle the flashlight inside.

Packing peanuts stuck to the liner of the box and threatened to go everywhere with one wrong move. He drove his hand inside and felt around.

Then hit something solid. He grabbed on to it, even as he felt every second slipping through their fingers, and pulled the object free. Big blue eyes stared back at him.

A baby doll—heavier than he thought it should be—closed its eyes the farther he leaned it back. Her purple pajamas were pristine with yellow-and-white stripes, but there was something wrong about the angle of her head. King gripped the doll's head with one hand and her body with the other and pulled.

The jolt dislodged hundreds of light blue pills from inside.

"Holy hell." Scarlett followed the spill, crouching to get a better look. "These are fentanyl tabs. Enough to kill a herd of elephants."

There weren't many people outside of the DEA who could identify a pill just by the look and color of it. He was impressed.

Cutting the flashlight back to the box, Scarlett shoved to stand and sank her hand back into the box. She pulled out nine more dolls before turning the beam out into the rest of the warehouse. "Ten dolls per box."

King followed her line of thinking. "In a warehouse packed with boxes. Shit. There has to be enough to here to OD fifty million people."

"Sangre por Sangre has never dealt in fentanyl before." There was something off in her voice. A combination of shock and anger and heaviness they didn't have time to sit with. "Do you think this has something to do with the overseas resources Agents Dunkeld and Roday uncovered?"

"I don't know." He pulled a small rectangular bag from his back pocket—a necessity for DEA agents—and bagged a few of the pills as evidence.

A trio of beeps echoed through the warehouse and singed every nerve King owned. "What the hell was that?"

"The security system. It's back online." Scarlett cast the flashlight beam down the row of boxes that didn't seem to have an end. "They know we're here."

Chapter Seven

The lights flared to life and blinded her for a split second.

The first bullet barely missed Scarlett's head.

The box at her left hit the floor from the impact and scattered ten baby dolls at her feet. Big wide eyes stared up at her. Hans and Gruber growled in unison, and every muscle down Scarlett's back hardened in battle-ready defense. A wash of adrenaline had her reaching for King. "Get down!"

She used her body weight to pull him to the floor, dragging him beneath her. The second bullet cut through the maze of boxes and pinged off the support column less than two feet from her. Right where he would've been standing.

"You just can't help yourself, can you?" King's breath mixed with hers. "Underneath me in the morgue, on top of me here. You're insatiable."

"Glad to know where your head is at." She rolled to her right. They couldn't stay here. Not without catching the next bullet. "The blueprints of this place outlined an emergency exit on the north side of the building. I can get you there, but I need you to do everything I say. Understand?"

Hans and Gruber were at the ready. Just waiting for her to give the command, but Scarlett wasn't interested in facing off with the cartel in a last stand to the death. Her job was to get them all out alive.

"I'm not leaving." King punctuated the three words by cokcing a round into the barrel of his sidearm. "I need to know if Julien is here."

"You don't get it, do you?" Low shouts echoed through the maze of aisles and stacks. Four distinct voices so far. Most likely more. The potential carved through her, hiking her heart rate higher until it was all she could hear. "We're in enemy territory. Outnumbered and outmanned. And the only way we're leaving this warehouse alive is if we go right now. Winding up dead doesn't help anyone, King."

"I'm not leaving without my son." An energy Scarlett used to recognize in herself lit up his eyes. Determination. Desperation. The line between the two was thinner than most people thought. He maneuvered into a crouch, weapon in hand, and chanced standing a bit taller to gauge the situation. "Where are the offices?"

"You don't have to do this." She hated the words coming out of her mouth. Hated the tension combing through her, the dryness at the back of her throat. She'd trained on blood-soaked battlefields and handled security that saved thousands of lives over the course of her military career. But she didn't want to do this.

Scarlett leveraged her heels into the cement floor, pressing her back against the nearest stack of boxes. She couldn't think. Couldn't get herself to move. What the hell was happening? "We have an evidence bag of pills. We can take what we know to the DEA and Socorro. We don't have to do this alone."

"Where are they, Scarlett?" His tone shut down any chance of changing his mind. Locking that hard gaze on her, King shook his head. "You know what? I don't have time for this. I'll find the offices myself."

He kept low as he cut down the nearest aisle.

"Wait." The sinking feeling in her stomach wouldn't let up.

She reached after King but only met thin air. It wasn't supposed to be like this. They were a team. But she couldn't make herself move. Even as those low shouts got closer.

He vanished into another row, out of sight.

Leaving her to fight alone.

Hans practically vibrated from her next growl. Louder. A warning.

"Move, damn it." Scarlett knocked her head back into a box in hopes of resetting her brain. She couldn't stay here. Sliding one hand farther out, she focused everything she had on going after King. He was going to get himself killed. Too blind to protect himself with only the slightest chance of protecting his son.

Movement registered off to her right at the head of the aisle. Gruber barked a split second before Scarlett's instincts brought the weapon up. She squeezed her finger around the trigger. A spray of bullets shot into the ceiling as the gunman fell backward.

Her position was compromised.

"Okay." She could do this. She had to do this. And she had to do it now. Scarlett shoved to her feet and took that initial step in King's wake. This was what she was trained for. What she was good at. She wasn't going to let him do it alone. Her feet felt heavier than they should have as she whistled for Hans and Gruber to follow. "I'm coming."

Another burst of gunfire exploded from somewhere else in the warehouse. Her entire nervous system homed on that sound. She picked up the pace. "King."

Return fire—deeper in tone—cut through the chaos. He was still alive. She could still make this right between them. Scarlett slowed at the end of the aisle.

A fist rocketed into her face.

Lightning struck behind her eyes. She fell back. Pain launched into her elbows as she failed to cushion her impact.

Hans and Gruber didn't wait for an order, launching forward. The attacker's scream bounced off the warehouse's metal walls as each Doberman took a piece of the cartel soldier for themselves. Stumbling to her feet, Scarlett struggled to breathe through the blood cascading down her face. Her nose was broken. *"Hier."* Come.

The twins released their death hold on the soldier and promptly fell back in line at Scarlett's feet. Blood spread over the gunman's arms and stained his shirt. The sight of which held her hostage for far too long. She'd signed on with Socorro to do good. This…wasn't it.

Groans escaped up his throat. Still alive. Swiping the back of her hand beneath her nose, she stood over him, weapon ready to finish the job. "How many of you are there?"

Cradling his arms to his chest, he spat at her boot. "You don't have a chance."

Scarlett was ready to leave him there. Ready to make him suffer, but she couldn't have him following after her. She slammed the butt of her pistol against his head, knocking him unconscious. "I already know that."

She moved slower than she wanted to. The click of Hans's and Gruber's nails kept her focused. In the present. On alert. Dead silence seemed to settle through the warehouse and vaulted her unease through the roof.

Something was wrong.

The return fire she'd identified from King's weapon had gone quiet. Did that mean…? No. She couldn't think like that. Couldn't let herself get distracted. Find King. Get him out. That was all that mattered. "Please still be alive."

A howl pierced through her ears.

Every cell in Scarlett's body fired in defense as she turned. Hans was down. Unmoving on the cement. *No. No, no, no, no.*

Gruber launched at the threat coming from ahead. They were surrounded, being pulled in two different directions. Gruber took down his target as strong arms locked around Scarlett's neck from behind. Oxygen locked in her throat and chased back that sinking feeling that'd taken control.

"I was hoping I would be the one to get my hands on you." The man at her back pulled her into his chest, his grating voice at her ear. "Scarlett Beam. Socorro's most feared operative. Let's see how feared you are on your own, eh?"

Scarlett didn't have time to think about how he knew her. Only that the attacker Gruber had gone after seemed to be wearing some kind of protective gear. As though the cartel had known they'd need it.

Because they'd been expecting her.

She brought the gun up, aiming over her shoulder, and pulled the trigger. The bullet went wide by a mile. But the resulting percussion did what she'd hoped.

Her attacker jerked her to the left, his grip around her neck faltering. High-pitched ringing drowned out the sounds of Gruber's growls not thirty feet away as Scarlett swung the gun up.

Too slow.

Pain spiked through her hand as the weapon ripped free and hit the floor. Giving her the first look at the man standing in front of her.

Muñoz. Not just a construct of King's investigation. But in the flesh. Her heart threatened to beat straight out of her chest as she tried to gauge movement elsewhere in the warehouse. No more shouted orders. No more gunfire. As though the fight had already been lost before it started. "Where is Agent Elsher?"

"Right where I want him," Muñoz said. "As are you."

No. She launched forward with a kick of her own and elbowed the son of a bitch in the chest. With no impact. She swung her fist toward his face as hard as she could, but he shoved her backward.

She hit the ground. Air seeped from her lungs, but she wouldn't give up. She wouldn't stop. Not until she couldn't fight anymore. Scarlett pressed herself up and went in for another strike.

Muñoz caught her fist in his palm and squeezed, but she wasn't going to let him slow her down. She spun to dislodge his hold and rocketed her knuckles into his face.

Disoriented, Muñoz stumbled back, and Scarlett took advantage.

She wedged her toes into the crease between his abdomen and thigh and hauled herself higher up his body. Wrapping her calf around the back of his neck, she increased the pressure until he was the one who couldn't breathe. But it wasn't enough.

Muñoz dug his fingers into her legs and threw her off.

Gravity gripped her insides a split second before she hit a packing crate. Boxes of fentanyl and baby dolls did nothing to counter the pain overtaking her entire body, but she couldn't let herself give in. Clawing from the mess, she grabbed for the blade tucked in her cargo pants. She rolled until she hit the strength of Muñoz's ankles and hiked herself to her knees.

Stabbing him in the back of the thigh.

His scream filtered through his teeth, just before the lieutenant locked his hands around Scarlett's throat and dragged her to her feet. He was strong. Stronger than her, but she had something he didn't. The will to save lives. And there was nothing that would stop her from keeping her word to King.

"You're going to regret that." Muñoz backed her into the

edge of the oversize metal support. "I'm going to take everything you love and kill it, Scarlett Beam. Those people you work with—even Agent Elsher and his son—I'm going to make you watch as I burn your entire world to the ground. Then I'm going to kill you."

She worked to pry his hands from around her neck, but his grip only seemed to intensify. White pinpricks invaded her peripheral vision. It was no use. He would strangle her if she kept trying to physically overpower him. Scarlett went for the blade lodged in the back of his thigh, but Muñoz had expected that, too. He swiped her attack away as easily as he swiped at a fly.

Then slammed his fist into her face. Once. Twice.

The world went black.

HELL. HE'D MADE a mess of things.

Pain pulsed in the back of his neck as he dragged his chin from his chest. Like he'd fallen asleep sitting up. Guess he technically had. Though the falling asleep part hadn't been his choice.

King put too much momentum into his neck, and his head fell back to stare up into a too-bright glow of fluorescent lighting. The office wasn't much more than a storage closet with foggy glass in the door. It was bland and empty, apart from an old metal desk the likes of which he hadn't seen in over a decade.

Damn it. His head hurt, but his pride had taken the biggest hit. He'd been so convinced Julien was here—desperate to be there for his son—he'd rushed in without a second thought as to what might wait on the other side. The attack had come fast, and the next thing he'd known was unconsciousness.

And now Scarlett and her Dobermans were out there trying to fix this. For him.

He'd never been the kind of man who would ask the people around him to do something he wasn't willing to do himself. But this… This wasn't going at all as he'd hoped.

A smattering of items on the metal desk a few feet away caught his attention. Phone, wallet, keys, badge, business cards. All his. No sign of his sidearm, though. His attackers had stripped him of anything he could use to his advantage.

King tried to break through the rope scratching through the layers of skin around his wrists. Muscles he hadn't used for far too long weren't interested in showing up for him now. He'd relied too heavily on his gear these past few years. All of which had been taken from him now. And it would cost him everything.

Shadowed movement shifted on the other side of the fogged glass. No sounds of gunfire or fighting. Nothing to suggest Scarlett and her dogs were still alive.

He needed to get out of here. Get them out of here. He'd brought her into this mess. He'd be the one to make sure she didn't pay the price. "Think, Elsher."

He studied every inch of the office. It looked as though it'd been stripped for parts. All this time he'd believed that original DEA operation had hurt Sangre por Sangre's growth. At least shut down one of their primary warehouses. Turned out, he, Adam and Eva hadn't done a damn thing to bring these bastards to a stop. The cartel had simply taken on a new face.

His head pounded in rhythm to his heart rate. Too hard. Too loud. Twisting his wrists opposite directions, he worked the rope digging in deeper, but there wasn't any bit of give. He was screwed in the leg department, too. No room for escape. The chair he was tied to wasn't anything special. Though steel posed a problem. Guess the Sangre por Sangre cartel had too many mishaps with wood. Or maybe they'd suddenly turned environmentally conscious. Decided to give back for once.

"And I'm the freaking tooth fairy," he said.

Oh, hell. He *was* the tooth fairy now. Julien had a loose tooth ready to come out any day now, and King would have to be the one to sneak into his room and leave a dollar beneath his kid's pillow without waking him.

No. He couldn't think about that right now. The thought of never getting to be the tooth fairy for his son only messed with his head.

There. On the back wall. A wire storage shelf stacked with paper boxes. No labels telling him what each of them housed, but it couldn't be paper.

He tipped his weight back onto two chair legs, his toes barely connecting with the floor. His shoulders screamed for relief, but King had to try. This was going to hurt, but it would be nothing compared to losing his son. Or Scarlett.

King shoved back against his toes. Gravity launched his stomach into his throat a split second before he hit the floor. The combination of the metal rim of the chair and his body weight threatened to break both of his arms, and he swallowed the scream ready to explode from his chest. He rolled onto his side, taking the too-heavy chair with him as he tried to catch his breath. That was going to leave a bruise.

Digging his heels into the floor, he shoved himself across the floor toward the shelf. Inch by agonizing inch. He was out of breath by the time he reached the base. Sweat beaded under his bottom lip. "Move, damn it." Though how he was going to get these boxes open without the use of his hands or feet was a mystery.

The shelf itself had been constructed of smooth stainless steel. No way to use the frame to cut through the rope. But the sharp edges where the grating held the boxes themselves might help. King leveraged one shoulder into the floor and circled his feet to the left, setting his back to the wire rack. And set his wrists against the raw edges of steel.

He couldn't move more than a few centimeters at a time, but that was all he needed. The fibers of the rope caught, and King put everything he had left into keeping the pressure on. Back and forth. Back and forth. He wasn't sure any of it did a damn bit of good, but he wasn't going to give in. Not to the cartel. And not to the doubt telling him he wasn't ever going to find his son. That he was too late.

A warning growl pierced through the fogged glass on the other side of the room. Shit. He was out of time. King scanned the room for something—anything—that would get him out of this chair, but it was no use.

The door kicked back on its hinges and slammed into the wall behind it. A cartel soldier fought with a Doberman at the end of a choke chain, trying to drag the animal into the room, but the K9 wasn't cooperating in the least.

Gruber—when had King figured out which was which?—wrenched his head from side to side as he dug his heels into the floor.

"Gruber," he said.

The dog set coal-black eyes on him. Accusatory. Scared. Pissed off to hell and back. The soldier managed to pull the Doberman fully into the room with a heavy tug. But if Gruber was here… Where was Hans? Where was Scarlett?

Another soldier fireman-carried the second dog into the room and not-so-gently deposited her onto the floor. Injured? Dead? King didn't know, but he sure as hell wanted to witness what Scarlett had done in return.

A scraping sound overrode Gruber's overly loud fight for freedom. A rhythmic sound that raised the hairs on the back of King's neck. A large man struggled to fit through the narrow door as he dragged something heavy and unconscious behind him. Recognition hit, and King's entire world tore apart at the seams.

Muñoz.

Age had gotten to Muñoz over the past ten years. Striations of gray chased back the muddied brown in the man's facial hair and eyebrows. The skin beneath those empty eyes sagged and folded as gravity didn't have much care for appearances, but there was still a hint of the man Muñoz had been. Physically lean, well-kept in the suit department. Much stronger than he wanted people to know. "Hello, Agent Elsher. I brought you a present."

Muñoz dragged the body forward, that thick accent carving into King's memory.

Scarlett hit the floor without protest. Unmoving. Blood dried beneath her nose and around her mouth. Gruber's low whine punctuated the ache in King's gut as he visually searched for a pulse or a chest fall. Something to tell him he hadn't gotten Socorro's security operator killed for nothing.

"Get him up," Muñoz said.

The cartel member who'd dropped Hans to the floor left the Doberman where she lay and closed the distance between him and King. Rough hands jerked King back to sitting, and feeling shot back into King's arms.

Despite the image he wanted to convey, that of a DEA agent who didn't give into threats, King couldn't control the tremors in his chin. He tried to breathe through it, to give his nervous system something other than Scarlett and Julien to focus on, but it was no use. Muñoz wasn't known for keeping hostages. Both Adam and Eva had learned that the hard way.

Palpable silence filled the room, only interrupted by Muñoz's advance. "How long has it been, Elsher? Ten years? You don't look like you've aged a day. You must take care of yourself." The lieutenant rounded behind him, lowering his face beside King's. "Such a waste."

King didn't answer. His gaze locked on Scarlett. She was alive. She had to be.

"You know, I've never understood all these elaborate tortures the people I work with like to use. The accelerants in tires. Countless days of beatings. Acid on the skin." Muñoz penetrated King's peripheral vision. The cartel lieutenant unsheathed a tactical blade, dark steel serrated in high peaks and valleys. The lights didn't even reflect off the surface. Not like King expected. "It's the simplest things that can get the point across."

Muñoz swiped the blade across King's thigh.

Stinging pain erupted faster than he expected and stole the air in his lungs. He bit back the scream trying to force its way free, but it was no use. His composure had been corrupted the second he set eyes on Scarlett. Blood rushed through the wound though the laceration was shallow compared to what it could've been. He stared straight ahead. Not willing to give Muñoz the satisfaction of breaking him.

A slap to one side of the face ensured King couldn't disappear. That he had to stay present. "There will be little for the DEA or your son to identify you as human when I'm finished, Agent Elsher. The only question is, will you give me what I want in time?"

King forced himself to take a breath.

"I want everything your partner and that bitch from ATF collected on me and my operation." The weight of Muñoz's attention intensified the pain in King's wound. One second. Two. The lieutenant nodded, backing off slightly.

The second cut went deeper. King couldn't contain the scream of pain this time. His agony filled the room and took

Gruber by surprise. The K9 howled in unison, but the man handling the choke chain cut him off short.

King's heart rate skyrocketed. Sweat slipped down the sides of his face.

"Perhaps your partner's wife will tell me where Agent Dunkeld hid the information he gathered. Jen, right? And the girls. Beautiful, beautiful girls. I can see them doing very well for Sangre por Sangre." Muñoz turned to the cartel soldier hovering over Hans and hiked a thumb toward the door. The subordinate left the room without a word, closing the door behind him. "In the meantime, why don't I remind you of what I'm capable of?"

Shuffling sounded through the door, and then the cartel soldier carried Julien—kicking and punching—in his arms.

Just before Muñoz stabbed the blade down into the top of King's thigh.

Chapter Eight

The scream ripped her out of unconsciousness.

Scarlett's heart thudded too hard in her chest as fractions of memory invaded. She sank in to the prickling numbness in her shoulder as she tried to gauge the situation without giving anything away. Until she caught sight of Hans.

The Doberman wasn't moving. Didn't seem to be breathing.

Instant grief burned in Scarlett's eyes. Hot and heavy and encompassing. She was slightly comforted by the fact Gruber seemed to be giving the man at the other end of a choke chain everything he had. With any luck, her defender would get the upper hand. Two cartel soldiers had positioned themselves off to one side from what she could see through the crack in her eyelids.

Her breath lodged in her nasal cavity, forcing her to part her lips. Pain kept rhythm with the ache in her face. Muñoz. He'd broken her nose. The crust of blood stuck to her face, but she couldn't worry about that now.

A groan called to something deep and protective as she pinpointed the source of the original scream. King had been restrained. Wrists, hands. And now a blade stabbed into his lower part of his thigh. But he wasn't the only one suffering—a third soldier tried to keep hold of a little boy struggling in his arms.

Julien?

The breath rushed out of her as a thousand different escape scenarios took shape in her mind. Each of them more unlikely than the one before, but one thing was clear. No matter what happened in the next few minutes, she'd get them out. All of them. Scarlett kept her senses trained on each threat as she worked her free hand toward the inside hem of her cargo pants. Muñoz had most likely stripped her of every weapon they could find, but there was hope they hadn't searched past the surface.

"All I need from you, Agent Elsher, is the location of Adam Dunkeld's and Eva Roday's investigation files." The cartel lieutenant dragged a chair from behind an old metal desk that resembled more of a cartoon anvil than a place to get any work done, the vibration of which rumbled through her.

A forced exhale reached her ears as she waited for King's answer. The files? All of this—the deaths of two federal agents, the kidnapping of a ten-year-old boy—for information for an off-the-books investigation. What the hell had Agents Dunkeld and Roday uncovered?

King's groan turned into more of a growl.

"The files, Agent Elsher," Muñoz said. "Please."

"I've got a little itch. On the right side of this blade." A hardness Scarlett had never witnessed seemed to roll through King as he faced off with Muñoz. "Do you mind?"

A frustrated laugh punctuated Muñoz shoving to his feet. He threw his chair backward, barely missing one of the cartel soldiers stationed behind him. The lieutenant latched on to the blade and twisted it deeper into her partner's thigh.

The sound of King's pain etched deep into Scarlett's memory, to the point she would hear it every time she closed her eyes. It took everything she had not to get to her feet and find another home for that blade, but she'd already failed

King once tonight. She wouldn't let it happen again. Gruber echoed King's lament and doubled the amount of agony washing through her.

She took the opportunity of distraction to make more progress on the inside of her waistband. To the razor blade she'd sewn into the fabric there.

It wasn't much, but it would have to be enough.

"No, to the right, Muñoz. I said to the right." A half laugh, half sob contorted King's usually even voice, shaking through him. His body wasn't going to be able to take much more. Shock hit everyone differently, but judging by the sweat coating his entire face and neck, Scarlett bet he didn't have much time before the laughs died. "Now everyone's going to know you died scratching my itch."

"I died?" Muñoz's voice didn't reflect his amusement.

"Yes." The tremors had settled in the past few seconds, giving her a raw look at the man holding out as long as possible to save the people he cared about. "Because no matter what you do, I'm not going to give you the location of those files, which means your bosses are going to hunt you down and cut you into tiny little pieces. And if you kill me, hurt my son or my partner, there will be nowhere for you to hide."

Scarlett pulled at the removable stitches and opened up the small slit in the fabric of her waistband. The razor blade was inside. No bigger than half of her index finger but deadly enough in a pinch.

"That's where we disagree, Agent Elsher." Muñoz leaned down toward King's face, his back to Scarlett. "Because even after I get rid of your bodies, the DEA would still welcome me with open arms. They need what I know."

"Seems you've thought this through." King was struggling to breathe. Exaggerated. Short.

"I have." Muñoz, out of breath, sank down onto one knee,

effectively ruining that pretty suit. Though maybe the blood stains on the right sleeve had beaten the floor to it. "Now, give me the location of the files, and I will at least let your son live."

But not Scarlett. Not Hans or Gruber. And not King.

Short bursts of breath escaped King's control as the dip in his brows suggested his inner fight with what might happen next. That intense gaze settled on her, and in that moment, she locked her full attention on him. And he knew. He knew that she wasn't going to give up or give in. Scarlett pulled the razor blade free, letting the sharp ends bite into her palms. She nodded. Just a little longer. That was all she asked.

Muñoz slapped the DEA agent's face, bringing him back to the present moment. "Do it soon enough, and Julien might even walk away in one piece."

King's laugh hiked his smile higher. Despite the blood loss and the overall agony he must have felt, he was going to hang on. To give them a chance of escape.

"You really aren't going to tell me, are you?" The cartel lieutenant wiped at his own brow, as though torture took more out of him than his victims.

"No." King shook his head.

"In that case." Muñoz shoved to his feet and kicked at King's chair. The agent tipped backward and landed with a hard thud against the cement floor. The lieutenant unsheathed a smaller blade than the one sticking out of King's thigh. "I'll start sending you back to the DEA one piece at a time."

Scarlett put everything she had into rolling, throwing herself into the back of Muñoz's legs, razor blade in hand. Her Kevlar vest threatened to slow her down, but that bright spot of determination was all she had to hold on to. Muñoz fell backward, slamming into the floor with his legs draped over Scarlett's side.

She swiped the blade across the tendon in the back of one ankle. "Can't have you following us."

Muñoz's scream outdid King's and called the other three soldiers to action. Only two of them were preoccupied with their captives. Julien and Gruber.

Eyes on the third soldier coming at her from across the room, Scarlett sawed through the ropes around King's wrists, then launched herself at the attacker closing in. "Get Julien out of here!"

The soldier pulled a gleaming steel blade and arced the knife down. Scarlett ducked, feeling every strike from her previous fight bruised into her sides and face.

Her attacker overextended, putting his back to her, and she took full advantage. She kicked him down as Gruber's growls grew louder with each passing second. She angled her back to the Doberman and the man at the end of Gruber's leash. Dragging her belt from her waistband, she wrapped it around her left forearm as the knifeman got back on his feet.

He came at her a second time, straight to the chest. Scarlett stepped to the side, letting him slide right past her. Into the cartel member at her back. The knife hit home, and the choke chain hit the floor.

Gruber was free, and he didn't waste a single second letting everyone in the room know about it. The Doberman launched at the knifeman as Scarlett caught the bastard's wrist and turned his own blade on himself. Shoving back with everything she had, she cornered both soldiers. Then kicked at the knee of the soldier with the knife.

Muñoz's screamed orders were nothing compared to the crunch of bone as the knifeman collapsed. Scarlett helped herself to his blade as the man who had held Gruber rushed forward with a knife of his own. She swiped at the bright steel in his hand but won a fist to the face instead. He launched at her, blade first, but missed her rib cage and embedded the knife into a metal filing cabinet as old as the oversize desk.

Scarlett knocked him out cold with an elbow to the face, but they were running out of time. The longer they stayed in this room, the sooner they'd be surrounded. The first soldier came at her again. She landed another kick to his chest and sent him backward, but it wasn't enough. He ran at her, and all she could think to do was tackle him to the floor. They hit as one, each struggling to get ahold of the knife in her hand.

Gruber latched on to the soldier beneath her and jerked his head back and forth to tear through clothing and flesh and anything else that might get in his way. The resulting screams triggered a high pitch in her ears as she let the Doberman keep himself occupied. Adrenaline gave her the false sense of being able to tear through anything else that got in her way. She turned to deal with the last soldier holding Julien against his will.

To see King standing over the body with his son tucked behind him. The tactical knife from his thigh was in his hand. His shoulders hitched as he tried to catch his breath. Blood and sweat combined across his skin, deepening the carved lines in his face.

Scarlett took an initial step forward, all too aware that his will to protect and defend could turn on her any second. His wound was bleeding freely. There was no way they were going to make it without an intervention. Soft whimpers escaped from the boy hiding as much of himself as possible, and she tucked the knife in her hand into her back pocket. They weren't finished. There was an entire warehouse of cartel members standing between them and their escape. "You good?"

"Yeah. I'm good." King headed for the items piled on the desk and shoved them back into his pockets. The last—his badge—seemed to weigh on him heavier than all of them together from around his neck. Shuffling back toward Julien, he hiked his son into his arms. "Let's get the hell out of here," he said.

Just before he collapsed.

HE COULDN'T FEEL his leg.

King tried to get a hold on his vision as a blurred shape rushed toward him. Everything seemed to slow down and speed up at the same time. Muñoz clawed across the floor like the snake he was, blood trailing behind him in long streaks.

But it was the woman running for him with a dog draped over her shoulder that held King's attention. Her features remained out of focus until she was fisting one hand in his shirt and hauling him to his feet. There was no mistaking her for his partner. Or what she'd done to try to get them out of here alive.

"Scarlett." Her name was strangled in his mouth.

Gruber lunged for Muñoz and took the son of a bitch straight back to the floor. King struggled to shift his weight onto his good leg as Scarlett reached for his son's hand. The boy kicked and punched with everything he had, but the security operator took every hit with hesitation. She yelled something at King, running for the door.

And all he could do was follow. Because she was carrying them. All of them. Hans, Julien, him. With her strength. With her determination, and he couldn't help but want to stay close. She was aggressive and rational and passionate. She was everything he needed as King forced himself to take that first step, and she was the one who was going to get them out of here alive.

King maneuvered around Muñoz, who was still trying to claw toward the door. Bloody hands locked around his ankle and threatened to pull him down, but Scarlett had already gotten his son out the door with Gruber on her heels. King would do whatever it took to make sure they left together. Leg be damned.

Muñoz's mouth formed words drowned out by the hard pounding of King's heart. The bastard's fingernails dug through the fabric of King's pants and bit into skin. "Not… over."

"Yeah, it is." King shucked the lieutenant's hold and lunged out the door, both hands on the frame for support. His leg was dead. No telling how bad the damage was, but it didn't look good. Didn't feel good, either, but it was nothing compared with the alternative. His son would not witness King's murder by the same drug cartel that had sentenced his mother to death. Julien had suffered enough. King would take a stab wound any day.

Full-blown chaos exploded from every corner of the warehouse as their escape party left the safety of the office. Scarlett forged on up ahead, leading them to cover behind a row of boxes that wouldn't hold up against a hail of bullets for long. Julien jerked out of her hold, and she couldn't get him back, surveying the fight in front of them.

His son bolted out into the open. Terrified. Confused. With no place left to go.

King had no choice other than to set weight on his bad leg to catch the ten-year-old around the middle as he ran past. A scream ripped up the kid's throat and tore King's last remaining strength from him. No one should ever have to hear a scream like that. Dragging Julien into the nearest aisle, he set his son's back against his chest as bullets impacted the wall in front of them. King covered Julien's forehead with his hand, setting the kid's head against his chest. "It's okay. I've got you, Julien. I've got you. Do what I'm doing. Just breathe, buddy. Follow what I'm doing."

It was the same thing he told Julien every time the nightmares came for his son. The same comforting hold that kept the ten-year-old from hurting himself or others. And it was all King could do now.

Scarlett chanced a glance toward them, exposing the situation in her expression. They were out of options.

The realization hit harder than getting the news about Eva or the call about Adam. Because this wasn't a bunch of operatives that'd been thrown together in the name of public safety. The men and women he served with had signed on to risk their lives for the greater good, and as much as King would give his own life to save any one of them, this was his son at risk now. The only person he had left to care about in his world.

"That's right. Breathe like me, and soon it will all be over." He kissed Julien on the crown of his head. "We're going to get out of here. We're going to go home. I just need you to be brave for a little longer. Okay?"

Julien's grip left half-moon impressions in King's hand, as though the boy had marked him as his own. His son nodded.

Blood seeped from his wound and settled beneath his leg in a pool that got stickier and thicker by the second. The knife hadn't penetrated all the way through, but it'd done a hell of a job on the way in. King was bleeding out. Slowly. Minute by minute. And the harder he pushed himself, the sooner he'd have to let Julien go.

Scarlett's gaze dipped to his leg, then back to his face. Understanding seemed to hit as they sat there warding off bullets.

"You're doing great, buddy." King tried repositioning the bad leg, but the damn thing wouldn't move. Not an inch. The pressure in his chest reached an all-time high. No matter how hard King had fought to be the father Julien deserved, he wasn't going to make it out of this. Wasn't going to be there for his son. Not like he'd come to hope. "Now, you see that pretty lady with the dogs? Her name is Scarlett. She's the one giving the orders. I need you to do everything she says. She's going to make sure you're safe."

Scarlett let Hans slide down to the floor—gently. She kept low as she came to sit by King and Julien, her mouth trying for a smile as the world around them threatened to collapse. "Do you like dogs, Julien?"

His son nodded, though from the angle of his head, King bet the kid wasn't looking at her. And he wouldn't. Not until he started trusting her. It was only in the past couple weeks, King had gotten the pleasure of his son's eye contact. It'd meant so much then. More so now.

"This is Gruber. Funny name, huh?" Scarlett tucked the Doberman into her side and planted a kiss behind the dog's ear. "Would you like to pet him? He likes scratches behind his ears."

Julien reached forward, and King couldn't help but memorize this moment. Where the three of them had somehow created a solid bubble between them and the evil that waited on the other side of these shelves. His son massaged behind Gruber's ears, and the K9 flicked a long pink tongue against Julien's wrist.

"Aren't you lucky? That means he likes you." Scarlett locked her gaze on King. Neither of them wanted to say it, but leaving the truth unsaid didn't make it untrue. King wasn't leaving this warehouse. Not as long as he couldn't control this bleeding. Which meant he had to trust her to keep her word. She had to get Julien out alone. Scarlett turned her attention back to his son. "And because he likes you, he's going to do whatever it takes to keep you safe. So am I. Okay? No matter what. I promise." She extended her hand. Waiting.

And Julien took it. Which was a miracle in and of itself. King couldn't remember a single time his son had reached out like that. Not since he'd come to live with King. It was just one more piece of evidence of Scarlett's effect on people.

She brought the boy to his feet as she stood.

But Julien hung on to King's other hand, unwilling to let go.

Tears burned in King's eyes. This wasn't like dropping Julien off at school every day, worried something would happen that King couldn't fix. This was goodbye. And damn it, he wasn't ready. "It's all right, buddy. You've got your very own personal guard dog. Cool, huh? And Scarlett here is going to make sure no one can hurt you again. You go with them. I'll be right behind you."

He'd never lied to his son before, and it didn't sit well now, but King couldn't destroy this boy's world all over again. King kissed Julien's hand, giving it a small shake. "It's going to be scary, but you've got this. You're amazing and brave and as stubborn as they come." King was losing it. Going right over the edge of being able to let go. "Go on now. Before you know it, we'll be back at home in our own beds with a big bowl of popcorn and your favorite movie."

Shouts grew louder. Closer.

They were out of time together.

Julien fell into King's arms, squeezing harder than ever before, and King's heart hitched in his chest. Just before his son pulled away. One hand on Gruber's collar, the boy kept close to Scarlett as she backed herself toward the end of the aisle. That brilliant gaze cut through him.

"I'll protect him. I promise," she said.

"I know you will." In the short time they'd partnered together, he'd learned that was the kind of woman she was. A woman of her word.

King watched as they got to the end of the aisle. Scarlett bent down, gathering Hans into her side, and whispered something to Julien, who nodded before taking her hand.

"I'll hold them off as long as I can," King said.

His son turned back to look at him one last time. Just as he'd imagined his mom had done when she'd slipped free of his bedroom all those years ago. Hell, King couldn't help but see her in that boy's face.

"I love you, Julien. Don't ever forget that." King didn't care if the cartel heard him. All he had to do was give Scarlett and Julien and Gruber a chance to escape.

Julien didn't answer. But King saw it there. The softening, the glisten of tears. His son loved him, too. In his own way and in his own time.

Two months wasn't enough for King. Wouldn't ever be enough, but he sure as hell appreciated the time they had together in the last few minutes of his life.

Scarlett led Julien out of sight, Gruber taking his job seriously at his son's side. And they were gone. Leaving King to fight off Sangre por Sangre alone.

The door to the office swung open, one of Muñoz's men dead center in the frame. Gun raised and aimed.

But King wasn't going out on their terms. Just as he would bet Eva and Adam hadn't. The last reserves of adrenaline dumped into his veins.

King was on his feet.

He lunged.

And tackled the cartel soldier a split second before the gun went off.

Chapter Nine

The shot punctured through the rhythmic pounding of her feet and Gruber's nails against the asphalt. Every cell in Scarlett's body knew the source, and instinctively she slowed their escape. Hans's weight nearly pulled her to the ground.

A hundred feet. That was all that stood between them and the SUV, but the need to go back—to pull King out—gutted her. But she couldn't turn back. She'd given him her word she would get Julien out, and there was no way she'd put his little life at risk. Not now. "Almost there."

Midnight air sucked the sweat off her skin and from beneath her gear. She picked up the pace. Julien was breathing hard to keep up, but he was alive, and that was all that mattered. Scarlett remote-started the car. "Get in."

No other gunshots came from inside the warehouse. Nothing to suggest the cartel was still fighting off the threat that had penetrated their walls. Which meant…

No. She didn't want to think about that.

She helped Julien into the back seat and fastened his seat belt. She had to keep her word. Rounding to the cargo area, she laid Hans—still breathing—across the carpeted space as Gruber jumped inside to settle down next to his sister. Any second Muñoz would order his men to expand the search area. They'd be found. They had to leave. Now.

But Scarlett couldn't help but slow when she caught sight of Julien with his hand pressed against the window. Waiting for King to be right behind them as he'd promised. Why was it people always said that? *I'll be right behind you.* Knowing the circumstances would force them to lie?

She followed Julien's line of sight to the side door of the warehouse that nearly blended in with the metal sheeting. All but for a single overhead light outlining the exit. Two seconds. Three.

King wasn't coming through that door.

He wasn't going to be able to keep his promise.

Unless she helped him.

Scarlett collected the remaining ammunition and her backup pistol from the cargo area, her mind made up. Gruber would kill anyone who tried to get into this vehicle. She reached for the Doberman, sliding her thumb across his head. *"Pass auf."* Stand alert.

Setting her palm against Hans's rib cage, Scarlett took in the K9's heat to settle the nerves trying to win out over her determination. "Take care of them. Okay?" She grabbed for the steel Hux tool all Socorro operatives carried to get through push bar doors in case of emergency. Two wedged prongs would create a gap between the locking mechanism and the frame while the solid length of the tool gave her leverage to pry it open from the outside. Not entirely legal. But useful.

"Julien, I want you to stay in the SUV. No matter what happens, don't open this car door for anyone but me. Okay? I'm going to get your dad. I'll be right back."

She didn't wait for an answer. King didn't have that kind of time. She slammed the cargo area closed and locked the running vehicle. Couldn't have the state taking Julien from her because she'd left him in a hot locked car. The air conditioning would keep him cool enough. Scarlett tucked the tool beneath her arm as she loaded a fresh magazine into her weapon and faced off with the warehouse, every nerve in her body on fire.

She moved fast, closing the distance between her and the exit. Couldn't go back the same way they'd gone in before. Muñoz and the rest of the cartel were already on alert. She leveraged her shoulder against the metal sheeting of the warehouse, the absorbed heat of the day working bone-deep.

She glanced back at the SUV, imagining Julien watching her through the heavily tinted bulletproof glass. She could do this. She had to do this. For that boy. And for King.

Holstering her weapon, Scarlett angled away from the building and inserted the Hux tool between the door latch and the frame. A gap in the frame increased with every pull. Until the door snapped free altogether. She slid the tool along her forearm. Bracing herself for what came next. Aches pulsed in her face from the last time she'd squared off with the soldiers on the other side of this door, but it wasn't going to stop her now.

Scarlett breached into quiet. As though the entire warehouse were waiting for her to come in far enough so they could jump out and yell, *Surprise!* But there wasn't going to be cake at the end of this party.

She kept her back pressed against the nearest shelf, moving slower than she wanted to. Taking in every change around her. Where was King?

Movement caught in her peripheral vision from a gap between shelves in the aisle off to her right. Coming straight at her if she didn't move fast. Forcing her legs to pick up the pace, she jogged to meet the soldier leading with an assault rifle aimed level for anyone who got in his way.

Scarlett's knees protested as she crouched. One bullet

would end this for all of them. She had to stay alive. Work smarter, not harder.

Wire shelves bit into the sensitive skin at the back of her neck as she waited. The soldier's boot crossed into the aisle.

Scarlett let the air out of her chest. And swung up with everything she had. The Hux knocked the rifle straight up, and a spray of bullets exploded into the ceiling. Like fireworks. Though this wasn't as pretty.

The soldier shoved her off.

She hit the floor and rolled, pulling her sidearm in the process. "Where is Agent Elsher?"

A low laugh and incredibly crooked teeth made dread pool at the base of her spine. Seemed this soldier liked to partake of the cartel's supply. He pulled an oversize blade from his back, swaying it back and forth in front of her. "You know the twenty-one-foot rule?"

Twenty-one feet. It wasn't as much as civilians might assume, but the rule was simple enough. Would she be able to get a shot off before he stabbed that blade through her? "I work for a security company. I'm pretty sure they taught that on the first day."

A gunshot exploded from behind the soldier, and his expression deadened right before her eyes. He collapsed to his knees. The blade pinged off the cement just before he fell face first. Revealing King standing behind him, weapon raised.

Sweat and blood and exhaustion clung to every inch of him as King's gun hand fell to his side. "You're not…supposed to be here."

Scarlett collected the discarded assault rifle from the floor, running to meet him. Another round of shouts told her there were more cartel members on the way. It was a big warehouse. No way to tell how many members were inside, but she didn't want to wait around to find out.

Slinging the weapon around her chest, she tucked herself underneath his left arm to keep King from eating the floor against his will. "I came to make sure you keep your promise to that kid."

"Where's Julien?" Two words made his priorities clear, and she had to admire that. He hadn't just taken on caring for a ten-year-old because a social worker and society expected him to step up as a father. He'd done it out of love. Raw, undying love for someone he barely knew.

"Safe. Come on. We need to get you out of here before you bleed out all over." She took the majority of his weight, in addition to her Kevlar and the rest of her gear. Her legs screamed for relief, but she'd trained and operated under worse circumstances. This was just a warm-up.

"Do me a favor." King shuffled forward at her lead.

"I'm kind of in the middle of the last favor you asked of me." She swung the rifle up as they passed each aisle on the way back to her entry point. "Not really sure I can take on much more at the moment. You know, facing off with a bunch of armed sociopaths and all."

King forced her to a halt. Pain and something along the lines of death infiltrated his expression. He swayed on his feet. Any second now, he wouldn't have the strength to stay upright. Hell, it was a miracle he'd gotten this far. "Tell Julien I'm sorry. I'm sorry I couldn't protect him the way he deserved."

Air lodged in her throat. Scarlett strengthened her grip on his T-shirt. "You're going to tell him yourself." She moved them forward. Fifty feet. Forty. They were almost there. She could see the outline of the door ahead. They were going to make it.

A gunshot exploded from behind them.

Searing pain thudded through her midback and shoved her forward. King lost his hold on her, and they hit the floor in a tangled heap of limbs. Agony spread beneath her waistband and up underneath her Kevlar vest. One hand stretched out in front of her, she reached for the door that would get them both out. Only it wasn't enough. Her lungs suctioned for air. The Kevlar had taken the hit, but she couldn't rush the recovery.

The gunman shouted something she couldn't decipher. Calling the rest of the shooters to his location.

No. She had to keep moving. Had to get King back to Julien.

"Scarlett." King's hand found hers.

"I'm fine." The lie slipped easily from her mouth, and right then she had her answer. People who promised they were right behind their loved ones in an impossible situation lied to make acceptance easier. To give hope. "We're going to make it."

Her heart thudded too fast at the back of her head, screaming for her to stop, to rest, to give up. But that wasn't her. Scarlett rolled onto her back and latched on to the rifle jutting into her rib cage. She squeezed the trigger, taking out the gunman advancing on them.

The soldier crumpled to the floor. A multitude of footsteps echoed off the metal warehouse walls. Three sources. Maybe more. This was her and King's last chance.

She latched on to King's hand as though it were a lifeline. It was. Pushing her upper body off the floor, she got her feet under her. Bruising intensity dug deeper into her back the more she aggravated the wound, but she couldn't stop. Not until she kept her promise. She reached for King, helping him stand. "We have to move. We have to go."

The door was right there. So close and so incredibly far away. The voices were getting louder. Closer. But she wasn't going to slow down. One foot in front of the other. And they were finally there. Pushing through the door she'd pried open, and then out into the night. They crossed the parking lot, leaning on each other for strength, but that strength was quickly running out.

Scarlett set her gaze on the SUV ahead. Only something wasn't right. The back door… It shouldn't have been open. Fear penetrated for the first time and intensified the pain in her low back. "Julien."

His son's name brought King's head up as they picked up the pace.

Desperation unlike anything Scarlett had felt before burned through her. She practically dove into the back seat of the SUV, hands spread wide in search.

But he wasn't there.

"Where is my son, Scarlett?" King nearly ripped the opposite door off its hinges. "You said…he was safe. Where is he?"

She clutched the SUV's frame as everything inside of her went numb. "He's gone."

THEY'D HAD HIM.

Julien had been right there in his arms.

Something heavy and uncomfortable seemed to be sitting on his leg. King couldn't move, and the instinct to fight bubbled up inside him. Pinpricks of numbness spread through his palms.

No. That didn't feel right, either.

A soft rhythmic beep broke through the pounding of blood in his head. Increasing. Like a heartbeat. This…wasn't him coming around tied to a chair after being knocked out cold. Something was different.

King fisted a handful of fabric as he forced his eyes open. Dim lighting and deep shadows played a game of dominance which neither was winning. There was the black outline of an open door off to his right. A blue glow came from a window next to it.

The room was small but private. The source of the rhythmic annoyance was right there beside his bed, along with whatever was monitoring the clear rubber tubes coming out of his forearm.

Hospital.

Made sense after taking a tactical blade to the thigh. The memory of which created a deep ache he knew he couldn't actually feel. At least not with whatever pain meds they had him on. More like remembered pain.

And it was nothing compared to the anguish of finding Scarlett's SUV empty once they'd escaped the warehouse.

He didn't remember much after that.

His son was missing. Again. They'd been so close to bringing him home. King had promised him. Promised him he'd be safe. That everything would be okay as long as they were together. And now Julien knew his father was a liar.

King had to go back. Had to take a look at the scene in the daylight. Sangre por Sangre be damned. He wasn't giving up. Not on his son. Not on their future together.

King sat up higher in the bed, though his muscles had filled with lactic acid that made every move hell. Too long spent unmoving. Tremors shook through his arms as he put most of his weight into his upper body. The bed rails had been raised, and he grappled for the release. The remote control for the bed slipped off the edge of the mattress and slammed into the bed frame, but he didn't need it. He needed to get out of here, to find his son.

The bed rail dropped with an exaggerated crash in the silence of the room, but he got the damn thing down. He'd take that as a win. Cold worked up through his bare feet as he pressed them to the floor. He was out of breath. The machine tracking his vitals was going haywire. Damn it. How the hell was he supposed to walk out of here like this?

"If I'd known you were this bad at escaping, I never would've let you follow me into that warehouse." Her voice urged him to lie back, relax into the bed and hang on her every word. As though it alone could get him through the pain. And the lies.

Scarlett.

A lethal dose of rage mixed with gratitude to the point he couldn't tell which way was up. She'd saved him. Kept Julien alive. Delivered on her promise. Yet if she hadn't come back for him, his son would still be safe. King twisted, putting her outline in his peripheral vision. He hadn't noticed her lying on the cushions shoved up against the window, but he knew enough about Scarlett now to know she only showed herself when she wanted to be seen.

Dryness graveled up his throat. "How…how long have you been sitting there watching me?"

"Long enough to know there's no way you're getting out of here without help." Her outline shifted forward, and he could see thin lines of light coming through the blackout curtains. Daylight. They'd made it through morning. "You can't go back, King. He's not there. I already tried."

"You tried." That rage wanted to keep burning beneath his skin, but it was nothing compared to the appreciation of knowing Scarlett had risked her life—twice—to bring Julien home.

The DEA wouldn't have done that. A failed mission meant escaping with the lives they had, regrouping and coming up with a new plan. Not trying to fix the one that nearly killed them in the first place. But he'd learned something else about her over these past two days. Scarlett Beam didn't accept defeat. Ever.

"We had him." Tears pricked in his eyes, and hell, he hated this feeling of helplessness, of powerlessness. Julien needed him at his best, and this…wasn't it.

Scarlett moved so gracefully, he barely heard her before the mattress dipped with her weight beside him. Damn it, she looked stronger than ever. As though the butterfly bandage across her nose had given her some kind of superpower while he was stuck in this broken body. "I'm sorry, King. I gave you my word I would get him out. I had him. He was safe. I could've brought him to Socorro, and there would've been no way for the cartel to get their hands on him. But I…"

"You couldn't leave me behind." How could King fault her for that? Choosing to save two lives instead of one? It was what any agent in her position would've done. Hell, he would have, too.

"I'm the reason he was taken again," she said.

King's senses adjusted enough for him to see her fist her hands in the fabric of her cargo pants. "You're the reason he's still alive, Scarlett." He set one hand over hers. Despite the low temperature of the room, a flurry of heat shot into his palm at the touch. The instinct to pull away charged through him, but there was something stable and balancing in that single touch at the same time. Something he needed. "Without you, we'd both be dead, and you know it."

Flashes of memory broke free of the pain med barrier, and his heart rate hitched higher. "I remember you carrying Hans out. Did she make it?"

"Hans is back at Socorro with the vet. She took a beating, but she's going to pull through. But Gruber…" Scarlett swiped a hand beneath her nose, then cringed in pain. As though she'd forgotten the break. "I left him to guard Julien when I went back into the warehouse for you."

"But he wasn't in the car, either." King remembered that now. The SUV had been empty apart from Hans's still frame. Which didn't make sense. "You think the cartel took him?"

"I searched that entire area after I brought you in." She

shucked his hand from hers, leaning to one side to pull something from her pants pocket. "All Socorro K9s carry responders in their collars. They're even trained to trigger the emergency signal. Gruber activated his while we were in the warehouse, and Socorro responded."

She handed off a leather strap, and King worked his thumb over the worn leather pitted with adjustable holes. A metal rectangle was etched with some kind of lettering—Gruber's information if King had to guess.

"Only problem is, they were too late," Scarlett said. "All my team found was this about twenty yards from where we parked the SUV. I have to assume Sangre por Sangre knew our K9s have transponders embedded in their collars, and Gruber wouldn't let the cartel take Julien, so they took him, too."

"Why not just kill him and take my son without the fight?" King hadn't meant to say the words out loud. As much as he didn't understand the connection some people had with their dogs, it was obvious the Dobermans had fought like hell to protect Julien. And he wasn't going to forget it.

"I don't know. Maybe as leverage," she said. "But for what, I have no idea."

"I'm sorry, Scarlett." He handed the collar back, feeling heavier than when he'd woken up. "I know how much you care about those dogs."

"That's the job, isn't it? We risk our lives to protect the ones we care about, but nothing is permanent." Scarlett skimmed her fingers over Gruber's collar. "And this isn't over. I gave you my word I would bring Julien home, and I'm not giving up."

"Neither am I." King reached for the side table to give himself something to hold on to. Shoving to stand, he put all his weight onto his good leg as he slapped a hand over his cell phone. "I need to check in with my supervisory agent. Get a raid party together to breach the warehouse and confiscate those shipments of fentanyl."

"King, you can't." Scarlett rounded back into his vision, supporting him with a hand beneath his elbow. She was everything he needed right then, and everything he'd missed in a partner.

"Not sure if you know this, but that's actually my job." He scrolled through his contacts and hit his SSA's information. The screen went black and started a countdown as the line rang.

"No. I mean the DEA is already aware of our attempt to recover Julien. They know about the drugs, too," she said.

"How?" The answer was already there, waiting for his brain to break through the pain killer haze and catch up. Scarlett had said she'd gone back. Her team had recovered Gruber's collar. King searched for his clothing, but it was no use. The authorities would've already taken them as evidence. "Where are the pills I took from the shipment we opened?"

"The DEA took custody of them after I provided my statement. One of their agents showed up dead yesterday morning, and another's son was abducted. They weren't just going to sit on the sidelines." Her expression collapsed. "They know everything, King. I didn't have a choice."

Defeat stole the last remaining energy he'd reserved as King sank back onto the bed. A voice cut into the surrounding silence. Voicemail. He ended the call. His SSA wasn't going to answer. "How bad is it?"

Her voice softened. Trying to ease the blow, he imagined, but he already sensed what was coming. "The DEA has put you on suspension, pending an investigation into what you've been putting together on the cartel the past couple of months. They confiscated everything in Agent Dunkeld's home office, including the case he and Agent Roday were working together. The FBI is on its way to handle Julien's kidnapping, and Socorro has been ordered to step aside."

A headache spread from the base of his neck, threatening to break him all over again as the last remnants of his life shattered in front of him. He wasn't just on the verge of losing Julien. His job was at stake, too. "All right. If the DEA knows about the warehouse, they can put together a raid party. Match the pills we took to the shipments in those boxes."

"They breached the warehouse about an hour ago, King, but it was cleaned out." Scarlett shook her head. "Everything that can corroborate our statements is gone."

Chapter Ten

It shouldn't have been possible. An entire operation gone within a few hours? With his injury, Muñoz couldn't even walk. How the hell could he have coordinated cleaning out that warehouse? And where did he run to?

The logistics didn't really matter. King's son did. They'd been so close to bringing him home, but now Julien seemed farther away than ever.

Scarlett flipped through another series of photos put together by Agents Dunkeld and Roday for the thousandth time. It hadn't taken much to create copies of the off-the-books investigation file and make it look like the original. The DEA could have the collection they left in Dunkeld's home. She'd piece this together with the raw notes she and King had uncovered in Dunkeld's office vent.

Only they were looking at the same information that'd brought them to that warehouse in the first place.

Sangre por Sangre was no longer accepting their position on the bottom rung of the ladder with their cocaine deals to high school students and underage recruiting parties. They were moving up in the world. Into fentanyl. And if history taught Scarlett and her team anything, it was the cartel didn't have the means or the resources to get the warehouse up and running on their own. Not like that. But who in their right mind would partner with a cartel?

Her head nodded forward without her permission, the photograph in front of her blurring for a moment. Any second now, her head would collide with the stir-fry she'd pulled from the fridge, uneaten. The pain in her face seemed to shift with gravity, and Scarlett leaned back in the chair. She couldn't stop now. Not while Julien and Gruber were still out there. She'd made a mistake, and she had to be the one to fix it. Before that little boy's body was the next to show up on her doorstep.

"When was the last time you slept?" King looked as beaten as she felt. He shuffled into the too-small galley kitchen of Socorro's headquarters, a crutch shoved under his arm. His facial hair had grown in over the past couple of days, revealing a single patch of lighter hair on one side. He'd changed out of the tight hospital gown that revealed more than she'd expected at the back and into what looked like a thrift store T-shirt with a popular cartoon cat and a pair of jeans that didn't quite fit around his waist. But damn it all to hell, being his center of attention still got her heart pumping.

She readjusted in her seat, leaning her elbows against the table to give her more stability. With a shake of her head, Scarlett put herself back in the game. It was the only thing she could do. They both knew who he blamed for losing Julien last night. "Shouldn't you still be in the hospital? How did you get here?"

His laugh shouldn't have had any effect on her while she was this tired, but Scarlett couldn't help but feel the tension seep out of her spine. "You'd think breaking out and calling a ride-share would be more difficult under the circumstances."

"You just signed the discharge papers against your doctor's orders, didn't you?" She didn't have the strength or the resolve to banter with him right now. Not with part of her brain focused on the file, another wishing she was asleep in her room down the hall and the last wondering when Ivy Bardot would descend from her throne on high to cut her from the team.

Scarlett had acted irresponsibly going to that warehouse without backup, without a strategy in place and without clearing it through Socorro first. And King's little boy had paid the price for her mistake. That in and of itself was unacceptable. She'd endangered lives. All to neutralize her own guilty past. Scarlett rubbed the sleep from her eyes. "You called a rideshare?"

"You wouldn't believe the going rate to get out here. Does Socorro expense travel for its operatives?" King dragged himself through the kitchen and pulled a chair from the end of the table that didn't get much communal use. He lowered himself down with the help of the crutch, his injured leg stretched out in front of him, and she couldn't help but imagine him here between assignments, as part of the team. A knife to his thigh had sliced through muscle and tendon, but the prognosis was better than they'd expected. He'd fully recover given enough time and physical therapy. "Scarlett, what are you doing?"

"I took photos of all of Agent Dunkeld's notes from his office. I'm going back through them. There are references here I haven't been able to make sense of yet. Random letters. Almost like it's some sort of code, but one I haven't seen before."

The letters seemed to jump off the page every time she looked away, as if they were calling her. Or maybe she was just hallucinating. She scrolled through another set, these written in more feminine handwriting. Eva Roday's, if she had to guess.

"My gut says if we manage to find the key to decode them," she said, "I think we'll have a better idea of where we stand. Maybe even who is partnering with the cartel and where they might be located."

"You need to go to sleep."

His voice intensified that exact need, like her body had been waiting for his permission. But she couldn't stop. Not yet. Not until she had something to bring back his hope. Because she'd been the one to kill it. The second she'd gone back for King in that warehouse, she'd broken her promise to get Julien out safely. And she couldn't live with that for the rest of her life. She could barely live with herself as it was now. "I'm fine. I just need… I just need some coffee."

"Coffee can fix a lot of things, but it can't fix this." King's breathing picked up as he got back to his feet. He wedged the crutch beneath his arm with one hand and offered the other to her. "Come with me."

His voice had been so clear a few minutes ago but refused to register in her brain now. He was right. Coffee wouldn't fix this. Neither would changing out her contacts or taking a cold shower. She'd given everything she had to recovering Julien, and she'd failed. Throwing herself back into the investigation wasn't going to change that.

Her attention latched on to the pattern of lines in his palm. Just before she slid her hand into his.

King didn't do much in the way of helping her up—couldn't in his condition—but the intention was still there. After everything they'd been through together, he wanted to help her. As a unit, they shuffled back through the kitchen and into the corridor before King pulled up short. "I'll be honest. I have no idea where I'm going. Every hallway looks the same to me."

"I've got you covered." Scarlett led him to the right, then took a left and shoved through a door at the end of the hallway. A deep heaviness clung to her legs as she caught sight of her bed. King-size suddenly had all new meaning as she considered whether or not to invite him inside. But her boundaries had been broken the moment she went back in to save him from Muñoz and the rest of the cartel.

Only this time King made the choice for her.

Maneuvering inside the room, he surveyed the space with its floor-to-ceiling windows making up two walls, the bed jutting out from the wall to their right and the simple layout with the bathroom and closet tucked out of sight. "This is…a lot of pink."

He was right. The upholstered headboard had been custom-made. The faux fur rug had been on sale in one of those huge home decor stores that were popping up all over. Pinks, whites and navy colors created a palette that made her happy every time she walked into this room. It was hers. Every inch. Hers. "Don't you have a favorite color?"

"Black shows the least amount of blood. Does it count if it's just good logic?" King was still taking it all in. The roses on the nightstand with a stack of books she'd read a thousand times. The built-in wardrobe where her gun safe was installed. He studied it all as though he was trying to understand the pieces of this room that made her…her.

And she liked it. Him being here. Trying to figure her out. Not in the way so many others had—how she could be of use, how she could benefit an operation—but pure curiosity.

"Sure." Suddenly blood seemed to drain from her upper body, pooling in her legs.

"Hey. I've got you." And then he was there, his hands anchoring around her waist. She wasn't sure how he'd moved so fast with that leg barely out of surgery, but it didn't really matter. "You've still got blood on you. I'll grab you a change of clothes."

Every cell in her body wanted to collapse as he led her to the edge of the bed and set her down.

Bending at the waist, he leveled his gaze with hers. “Don’t move.”

She wasn’t sure she could even if she’d wanted to. Her body had hit a wall, and there was nothing that was going to get her to the other side until she gave in. Her pulse pinged a steady rhythm underneath the butterfly bandage across her nose as her partner pried the built-in doors wide.

King returned to face her with a set of her favorite pajamas in hand. Silk shorts and an oversize T-shirt. Ridiculous, really. That someone like her—someone who thrived in knowing and exploiting the enemy’s weakness and who’d become comfortable with the violence that ensued—needed her pajamas to be soft. That she relied on that small bit of comfort every night.

He tossed the crutch on the bed, his weight on his good leg as he took a seat beside her. Hints of soap tickled the back of her throat. He’d showered—most likely at the hospital—and she couldn’t help but wonder if she smelled anything close to clean. “Lie back and give me your foot.”

She didn’t have it in her to argue as the mattress came to meet her, and she dragged one foot away from the floor.

He grasped it between both hands, and a flurry of nervous energy spiked through her. There was a lot he could do with that one foot given the chance. But King wouldn’t hurt her. That was how it worked when you went to war together. When you saw past the mask a person wore for the world, you got to witness the truth of them. And she knew King Elsher.

He tugged at the laces of her boot and slipped the heavy gear free, and Scarlett couldn’t help but let her anxiety win. This was…slow. Uncomfortable. Out of her range of experience. No one had taken this kind of care with her since before her discharge from the army, and she wasn’t sure what to do with it.

“Now the other one,” he said.

She followed his orders as relief spread through her socked foot and nearly sighed as he dropped her other boot to the floor. He reached for the elastic of her socks and started pulling them free, one by one, but Scarlett bolted upright to stop him from going farther.

King waited. Held perfectly still until she made the decision. "I've got you. No matter what happens."

The words slid through her defenses as easily as the blade had gone through his leg, and she lay back down. Cool air added relief between her toes…just before King started massaging away the tension in her heel and the ball of her foot.

And she drifted to sleep.

KING COULD SPEND the rest of his life in this bed. He could even ignore the pink pillows underneath him, as long as he didn't have to give up this view.

Of Scarlett. Of her hair trailing around her shoulders and into her face. The clock on her nightstand warned him he was wasting time, but he couldn't seem to stop memorizing the way she'd lost that defensive edge while asleep.

She was beautiful. Definitely stronger than him, and more than he'd initially judged when they collided in the morgue—hell, when was that? Two days ago? The bruising fanning out from around her nose had darkened to shades of blue and purple but didn't take away from the spread of freckles peppered across her cheeks. He'd counted them. Over and over while she slept. One hundred and thirty-eight of them, each distinctive in its own right. Each one perfect.

"If you're going to keep staring at me like a serial killer stares at his prey, I'll require breakfast." Scarlett's voice cracked, but she gave him a half smile. Bright green eyes locked on him, and everything outside of these four walls didn't seem so important. "I like bacon."

"If that means I have to find my way through this maze back to the kitchen, you're out of luck." King's laugh rolled through him easier than it should have.

He'd been suspended from the DEA for running an off-the-books investigation into a cartel. The last woman he'd partnered with had been murdered in her own home. Adam had been tortured and slaughtered, and his son had been kidnapped. There shouldn't have been room for the lightness flooding through him. But Scarlett somehow made that possible.

She reached out, her fingertips brushing against the stubble across his chin. Heat cut through him, blistering and driven by something he hadn't experienced in a long time. Desire. "I believe in you."

The second laugh hurt more than it should have. His pain medication had worn off sometime during the night, but exhaustion had won out. Until now. He felt every blow as clearly as when they'd landed. In his ribs, his hands, his leg. They both knew getting lost in these halls wasn't going to end well for him.

Scarlett lowered her palm to his chest, directly above his heart. "I don't remember changing into my pajamas. Last night, did we…"

The question hung between them, and King didn't really have an answer. On the surface, it was easy. They hadn't slept together, but there was a part of him that was convinced they had. Mentally, emotionally. She'd trusted him to touch her, to take care of her, and while he didn't know her past as well as his own, King got the feeling that didn't happen often. If rarely. "No."

Her mouth formed an O for a split second. Surprised? Disappointed? Grateful? He couldn't tell. Scarlett pushed upright, angling long, lean legs over the edge of the bed. "Thank you. For getting me here."

"Figured you'd probably pass out at the dining table with your tablet stuck to your head." While that may have been true, he also knew that keeping her from falling asleep in the communal dining room had little to do with it. "Wanted to save you the embarrassment."

She laid her head back on the pillow. Silk. Another element of this personal space he hadn't expected. Everything he'd known about Scarlett Beam up until this point had given him ideas of a dusty room with little to no personalization. A waystation between here and wherever she ended up next. But this…

This single room felt like a piece of home. Cared for. Lived in. Hell, he and Julien had been living together for nearly two months, and their place looked nothing like this. Didn't feel like it, either. As much as he wanted to credit the decor, King understood that all this warmth came from Scarlett. She was the one who added life to every room she walked into. Including the one where he'd been bound, interrogated and stabbed.

Scarlett tucked her hands beneath her chin, studying him. "Is this what you really look like in the morning?"

"Disappointed?" he asked.

"Not at all. I can finally see your face without all those tight lines in it." Her smile stretched from one side of her face to the other. The effect released her own set of tight lines from around her eyes and hitched his heart rate into overdrive. There was something about that smile. About that smile in this place, in this bed.

"I'm not sure if I'm supposed to take that as a compliment or an insult." He itched to close the small space between them, to feel her without a Kevlar vest getting in the way. To experience that heat she generated not just in his hand the few times they'd touched but over his entire body.

The truth was, he hadn't felt anything for a long time. And painkillers had nothing to do with it.

King reached out, sweeping long red hair behind her shoulder. His finger brushed against the underside of her chin, and Scarlett closed her eyes as if she'd been waiting for that physical contact as long as he had. Hell, she was so damn beautiful like this. Raw. Without any threats driving her from minute to minute. Right here, right now, she looked…at peace.

And despite the danger and the violence and the worry outside of this room, King felt the echo of that peace for the first time in… Damn, he couldn't remember how long. When his life hadn't become his job. When he hadn't been blindsided by a ten-year-old who'd been kept from him for the past ten years. When he hadn't lost the closest thing to a best friend he'd had. How long ago was that?

Seconds blurred together as they lay there. King wasn't sure how many. Didn't matter. Because he finally had the chance to breathe. To slow down. To just…be. In this bed he wasn't a DEA agent, the cartel didn't exist, he wasn't a father, and he wasn't grieving the loss of the loss of his job or everyone he cared about. He was King. A guy who'd dreamed of being a hero all his life, who'd fallen in love for the first time as a junior in college and had his heart broken, whose bucket list included things like visiting the Grand Canyon and seeing a real-life volcano and running a marathon. Someone who didn't feel the need to protect everyone and everything all the time, his own happiness be damned. Here, he was that man. Because of her.

King swiped his thumb beneath her chin, memorizing the feel of her skin, of a thin scar he hadn't noticed until now. He ran the pad of his finger over it a second time. She'd told him not to ask about the scar across her stomach, and he'd do as she asked. "What about this one? Will you tell me about that?"

"You're going to laugh at me." Sliding her hand over his, Scarlett pressed her face into his palm. "My nana used to make my cousins and me take naps when we were growing up. My mom and my aunt were working single moms at the time, and the four of us cousins would get dropped off at my nana's house. At the time I didn't understand why we had to take naps, but looking back I can see she just wanted a break. She was the one who needed the nap, and she didn't trust us to let her sleep without getting into trouble."

"You were one of the kids that got into trouble, weren't you?" He could see it now. Her curiosity, her determination to challenge and learn and figure the world out for herself. Nothing had changed in that sense.

"You're not wrong." Her laugh shook through his hand, real and bright. "We'd all pile in her king-size waterbed, but I never actually went to sleep. Instead, I would keep my brother and my cousins from going to sleep by poking them in their faces. Turned out, they didn't like that so much. My brother scratched me, leaving this scar, and I never poked him in the face again."

"Here I thought you were going to tell me you'd sneaked out of bed and gone to do something against the rules. Like climb the pantry for cookies. Seems more your style." He'd meant it as a joke, but the smile disappeared from her face.

Scarlett drew his hand along her neck, down over her collarbone. His fingers trailed between her breasts and over her stomach, lifting the hem of her shirt to expose the angry jagged pink line underneath. "The last time I broke the rules, my unit turned on me."

He didn't know what to say to that, what to think. "Your unit?"

Her gaze dipped to the raised scar tissue. "We were stationed in the Middle East. Security. Our job was to keep everyone safe, escort any high-value property on and off the base, investigate criminal activity, the works, but it turns out, the best people to break the rules are the ones who are there to enforce them."

Her skin warmed against his, her breathing coming faster, and King couldn't keep his distance any longer. Shifting, he closed the space between them and speared his fingers into her hair. "Hey. You don't have to do this. You don't have to trust me with this."

"But I do." She brought her gaze to his. Clear and soft and brilliant. The kind of eyes that could see right through him. And, damn it, King wanted her to see him. To be someone she could know and rely on in a world where she gave so much of herself to everyone else. "Which seems like a very dumb idea on my part, but here we are."

"Here we are," he said.

"I noticed things. Whispered conversations between a couple members of my team while we were on shift. I didn't think anything of it at first. Our unit wasn't exactly tight. More of a bunch of misfits thrown together, and I figured they had a closer relationship. They were friends, and I was the rookie. We got along. Drank together, told war stories and played Monopoly off duty, so I figured it was just a matter of time." Her next laugh wasn't as real as the last and died almost as quickly as it escaped. "But then I noticed a routine whenever the rangers brought in confiscated goods from their missions."

"What kind of goods?" He hadn't meant to ask, but it seemed important.

"Weapons, money." Scarlett tightened her hold on his hand. "Drugs. It didn't take me long to put it together. They had a protocol they followed whenever one of those shipments came in to be processed, and we were the ones in charge of processing."

"They were helping themselves." King pressed his thumb

into end of her scar, where the tissue had built up more than the others. “What did you do?”

“Threatened to rat them out to our commanding officer and have them all court-martialed. Problem was, he was in on the operation, too.” Her voice softened as she studied the line across her stomach. “And then one night, he decided he couldn’t risk me telling anyone.”

Chapter Eleven

She hadn't told a single soul.

Not outside of the court of JAG lawyers and the judge who'd been all too ready to throw her in the darkest hole after everything that went down.

Scarlett didn't want to think about any of that. About what had happened after she'd woken soaked in her own blood. She wanted to be in this bed. With King. He'd told her they hadn't slept together, but this somehow seemed far more intimate than mutual pleasure. As though she'd allowed him to dig through the scar across her stomach and peek inside. She'd never forget these moments. No matter what happened.

"How did you make it out of that alive?" he asked.

"I don't remember." It was the truth. She should've died from her wound. Part of her did and was continually trying to convince her none of this was real. That she'd been sent to purgatory to fight an impossible opponent for the rest of eternity. If she believed in things like that. Her brain provided the memories she'd tried to shove into a box at the back of her mind for over a year. "I remember my CO coming at me with the blade. I fought him off. As hard as I could. But it wasn't any use. I remember the knife going in. It burned more than I expected. I'm sure you can relate."

"A little." His thumb followed the length of her scar, back

and forth, back and forth. Trying to hypnotize her. And it was working. Keeping her in the moment. Giving her an anchor when it would be so easy to let go and fall into the past.

She'd never had that before. Someone to hold on to. During her military career, she'd believed deep in her core that her unit would have her back. No matter where she was assigned. But that belief had been cut out of her. Literally. "He left me to bleed out. Stood over me until I lost consciousness to make sure, I guess. But next thing I knew, I was waking up in a small hospital room barely holding itself together. I was off base. I could tell that much right away. The surgeon who stitched me back together didn't even speak English. The army took my being off base as an act of treason. I was branded AWOL within hours."

"They charged you?" Distinct lines deepened between his eyebrows.

"After my unit was sent to find me, yeah." Her pleas echoed through her head as the scene played out like it had happened yesterday. "I tried to run, but the hospital I was brought to didn't have the resources to give me any pain medication. It hurt too much to move. I could barely stand on my own after what happened. So I was court-martialed. Dragged back to base. My CO stood in front of the judge, the attorneys and everyone in that room and told them he'd uncovered a smuggling operation within his own unit. That I was the ring leader, and he'd tried to stop me."

"And most likely used the fact you ended up in an off-base hospital to prove you were a flight risk," King said.

He was good at this. Putting the pieces together. It was what made him such an excellent agent, and she couldn't help but admire that. Maybe if she'd been as committed to looking at the people closest to her as she did for outside threats, none of this would have ever happened. Maybe she could've seen the end of the tunnel before the train hit her.

King's breathing had grown shallow, matching hers, and Scarlett wondered if his heart was threatening to pound straight out of his chest like hers. If his hands were sweating like hers. Probably not. This wasn't his story. It was hers. Dark and violent and full of secrets she'd hidden inside herself. But King made her feel safe. Good, even. Like someone worthy of being in his and his son's orbit. That feeling called to something deep and closed off inside of her. Something she'd left untouched for…forever.

"I was sent to the base hospital. Under guard. Handcuffed to the bed. No matter what I said, no one would listen. Not even my defense attorney. I didn't have any proof of my claims, and my CO knew it. And having me in custody gave my unit enough time to slowly shut things down in case someone else caught on. Lucky for me, I was isolated. No chance for them to slip by and finish the job."

"The investigators had to have found evidence somewhere. Someone must've come forward with information." King slid his hand along her hip, and instant defensiveness carved through her. But she was more convinced than ever he wasn't the threat. It was her own vision of herself. The crystal clear version of the woman who failed to bring Julien home as she'd promised. "You're here. You're with Socorro instead of in some prison the military keeps off the books."

"It was Granger." A chill tremored through her as she realized King had gotten closer. Mere inches between them.

He was absolutely beautiful. Impossible to look away from. Dangerous in his own way, but only to her sense of mission. Even so, she didn't want to pull away. She wanted to taste his mouth and didn't even care if that was weird. Had she ever wanted to taste someone before?

"We were stationed overseas at the same base," she said. "Overlapped by a few months as he worked counterterrorism in that part of the world for a brand-new private military contractor that hadn't gotten on its feet yet. I didn't know about him until I was being released from custody and handed my discharge."

"He's the one who brought you to the hospital. Gave the judge proof you weren't involved in the ring?" he asked.

She didn't really know how to answer that. Not with so many pieces still missing. "I know he found me in that hangar. If Granger hadn't been there, I would've died. He told me later he was already aware of the smuggling ring. He'd been closing in. And that made my CO desperate. Granger had gone in to that hangar to find the confiscated goods my unit stashed. Instead, he found me. Later, when he offered me a job working for Socorro, I took it without looking back. And here I am."

"Here you are." King's voice softened. His fingers brushed against her lower back and dug into the skin there. "Keeping your team and everyone else you care about safe."

"Almost everyone." She expected the past to rush into the present, to take these electrically charged moments from her, but it didn't. It stayed where it was supposed to. Firmly behind her. And left her all too aware of the hole consuming her from the inside. Which shouldn't have been possible as long as King held on to her.

"We're going to get them back, Scarlett. Both of them. Julien and Gruber. Together." Before she had a chance to argue, King crushed his mouth to hers. Claiming her. Fiercely. Intensely. As though he needed her as much as she needed him. And it didn't make sense. But his kiss was slick and hot and sweet, and all common sense had gone out the door the moment he touched her.

He angled his head, accessing her more deeply, and Scarlett had the impression if he hadn't been holding on to her waist, she would've fallen right off the bed. Heat charged up her neck and seeped into her face.

She'd kissed a few good men in her lifetime, starting at fifteen when her mouth had been full of braces and her boyfriend's bad breath. None of those compared to this. Her body responded as though she'd been waiting months—years—for this moment. Maybe all of her life for this kind of desire, and parts of her body she'd never fully engaged with were starting to wake up.

She met him stroke for stroke, with each ferocious pass of his tongue, and managed to keep the pain in her nose from taking over. Her heart thundered in rhythm with his, her whole body shaking for release as she clamped a hand onto the back of his neck and refused to let him separate from her. She was supposed to be in control, on alert for any kind of threat, but King made her feel desperate. Wanted. Whole.

Her body pressed against his from chest to toes. She was ready. For this. For them. For his forgiveness.

A knock punctured through the pounding in her temples, and King broke the kiss. "Expecting someone?"

"Not unless that's the breakfast I asked you to get." The pressure that'd tried to suffocate her since being forced to get King to the hospital last night had lightened. To the point she was able to take a full breath for the first time in hours.

"Can you have food delivered here?" he asked.

"Only if you want to traumatize poor delivery drivers." She released her hold, hating the emptiness in her gut that followed. But as much as she wanted to pretend these walls could protect them forever, reality didn't play that way. Hernando Muñoz was still out there. Still terrorizing the people of New Mexico, increasing his reach by merging with an unknown partner and holding a ten-year-old boy against his will.

Scarlett left the warmth of the man in her bed and padded to her bedroom door. Every muscle in her body ached with a reminder of her failure. She opened the door to Granger on the other side. "You have something for me?"

The counterterrorism agent handed off a single piece of paper. "You were right. We were able to trace the signature in the fentanyl pills you recovered from that warehouse back to a supplier."

"I thought you said you handed the evidence over to the DEA." King straightened to the edge of the bed but didn't bother trying to stand with his wound.

"I did. All but one of the pills." Scarlett read over the report of ingredients broken down line by line, looking for the one that would give them everything they needed: the cartel's new partner. "Once we breached that warehouse, there was no way Sangre por Sangre was going to stick around for the authorities to confiscate that much product. Given how much fentanyl is worth on the street, I'd say we uncovered a six-million-dollar operation. That kind of loss would destroy the cartel and any chance Muñoz had of making it out of there alive."

"So you kept one of the pills to have tested." A hint of admiration reached through the buzz he'd left behind from that kiss. "The DEA will be running their own tests. They're going to find out where those drugs came from."

"Yes, but federal crime labs take weeks to process evidence, and they're certainly not going to know where to look before we do." Bingo. The last ingredient. Scarlett glanced up at Granger to confirm the dread seeping through her. "Are you sure?"

"Had Dr. Piel run the results twice. She says it's not a

mistake. We can do it again, but we're going to need another source. She went through the single pill you gave us. But unless you know of someone else using dextromethorphan in their fentanyl, I think we have our answer as to which organization Sangre por Sangre is using for new product."

"Dextromethorphan." King grabbed for his crutch and dragged himself to their position at the door. She handed off the toxicity results, and his gaze locked on the paper in his hand. "I only know of one organization that uses that as a signature in their product."

"Yeah. Me, too." Scarlett wanted to sink back into bed, to rewind the past few minutes and pretend wolves weren't waiting at the door all along. "Sangre por Sangre has teamed up with the largest triad in the world."

THE TRIADS CONTROLLED the drug trade through bribery, extortion and murder in the extreme. To the point western law enforcement couldn't even penetrate the organizations without inside help. They were the sole hands-off source of the opioid crisis ripping through the world.

And Sangre por Sangre had taken them on as a partner.

Providing them with unlimited resources in product, weapons and manpower. New Mexico would never stand a chance once the cartel took full advantage.

King couldn't just sit here. He dressed as quickly as his leg allowed. The wound was pulsing, trying to hold him back, but this new intel wouldn't wait for him to recover. The cartel was in over their heads, and his son was stuck in the middle. "Adam and Eva must've figured out the connection. They were getting too close to exposing the triad's involvement."

King aggravated the stitches in his leg, and he fell back against the mattress. Nausea surged as pain stabbed through his thigh, and all he could do was wait for it to pass. Sit here. Useless in his own body. "Damn it."

"Take it easy." Scarlett was there, securing her hands around the back of his calve. "That wound isn't going to magically fix itself in under twenty-four hours, King. You've got to give it some time."

"I don't have time." He hadn't meant his explanation to sound so harsh, but King couldn't help it. They were running out of time. Julien was running out of time.

"I know." She massaged her fingertips around the wound, careful not to touch anywhere close to the bandages. "That's why I had Granger take what we know upstairs. Ivy and Socorro have been taking a lot of heat as to why the cartel only seems to be getting stronger despite our efforts to take down the key players. Now we know the answer. They're not the only ones we're up against, and I have a feeling it's been that way for a while."

Every muscle in his body prepared for the pain she'd trigger if she kept touching him. Only it never came, and he seemed to be relaxing, inch by inch under her touch. And, hell, he didn't know how that was possible. A live wire of defensiveness had been sizzling beneath his skin his entire life. And this woman had somehow worked her way around it. That was her job though, wasn't it? To figure out a system's defenses and either build it up or take it down? Tough part was, he wasn't sure which she was doing to him.

"What do you mean?" he asked. "We only got to this point because Eva was killed two months ago."

"In your world, yes. You started looking into Muñoz because you suspected he had something to do with the murder of someone you knew." She slid her hands along the back of his calf, starting from the base of his leg and working up again, and King couldn't move. Didn't want to move. "But

Socorro has been focused on Sangre por Sangre for close to a year. We've been mapping out their entire organization through surveillance, financials, property records and inside intel to find their weakness. Everything we've uncovered points to a simple hierarchy with no outside influence. One man at the top with lieutenants protecting their territories across the state. Now it seems we were wrong. We're up against something much bigger than we or the Pentagon imagined, and I'm starting to think it's only a matter of time before Sangre por Sangre stops trying to hide that fact anymore."

Truth rang deep through his chest. She was right. Of course he'd carried out assignments that involved the cartel for years—a lieutenant here, a search-and-seizure there, border checks every few months—but he'd never tried to put the whole picture together before now. Before it became personal. A monster had been growing within the organization all this time and no one—not even the DEA—had suspected anything had changed. "It's Muñoz."

Scarlett lightened the pressure on his leg, the only evidence she'd heard him at all. "What do you mean?"

"He has to be the liaison between the two organizations. That's the only reason I could see him being so desperate to go after federal agents and their families to keep the triad off the DEA's radar. To come after me. He's scared."

The pieces were slowly starting to make sense, but there was still so much missing from the overall picture. Something they weren't seeing.

"He makes the connection with the triad," King said, "proposes that Sangre por Sangre can be a gateway into the United States. Only problem is, his cartel isn't the only one on the map, let alone the only one near the border. So he starts going after other organizations that can provide the same kinds of services and taking them out."

"Like the Marquez cartel. The one whose leadership was taken out in a bombing in Sangre por Sangre's warehouse ten years ago and the DEA called in Agent Roday." A brightness King had come to anticipate lit up Scarlett's eyes. She shoved to her feet as though the same kind of energy sizzling through him had transferred into her. "But why take the risk of bringing down the DEA, the ATF and Socorro on his own head? What does Muñoz get out of all of this?"

"What do lieutenants like him always want inside these organizations?" he asked.

"Power. Respect. Fear, in a lot of cases. You think he wants to be the man at the top." An audible inhale shuddered through her as she crossed the room, back and forth. "If that's the case, our intel was right. Muñoz is planning a hostile takeover from the inside. Which isn't easy. I've watched lieutenants kill each other to claw their way up that ladder, but it never works. The guy at the top isn't easily impressed. But Muñoz would have all the support he needs if he pulls off a deal moving triad product. It's a hell of a theory, but all we have to corroborate it is an empty warehouse and single fentanyl pill that was used up during testing."

"We have more than that." Though King wasn't sure how far it would take them. "Julien recognized the woman who checked him out of school the day he was abducted. Kidnapping a federal agent's son isn't something Muñoz would leave to just anyone, especially one of his soldiers. Too risky."

Scarlett stilled. "You said the only female soldier that matched that woman's description in Muñoz's inner circle was killed a few months ago."

"There's one I hadn't considered." And he hated himself for not realizing it until now. "Though up until now, I was positive she only benefited from Muñoz's lifestyle. There's no evidence she's involved in the business."

Scarlett pointed a soft finger at him. "The wife. You think he sent his own wife to get Julien? But how… How would he have recognized her at the school unless…"

"Unless she was there the night Eva was killed." King ran through every ounce of intel he'd gathered over the past two months. None of it fit in an obvious kind of way, but he needed something—anything—he could use to get his son back. And Muñoz's wife was all he had.

"Okay." Scarlett darted to the tablet charging on her room's built-in desk. "I can work with that."

"I don't know how." Grabbing for the crutch he'd tossed on the floor last night, he wedged it beneath his arm to hike himself off the bed. "It took me a month to map out Muñoz's organization on my own, and the DEA has most likely already been by my place and seized anything pertaining to my investigation. I'm not exactly sure what you think you're going to come up with in a few minutes."

His phone fell free of his pants pocket and revealed a handful of missed calls. His supervisory special agent was most of them with a couple missed from an unknown number.

Given that the FBI had officially taken on Julien's abduction, King imagined whoever had caught the case was trying to reach out as well. The FBI didn't know Sangre por Sangre or Muñoz like King did, but damn it, he needed as much help as he could get. Covering every angle. A quick review of his voicemails assured him the FBI and local police were working the case as best they could.

But he and Scarlett were onto something here. He could feel it.

"I don't need your files. I just need…" She was lost to a series of taps and screens his brain couldn't keep up with. "Got it."

"Got what?" he asked.

"Catalina Muñoz. Forty-six. Originally born Catalina Lemos in Mexico but soon applied for citizenship once her parents immigrated into the US on a work visa when she was ten. Her parents were denied and returned to Mexico, but they left Catalina with…an uncle. Metias Leyva." Small lines creased in a half-star pattern along the edges of her eyes.

Seconds seemed to pound at the back of his head. "What is it?"

"I'm not sure yet. I feel like I should know that name." Scarlett shook her head as though to rewind the past few seconds and made a few other swipes across the screen. "Catalina managed to gain citizenship and went on to graduate with the highest marks from Columbia at the age of twenty with an MBA before marrying Hernando Muñoz a year later. No children or dependents. They own their home in Albuquerque. No work history on her part that I can see from filed joint taxes in the last seven years, but if these financials were filed right, she's never had a reason to work a day in her life."

"Where are you getting all that? Because everything you just listed requires a warrant." King tried to get a good look over her shoulder, but Scarlett pressed the tablet to her chest.

"One look at this screen, and you make yourself an accomplice. I'm pretty sure you want to keep your job with the DEA when this is over, don't you?" She eased the screen away from her chest and continued the digital flip through whatever information she'd found. "So let's just say I have my ways."

She had to be kidding, right? "Your ways? You know nothing is going to hold up in court if you can't prove you searched Muñoz's financial history legally. Even cartel lieutenants have rights."

"I'm not interested in taking Muñoz or his wife to court," she said. "All I want is to bring your son home alive. This is how I can do that, King."

The shock of her words sucker-punched him. It took him longer than it should have to get his head on straight, but he guessed that was why it was good to have a partner. Someone he could count on to keep him grounded. “I already put all this together on my own, and unless you think Catalina’s background will give us an idea of where my son is being held, none of this means a damn, Scarlett.”

“What if I told you I know where I heard that name? Metias Leyva. Catalina’s uncle who raised her.” She turned the tablet toward him and slid her finger across the screen to narrow the bird’s-eye view over a property he didn’t recognize. Rural, almost deserted from the look of it. “Socorro has dealt with him before.”

“He’s Sangre por Sangre? I mapped out Muñoz’s organization during my investigation, even going as far as checking into extended family members for a lead. His name never came up in connection to Catalina,” he said.

“He was Sangre por Sangre. Pretty high up, too.” Scarlett set her attention back to the tablet screen. “He threw a raid party in a small town called Alpine Valley in search of his ex-wife and came up against one of our operatives. He survived the encounter, but the cartel found out he’d put his own agenda before theirs, and he couldn’t face upper management without punishment. So he ran. Cops found him with a tire around his neck outside Albuquerque.”

“Let me guess. Lit with accelerant and a match to make it harder to identify him. Not to mention the message it sent to the rest of the organization.” King took the tablet, studying every pixel on the screen. Especially the dark rectangle positioned on a long dirt driveway. “If he’s dead, then why is there an SUV parked in front of his house?”

“That’s a great question.” Scarlett pried open one of the doors to her built-in shelving and pressed her thumb into a safe installed inside. The keypad lit up, releasing the locking mechanism, and she handed him a sidearm. "Are you up for finding the answer?"

Chapter Twelve

The last time she ran into a suspected cartel hideout, she'd lost Gruber, Julien and almost King. This time would be different. This time she had her team. And she wasn't going to fail.

"Metias Leyva. Hell, who knew the son of a bitch would keep giving us trouble even after police had to pry that tire off what was left of him?" Granger Morais's words didn't match the gravelly voice she'd never heard raised above a warning.

The counterterrorism agent studied the property from the passenger seat of the SUV with the help of the tactical binoculars all Socorro operatives carried in their kits. Completely at ease. As though he'd done this a thousand times before. Which, she imagined, he had.

"You encounter him yourself?" King had been relegated to the back seat. More room to stretch out his leg. The plan was set in stone. He would remain behind until Scarlett and Granger cleared the property. With any luck, they'd have Julien when they returned. And if anything went south, he could call the rest of the team.

Granger lowered the binoculars and tossed them into the console between the front seats. "Not personally. No. Though cleaning up what was left of his operation got put on me. Took a few weeks, but I managed to trace every one of his soldiers back into their dark holes or into the shallow graves where the cartel left them."

"What about Hernando Muñoz?" King asked. "The husband of Leyva's niece. Did you uncover any evidence he had something to do with Leyva's operation or have any reason to believe Muñoz was using his wife's uncle for his own agenda?"

Granger faced off with King in the rearview mirror. "None, and I dug deep. If your guy was involved in Leyva's business, they kept it off the books."

"I'm sensing a theme." Scarlett studied what she could see of the oversize mansion down the block. The DEA couldn't condone an independent investigation into the cartel led by one of their own agents. All matters concerning Hernando Muñoz would be shut down and placed under review for actionable leads, but that still left a ten-year-old boy out here on his own. The FBI didn't understand what they were dealing with. Scarlett did. She grabbed the driver side door handle. "You ready?"

"Ready as I'll ever be." Granger shoved free of the vehicle.

Scarlett craned her neck to face King. "You know the deal. You leave this vehicle only—and I mean only—if Granger and I recover Julien."

"Couldn't break out of here if I wanted to." He adjusted his weight in the seat.

A small part of her wanted to believe he'd listen to his body and not aggravate the wound. But King had proven the lengths he would go to for his son before.

"I'll be on the radio. Talk to you soon." Scarlett secured King inside the SUV, then latched the radio on to her belt and unholstered her sidearm. Sweat had already built in her hairline. "You think I should crack the window for him or something?"

Granger's laugh did nothing to release the unease building inside her as they approached the one-story mansion surrounded by nothing but desert. No cover to hide their approach. If Muñoz had a team surveilling the perimeter, they'd be made in seconds. "He's not a dog, Scarlett. The man can take care of himself."

Her unease darkened into discomfort. Her Kevlar suddenly seemed much heavier despite years of getting used to the weight. But it wasn't that. It was the feeling of something missing. Gruber and Hans, King even. In a matter of days, she'd gotten used to their team. However scattered and mismatched they were. They'd done something amazing together in that warehouse.

Scarlett looked back, putting King in her sights through the tinted window, and the pressure let up. Just for a moment. It was enough to clear her head as she turned back toward the house. The SUV was there. Right where overhead satellite footage had put it.

She and Granger jogged low, using the vehicle as cover. Scarlett pressed her hand against the SUV's window to block out the sun distorting her vision. "It's empty. Judging by the fact our footprints are the only evidence of life on this driveway, I'm guessing it's been sitting here for a couple days." Panic was starting to set in. That she'd made the wrong call. That she'd wasted another couple of hours of Julien's precious life. Of Gruber's. "Why is nobody shooting at us?"

"Your guess is as good as mine. On me." Granger raised his weapon shoulder-level and left the cover of the SUV. He and Scarlett moved as one toward the front door of the home.

Property records still put the home under Metias Leyva, the uncle. No new homeowners. Only next of kin listed was Catalina Muñoz, but this place… She didn't like how quiet it was.

It was massive. More than the two of them could search in

under ten minutes. The structure sprawled out at the foot of the low-rising mountain at its back. Massive windows overlooked their position as she and Granger approached. Decorative pavers led them straight to a large overhang protecting the front door. Sunlight could barely reach into the cave-like space, and a tightness started in Scarlett's chest. Etched glass rimmed gray double doors, but no light escaped from within.

They pressed their backs into the structure on either side of the door, weapons in hand. Waiting. Her breathing was headed toward the rafters, too high to control. Granger held up three fingers, and Scarlett nodded acknowledgment.

Three. Two. One.

She put everything she had into her heel and slammed it into the space beside the dead bolt. Aged wood gave under the force, and the door slammed back on its hinges. A wall of dust rained down into Scarlett's face and collected at the back of her throat as she and Granger breached the door. This was it. This was how she made up for her mistakes.

They stepped into an oversize entryway—empty apart from a single circular table stylized with faux flowers and a stack of books. A cavern of white tile and double-story ceilings threatened to swallow them where they stood. Arches gave Scarlett a view into a sitting room off to the right decorated with ornate chairs she never would've felt comfortable sitting in. If she'd ever been invited to a cartel lieutenant's home for dinner. Over-the-top vases stuffed with dead flowers peppered the room as they followed the flow of the home.

"Something's not right here." She didn't know how else to explain it. This…knot behind her sternum. That part of her that wished she had Hans and Gruber at her side ached. She hadn't realized how much she relied on them until now. How much she needed them. "You feel that?"

"Yeah. I feel it." Granger moved into the kitchen, weapon

raised high, as Scarlett pinpointed the command panel for the security system.

Holstering her weapon, she faced off with a rectangular gray cover equipped with a keyhole at the top, a camera to identify the user to the left, a card reader off to one side and a keypad with twelve digits on the other. The Ascent K2 model worked off a homeowner's cellular data with a special SIM card installed in the phone with cloud-based access from anywhere in the world. She scanned the ceiling, spotting two cameras capable of visually identifying visitors or intruders just within range. More were likely installed throughout the house and around the property, but there wasn't any indication the system was operational. The equipment wasn't affected by temperature or power outages. So why hadn't she and Granger set it off? "The system should've sent an alert the second we stepped onto the property."

"I'm guessing whoever was here didn't want to draw attention from law enforcement." Granger's even voice once again contradicted the words coming out of his mouth.

"Why do you say that?" She prodded both thumbs around the frame of the security panel, looking for a way past the keypad, keyhole, camera and card reader. Though if that were possible, this brand wouldn't be one of the top-of-the-line systems in the world.

"Because of the dead guy in the kitchen," Granger said.

Scarlett dropped her hands away from the panel, every cell in her body homed in on the pool of blood peeking out from behind the nearest kitchen cabinet at Granger's feet. Dead guy. Not dead boy. Hope expanded in her chest as she rounded into the kitchen.

And froze.

"Hernando Muñoz." Crude bandages had been wrapped around the ankle where Scarlett had sliced through the lieutenant's Achilles tendon that night in the warehouse, but that wasn't the source of all the blood. The handle of the blade dented Muñoz's chest around the wound. "Stabbed. Like Agents Roday and Dunkeld."

"Only whoever did this didn't leave a badge this time." Granger bent down, careful not to compromise the body. He pointed at one side of the bloody hole in Muñoz's chest. "There's something at the edge of the wound. Wedged in there. A business card, maybe. Hard to tell with all this blood."

"It's mine." The voice cut through her, setting every nerve ending in her body on fire.

Scarlett confronted King as he shuffled into view. "What are you doing here? We haven't cleared the rest of the house yet, and you agreed to stay in the car until I radioed you."

"There's nobody here." Those three words shouldn't have held so much weight to them. But King was right. They would've already come into contact with Muñoz's soldiers already. King nodded at the body, his crutch offsetting the shift in his weight to the point he looked as though he'd fall at the slightest touch. "The card. It's mine."

"How can you be so sure?" Granger shoved to stand, holstering his weapon.

"Muñoz pulled it out of my pockets before tying me to a chair in his warehouse and handicapping me," King said. "Whoever did this has my son. They knew we were going to come after Muñoz, so they killed him, and now we have nothing to go on to bring Julien home."

"He's still alive, King. We're going to find him." Nervous energy shot down into Scarlett's fingertips. She needed to keep moving, keep uncovering lead after lead until she fixed this. "Granger, check the rest of the house. I need Muñoz's phone, a tablet, a laptop—anything that connects to the security system. If we're lucky, we might get something off the surveillance."

"You got it." The counterterrorism agent slipped into a parallel hallway and out of sight.

"You really think whoever did this was careless enough to leave evidence of murder behind?" King's gaze bored into her. Desperate for the answer.

"It's worth a try." Because digging through security systems and building defenses was all she knew how to do. It had to be enough. Otherwise… Julien didn't stand a chance. And that was what scared her the most. "But there is one more option. Someone I could reach out to."

King's chest and shoulders stiffened, pulling him up as straight as if a puppeteer had a hold of a string connected to the crown of his head. "What do you mean? Like a contact within Sangre por Sangre?"

"No. Not exactly. Though this person is involved in the same kind of smuggling as the cartel, and he might know where we need to look for Julien first." Her skin caught fire from the weight of his attention, but not like it had when they'd slept in the same bed together. "Before, when I told you about how I got the scar across my stomach, I didn't give you the whole story. I…couldn't."

He didn't have an answer for that, and she didn't have time to get into every detail if they wanted to recover Julien.

"The truth is my commanding officer brought me into the smuggling operation months before he tried to kill me." Her lips dried in an instant, begging for relief. Everything she'd worked to hide about her past wasn't worth the life of a child. No matter what happened next, she'd keep her word to bring Julien home. "I saw him do things I wasn't supposed to in that time, and I think I can use it to get him to help us."

He couldn't breathe. Couldn't think.

"Wait. You..." King tried to get his head around what she was trying to tell him while also trying to ignore the dead body at her feet. "He brought you in before the night you were stabbed and left for dead? Which means, you were in on the smuggling operation from the beginning."

"Yes. I was one of the soldiers stealing cash, weapons and drugs the army confiscated from the enemy forces in the area." Her voice cracked. As though she'd never admitted any of this out loud. And given the fact she wasn't sitting somewhere in a cell that didn't exist on paper, King put his money on the idea she hadn't. "My commanding officer believed my skills for security systems and defense could work in their favor. And he was right. I made sure none of us were caught."

Scarlett took a step forward but stopped her approach as every muscle around King's spine hardened with battle-ready tension. "King, I give you my word, I thought we were putting those resources to good use. I didn't know the full extent of what they were doing, and I needed—"

"What did you need, Scarlett? The drugs? The money?" The answer didn't matter. Blood drained from his upper body in a rush, nearly knocking him over. The woman standing in front of him wasn't the one he'd partnered with over the past few days, the one who'd given him her word to bring his son home.

"No. I just..." Her gaze cut somewhere past his left arm. "I thought we were doing something good. They told me everything was going back to the people we were trying to help, but it was a lie." A glimmer of tears reflected in her eyes. "Two weeks before I ended up in that hospital, I found out about the human trafficking. My CO and the rest of my team were selling off women and kids to the highest bidders, and I pulled out. I made a plan to expose the entire operation, but I made a mistake. I trusted the wrong person. That's when my commanding officer decided I couldn't walk away alive."

"And what? You want to get in contact with him and ask for help to find my son?" King tried to thread his hand through his hair, for something to distract him from the churn of rage and betrayal, but his balance shot to one side. "No. You know what? Don't answer that. Because you're just digging yourself deeper. I have grounds to arrest you and hand you over to the army, Scarlett."

"Not as long as you're suspended from the DEA, you don't." She took another step, her voice softening, but it wouldn't work. The manipulation, her proximity—none of it would affect him. Not anymore.

"You lied to me." And that was what hurt the most, wasn't it? That Eva had lied about his son's existence for ten years. That Adam had lied about running his own investigation into Sangre por Sangre while preaching they had to work by the book. But of all the people he'd trusted to have his back, Scarlett was supposed to be different. A partner. Someone who didn't break their ideals and proceeded on logic and truth. Someone he could rely on to bring his son home.

Only that hadn't been the case at all. He never knew that person.

That was all anyone was. Appearances.

And he'd taken them all at face value.

"King, listen to me. Hernando Muñoz is dead. The man who orchestrated Julien's abduction is dead and so is any reason or personal revenge he had to do it. Muñoz had leverage by keeping Julien alive, which gave us time to strategize until he made his move." Her breathing picked up, making her words wispier. Urgent. "Whoever killed Muñoz has your son. Only now they have no use for Julien. They'll use him until he doesn't serve a purpose, and it already might be too late, but I can help. I can reach out to my former CO with where to start looking. I gave you my word—"

"What does your word mean, Scarlett?" The cavern of emptiness he'd tried to fill with his job ached around the edges. For the first time in…ever, he'd finally felt as though he was on the right path. Becoming a father, claiming justice for Eva and Adam, trusting Socorro with Julien's life. But it'd all been a lie. "You just admitted to being an active participant in an international smuggling ring during your service. Anything you've said up until now has been corrupted. Your word means nothing to me. You mean nothing to me, and as of this moment, we're done."

He regretted the words the instant he said them, but there it was. Seeping into the silence between them.

Her mouth parted, and a vulnerability he hadn't witnessed escaped on her next exhale. Color drained from her face and neck, and King half expected her to collapse, but in an instant that raw part of her was contained. As though it never existed. That guarded armor he'd managed to crack through the past few days returned, agonizing second by second, until King couldn't read anything in her expression.

Scarlett shifted her weight center, almost a full inch taller as she faced off with him. "Well, I'm glad we cleared that up. Consider your deal with Socorro void, Agent Elsher. Should the DEA require statements as to your investigation in Hernando Muñoz from our operatives, please have them reach out to Granger Morais. He'll be happy to assist."

Agent Elsher. Not King. The formality stabbed through him as effectively as the blade in his thigh and sent an earthquake of renewed pain into his nervous system. But King wouldn't break. Not as long as Julien was still out there.

"House is clear. No signs of clothing or toiletries left behind. Whoever was here didn't stay long. Must've taken Muñoz's devices, too." Granger rounded back into the kitchen and stopped dead cold. With palpable tension, his hand eased toward the sidearm at his hip as the counterterrorism agent's gaze bounced between King and his teammate. "Everything okay?"

"We're done here." King's own words seemed to hit harder when coming from Scarlett's mouth. She tried for a smile, but everyone in the room saw the forced nature behind it. "We can call the body into Albuquerque PD from the SUV. Agent Elsher is going to babysit the scene until they arrive."

King hadn't volunteered. But without Socorro resources, staying behind would give him the chance to search the place himself before police arrived on the scene. There had to be something here that could tell him where Julien was. It was Locard's principle. Anyone coming onto a crime scene left a piece of themselves behind, and anyone leaving took pieces with them. No matter how small. "I just want to find my son."

He sounded hollow. Way too calm and casual about the fact she was about to walk out that door and out of his life forever. Possibly taking the only chance Julien had with her.

"So do I." Scarlett gave a final nod before maneuvering around him. Her boots echoed off the fancy tile until the pitch changed, and King couldn't hear her or Granger's steps.

He was thrown into a silence punctuated only by his own thoughts.

King forced his weight onto his good leg and took a step forward. The island with the body on the other side of it spanned the length of the entire kitchen and didn't leave a whole lot of room for an injured former DEA agent with a bad leg to navigate.

His heart seemed a whole hell of a lot heavier than it had a minute ago as he caught Socorro's SUV pulling away from the house. Albuquerque PD would arrive to investigate the body. He had ten, maybe fifteen minutes before he'd be forced to take a back seat. He needed something now.

King set the crutch against the counter, not caring when the damn thing slid out of reach and hit the tile with a metallic bounce. His good knee collapsed onto the cream tile, and it took everything he had not to fall onto the body while trying to hold himself together.

Moving or searching a body before the medical examiner had a chance to catalogue the remains wouldn't help his case with the DEA, but King couldn't wait. Because Scarlett was right about one thing. They were already out of time. Julien was out there. Without anyone to look after him or use him for their own agenda. Alone. Scared. Possibly hurt.

"Come on, Muñoz. You gotta give me something. Where would you have stashed a ten-year-old kid?"

King plucked at the blood-soaked business card stabbed into the bastard's wound. Why the hell had Muñoz hung on to it? The son of the bitch had his son. Having King's contact information wouldn't have done him a damn bit of good.

King memorized the bruising settling at the back of the lieutenant's neck. Tortured. Thoroughly. And for an extended period of time. But that didn't make sense. Muñoz served the cartel. Why kill him with his own MO unless…

Acid surged up his throat as he pieced the business card back together. Muñoz's blood raced into the whorls and loops of his fingerprints. The front looked like every other business card King handed out to witnesses, victims and sources. Apart from one element. His first name had been circled in smeared dark ink.

Turning the card over, King stared at the scrawled handwriting across the back. Recognition iced through him as he read the phone number over and over. Not in his handwriting, but Adam's.

He cut his attention to Muñoz's face, trying to come up with why his former partner would've had any motive to reach out to Muñoz one on one. Close enough to hand the lieutenant one of King's business cards. And only came up with a single answer. "Son of a bitch. You were helping them, weren't you? You were Adam and Eva's source."

Muñoz had wanted the DEA to breach the warehouse. Had given Adam and Eva what they needed to investigate. Which meant Muñoz hadn't ordered Eva's murder or had anything to do with Adam's death. Someone else had. Someone who'd caught onto Muñoz's betrayal and killed him for it.

That was why the lieutenant had been so desperate for King to hand over Eva and Adam's investigation files. He'd needed something from them. A way out of the cartel? A chance to get away from someone within? Then he'd used Julien to try to force King's hand.

Only Scarlett and King hadn't been able to break the cipher Adam and Eva used to manually encrypt their notes, and Muñoz wasn't talking anymore. King had nothing to support his theory, but the pieces fit the violent and bloody puzzle scattered around him.

He stared at the inked circle around his name.

"It can't be that easy." His name. It was the four-letter word that linked them all together, wasn't it? Except now the DEA had the physical case files, and King had left the copies with Scarlett. It would take a court order for her to hand it over after the way they'd left things.

Pounding footsteps charged his defenses into overdrive, and King used the edge of the counter to bring himself to his feet.

"Police! Is anyone here?" Two officers penetrated his vision, weapons aimed. At him. "Sir, I'm going to need you to step away from the body with your hands up."

"Agent Elsher, DEA." One hand raised in surrender, King

dragged his badge from beneath his shirt for the officers to inspect for themselves. “I know this is bad timing, but I’m going to need a ride.”

Chapter Thirteen

Her heart hurt.

It wasn't the shame of her past that pinned her to the back of the seat. It was King. His parting words circled her brain until they blurred together in one long streak. She'd meant nothing to him. After everything they'd been through together. After risking her own life—and the lives of her K9s—for him. She was nothing but something to be used for his own gain.

Just as she had been for her former commanding officer.

"You want to tell me what happened back there?" Granger slid his palms along the steering wheel's frame as he checked the driver side mirror. "Last I checked, Elsher is the one who brought us into this mess."

Scarlett forced her gaze out the window as the tears burned. Dirt kicked up alongside the SUV and pinged off the metal frame as they carved through the desert. The suspension failed to absorb every bump in the road, knocking them around in their seats, but the internal beating was so much worse. "I told him the truth. About what happened overseas."

"How much of the truth?" A small inflection in his voice was the only evidence Granger Morais had an opinion about any of this. It warned her to choose her words very carefully. Because what she'd done on tour didn't just involve her. Her teammate could be brought up on conspiracy charges for hauling her off base to that hospital if the army identified him.

"All of it." She saw the mistake now. Trusting a federal agent with information that could put her behind bars for the rest of her life. "He didn't take it well, and I don't know what he's going to do now."

"Damn it, Scarlett." Granger's disappointment burrowed beneath the hurt and the invisible pain suffocating her second by second, stealing the last of any remaining self-compassion she had. "We had a deal. I risked everything to save your life, and the only thing I asked in return was for you to keep the details of your involvement in the smuggling ring between us. You're less than a year from your discharge. The army can still court-martial you. They can come after us both."

"I know. I'm sorry. I just… I wanted to fix this." She didn't know what else to say, what to think. Tears escaped her control. Humiliating and hot and uncomfortable. She swiped at her face to get rid of the evidence of her grief and triggered the underlying pain of her broken nose.

This wasn't her. She was the one who was supposed to keep Socorro safe. She was the one who held it together for the sake of everyone else on the team. That was her job. To remain logical and strong and perfect so as to keep the people she cared about alive. But she wasn't any of that. Hadn't been for a long time.

Had she ever?

"Muñoz was the only one keeping King's son alive. With him dead, there's no telling what the cartel will do with a ten-year-old kid. My gut is telling me they'll sell him as soon as they get the chance. I thought if I could reach out to my former CO—"

Granger slammed on the brakes, and the SUV jolted forward.

She threw her palms out first to keep herself from hitting the dashboard as the entire vehicle groaned to a stop.

"Tell me you didn't." The counterterrorism agent faced off with her from the driver's seat. "Tell me you didn't put us both at risk for a DEA agent you've only known for three days."

Her stomach felt as though it'd shot up into her throat as the dust settled around them. Three days. Was that really all it had taken for King to convince her the past couldn't hold her back anymore? That she could make up for all the wrong stacked against her by bringing a little boy home to his dad and solving a case he so desperately needed to end? That she was good enough?

Didn't seem like any time at all, and in the same moment, an entire lifetime. Of her prodding him with jokes and getting a glimpse of that off-center smile in return. Of his hands on her waist as she dared to reveal the darkest parts of her soul. Three days had slipped through her fingers and into the void. She'd wanted more. So much more.

Mornings of waking up to him in her bed. Foot massages after hard days. The scent of him filling her lungs. King watching her back in the field. Him. It was all him. The one man who'd convinced her she could be the good in the world. Gravity suctioned her deeper into the seat and stole the air from her lungs. She hadn't just left King back at that crime scene. She'd left her heart, and she wasn't sure she could ever get it back. "No. You're safe. I'm the only one who's at risk. And if the army court-martials me, I'll make sure your name never comes up."

"That doesn't make me feel any better." Pulling onto the road, Granger pushed the SUV through a dip and maneuvered them back on track. The hum of the engine and crunch of rock under the tires settled between them. "You want to know why I pulled you out of that hanger after your CO tried to gut you?"

"It wasn't out of the goodness of your heart?" She'd meant it as a joke, a way to get rid of the heaviness constricting her chest, but the memories were there. Just waiting for her to give them the attention she'd fought against for close to a year. It'd been easier the past few days. Believing once she and King brought Julien home that she'd never have to think about them again.

"I clocked your operation while running my assignment for Socorro. I knew you and your crew were skimming from the resources the rangers confiscated from the other side." Socorro's headquarters—tucked back into the mountains with gleaming sharp black lines—came into view, and Granger hit the overhead button to signal the gate. The crowd of picketers had thinned over the past few days, but the ones left swarmed the gate with their neon signs and harsh words. No sign of added security though. Ivy must've decided a few protestors weren't worth the extra effort. "And I followed you that night so I could use you to lead me to the others. It worked."

Surprise pulled her attention from one of the protestors. A man wearing a thick coat in the middle of the desert. All this time, she'd imagined Granger Morais as the knight in Kevlar who just happened to come across her broken body and save her life. Not the one who could've put an end to it. "You could've turned me in. Why didn't you?"

"Because of all the moving pieces in the smuggling operation, you were the only one who was doing what your CO told you everyone else was." He locked that crystal clear blue-green gaze on her as the SUV dipped into the underground parking garage. "You were the one giving back what you took to the people in the region who needed it. Yeah, you were stealing cash and guns and drugs, but that money made it into the hands of women having a hard time feeding their kids and to organizations who were trying to help conditions in the villages."

Her throat threatened to close in on itself.

"I heard you that night. Telling your CO you were going to expose them for the human trafficking." Her teammate pulled the SUV into his assigned spot and cut the engine. Only he didn't move. Shadows carved across his face, like he was some kind of villain trying to hide in the dark. "I saw the knife. I still remember the sound of it cutting into you. How you seemed so surprised. And I knew right then what kind of person you were."

Pain flared through her midsection, and a rush of nausea pushed up into her throat. "What kind of person am I?"

"Broken." That single word punctured through the pounding in her head, aggravated by the evenness of Granger's voice. "Like the rest of us. The only difference is you don't want to accept that being broken is what makes you stronger than anyone else on this team. You put everyone's needs ahead of your own for that exact reason. Because you don't want them to end up broken like you."

"It's still not enough." Her lungs felt too tight. Like they'd somehow overfilled and emptied at the same time. "No matter what I do—how hard I try—it doesn't work. I'm still the woman that got conned into believing I was making a difference."

"That's the woman I recommended for this job, Scarlett," Granger said. "The one who fought to fix her mistake. And I know for a fact that's who Agent Elsher believes in—"

An explosion rocked through the entire garage.

"Get down!" Scarlett brought her hands to her head as though she could stop the entire parking garage from coming down on top of them. Debris slammed against her side of the vehicle and cracked the bulletproof glass. A tingling sensation swept from crown to toe as cement dust cleared.

Shouts penetrated the SUV's glass as she watched the armored garage gate hit the floor. She unholstered her weapon. "We're under attack. I can't see how many, but they brought more than guns."

"Get to the elevator." Granger pulled his weapon, keeping his head well below the window. "I'll hold them off as long as I can and get them away from the civilians."

"I'm not leaving you down here alone." Trying to gauge the manpower waiting outside the vehicle was useless. There was too much debris. "You have no idea how many of them are out there."

"Yes, you are. You're the only one who knows how to trigger the building's backup defense system." Granger shouldered his door open and motioned her over his lap. "Go. Now."

The structure's alarms pierced through the garage. Red lights circled in distress to inform the entire team they were under attack. "You better be alive at the end of this."

"Ditto. Now get out of here before this place collapses on itself." Granger backed out of the driver seat, using the SUV as cover to get a count of how many attackers waited at the entrance.

She followed his retreat. Only she kept moving, past the back of the vehicle, weaving between the SUVs parked between her and the elevator. A light outline stood out against the black backdrop. She was almost there.

Gunshots popped in succession. A bullet whizzed past her ear, and Scarlett lunged for the keypad as Granger returned fire. A groan broke through the drone of lead. She punched in her security code and turned to face the onslaught of the attack as the elevator doors took their time. Weapon raised, she caught sight of movement to her left and took aim. She compressed the trigger. The gun kicked back in her hand a split second after the round found its mark. The man she'd noted outside, dressed in a coat. The cartel was among the protestors. Using them as cover. Damn it. The attackers were inside, maneuvering behind Granger's position. One wrong move, and she'd lose a member of her team.

The elevator announced its arrival.

Two more shots. Another moan of pain.

"Move it, Beam!" Granger retreated behind his vehicle and repositioned. He fired another round of shots. "Get out of here!"

Scarlett stepped backward into the elevator against her heart's will. He was right. She was the only one who could put a stop to this attack before it had a chance to reach the others. The doors started to close.

Just as Granger took a bullet and hit the ground.

KING HAD THE CIPHER. Now he just needed Eva and Adam's notes to test his theory about Muñoz's involvement in the case.

Except smoke was spiraling up from Socorro's headquarters a mile out. Black and wispy. Like the place was on fire.

"Step on it." King held on to the dashboard and the passenger side door as the Albuquerque PD officer hit the accelerator. His heart rate rocketed to dangerous levels as the last curve onto the one-lane dirt road gave him a straight view of the building. "Call for backup. Albuquerque, Alpine Valley. Everyone. Socorro Security is under attack."

The officer detached the radio from the dash and called in the orders to any available officers in the vicinity as King mapped out the source of the damage.

"Head for the garage." He pointed to the west side of the structure, automatically leaning forward as though he could somehow make the patrol vehicle go faster.

"Sir, we need to wait for backup and fire and rescue. There's no telling what we're walking into," the officer said.

"Then wait, but I'm going in there." His leg be damned. There was only one organization stupid enough and with enough resources to attack a private military contractor like Socorro. The cartel wanted whatever intel Muñoz had given up to the DEA and ATF. They wanted the case file King had left in Scarlett's possession.

His ass left the seat as the patrol car throttled over the uneven landscape. Unholstering his weapon, King released the magazine and counted the ammunition inside. Hell, he'd gone through it all while trying to give Scarlett and Julien an escape in the warehouse, and he hadn't slowed down long enough to restock. He couldn't go in there without a weapon.

"Drop me here. Wait for backup and tell whoever's in charge that Sangre por Sangre is inside, armed and highly dangerous. Oh, and if you have any extra 9mm Luger ammunition, that would be greatly appreciated."

The car skidded to a stop, threatening to throw him through the windshield, but King didn't have time for any other injuries. Scarlett was in there. He had to go. King kicked the passenger side door open. He reached back in and threw a thank-you to the officer who handed him a box of fresh ammunition. "Reach out to the supervisory special agent of the DEA in Albuquerque. Tell him Agent Elsher is on the scene. He'll know what to do."

King slammed the door behind him, effectively putting an end to any change of mind. He packed the magazine of his weapon and jammed the heavy metal casing into place. Intense desert heat beaded sweat at the back of his neck, but it was nothing compared to the heat coming off the building. Flames licked at the garage entrance he and Scarlett had slid beneath two days ago. She'd spent her entire career with

Socorro building defenses against attacks on this place. He wasn't going to be able to walk through the front door.

He had to go straight into the belly of the beast.

King tested his weight on his bad leg and regretted the choice immediately. But there was no other option. No other way for him to get inside. And he had to. He had to get to Scarlett.

She was the only reason he was standing here.

The past three days had blurred into a chaotic stream of bullets and blood and loss, but all the while, she'd been the one to keep him grounded. Their ridiculous debates and jabs at one another had kept him from spiraling. For the first time in years, someone had made him laugh, but it was her determination to leave the world better than how she'd found it that had convinced him she could bring Julien home.

And he wasn't letting her go. Not yet.

Scarlett's personal mission to make up for the past by giving her all—including her own life—for a kid she hadn't even met outweighed everything she'd told him about her involvement in the smuggling ring overseas. And he'd been an idiot to think a single cell in her beautiful body could be corrupted so easily. That she could hurt anyone.

All she'd done was prove over and over again that he needed her. Back in the warehouse. In this case. In his life. And, damn it, he wasn't ready to give that up.

Because he loved her.

In a matter of days, Scarlett had broken through the wall he'd built around him and Julien over the past two months and given him something to look forward to. A reason to keep going.

"I'm coming. Just hang on a bit longer." King added weight to his leg and took that first step toward the garage. Adrenaline raced to block the pain in his nerves, but it wouldn't be enough. The stitches around his wound screamed for his crutch. No. He could do this. He had to do this. His heel caught on a rock and worked to tip him off balance, but he was stronger now. Because of Julien. Because of Scarlett. Everything they'd been through had led him to this moment.

A gunshot echoed from the garage entrance.

He took a second step. Then another. His body adapted to the barbed wire curling through his thigh muscle, and he picked up the pace. He had no idea what he was walking into, but it didn't matter. His future was in that building, and he wasn't going to turn his back on it anymore. They were going to get through this. Together.

Two SUVs angled inward on either side of the entrance ahead.

King took position behind the one on the left, scanning the interior for movement. Instead, he found an arsenal. "Don't mind if I do."

Grabbing for the hatch release, he let the cargo door swing upward on its hydraulics and exposed an entire selection of automatic weapons, grenades and ammunition. He tucked a flash grenade in each pocket, cutting his gaze around the vehicle to keep an eye out for anyone left standing guard. Then grabbed for the nearest rifle. "I'll just ignore the fact it's illegal to drive around with all this."

Leaving the cargo area open, King maneuvered to the front of the SUV along the driver's side. Fire raged mere feet from the bumper and flashed hot along the exposed skin of his arms, face and neck. The longer the flames burned, the more unstable the building would get. He couldn't wait for fire and rescue. He had to go now. "It's just a couple arm hairs. They'll grow back."

King took two deep breaths, then held the third. And took the leap.

He hauled himself over the threshold of the entrance, barely missing the reach of flames. Colliding with a wall of human muscle on the other side.

The cartel soldier stumbled forward and slammed into another SUV parked a few feet ahead. King tried to get his strength back into his legs, but the added gear was holding him down. He dropped the assault rifle as the soldier turned on him.

A fist connected with the left side of his face and sent King spiraling toward the cement. Fire licked at the back of his neck. He rolled to avoid the flames and took out the soldier's legs in the process. The two-hundred-pound attacker landed directly on top of him, shoving the air from his chest.

King grabbed for one of the grenades stashed in his pants pocket, pulled the pin and shoved it between the soldier's Kevlar and rib cage. He kicked the son of a bitch out of reach and, plugging his ears, he scrambled out of the blast radius as fast as his leg allowed.

A panicked scream was cut short as the device exploded.

Smoke drove into King's lungs as he forced himself to his feet. He collected the assault rifle and set the butt of the weapon into his shoulder. "Who's next?"

A gunshot burst from his right, and King turned the rifle on the shooter. His bullets cut through the thick smoke pouring down from the garage ceiling.

Something heavy hit the ground. No more gunshots.

King kept moving, working his way through the maze of parked vehicles. The elevator access into the building had to be close. He pressed forward, putting everything he had into staying on his feet. He rounded the final vehicle.

And faced off with a gun pointed directly at him.

Granger Morais's hands bobbed with every exaggerated breath. One second. Two. The counterterrorism agent seemed to think better of pulling the trigger and let his arms collapse into his chest. Lying back, Granger stared up at the ceiling. "Where the hell did you come from?"

"Outside." King noted the dark puddle of liquid pooling beneath the operative's right side and took another step forward. "You don't look so good."

"You think I'll be ready for my date later tonight?" A half scoff, half laugh seemed to aggravate whatever wound Granger had sustained in his shoulder. Pain contorted his expression and tightened the muscles along his arms. "It's just a scratch. She won't notice, right?"

"You might want to reschedule. Or, hey, hospital food isn't as bad as everyone thinks. It's not every day you get to visit a cafeteria. She'll certainly remember it." King swung the rifle to his back, the strap digging into his shoulder. He offered Granger a hand. "What happened here?"

Granger didn't hesitate and slid a calloused palm into King's. A groan escaped the operative's control as King hauled him to his feet. "They blew through the gate. My guess is with C-4. Never saw them coming."

Dread pooled at the base of King's spine as he scoured what he could see of the garage. Wide cracks splintered across the ceiling. The weight of this entire building could drop right on them without warning. They had to get everyone out of here. "Where is Scarlett?"

"I sent her upstairs. We needed her to call the shots." Granger rolled his shoulder back, pulling a scream from his chest a split second before he doubled over. Not even the most experienced operators could outrun a bullet.

"Have you heard from her since?" They got to the elevator, and King swept the area one last time as Granger set his key card against the reader. Seconds ticked by—slower than he wanted.

“I kind of had other things on my mind.” The counterterrorism agent collapsed against the wall near the key card panel. “Not dying, for one.”

Movement registered from the crumbling gate.

An armored vehicle tore through the mess and rammed into the first two SUVs in its way. The crash threatened to trigger an avalanche of steel, cement and wood and bring the entire building down on top of them.

King checked the elevator’s progress, swinging the rifle into both hands. “We’ve got company.”

“We already had company,” Granger said.

The elevator pinged before opening its doors. King fisted the operative’s shirt and dragged him inside the car as an army of cartel soldiers spilled out of the armored truck. “That was just the first wave.”

Chapter Fourteen

Her feet slipped out from under her. Scarlett hit the clean black tile with a thud. Oxygen stretched out of reach the harder she tried to control the impact. Her fingernails clawed into the thin grout, but it was no use getting to her feet.

Alarms screeched from every hallway. Socorro was under attack. Whoever blew through the gate had tripped the system. Any operatives inside would already be taking battle positions. Cash and Jocelyn on the roof with their high-powered rifles, Jones armed with his personal arsenal on the elevators and Granger… She'd left him in the garage. Watched him take a bullet.

But she couldn't think about that right now.

Her job was easy. Get to the security room. That was where she could do the most damage. Scarlett shoved to her feet. The aches and bruises from the past few days wouldn't slow her down. She wouldn't let them. She dug her toes into the floor to propel her forward. Right, then two lefts. She collided with the door that prevented anyone but her and Ivy Bardot access to the security room and scrambled for her key card.

Every second counted on the battlefield. One wrong move. That was all it would take, and she and her team would lose everything.

Scarlett nearly fell over the threshold as the door released.

Loud voices punctured through the radio sitting in its charging station on the desk. An entire array of monitors cast a blue-white glow across the darkened room. Cameras covered every angle of the structure, and Scarlett worked to get eyes on the rest of her team. She grabbed for the earpiece left in its power cradle.

"Gotham and I are in position on level two." Jones's voice was staticky in her ear. "Anyone manages to get inside, they won't make it far."

"Hold your position. Scarlett, shut down the elevators. We're not going to make it easy for them." She imagined Ivy Bardot secured in her office, armed, with both eyes on the surveillance.

"Granger's in the garage trying to hold them back," Scarlett said. "That's his only way out."

Thousands of possibilities screamed for attention at the back of her mind, but only one stood out. Sangre por Sangre. Scarlett scanned the multitude of monitors for her teammate, but there was something else in the garage. Something that shouldn't be there. Her skin tightened to the point she was convinced her bones would crumble to dust inside her own body. "Be advised, hostiles have brought in an armored vehicle. I count fifteen—no, sixteen—armed enemy combatants in the garage, but I don't see Granger."

"Damn it. Get eyes on him. Now." Ivy's voice notched an octave higher.

Socorro had never been attacked in its own territory. For as many years of experience each of Ivy's operatives had gathered, this was a first for all of them outside of their military careers. And it was showing. "Cash, Jocelyn. I need you on that roof in case more are on their way. Where the hell are you?"

"Almost there." Socorro's forward observer—Cash Meyers—sounded out of breath. "Do you know how many stairs there are in this place? Not to mention how much gear I'm carrying."

"Just keep climbing. Just keep climbing." Logistics coordinator Jocelyn Carville sang her own personal mantra.

"I will end you." Cash's threat meant nothing when an entire drug cartel had breached their home base.

"Has anyone contacted Dr. Piel or the veterinarian?" Jones Driscoll looked up into the camera set on him. "Might be a good time to let them know to stay in their offices."

"On it." Scarlett took out her cell and tapped out the message to both physicians. An instant reply buzzed through from the vet.

Hans ran when the alarms went off.

"What?" The question was more for herself as Scarlett instructed the vet to shelter in place. Her female K9 was missing with the other one unaccounted for after the fight at the warehouse. In a matter of hours, she'd lost everything she held dear. She wasn't sure she could take much more.

"I've got movement on the elevator." Jones hiked his rifle into his shoulder on the monitor, but all Scarlett could see was a bunch of blurred pixels as her world unraveled right before her eyes.

"Scarlett, where is Granger?" Ivy's voice tried to keep her in the present, but grief and a stabbing of fear kept her from engaging in the moment. "Scarlett?"

She tossed her phone on the desk. Tears prickled at her eyes, but she couldn't focus on that right now. Her mind was being pulled in a thousand different directions, and she couldn't make sense of a single one of them. She scoured the monitors. Hans had to still be in the building, and there was nothing Scarlett could do about it.

"Uh, guys. Elevator. On the move." Jones backed up a step, ready to engage anyone who came through the elevator doors.

"Working on it." Scarlett ran through the elevator protocol as fast as her fingers allowed and found the line of code to take the system offline. "There."

The elevator's LED panel froze on the screen. Whoever was hoping to get onto the level would be stuck until Scarlett deemed otherwise.

"Wait. I hear something from inside." Jones took a hesitant step forward. The combat controller let his weapon swing free as he pressed one side of his head to the doors on the screen. "Oh, hell. It's Granger. Bring the elevator back up."

Her heart jump-started at the news. Granger was alive. "I shut the whole system down. It's going to take at least two minutes to bring it back online."

Two minutes Granger might not have.

"We don't have that kind of time." Jocelyn's voice was no longer singsongy. "I've got five more vehicles headed our way. Cartel based off the makes and models. No telling how many more soldiers inside. A half mile out."

"I've got another dust cloud coming in from the east," Cash said. "Can't be sure who it is yet."

"They're cutting off any chance of escape." Ivy went silent for a series of seconds, every single one of them waiting for the next order. "Scarlett, I need you to get the secondary system ready."

Shock stole Scarlett's confidence to win this battle. "Are you sure?"

"This firm is a direct connection to the Pentagon and every other federal organization we've partnered with to undermine Sangre por Sangre." Socorro's founder didn't wait for an answer. "If the cartel gets their hands on any of the intel we've used, they'll be able to identify our inside source, and there will be no stopping them, and that is something none of us can come back from. Get the system ready."

Jones let his rifle drop to his side as he threaded his fingers between the elevator doors. Muscles Scarlett would never have in her life flexed as he tried to pry the doors open by hand. "Why does that sound like we're launching a nuclear missile?" he asked.

"Because that's basically what we'll be doing." Scarlett brought up the program she'd built from the ground up. One press of the button. That was all it would take to appease Socorro's enemies and ensure the team never interrupted cartel operations again. Because none of them would make it out of here alive. A chain reaction of fear and determination and grief knotted her nerves. "The entire building will be demolished."

"Whoa. What the hell are you talking about?" Wind caught Cash's last word from the roof and made it difficult to hear through the earpiece. "What is the secondary defense system?"

Scarlett took a deep breath as a flood of cartel members spread through the garage. They searched every SUV and confiscated individual weapons from the back of each vehicle. She let her hand slip to her sidearm, hoping beyond hope it would be enough. "C-4. Wired over every square inch of this place."

"It's not every day you get a front row seat to the end of the world, but at least we're all together." Jocelyn's voice cracked a split second before a dog bark pierced the open channel. Her German shepherd, Maverick, had been the logistic coordinator's partner as long as Scarlett could remember. "I'm going silent. I need to call Baker."

The green LED connected to Jocelyn's earpiece on Scarlett's monitor went red as her teammate reached out to her life partner, Alpine Valley's chief of police.

"Got it!" Jones pried the elevator doors apart and leveraged one leg into the gap to keep it from closing.

Granger slapped a hand onto the tile and hauled himself free of the elevator that wasn't quite level with the floor yet. Only he wasn't alone.

The desk bit into her sore midsection as Scarlett tried to get a better view of the man following the counterterrorism agent, but her instincts had already put two and two together. Her nails bit into her palms as she recognized the sharp jawline and dirty blond hair. "King."

She pushed away from the desk to intercept him but caught another range of movement on a monitor. One of the armored vehicles. An outline of white in the middle of so much darkness and destruction.

A woman stepped down from the back of the vehicle. So out of place. Long dark hair lay in tendrils past her shoulders and framed a heart-shaped face. Her white blazer and pant set put her in a whole other category of wealth and security as the soldiers around her fanned out.

Catalina Muñoz.

"It's her." Scarlett wasn't sure who she was talking to, but the comms were still open. "Catalina Muñoz. She's here. This is all happening because of her."

"Who the hell is Catalina Muñoz?" Jones's question seemed to catch King's attention on the monitor.

"Who are you talking to?" The DEA agent fought her teammate for his earpiece and won out, shoving the device into his own ear. "Who is this?"

Their last conversation—his accusations—undermined everything she knew about herself and her ability to get her team out of here alive. "Agent Elsher."

"Scarlett." King searched the corridor until he found the nearest camera and limped toward it, his gaze searing straight through the monitor. "I put it all together. Hernando Muñoz was a source. Adam and Eva were using him to get to the triad. If Catalina's here, that means she's the one who killed him. She's the real brains behind the operation. Taking out the other cartels, partnering with the triad, abducting Julien. It's all because of her. Where is she?"

Scarlett turned her attention back to the monitor overlooking the inside of Socorro's garage. Instantly on high alert as Catalina stared into the camera lens. "In the garage."

Catalina turned toward someone or something still in the truck before facing off with the surveillance. Another pixelated outline—smaller—appeared on the screen. And then Julien came into view.

"King," she said. "She has your son."

KING DISLODGED THE EARPIECE.

"King! There are more on the way!" Scarlett's voice crackled just before he handed the device back to the operative in front of him.

Pointing to Granger, King backed toward the elevator car still uneven with the floor. "You're going to want to get him to a doctor."

"There's no way out of here that doesn't put you in their sights, Elsher." Granger's usually frustratingly even voice dipped as he latched on to his shoulder. "They'll kill you the second they get eyes on you."

"Not before I kill them first." King's gaze caught the surveillance camera. He knew Scarlett was watching, and he got as close to it as he could. He didn't know whether or not they had sound or if she could make out his words, but it didn't matter. He had to tell her. That he was wrong, that she meant something to him, that she was everything he'd tried to avoid in his life and everything he needed at the same time.

"I love you." There wasn't any more he could say.

King turned his back on the camera—on whatever future they might've had—and headed for the elevator door. He set the rifle against his chest, ready for whatever waited on the other side. Because it was the only way to get to his son. And save the woman he loved. If he could slow Sangre por Sangre down, there was a chance the entire Socorro team could live to fight another day.

Only one way to find out.

"You really think you're going to survive whatever is down there without a vest?" The operative King hadn't met before—the one who had forced open the elevator doors for them—stripped the Velcro from the side of his ribs and pulled his Kevlar vest over his head. Offering it with one hand, he hiked Granger's arm around his shoulder for support with the other. "Thought you DEA types were smarter than that."

"You'd be surprised." King hauled the rifle strap over his head, took the vest and slipped into it before replacing the weapon. There were more on the way. That was the last thing he'd heard Scarlett say. The cartel had most likely surrounded the place, cutting off any chance of escape. Socorro operatives would have to prioritize, Scarlett included, leaving him to fight this particular battle alone. "Thanks."

Electricity powered up behind him, and the elevator car closed the distance to the last level. Scarlett. With a half salute toward the camera, he smiled. "Wish me luck."

King stepped into the elevator, facing off with his own reflection as the doors closed down the middle. Gravity suctioned his stomach into the bottom of his torso as the floors counted off on the LED panel overhead. "I'm going to need it."

The elevator pinged just before a thud registered from under his feet as the car landed on the garage level. One second. Two.

The doors parted.

Smoke and dust and diesel infiltrated his senses as King stepped out. A circle of soldiers took aim, and he raised his hands in surrender. "I come in peace."

"I'm not entirely sure that's true, Agent Elsher." The semicircle parted down the middle, exposing the source of the voice. Catalina Muñoz, in the flesh. "I seem to recall having to clean up quite a few bodies at my warehouse two days ago. You wouldn't believe how hard it is to get blood out of cement."

He wasn't going to apologize for that. He wasn't going to apologize for anything concerning this investigation. "Where is my son?"

"Right here." Catalina half turned and reached behind her. Long fingers wrapped around the back of his son's neck and drew him forward away from the soldier guarding the ten-year-old. "Julien has done a fine job of keeping me company, haven't you, dear?"

"I'm here, buddy." Every cell in King's body wanted to rip Julien out of Catalina's grasp, but that would surely get him a few bullet holes of his own. And Julien had already watched one parent die in front of him. King couldn't do that to him again. He balanced his weight onto his good leg, just in case he had to move fast. "Everything's going to be okay."

"The lies parents tell their children," Catalina said. "No wonder betrayal trauma has become so prevalent these days."

His son flinched at the comment. Or maybe from the woman's grip around his neck. King couldn't tell which, but one thing was clear. Nothing was going to stop him from getting Julien out of here alive. "Let me guess. You're here for the intel your husband handed over on your operation."

"You're smarter than you look, Agent Elsher." Catalina stepped fully into the ring of armed cartel members, putting Julien that much closer to the barrel of an assault rifle. "I'll make this easy for you. Give me what I want, and you and Julien are free to leave this place."

"While you burn Socorro to the ground." That wasn't an option. "Why? Why dump Adam's body at Socorro's doorstep? They didn't have anything to do with this until I approached them for help finding your husband."

"Is that what she told you?" A weak, sad smile creased crow's feet at the edges of Catalina's dark brown eyes. "Ivy Bardot knew about your partner's investigation long before you recruited Socorro into your little revenge plot, Agent Elsher. How else would he and that ATF agent access satellite images and intel about my operations over the years without raising federal suspicions? I imagine that's why she offered you her resources in the first place. Because once I took care of your partners, Socorro lost their hold in my dealings. And she couldn't have that."

Was that true? Had Ivy Bardot already known exactly who he was and what he wanted before he'd stepped into that conference room? Had she used him?

"Only now it seems I'm presented with the opportunity to take out two birds with one stone," Catalina said. "My uncle would still be alive if it weren't for Socorro. Metias raised me, you know. Taught me everything I know, made sure I went to the best schools, supported me. He shaped me into the woman I am today. One who's going to lead Sangre por Sangre into the future."

Blah blah blah. King didn't have time for this. Cartel reinforcements would only skew the chances he and Julien had of making it out alive. "Then I was right. You were the one behind taking out the other cartels in the area. Not your husband."

"Hernando served his purpose well. Kept the DEA and other federal agencies focused on him while I moved the deal with the triad forward," she said.

A ferocious growl resonated from the back of the armored truck, and Catalina let her hand slide from Julien's neck.

"It worked for a while." She backed toward the truck. "But after you and your friend—Scarlett is her name?—breached my warehouse, I discovered Hernando hadn't been as true to me as he promised in our wedding vows. And, well, I couldn't have that."

The widow motioned for one of the gunmen, and Gruber lunged from the darkness. A restraint prevented him from opening his mouth wider than a few centimeters while the choke chain kept him from attacking. The K9's dark eyes focused on Julien before the animal went wild all over again. As though he were trying to live up to his orders to protect King's son.

King locked his gaze on Julien. "Stay with Gruber."

His son's terrified face relaxed slightly.

"I've given you my terms, Agent Elsher." The widow was losing her patience, her voice icier than a moment ago. "But you seem to have come down here empty-handed. Am I to understand you won't be giving me what I came for and that I'll have to do to you what I did to the other two agents who crossed me? What were their names again? Eva Roday and Adam Dunkeld, right? Were they friends of yours?"

Rage bubbled up his throat. "You were there that night. The night Eva was killed. You ordered her murder."

"No, Agent Elsher," Catalina said. "That's one tradition I don't follow in the cartel. You see, I do my own dirty work."

Eva. Adam. Muñoz. This woman had killed them all.

The elevator pinged again, drawing the attention of every gunman in the garage.

"You might've gotten away with the murders of my partners, Catalina, but you're wrong about one thing." He heard the doors part. "I didn't come empty-handed."

Something hit the cement.

King didn't have to know what it was. He lunged for his son, securing Julien in his arms as the explosion rocked through the garage. Cement rained down on top of them as King rolled to put his son underneath his body.

Gruber's growl pierced through the cacophony of screams and gunshots, and King stuck a hand out. "Gruber!"

The K9 collided into King's back, every muscle the dog owned rippling in response to the attack. King loosened the choke collar from around the Doberman's neck and tore at the muzzle. *"Pass auf."* That was what Scarlett had said to get Gruber to protect Julien, and King needed the K9 on that job now more than ever.

A second bark registered from near the elevator, and a dark blur of lean muscle and sharp teeth burst through the circle of gunmen. Hans pounced on a soldier coming up on King and Julien, taking him down in a mess of claws and teeth.

King kissed the top of Julien's head. "Remember what I said, buddy. Stay with Gruber."

"Shoot them!" Catalina's voice was broken up by a series of coughs. Distant. In retreat.

King pushed upright as a glimpse of Catalina's white blazer disappeared into the back of the armored truck. The engine growled to life. "You're not getting away that easily."

Return gunfire cut through the haze of dust and debris still clouding the garage, and Scarlett shoved her way into the fight. She took aim at a soldier coming up on King's left and pulled the trigger. The gunman dropped. "Go! We've got this!"

It was then King realized she hadn't come alone. The operative who'd loaned King his vest rocketed his fist into a cartel member's face off to the left as another Socorro contractor unsheathed a knife from her cargo pants and sank it deep into an attacker's side. One by one they were picking off threats to give King the opportunity to finish this.

"Take care of my boy." He scratched behind Gruber's head, then ran for the armored vehicle. His leg protested every step, but he wasn't going to slow down. He wasn't going to let Catalina get away with what she'd done.

Her smile cut through the interior of the cargo area a split second before the door secured.

He ran into the two-inch steel and slapped his hand against the door. The vehicle lurched backward toward the entrance. "No!"

"King!" Scarlett's voice penetrated the haze of adrenaline and anger combining into a toxic cocktail under his skin.

He turned to face her just as she tossed him a brick of white clay. Only it wasn't clay.

King caught the mass and hurried to stick it under the armored vehicle's front wheel well. Catalina was in the passenger seat, that smile still in play. Until he unholstered his sidearm and took aim. Not at the windshield. At the brick of C-4 he'd planted on the armored truck.

He pulled the trigger.

The truck shot into the ceiling of the garage, the entire engine bursting into a thousand different pieces.

Strong hands grabbed the shoulders of King's Kevlar vest and dragged him to the ground. He slammed into the cement as a wall of gear and muscle and red hair shielded him from the blast. The explosion triggered a high-pitched ringing in his head, but through the aftermath, Scarlett's voice crystalized. "And you made fun of me for preparing for the zombie apocalypse."

Sirens screeched through the garage as two police patrol vehicles cut off the cartel's exit. The passenger side door of the armored vehicle fell open, depositing Catalina Muñoz onto the ground with a huff. Her white pantsuit would never be the same.

Nondescript SUVs skidded to a halt beyond the police wall and unloaded a dozen DEA agents, and Catalina had no other choice than to raise her hands in surrender.

The fight was over. King's son was safe. His leg would heal, and the world would keep turning. Without Eva and Adam in it. And all King could think to do was pass out cold.

Chapter Fifteen

Scarlett reset the ceiling tile in place.

Despite two explosions in the garage, her secondary defense system sat untouched. Everything was stable. Well, apart from the fact the entire building could suddenly collapse underneath her without warning. The engineers were working on it, and she'd have to remove the bricks of C-4 she installed through all four levels, but she wasn't able to stay away from this place. Socorro had become a home. A safe haven that'd given her life purpose after she'd thrown it away at the slightest misguided chance to do something good.

Only now she really had made a difference.

"Come on." She whistled low for Gruber to follow.

The K9 had followed her orders and protected Julien to the very end, taking a few samples of cartel member DNA in the process. There were more than a few gunmen sporting bite marks, and she'd made sure to give Gruber extra treats as a reward. Though it had been hard to separate him and Julien once the chaos of the attack had settled down. Even now, she was convinced the Doberman wanted to be with the kid instead of her.

Hans was still recovering from a broken rib sustained during the fight in Muñoz's warehouse. Socorro's alarms had triggered her training to defend the team, but after reuniting with Gruber, the K9 finally seemed convinced that she could go to the vet clinic in Alpine Valley to serve out the rest of her recovery. And Scarlett made sure to check on her every chance she got between disarming the building so the construction crew could get to work.

As for Catalina Muñoz, her admission to killing Agents Eva Roday and Adam Dunkeld and her husband had been recorded on Socorro surveillance, which Scarlett had been all too happy to hand over to law enforcement. The medical examiner's office managed to collect a single sample of DNA from the blade stabbed into Adam Dunkeld's chest, and with a compulsory court order for a comparison, Catalina had written her own life sentence. Seemed stabbing a knife through an officer's badge took more strength than Catalina possessed. The blade had slipped, cutting her hand in the process.

Detectives had found a matching scar on her other hand, most likely from when she stabbed Agent Roday two months ago. Though they couldn't prove it, and Catalina wasn't talking to anyone without a lawyer.

Adding abduction charges on top of everything else had almost been too easy with eyewitness statements from the women in the front office of the school identifying Catalina as the woman who checked Julien out the day he went missing, as well as surveillance video from the principal. DNA comparison from the scene inside the freezer of Muñoz's restaurant matched that of Adam Dunkeld, and though they couldn't tie Catalina directly to the scene, her admission of the agent's murder was enough for the prosecutor. And charges filed by the DEA once they concluded their investigation into the fentanyl from the warehouse would ensure the widow never saw the outside of a prison ever again for what she'd done.

The triad was still a problem. Sangre por Sangre's newest partners had lost their supply line into the country, and from what little she knew of organizations like theirs, this wasn't over. They would try to reestablish contact, maybe take on a new liaison given they'd lost both Muñozes. If anything, Scarlett had the feeling the fight ahead would be much, much worse than what they'd survived this week.

But she wasn't fighting this war alone. Agents Roday and Dunkeld had given the feds a huge leg up now that Scarlett had been able to decode the ciphered notes. Identities of triad contacts from Muñoz, bank account numbers for deposits to Sangre por Sangre, operations that spelled out which competing cartels were targeted in the purge. It was all there.

Ivy Bardot had taken the intel straight to the Pentagon. Socorro would take the lead with the support of the DEA, ATF and the CIA to keep the triad off American soil. Though King's and Ivy's professional relationship had been put on hold since they'd learned of Ivy secretly funding his partner's off-the-books investigation. But maybe in this case, the ends had justified the means.

But best of all, King and Julien had been reunited once Scarlett's partner had been allowed to receive visitors in the hospital. The wound in his leg would heal if he actually stayed off his feet and followed his physician's orders, but Scarlett had the sense his recovery wouldn't go as smoothly as they hoped. King's suspension from the DEA hadn't been lifted despite solving his personal investigation, and the man wasn't the kind to sit still for long. Especially not with Adam's funeral scheduled for tomorrow.

Scarlett hefted the container of C-4 and wiring she'd ripped out of the ceiling tiles from the floor and headed for the security office. It was a shame Ivy had made her take it all down. Then again, with the team working out of Alpine Valley's doublewide trailer-slash-police-station, there wasn't much here left to protect.

Her steps faltered as the weight of that realization set in. Everything looked the same, yet her entire world had changed. There wasn't anything left for her to protect.

She shouldered into the security room. And froze at the realization she wasn't alone.

Gruber huffed before circling the room and then lunging at the ten-year-old boy standing off to the left of the door. Traitor.

"You certainly know how to throw a party." King twisted in her desk chair. As though he'd been waiting for her all this time. Considering he couldn't get around with a crutch, she bet sitting grated on his nerves. "What do we got here? Bricks of C-4 and wiring. It's not much, but we can sure as hell put on a show."

Her grip tightened on the edges of the box. "Aren't you supposed to be recuperating under professional supervision? I thought I told security not to let you out of the hospital."

"Julien couldn't wait until I got out to see Gruber." King's smile broke at one side of his mouth as he watched his son and Gruber start wrestling. The Doberman was gentle. More so than he'd ever been with Scarlett, and she couldn't help but imagine they would be friends for a very long time. "See? How can I say no to that face?"

Scarlett set the box of explosives on the corner of her L-shaped desk. "Has he said anything about what happened?"

"Nah." King set his elbows on his knees, shaking his head. "I'm not sure he ever will, and I'm okay with that. When he's ready to talk to me—or to anyone else for that matter—I'll be there. I'm just happy to have him home."

"Right." That was what was important. That was what they'd fought so hard for. But the hollowness that had tried to break her so many times before wouldn't let go. They'd exposed a monumental shift within the Sangre por Sangre cartel, taken out one of their key players and managed to bring

Julien home alive. She should've felt relief. Felt…something more than this deep ache that had set up behind her sternum the moment she partnered with King on this case.

"You weren't there. When I woke up." King raised his gaze to hers. "Hell, the last thing I remember before coming around in the hospital is you tackling me to the ground. The DEA came onto the scene, and then… I'm not even sure how I got out of there, but I knew who I wanted to see on the other side."

"Yeah." She clutched the handles of the box as though her life depended on it. She'd wanted to be there. At his bedside. She wanted to be the one holding his hand when his eyes opened and tell him everything was going to be okay.

But she'd frozen outside his hospital room, hand on the doorknob. The only thing she could hear were his final words cutting through her all over again.

The security monitors blurred in her peripheral vision. "There was a lot going on. I needed to coordinate with Alpine Valley PD and the DEA to make sure there were no other threats inside the building. And the engineers said they couldn't assess the damage until all explosives were removed off-site."

"Scarlett." King dragged himself out of the chair and shifted his weight onto his uninjured leg, somehow closing the distance between them. The room suddenly seemed so much smaller than before. "Granger told me what he uncovered while he was on assignment overseas. About the smuggling ring you were involved in."

Her throat constricted in defense, but she wasn't going to give him more to hold against her. Because he'd been right before. Admitting her involvement had given him everything he would need to have the army court-martial her and send her some place no one would ever find her. The DEA would come around. Sooner or later his suspension would be lifted, and King would be allowed to work in a federal capacity. With the power to destroy her and another member of her team.

"He told me you and your crew stole cash, weapons, drugs—anything you could get your hands on under the radar," he said. "He told me while the other soldiers you worked with were in it for themselves, you were the only one who took what you stole, turned it into cash and food and supplies and gave it to dozens of families stuck in their villages."

He put his hands on her. Soft at first, then tighter around her biceps, and she couldn't help but want that contact. To feel him holding her upright instead of her trying to hold up the entire world on her own.

"But even before Granger explained your involvement, I knew. In my heart, I know you're a woman who keeps her word. I know you were willing to risk your and Granger's freedom for my son, and I know there isn't anything you wouldn't do for the people—and the dogs—you care about. Even for the kid of a DEA agent who tackled you in a morgue."

Her burst of laughter took her by surprise.

"I was wrong, Scarlett. About everything. If it weren't for you, I wouldn't have my son back, and I owe you my life. I owe you more than that." King threaded one hand into the hair at the back of her neck, closing the last few inches of distance between them. "But most of all, I owe you an apology. Because I didn't mean what I said before. About you not meaning anything to me."

Her skin constricted around her bones. Too tight. "Oh?"

"The truth is, I was scared of caring about one more person after I've lost everyone in my life, and I ran at the slightest provocation," he said. "You carried me through this investigation. You saved me, and not just in that warehouse or downstairs in the garage. You kept me focused on what mattered, and you made me realize what I've lost is nothing compared to what's possible with you at my side. You mean everything to me."

Her mind automatically raced to fill in the blanks around that last statement, though she'd never been one to make a move while emotionally compromised. But she sure as hell wanted to start. "I'm going to need you to spell it out for me, King. And not on a camera without sound."

"All right. I love you." He traced his thumb along her bottom lip, and a rush of sensation filtered through her system. "I used to think being a DEA agent was all I was worth, but now I know I'm meant to be your partner. In the field or out. I'm there for you. Whatever happens with my job and the suspension, wherever I end up, I don't care. Because I have everything I need right here in this..." he surveyed her dark corner of Socorro "...surveillance room."

"You love me?" Scarlett interlaced her hands behind his neck, drawing his mouth to hers. She was still trying to make sense of the past few minutes, but even off balance by the course of events and finding him in her security room, she hadn't felt this full in...ever. Whole. And yeah, she felt good, too. King had taken all those broken pieces she'd believed couldn't be put back together and shown her reality. "I love you, too."

"Ew!" Julien's protest broke through the bubble she and King had created around themselves, and Scarlett couldn't help but enjoy the sound of his voice for the first time.

She pulled back, swiping her hand across her mouth, and couldn't contain her laugh. Of all the times Julien could've broken his silence, she was glad to be part of it. "You're the one who wanted him to talk so badly."

"Sorry, buddy." King held on to her, and she caught sight of a line of tears reflected from the blue-white glow of the monitors. He'd been waiting for this moment for so long, and she couldn't help but feel that awe in his expression. "We'll try to behave ourselves."

Scarlett pressed her index finger into her partner's chest. "I guess now's a good time to tell you I've already drawn up plans to secure your house. Can't have the cartel or the triad coming for you or Julien again."

"Not with C-4, though." King studied the box not a foot from where they stood. "Right?"

Scarlett hefted the explosives off the desk to bundle with the three she'd already collected from the other floors.

"Scarlett." King followed after her. "Not with C-4."

"You said it yourself." She stacked the boxes together and dusted off her hands, getting a good look at Julien, King and Gruber. Her only wish was that Hans could be here with them, but the K9 would be up and running soon enough. And Scarlett couldn't wait for what came next. "I'll do whatever it takes to protect the people I care about."

* * * * *

WYOMING DOUBLE JEOPARDY

JUNO RUSHDAN

For Gloria

Chapter One

It was another typical Thursday evening until it wasn't. A fourteen-hour workday. Always the first one in. Always the last one out.

Gathering her things, she grabbed the fragrant bundle of flowers from a chair and then closed the door to her office. She glanced at the plaque on the door, engraved Assistant District Attorney, Melanie Indira Merritt.

"One day it won't be assistant," she muttered to herself. Her time would come.

Melanie had put in tremendous effort and had the keenest talent when it came to picking a jury, leading to her pristine victory record and earning her the nickname of *The Closer.*

Her previous boss had had a bad habit of taking credit for her work, but things were different at her position here in Laramie, Wyoming. This DA didn't use her and didn't try to sleep with her. More of a father figure, Gordon championed her successes, invited her into his home for meals with his wife, and helped make her transition to the Cowboy State a smooth one.

She walked down the hall of the third floor of the county courthouse where the prosecuting attorney's offices took up the entire space and locked the inner door. Her stomach grumbled, reminding her she'd missed dinner.

Adjusting the straps of her laptop case and purse on her shoulder, she glanced at her watch: 9:10 p.m. Too late for anything heavy. A Caesar salad waited for her in the fridge.

She pushed through the outer door into the attached covered parking garage. The muggy July wind had died down and cooled off. A light rain had started. In the Wyoming valley, where Laramie and Bison Ridge sat, surrounded by the mountains, the temperature in the summer evenings was often mild and pleasant, which beat a blustery winter breeze slicing through her.

She watched Darcy Rosenfeld pull out of her parking spot. The paralegal was great at helping her prepare for meetings and trials. The young woman was thorough, saving Melanie tons of time.

At the trash receptacle, Melanie stopped and took one last whiff of the bouquet of flowers cradled in her arm. Roses, freesia, sweet pea, peonies and hyacinth. Her favorites. They smelled divine, rich in summer colors that would brighten anyone's day.

She read the card once more.

To M&M–no nuts,
This sucks. I hate it. I miss you. Miss the us that might've been. Please rethink this. Soon. Can't wait forever.
Your Cowboy.

Melanie bit back a sad smile. Waylon was holding on to false hope that she would backtrack, go against common sense and a healthy instinct for professional self-preservation. At least he'd stopped calling, leaving enticing voicemail messages that tempted her willpower.

He needed to move on. They both did. But she was far too

busy to find someone more suitable, who wasn't a threat to her career.

She tossed the gorgeous bouquet into the trash bin.

Darcy pulled up and rolled down her passenger's-side window. "I'd kill for Hank to buy me a bouquet like that," she said, referring to her boyfriend, a sweet paralegal at a local firm. "Maybe I'll drop a hint. Hey, even if the relationship is kaput, you should keep the flowers. Must've cost a fortune. Sure you don't want to tell me who the cowboy is? It'll be our secret."

Sharing was how secrets ceased to exist. "Good night, Darcy. See you tomorrow."

"Your cowboy, whoever he is, has excellent taste. Not only in flowers." The grinning paralegal waved bye and drove off.

Waylon was definitely unlike any man Melanie had been with. A salt-of-the-earth straight shooter. Humble. Handsome despite his scars or perhaps because of them. Emotionally available.

A great lover.

And a crackerjack detective with the Laramie Police Department, constantly arresting dangerous criminals she had to prosecute.

Therein lay the complicated problem.

When it came to choosing the right guy, she was a horrible failure.

Loneliness crowded in on her, making her ache for something she couldn't have. Not with Waylon. She reached into the trash bin and took out the flowers, against her better judgment. They'd die in a week on their own. No need for her to hurry their demise. Besides, Darcy was right. Waylon had paid a pretty penny for the huge bouquet. She'd never chuck a hundred dollar bill out the window because the wrong person had given it to her.

A yawn took hold. She needed to get home, eat and rest.

So, she could rise and shine at the crack of dawn, go for a run, and do it all over again.

Yay, me.

Pulling her car keys from her purse, Melanie headed for her SUV, the lone vehicle remaining on the top level, tucked beside a concrete pillar. Her keys jangled in her hand and her high heels click-clacked across the pavement, echoing in the garage. Raindrops pitter-pattered on the roof of the building and asphalt on the street. She liked to park midway in the lot. Far enough to get in some extra steps on her pedometer. But not too far to make her uncomfortable at night in the public parking garage alone.

These past six months without Waylon, she was always alone.

Maybe time to get a pet. A fluffy, warm independent cat to cuddle. Too bad she was allergic.

She pressed the button on her fob—the horn beeped and the lights flashed—unlocking the SUV, and dropped the keys in her suit pocket.

Footsteps shuffled somewhere behind her. The nape of her neck prickled as she wheeled around toward the sound.

No one. Not a soul in sight.

She listened.

Silence, other than the rain.

She scanned the nearly empty upper floor, searching for anyone lurking, any sinister shadows in dark corners, but she didn't see anything of concern. Nothing out of the ordinary.

Was her mind playing tricks on her? Served her right for working herself to the bone every day.

Dismissing it as fatigue, she started for her SUV. She walked with care, trying to lessen the clatter of her heels.

More footsteps—the sound whispering beneath the noise of her shoes.

Unease slid down her spine. She stopped and surveyed her surroundings again with even more vigilance.

This was a small town, where everyone knew everyone. None of the dangers of a big city, like random muggings, drug addicts driven to desperation. Crime still existed. Usually of a higher order.

Looking around, she didn't see anyone.

The lot was well lit, the street below quiet. The sheriff's office was in the same building on the first floor, and she was well acquainted with everyone in the department. An attendant was in the booth on the main level until ten. She was fine.

Perfectly safe.

Still…

Tension gnawed at the base of her spine.

Trust your instincts. That's what her parents and self-defense classes had taught her.

She tightened her grip on the leather straps of her bags. Digging in her purse for her cell phone just in case, she quickened her pace to her SUV. Her pulse picked up. Sweat trickled in a cold line down her back. Almost there.

Almost.

Movement out of the corner of her eye snatched her attention. She whirled back around.

A man lunged from behind a concrete pillar and rushed toward her. Dressed in dark clothing. Wearing a full-face helmet. Dark-tinted visor. Something long and metallic in his hand.

A crowbar!

Her heart seized. She stumbled backward.

He plowed into her, shoving her up against her vehicle. The flowers tumbled from her arm. He raised the steel bar and swung. She ducked, narrowly missing the blow intended for her skull that crashed against the roof instead.

Melanie punched his stomach and rammed her knee up into his groin. With a grunt, he doubled over and staggered away. She jerked sideways and ran. But he snatched the back of her suit jacket, stopping her.

"Help! Help me!"

Grabbing the laptop case's strap, she swung the bag, using it as an improvised weapon. She slammed it down against his arm, freeing herself of his grip. But her purse slipped off and fell. Another swing with all her strength knocked the crowbar from his other hand and it clattered to the concrete floor. She kicked the steel bar, sending it skittering under the SUV. Then she slung the laptop case up at his head.

He lurched back, his arms flailing.

She dropped the bag and took off running, cursing her stupid heels and the tightness of her skirt. Taking the ramp would lead to the attendant's booth and the sheriff's office. But her assailant was faster and stronger. He could easily overtake her on the way down two stories. Same problem with the stairs.

Keys jangled in her pocket. Avoiding the ramp and staircase, she bolted back toward the building.

Footsteps thundered after her. Melanie flung the exterior door open and ducked inside. She dared to look back. Through the glass panel, she spotted him. He was up and running straight for her.

She raced for the interior door to the office space and snatched the keys from her pocket.

Faster, faster! Run faster!

The keys slipped from her fingers, hitting the carpet. She dashed back and grabbed them. With shaking hands, she fumbled for the right one.

Hinges squeaked behind her. She cast a terrified glance over her shoulder. He stormed through the outer door leading from the garage. She shoved the key into the dead bolt and unlocked the frameless glass door.

He was closing in, charging toward her like an angry bull.

Oh, God!

She pulled the key free, darted inside and flipped the latch on the dead bolt just as he raced up to the door. Now there was a locked barrier between them.

He yanked on the handle, making the glass vibrate.

What did he *want*?

Unable to get inside, he slapped the door. She backed away, watching him. He tilted his head to the side and studied the door from top to bottom.

The eerie movement sent a chill over her skin.

Then he smashed his head against the door. Once. Twice. Under the force of the helmet, the glass splintered.

Melanie's heart clenched. She had to get to a phone. Call for help. Once the sheriff's department got the message, a deputy could get to her in less than two minutes.

Unless that man reached her first.

The cracked webbing of the door spread. Panic zipped through her veins hot as an electric current, driving her to move.

Melanie spun around and ran. Not to her office. If he knew who she was, and this wasn't some random attack, then he'd expect her to head there.

But where to go? None of the office doors locked.

Her pulse skittered. Her legs shook. Her mind raced even as time slowed to a crawl.

The glass shattered. He was coming. He was behind her, erasing the distance between them at a frightening rate.

She darted to the left, down a walkway. Her heel caught on the carpet. She tripped and fell hard, scraping her bare leg. Climbing to her feet, a shoe came off. She surged forward, leaving the heel behind, and scanned the open cubicles where legal assistants, witness advocates and interns worked. With only half walls dividing the section, hiding there, virtually out in the open, wasn't a possibility.

No time to hide. She had to call 9-1-1. Reaching over the half wall, she grabbed the receiver. Stabbed the number nine.

The next thing she knew he was on her.

Strong hands flung her against the back wall and clamped around her throat. Melanie struggled and bucked to break free. Tried to throw another knee in that tender spot that would hurt him most.

But he turned at an angle, wedging one of his legs between her thighs. The stench of tobacco registered in her brain. She punched his forearms, hitting solid muscle, not making his grip budge in the least. Ice formed in her chest. She fought to get him off her. Every cell in her body strained with effort.

He had her, his hands locked in a viselike grip around her neck. She tried to scream. No air. Her lungs burned.

Fingers dug into her skin, pressing down on her windpipe, filling her with bone-deep fear. It felt as though her heart was being squeezed in a fist. He slammed her head into the wall. The stunning blow shook her hands loose from his arms. He did it again.

Pain exploded in the back of her skull, blurring her vision. Tears stung her eyes. Much more of that and he'd knock her unconscious.

Melanie prayed he wasn't wearing steel-toed boots and thrust her remaining heel down onto his foot. He flinched.

His feet were vulnerable.

She stabbed the pointed heel down again with far more force. His hands loosened and he reared back a step. She kicked his shin, aiming the heel at bone and then launched her foot into his groin.

Turning, she fled. But she didn't make it far.

He pounced, tackling her to the floor. They wrestled, each struggling to gain the advantage. She threw an elbow into his throat.

Melanie scrambled up from the floor. And so did her attacker.

He grabbed her and threw her into the wall. His gloved hands seized her throat again. He maneuvered his lower half, pressing his knees between hers, protecting himself. His grip on her tightened, shutting off her airway.

A scream was strangled and died in her throat. She wanted to ram the heel of her palm up into his nose to break it the way she'd been taught in self-defense class, but the helmet protected his face.

His face.

If she could see him, identify him, scratch him, claw his eyes, get his DNA under her nails in the event of a worst-case scenario in which she didn't make it out of this alive, that would be something.

A fierce sense of determination rushed through her veins. No matter what, she was going to take this guy down. Regardless of the personal cost.

Melanie resisted the instinct to pry his hands from her throat and reached for the visor. She shoved it, but the face shield didn't move. Like it had been glued shut.

One of his hands released the pressure against her windpipe. She sucked in a ragged breath.

A fist blasted into her jaw, knocking the air from her lungs. She reeled from the blow, but if he didn't like her messing with his face shield, then she had to get it up.

She scraped and clawed at the visor, prying her nails into the seam. Breaking several gel tips down to the nail bed, she forced a sliver of the dark-tinted shield up. He slammed another fist into her.

Agony left her dazed, struggling to stay on her feet.

Letting her go, the man spun away, lowering his head and adjusting the visor while she pressed herself against the wall, hauled in desperate breaths through the gut-wrenching pain and felt around for something, anything, to help her get out of this nightmare.

Her fingers grazed cold metal.

A fire extinguisher.

She unhooked it from the wall and swung the extinguisher like a baseball bat, smashing it into his head. He spun, thrown off balance. Not giving him a chance to recover, she rammed the butt of the extinguisher into his gut. She hit him again and again, this time over the back of the head, wanting to crack the helmet open.

He dropped to his knees and pitched forward, putting a hand to the floor to steady himself. She pulled the pin on the fire extinguisher, breaking the tamper seal, pointed the nozzle at him and squeezed the handle, spraying him with the extinguishing agent.

The man coughed and grunted.

Melanie spun on her heel and ran to the district attorney's office at the far end of the hall. She slammed the door shut behind her. Dropped the extinguisher. Grabbed a chair. Jammed the sturdy back under the lever door handle.

The next best thing to a lock.

But was it enough?

She hurried to the desk. Shoved it across the room with items on the top clattering to the floor. Pushed it against the door as a barricade.

Dread clogged her throat. She wiped moisture from her nose with the back of her trembling hand. Her face throbbed where he'd hit her and her heart hammered against her ribs. She picked up the extinguisher and clutched it to her chest. Something inside her needed to keep the makeshift weapon close.

She searched the floor and saw the landline phone.

On quivering legs, she stumbled to it, dropped to the floor in a shaking, terrified puddle and picked up the receiver.

Blood was on her hands, on the phone. Her blood.

Pressing her back to the desk, digging the heels of her feet into the carpet, pushing against it with all her weight to prevent him from getting inside the room, she dialed for help.

"This is 9-1-1, what's your emergency?"

Chapter Two

Detective Waylon Wright cut his gaze from the deputy assigned to do forensics work near Melanie's car and eyed the bouquet he'd sent her that had been trampled to pieces. He stalked toward the building, ducked under the crime scene tape and headed down the short walkway.

At the shattered door, he stepped on broken glass, the shards crunching under his boots.

Entering the offices of the district attorney, he wiped any trace of the feelings roiling through him from his face and walked down the hall. He was about to make a right toward Melanie's office but noticed the gaggle of deputies at the other end of the floor.

On his way there, a spot in the hall caught his attention and he stopped. There were signs of a struggle and remnants of fire-extinguishing agent. He looked around before he made his way to the DA's office. Deputies Cody and Lee blocked the threshold with their backs to the hall. Waylon put a hand on Lee's shoulder. The guy glanced at him and stepped aside, letting him through.

The office was in shambles. Melanie sat in a chair. An ice pack pressed to her cheek. An EMT examining her. Mel's nose was bloody. The usual slick twist she wore was loose and messy, with wild black strands hanging around her face.

She spoke in a firm, steady voice, giving a statement to chief deputy Holden Powell, who was crouched in front of her.

Waylon's mood darkened as he listened. Rage filled him, his fingers curling into fists. But relief seeped through, too. She was alive.

"Once I managed to get away from him, I called 9-1-1." Mel's gaze flashed up to his. A flicker of unguarded emotion crossed her face, horror suddenly alive in the depths of her brown eyes. Tears glistened and one rolled down her cheek.

Looking away from him, she lowered her head and whisked the moisture from her eyes.

Holden glanced over at him and stood. "Waylon. What's the LPD doing here?"

"I was getting ready to head home, heard about the attack on the radio, and the APB for the suspect." Not that the all-points bulletin had provided much to go on. Male. Dressed in all black. Wearing a dark-tinted motorcycle helmet. Approximately six feet tall. Medium build. "Figured I'd swing by. Take a look around. Unofficially, of course. Make sure the town's favorite ADA is okay."

"Hope you're not planning to try and steal this case." Holden put his hands on his hips.

Melanie straightened. "I don't want him working on this one. He shouldn't even be here."

Gritting his teeth, Waylon gave a slow nod of acknowledgment. "As I was going to say, I had no intention of doing any such thing." Not that he could steal it even if he wanted to. This attack had happened on the sheriff's turf. Literally. Made the case personal for them. It was personal for him as well, but Mel didn't want anyone to know that, which he'd respect.

"Good," Holden said. "Then you're welcome to stay."

Thanks for your permission. He was staying whether Holden liked it or not.

"But we've got this well in hand," Holden added.

Waylon stepped deeper into the room. "No doubt in my mind you do. I'm here informally."

The chief deputy's gaze swung back to Melanie. "Did the assailant say anything to you? Threaten you? Indicate what he wanted?"

She shook her head. "No, he didn't."

"Not in the garage where he first attacked you," Holden said, "or here in the offices? Anything?"

"As a matter of fact, not a single word from him."

Holden made a note in his pad. "And when you managed to get his visor up, you didn't get a look at him at all? Could you see his skin color? Was he white, Black, Hispanic? What about his eye color?"

Taking a breath, Melanie shook her head again. "I don't know. Sorry. I tried to identify him, to get a sample of his DNA, but he had the visor glued shut. It took everything to get it up half an inch." Her gaze fell to the trembling hand in her lap.

Her fingernails were broken and bloody, her knuckles bruised. A bad scrape on her knee looked tender and when the EMT cleaned the wound, Melanie flinched.

Waylon could only imagine how terrified she must've been, how hard she had fought to survive.

"After I got the visor to budge a little, it only enraged him. That's when he hit me." She gestured to her face, moved the ice pack from her left cheek and pressed it to the back of her head, giving him a good look at her.

A nasty bruise had already formed on her brown cheek. The ice had done little to prevent swelling. Blood oozed from a cut on her lower lip and a black eye was blooming. He reckoned she was going to have one heck of a shiner in an hour or two.

Fury pierced Waylon deeply, taking root in a dark place inside him he seldom acknowledged. Melanie had taken brutal blows, but she hadn't gone down without a fight—fueled by fear and adrenaline, he supposed.

Weariness and pain glimmered in her eyes, right along with strength and determination. Tonight, he could've lost her forever. Regardless of whether they were together in some capacity, Melanie was a bright light meant to shine and do so much good. The world would be a darker place without her.

He swore under his breath and swallowed around the lump of raw emotion lodged in his throat. The need to tear apart whoever had dared to hurt her surged through him, but he tamped it down.

"Any identifying marks?" Holden asked.

"He was completely covered. Helmet. Long sleeves. Gloves."

"Did you smell anything on him?" Waylon treaded closer. "Aftershave? Alcohol? Weed?"

Shooting him a fierce glance, Holden heaved a breath.

"Uh, yeah, I did." She nodded. "Cigarette smoke. Menthol."

"How can you be sure it was menthol?" the chief deputy asked.

Her father was a smoker. A bad habit she tried to get him to break.

"A guy I knew in Denver only smoked menthols. We spent a lot of time together. Sometimes the smell would get into my clothes."

They'd spent a lot of time together in close proximity if the smell had permeated her clothing. News to him.

A lot about Melanie he longed to know, but only a brief window had opened after they'd made love when she'd been willing to share. If she had to work the next day, once the sun rose, she threw on clothes, had coffee, and either kicked him out of her house or skedaddled from his place.

They'd been doing that tango for almost three years. One night a week had turned into three, sometimes four. Strictly sex had shifted to takeout beforehand, cuddling afterward, along with pillow talk—a sure sign that things had been more than physical, coffee together in the mornings and a few hurried kisses. Some holiday weekends they'd spent several days in a row together.

Fed up with the bare minimum, he'd finally pushed for a real relationship. He'd wanted to go out to dinner, hold her hand in public, take a vacation, wake up every day with her. Discuss their future.

The sex was off the charts. No woman did it for him the way she did. But he'd wanted more.

She hadn't, and had ended it. Lectured him about professional boundaries. Spouted bad-timing mumbo jumbo in a rather cold and impersonal manner, like she was delivering a closing argument in a courtroom, without bothering to give him a chance at a rebuttal.

Deep down, he suspected she simply didn't want distractions from her job and was willing to burn any bridge to make district attorney.

Maybe she'd burned one too many bridges in Denver.

"Did the relationship end badly?" Waylon asked, eliciting another sigh from the chief deputy.

"It did." Melanie hung her head. "It's one of the reasons I moved here from Denver." The EMT bandaged her leg and she winced. "But he wouldn't do this."

"Are you sure?" Holden asked and she nodded.

Waylon stepped within easy reach of her. "What's his name?"

Melanie stiffened, avoiding any eye contact.

"Give *me* his name," Holden said, throwing him a scathing glare. "*I'll* have a chat with him, feel him out. That way we can be sure and eliminate him as a possible suspect."

"That won't be necessary. You don't need his name." Her tone changed, the unyielding ADA coming through. "He isn't violent and has no reason to physically hurt me," she said to Holden. "He was glad when I left Denver and we've had no contact since. Except for an email he sent me, a couple of years ago. An invitation to an event, which I declined to attend. This wasn't him."

Physically struck Waylon. This guy might want to hurt her emotionally. Or maybe she'd been the one hurt in the fallout of the relationship.

"Okay." Holden pressed his lips in a firm line. "Has anyone made any threats against you lately? Have you received any hate mail?"

Convicted felons sometimes said reckless things after sentencing, but he wasn't aware of anything recent, and he made it his business to keep track.

"Nothing. It's been quiet." Her delicate shoulders hunched. "Until tonight."

Another deputy pushed past the other two, entering the room, holding a tablet. "The perp waited two hours for her." Deputy Platt turned the screen toward them and tapped it, playing back the surveillance footage from one of the security cameras.

Melanie got up from the chair and came over, standing between them. Her gaze fell to the tablet as her hand held the ice pack lower.

He looked at the side of her jaw. Swollen and quickly turning purple. His gut clenched as he imagined a meaty fist connecting with her face.

She stepped closer to him, on purpose or unconsciously, shifting his focus.

Waylon took in the scent of her. Jasmine and musk and something else warm particular to her. Whenever they'd been together at his place, he hadn't washed his sheets immediately, just to hold on to the smell of her for as long as he could.

Their fingers brushed, the slight touch sending a spark shooting through him.

She moved her hand away, putting the cold compress back up to her face.

He guessed the contact had been purely accidental. But the proximity to Mel pulled at his emotions, a dangerous thing in a room full of people. He turned his attention back to the surveillance footage. Away from Melanie and the need he felt for her.

They watched the perp creep up the garage ramp, hugging the wall, to the third level. Helmet on. Gloves. Sneakers. He glanced at the cameras, like he already knew their locations, and made a beeline for her SUV. Dropping down on the side, out of view of the camera, he stayed there a moment and then crept over to one of the concrete pillars.

"Wonder why he decided to move so far away from her SUV and stopped there instead of hiding closer?" Holden said as if thinking aloud.

"Because of the position of the other two vehicles beside the ADA's still in the lot." Waylon pointed to them. "One of the drivers might have spotted him as they left."

The perp ducked down behind the pillar, taking a seat on the ground. From that angle, with the low wall of the parking ramp that curved around as a shield, he was completely blocked from the view of the camera. The helmet lifted—he must've removed it, but they couldn't even see the top of his head to refine the description of who they were looking for.

Seconds later, a thin trail of smoke wafted up in the air from his position.

"He planned this out carefully," Waylon said. "Knew exactly where to hide and brought cigarettes to smoke while he waited. You need to have your deputies check the spot for cigarette butts and review all the footage for the last two or three weeks. Look for anyone scoping out the place, monitoring Mel—Merritt's—comings and goings."

"I know how to do my job," Holden said, the words emerging like a sigh. He looked at the deputies lingering in front of the door. "Go take care of it, will you?" He turned the tablet toward them, showing them where to look.

Cody hurried off down the hall.

Waylon would've apologized to Holden, but he wasn't sorry. He didn't care if he stepped on someone else's toes. This wasn't simply any case.

"I have no doubts about your competency or that of your department," Waylon said. "I just want to get this SOB. A dedicated detective should be helping you on this one." They were experts, after all, and unlike the sheriff's department, they wouldn't have their focus spread thin by everything else going on in the entire county. This sort of thing would put a squeeze on their resources. The sheriff's department didn't even have the budget to keep crime scene investigators on staff. A handful of deputies had taken some training courses, making them capable of handling routine things such as thefts and burglaries. But their most experienced person, who had worked homicides, had been killed recently. "Maybe Hannah Delaney, Kent Kramer or Brian Bradshaw." All were excellent and, more importantly, he trusted them.

"I'll give it consideration," Holden said. "Run the idea by the sheriff in the morning." He fast-forwarded the footage.

The perp finished smoking and put the helmet back on.

The district attorney, Gordon Weisman, had left a half hour later. At nine, one of the paralegals he recognized, Rosenfeld, walked out while talking on the phone. The young woman popped her trunk and rummaged around in the back for several minutes, engrossed in her conversation. No clue the guy was there, lurking only a few feet away. The woman hung up and climbed into her car.

Mel left the offices. She marched over to the trash can, hesitated a moment, and threw away the flowers.

Waylon snuck a furtive look her way that she ignored without even a glance in his direction.

"Who were the flowers from?" Holden asked, pausing the playback, and Deputy Platt lowered the tablet.

"No one important," she said, her tone nonchalant. She tucked loose strands behind her ear, like a nervous habit.

He'd never seen the formidable Melanie Merritt nervous. Except for when he'd admitted his feelings for her.

"The guy is just an ex," she added, still fiddling with her hair. "Not even that. Simply someone I saw from time to time to scratch an itch, if you know what I mean, before I decided to end the dalliance."

No one important. Scratch an itch. Dalliance.

The words stung, wounding his heart more than his ego.

"The name of this spurned lover?" Holden held his pen, waiting for an answer.

"I never said spurned."

"Maybe he didn't like you ending things," Holden said. "Maybe the message didn't sink in. Could be a situation where if he couldn't have you then no one could."

Waylon restrained a groan and swore to himself. He was about to make the list of suspects.

"He's a good guy," she said. "Not the perp you're after. Trust me."

The chief deputy folded his arms across his chest. "For a victim, you sure are reluctant to give us the names of these two men who could be responsible," he said and her chin jerked up at that. "Nothing I can do about identifying Mr. Denver without your assistance. But Mr. Flowers is a different story. If there's a card from the shop out on the ground, it might have his prints."

Another curse prickled Waylon's tongue. It definitely had his prints.

"In the event it doesn't," Holden continued, "he probably used a credit card to pay for the flowers, or someone will remember him buying such an extravagant bouquet. We'll track him down with or without your cooperation, though I'd prefer the former."

Melanie pivoted, facing the chief deputy. "You're barking up the wrong tree. Any time you invest in looking into him is a waste. You should focus on anyone who seemed like they were surveilling the garage or monitoring my comings and goings, like Detective Wright suggested. Whoever attacked me obviously knew I leave late every night."

"Excuse me, ma'am," Cody said, coming back into the room, his hand outstretched. Her designer purse and leather laptop straps dangled from his fingers and her shoe was in his other hand. "Here you go. You can have these back now, and your wallet is in there."

"So, this wasn't a mugging." Waylon looked between Holden and Melanie. "I'm guessing that purse is worth a few hundred dollars." Not that he needed to guess. She'd spent more on some of her handbags than most folks in the area did on the monthly mortgage for their house. "And he didn't bother with your wallet. He targeted you and attacked you for some other reason."

Deputy Cody turned to Holden. “There were no cigarette butts in the spot where he hid. Only ash on the ground.”

“If he was smart enough to pick it up and take it with him,” Waylon said, “then surely he didn’t send her flowers that could be traced back to him.”

Holden frowned and it was obvious by the way his mouth twitched that the chief deputy was biting his tongue.

Melanie slipped on her second shoe. “Can I go now?” She stashed the ice pack in her purse. “If there are any other questions, I think it can wait until tomorrow. Don’t you agree?”

Holden glanced past her at the EMT. “Is she medically cleared?”

“Are you sure you don’t want to go get checked out at the hospital?” the tech asked.

She turned her attention to the EMT. “I’m good. Really. I need to get home.”

“It’s entirely possible you could have a concussion,” the paramedic said.

“No blurred vision. No nausea. Or confusion. Or dizziness. If something changes, I’ll go to the hospital. Right now, a trip to the emergency room is the last thing I want. I’m leaving.”

The EMT shrugged and shut the lid to the first-aid kit. “I can’t force you to take reasonable precautions, ma’am. You’re cleared to leave if you want.”

“I’ll give you a ride home,” Waylon said to her.

Melanie looked surprised. Then guarded. “Thanks, but I can drive myself.”

“Afraid not, ma’am,” Deputy Platt said.

Mel’s brow furrowed. “Why is that?”

“When the perp dropped out of view on the side of your car, he flattened two tires,” Waylon said. They had been slashed down to the rims. “He made sure you weren’t going anywhere.”

"We can give you a ride to your house," Holden said before Waylon had a chance to.

"No, no, that won't be necessary." She hitched her purse and laptop bag on her shoulder. "You all have better things to do and it's late. I'll call for a rideshare. I'm fine."

Mel could be stubborn, but this wasn't the time for her obstinate independence.

"It is *late*, and you are *not* fine. You were just assaulted." Waylon marveled at her fierce determination to want to go home alone, in the dark, after what she had gone through. "I'm off duty." Which was relative. For him, he was always working. "I'll make sure you get home safely. Frees up the deputies so they can get back to work finding the guy who did this to you." He gave her an unflinching look to let her know this was nonnegotiable and stressed, "Let's go." He extended his arm and waited for her to walk out first.

Her gaze narrowed, always a lawyer up for a fight, and he braced for her to debate the matter. Whether she liked it or not, she would be driven home. By him.

With an annoyed shake of her head, she left the office without protest.

In the hall, he came up beside her but didn't say anything until they had cleared the busted door. "Mel—"

She raised her palm, cutting him off. "Not here, Detective, and for the record, I'm capable of deciding how I get home."

Not wanting to argue, he walked her to his compact truck and unlocked the door. His GMC Sonoma was an older model that sat lower to the ground than newer trucks and lacked a running board. Putting his hands on her waist, he gave her a slight boost up inside since she was wearing a tailored slim-fitting skirt that restricted her movements.

Off to the side, he couldn't help noticing the card from the flower shop bagged as evidence.

Maybe it was best to have a frank conversation with Holden and tell him he'd been the former nobody in Melanie's bed. Sooner or later, Holden was going to find out anyway. But Waylon needed her permission first.

He hustled over to his side and took off. Once they cleared the garage, he glanced over at her. "Melanie."

"I know where this conversation is headed, and I don't want to have it."

If she thought he was going to bring up their former relationship, she was wrong. This wasn't the time and/or place for that kind of discussion. His only concern was her well-being and the case. "You've got no idea what I'm going to say."

"Your protective cowboy instincts are in overdrive right now because you have feelings for me."

"Apparently, they're one-sided."

"I didn't say that." She rubbed her temple. "I should've asked the medic for a painkiller for my head."

Waylon leaned over, popping the glove box, and handed her some Tylenol. His attention snagged on how her skirt rode up, exposing a bit of her sexy, toned thighs. Just enough silky-smooth, chestnut-colored skin to scatter his thoughts for a moment.

Clearing his head, he opened the center console and gave her a bottle of water. She dumped two gel capsules into her palm and washed them down with a little water.

"This conversation is going to get heavy. I don't want to say anything that'll hurt you," she said, but too late for that. "Let's not do this right now. Okay?"

She phrased it like a question, as if up for discussion, but that wasn't the case. He was fluent in Mel-speak. She cracked her window several inches, letting in fresh air, and switched on the radio.

The sound of Garth Brooks crooning something about

thunder rolling filled the truck cab and the empty space of silence between them.

His intent wasn't to cause more stress. They were going to discuss the way she'd blown up their relationship, but at a different time. Tonight, he only had one more thing that he had to mention. "In the morning, I need to tell Holden about us."

She opened her mouth to object.

"Stop." His voice was soft yet firm. "Listen to me. We both know it won't take him long to figure it out when he traces the flowers. But by then, he won't be the only one to know. The whole department will. I can get him to keep it quiet if I get out in front of it." He was on somewhat good terms with the Powell family these days. After he'd set aside old resentments with Holden's brother Monty and had helped them all out on a mission across the state line, Waylon had earned the right to call in a favor. "I won't unless you agree, but it's the smart thing to do."

Melanie was brilliant. She had an uncanny ability to read people, making her great at picking juries, spoke six different languages, attended a fancy prep school as a teen, went to Harvard and Yale, and was highly respected for her good judgment by most people he knew in law enforcement.

Once she eliminated emotion, she would see that this was the best way to handle it.

Flattening her mouth in a thin line, she simply nodded. "Are you sure he won't say anything?"

"Positive." Waylon frowned at the cut on her lip. When he got his hands on the guy who'd done that to her, he was going to make him regret it before he brought him to justice. There was no way he wasn't working on this case unofficially.

Officially, he needed to have a detective of his choice assigned to her case. The chief of the LPD, Wilhelmina Nelson, trusted his judgment and if anyone could persuade Sheriff Daniel Clark, it was her, considering they were married.

In what felt like no time, they turned down her street. Melanie only lived fifteen minutes away in a house on a cul-de-sac, in a quiet, middle-class neighborhood that had good-sized yards with decent space between the homes.

Waylon parked in the driveway. He was out of his truck and by her passenger's-side door when she stepped onto the asphalt with her bags.

"I'll check inside before you go in," he said.

"If you insist."

"I do." He was grateful she didn't argue with him. They headed for her covered front steps. "I can stay the night if you want," he offered, and she tensed. "On the sofa or in the guestroom, Mel." Goodness, he didn't want her to think he was trying to make a move on her at a time like this. She'd just gone through something traumatic and needed to rest without worry. "It's not good for you to be alone tonight. I'd prefer to be inside instead of sleeping in my truck, parked in your driveway." But he wasn't leaving her alone.

"You should go home." She tucked more strands behind her ear. "I don't need a babysitter, especially not..." Her voice trailed off as she stopped near the steps.

He tore his gaze from her face and looked to see what she was staring at.

On her front stoop, under the portico, there was a circle of sand. Two feet in diameter. In the center was an impression, resembling an angel. Like someone had made it in the sand using a large doll.

"I-I-It can't be," she whispered, her face growing ashen. "It can't be."

"Mel, what are you talking about? Can't be what?"

Shaking her head slowly, she looked terrified. “It’s not possible. I made sure he was convicted and put behind bars.”

“Who?” Waylon looked back at the front stoop. “What is this?”

“He swore he’d make me pay. Me and everyone else responsible for his conviction.” She started trembling. “But he’s serving a life sentence in a Colorado prison. It can’t be him. He couldn’t be the one who attacked me.”

Waylon took hold of her shoulders, turning her toward him. “Who are you talking about?” he asked gently.

She swallowed so hard it was audible. “That’s his calling card.” She pointed back at the stoop while staring at him, her eyes filling with tears. “Drake Colter. The Sand Angel Killer.”

Chapter Three

Never-ending.

The night was never-ending, with the horror and the necessary presence of the sheriff's deputies.

She could only presume her masked attacker had left the sand angel on her doorstep as a message for the police. To give them an indication of what would have happened to her if he had been successful.

A shudder slipped through Melanie.

Not a close-call mugging or an assault. The man wearing the helmet had intended to kill her.

He must've planned to incapacitate her, transport her to a different location, a sand dune, where he would've killed her and left her body.

That's what happened to the Sand Angel Killer's victims. The weight of that hit her full-force and she swayed on her feet.

Waylon put a hand to her back, steadying her.

She appreciated him risking the small gesture of comfort, considering Holden was going to find out about them anyway.

"Maybe you should take a break," Waylon said.

Holden had been firing off question after question, and she didn't have any concrete answers.

"No, I want to finish." Better to press through and get it over with, so this night could finally end.

Melanie glanced back over at the sand angel impression by her front door. The knot in the center of her chest tightened.

A deputy finished taking pictures. She was anxious to wrap up and get out of there. No way she'd be able to sleep inside her own house tonight.

"It must be a copycat," she said. Drake Colter, the SAK, was locked up in a supermax prison in Florence, Colorado. Not just any jail, but the most secure prison in the world, often called the Alcatraz of the Rockies. Experts in prison design deemed it to be one hundred percent unescapable. "Someone who admired the Sand Angel Killer and decided to target me for some reason."

"That's what I don't understand," Holden said. "You prosecuted this murderer, Colter, and he was locked up three and a half years ago. Why would someone go after you now?"

The same question ricocheted in her mind.

She gave the chief deputy a weary shrug. Her temples throbbed. The back of her head ached. Her face was sore. She was exhausted, more so mentally and emotionally than physically. "I don't know."

"Do you need another cold compress for your head?" Waylon asked, his warm sturdy hand still on her, making her pulse pound.

"I'll be okay."

When they'd first started spending time together, somehow, with no effort at all, they'd slipped into the same frequency, a special channel for only the two of them, where they could read each other so easily.

Too easily.

Months apart should've destroyed the connection. Diminished it at the very least. Now they were in proximity to each other again, dialed back in and attuned. The prospect of him sensing what she felt or thought unnerved her.

She didn't want him to realize that despite her façade of not needing anyone, she did need him tonight, after the attack on her at the office and this violation at her home.

But that wasn't a door she dared reopen. Too complicated. For them both.

Melanie fought off another wave of dizziness, a bitter bite on her tongue.

"Do you need to sit for a minute?" Waylon's deep voice, a protective growl mixed with concern, pushed at the barrier she'd set between them.

"This has all been a lot." She struggled to maintain her composure, to keep tears from her eyes. Breaking down under emotion wasn't like her at all, but her bruises were fresh, painful, and far more than skin deep. "I need to get cleaned up, catch my breath. Process everything with some quiet." Another ice pack wouldn't hurt, either, but she wanted to leave.

"Okay." Holden nodded, closing his notepad. "I think you've answered my questions for tonight. Too bad we don't have more to go on."

The security camera mounted near her front door had captured the perp. Same guy who had attacked her at her office, wearing a black helmet, making it impossible to identify him. The front side of his vehicle had been in the frame.

Not a motorcycle. A white nondescript van.

None of her neighbors had noticed anything unusual and the use of home security systems in the area was rare. If the neighbor to her right had had one, they would most likely have the license plate number or the make and model.

The bad thing about Laramie and Bison Ridge was the lack of a robust traffic camera system. The ones they had were few and far between, and only at major intersections.

Someone as careful as her assailant would be clever enough to avoid them.

Holden put his notepad away, slipped his pen in his shirt pocket and glanced at the deputies collecting evidence in front of her house. "We'll need to go inside as well. Just to be sure."

She wrapped her arms around herself. Nothing on her security footage indicated that the perp had gone inside, but it was best for them to be sure and check.

"I don't recommend you spend the night here," Holden said.

"I wasn't planning on it."

"And you shouldn't be alone," the chief deputy added.

Waylon dropped his hand from her back, but she was aware that was probably contrary to what he wanted to do. He was an affectionate, emotionally transparent type of guy.

In many ways, they were opposites.

Soon enough, the chief deputy would know that she had been sleeping with Waylon. Still, appearances mattered for the others who were starting to turn their attention toward them.

Her cheeks burned with embarrassment over the impending exposure of their secret.

"She won't be alone," Waylon said. "I'm going to take her somewhere safe."

"And where would that be?" Holden asked.

Melanie and Waylon exchanged furtive glances. He inclined his head in a silent question to her.

Was it okay to tell Holden here rather than waiting until tomorrow?

A different kind of man wouldn't have sought her permission and simply would've done what he thought best regardless of her feelings. Not Waylon. Never.

He was good, decent. Thoughtful.

Melanie gave a little nod of consent and the burn crept down her throat.

Now was as good a time as any for him to talk to Holden about their relationship. Little point in waiting.

"Do you mind if she goes inside her house to grab a few personal items?" Waylon asked, redirecting the conversation to her surprise.

"It would be better to wait until after we've finished up," Holden said and looked at her. "You might want to just come back in the morning."

Melanie nodded. "That's fine."

"I need to speak to you for a minute," Waylon said to Holden. "Privately. Let me get the ADA inside my truck first."

"Sure." Holden traipsed behind them, giving them space.

Relief eased a bit of tension from her shoulders. Waylon intended to do it one-on-one, sparing her from the conversation and the in-your-face humiliation of having her personal life revealed.

She slid a glance at Waylon, catching his eye. "Thank you," she whispered.

"I'll take care of it. Cop-to-cop, cowboy-to-cowboy, is better anyway." His voice was low and reassuring. "You've been through enough tonight."

Waylon helped her climb up into his old truck, shut the door and then he pulled the chief deputy aside.

The two men stopped out of earshot of the other deputies and away from her direct line of sight.

Looking in the side mirror, she could see them and, thanks to the open window in the truck and their proximity, she could also hear them.

"Holden, I need to ask a favor of you."

"Well, that's a first. Waylon Wright asking a favor from a Powell. Sure, what is it?"

Flicking a quick glance at the others working the crime scene, Waylon crossed his arms over his chest and looked back at the chief deputy. "You don't need to dig into the guy who sent ADA Merritt the flowers."

"Why is that?" Holden asked quickly before Waylon finished.

"Because it was me."

Holden put his hands on his hips. "Come again?"

Melanie fidgeted with her hands, wishing Waylon had never sent those extravagant flowers. Even though they'd been beautiful and the gesture undeniably sweet.

"We've been seeing each other," Waylon said. "Discreetly. Or rather, we were until she called it off. She would prefer it if no one else knew. We would both appreciate it if you could keep it quiet. Not tell anyone else."

Holden scratched his chin, mulling it over. "I guess I can do that. Keep the flowers out of the report. Not as if you were the one who attacked her. But I will need to let the sheriff know. Only him, though, and he won't say anything."

Holden's boss was also his brother-in-law. Small town.

The exception seemed more than reasonable to Melanie, and she released the breath that she had been holding.

"Thank you," Waylon said.

She planned to share her appreciation as well later.

"It's not a big ask on your part, considering you put your life on the line to help my family last year. We needed assistance, off-the-book, and you were there. That's not something that'll soon be forgotten," Holden said.

Melanie had also helped with the awful situation, completely by accident. She'd gone from thinking she might have to bring Monty Powell up on charges of murder, to helping Holden's eldest brother and Waylon—the lead detective—crack the case and identify the person responsible for Monty's troubles.

The circumstances had spiraled, turning deadly, and Waylon had jumped right into the fray, joining their mission. No hesitation. No questions asked. The Powells had needed help and Waylon had been there for them.

She'd been so thankful he had come back unharmed.

Then, only a couple of weeks later, on Christmas, everything between them changed and she'd had to end it.

"So," Holden said, "when you say you're taking her somewhere safe, I assume you mean to your place and that you'll be the one keeping her company."

Waylon nodded. "I do."

Melanie stiffened. She wanted protection, and if she were being honest with herself, also comfort. No one was better suited than Waylon, but she wasn't foolish enough to assume it would be a good idea to accept either from him.

People always disappointed her, failed her in some way eventually. Her biological father acted like she didn't exist. Even her mom and stepdad, whom she considered her real dad, let her down time and time again. The only person she could ever rely on was herself.

"No need to mention that she'll be staying at my place to anyone else," Waylon said. "Besides the sheriff."

The bed-and-breakfast in town would be more than adequate. That's where she was going to spend the night. Not under the same roof as Waylon Wright.

"I appreciate you telling me. Saves time and resources investigating Mr. Flowers. Well, you. It also explains why you showed up tonight. Truth be told, I found your presence at my crime scene particularly irksome, but I get it now. Whether you two are broken up or not. If it had been Grace," Holden said, bringing up his wife, "who'd been attacked and it was your crime scene, I would've been there. Probably getting in the way, trying to take over and give orders, too. No hard feelings." Holden shook Waylon's hand. "My gut tells me this guy who attacked her, whoever he is, Sand Angel Killer serving a life sentence, or more likely some nut-job copycat that left the sand on her front stoop, might try again."

After seeing the sand angel at her home, Melanie's instinct was telling her the same thing.

"I figured that, too," Waylon said.

"The ADA might need a bodyguard until we catch this guy."

"She's got one. Nothing is more important than her safety. Let us know if you find anything inside her house."

"Will do." Holden rejoined the other deputies.

The sheriff's department was going to have an even longer night ahead of them.

Waylon climbed into his truck and started it up. The engine always rattled the first few seconds, like it might give up and die, then purred as though it would run forever.

"You can take me to the bed-and-breakfast in town." She had stayed there for three months when she'd relocated to Laramie from Denver and waited to close on her house. The owners, Mr. and Mrs. Quenby, were a lovely couple and provided free breakfast. "The place is clean and comfortable. Close to my job. It's fine for a week or two."

"No, it's not."

"Yes, it is. The B and B is homey. I'd prefer to stay there. I insist." Melanie gave him one of the long lingering stares she'd realized made most men stutter and back down.

Waylon merely stared back at her. "I'm taking you to my house." He threw the truck in Reverse and backed out of her driveway.

"That's not a good idea or what I want."

Hitting the road, he took off. "Are we really going to do this?"

"Do what?"

He sighed, taking the road that led to Wayward Bluffs, where he lived, rather than heading back into town.

"You're going the wrong way," she said.

"Am I?" His voice was tight. "Because I believe this is the correct way to my house."

She folded her arms. "If you don't take me to the Quenbys' B and B, I'll simply call a rideshare to take me." Going to his house wouldn't put her in the detached headspace she needed to be in to rally. His cozy cabin was filled with memories—passionate, steamy, sweet memories—that would only bring unwelcome emotions to the surface. She was on the verge of cracking when she needed to pull herself together. Being in his home would be hard, but then he'd touch her and she'd fall to pieces. Having a relapse with him, falling back into bed, making love to him, would feel incredible in the moment. Like a junkie getting what they craved. But the sun would rise, along with her shame and regret and anger at herself for being weak. "You have two choices." She spoke with the right amount of conviction, but underneath her confidence was a twinge of anxiety. "Turn around or I pull up the app and request a ride."

"The B and B isn't safe. This guy has been watching you. We have no idea for how long. When you go back to work, he can follow you to the B and B. Book a room. Pretend to be a guest to see which one you're staying in. From there, it would be simple to pop the lock, which isn't a dead bolt, while you're sleeping and finish what he started. Heck, he doesn't even have to go to the trouble of getting a room. All he has to do is watch you go inside and wait to see which room light turns on shortly thereafter."

Icy fear scuttled up her spine and froze her brain.

"This is a small town," Waylon added, "usually so safe and quiet that Mr. and Mrs. Quenby didn't put on a proper lock that's only accessible to guests on the exterior upper door. The perp could get inside in less than sixty seconds guaranteed. If necessary, he might kill the Quenbys, too, or any other guest there to make sure no one hears you scream. Staying at the B and B alone leaves you vulnerable. It's one of the worst places for you to be."

Fighting off a shiver, she clenched her hands. The grim reality of the situation had her rethinking her stance. "I hadn't thought of that."

"You're not a cop or ultra paranoid, why would you?"

Waylon was only looking out for her. As always. "I just don't want you to get the wrong idea about us. We're simply friends now. That's all we can be." If she cared anything about her job, about advancement and realizing her professional dream, he needed to stay off limits.

"Mel, this isn't a romantic overture. I'm only taking you to my house for your safety."

"This is a big deal, Waylon. I'm the ADA. You're a detective. I can't be shacked up with you."

"We're not shacking up. It's protective custody." His grip tightened on the steering wheel. "You're used to controlling everything and all situations. But this is something you can't control. As a prosecutor, you rely on the expertise of others on a regular basis. Use mine now. Don't think of me as your ex. Only as a professional who also happens to be your friend. Let me keep you safe and stop fighting me. Can you do that until we figure out what's going on and put a stop to it?"

She was fighting their chemistry, his raw sexual magnetism, an attraction to him still as strong as ever, and her desire for something with him that she couldn't have, more than she was fighting him.

Not that he would appreciate the distinction.

Her whole career, she had never been anything *but* careful. Until she'd gotten involved with Waylon Wright.

Melanie drew in a ragged breath. "I can try."

Chapter Four

Once they made it to Wayward Bluffs, the knot at the base of Waylon's spine still hadn't loosened. Melanie's situation was even more dire than he'd first feared.

Keeping her safe was all that mattered.

By the time he got Melanie settled inside his house, it was after midnight. Waylon had to restrain the impulse to physically comfort her. A hard thing to do considering what she'd endured.

The shower started running in the one full bathroom he had in the log-sided home. He lived a good thirty-minute drive from Laramie. The one-story place sat on four acres and had expansive views in every direction with the mountains to the north.

Peaceful and priceless in his opinion.

The funny thing was, he never would've met Mel—not ADA Merritt—if he hadn't lived in Wayward Bluffs. He'd trudged into Crazy Eddie's, the little honky-tonk bar two miles down the road from his house. Hunger had driven him there without showering, shaving or putting on fresh clothes after spending the entire day painting his kitchen and living room. Friday night. Famished. Ordered a beer and burger. Ready to unwind to some good music. Not really interested in much else.

She had sidled up on the bar stool next to him, the scent of her perfume registering along with her presence. "Drinking alone?" she'd asked in a sultry voice.

He'd cast a glance at her and been awestruck.

Leggy, big-breasted blondes were his usual go-to. Uncomplicated gals who didn't expect much from him since he had a demanding job and modest lifestyle, but this woman was the opposite.

Petite. Dark hair. A warm, smooth, brown complexion. Sophisticated.

Nothing basic about her.

And way out of his league.

Taking off his cowboy hat and setting it on the other stool, he smiled at her, his attention roving over her lithe frame from the front of her light blue sweater that hugged a nice set of breasts, trim waist, down her lean legs clad in tight-fitting jeans and to the sexiest strappy black heels.

"Not if you join me," he said, and she turned slightly so that her thigh brushed up against his. And just that light touch sent excitement coiling deep inside him. "New to the area?"

He'd never seen her around before and certainly would've noticed this lovely lady.

"Sort of. Just moved to the great Cowboy State, but I'm about thirty minutes away."

That could put her in Laramie, Bison Ridge, Centennial or Cheyenne, which was in an entirely different county. "What brings you to Wayward Bluffs?"

She flipped her hair over her shoulder, kicking up that enticing, expensive scent. "I don't want to start anything with someone in my backyard, if you know what I mean."

He raised a brow. "But you're interested in starting something with me?"

"I am," she said with suggestion, "provided we can reach an understanding."

Boy oh boy, he loved her confidence. And she was a beauty. Too beautiful for him. Glossy raven hair. A killer body. She looked like a shorter, slightly younger version of Freida Pinto, the actress, and she had the most direct personality he'd ever encountered.

No woman had ever picked him up. Especially not one drop-dead gorgeous. He was a big guy. Six-five. Two hundred forty pounds. His build was intimidating. Something he was cognizant of around women and did his best never to do anything to make them uneasy, but she didn't act the least bit daunted.

"I'm all ears." He took a sip of his beer, tapping his foot to the beat of the music the band played.

"My terms. I say when. I say where." She shifted on her stool, sliding her knee along the inside of his, cozying up even more to him. "Let's start with one night. No last names. See how it goes." Dark eyes teasing and hot, she gave a smile that could wound.

He did his best to keep from grinning like a fool, but he felt as though he'd won the lottery. Strange. He was a serial monogamist and had never had a one-night stand.

But he'd take whatever he could get with this woman.

"What do you think?" she asked. "Are you game, cowboy?"

Yes. Yes. Yes! "I'm your huckleberry."

That smile of hers spread, knocking the breath from his lungs. "There's a motel not far from here."

The bartender, Steve, set his food down on the bar top in front of him.

"I know the one," Waylon said and nodded his thanks to Steve. "But my house is closer and free."

She swiveled and looked at the bartender. "Do you know this fellow?"

"Yeah, sure do," Steve replied, having full knowledge of him and his family since they'd both grown up in the area. "That's Waylon—"

"I don't need to know his last name, as long as you do, in the event a woman fitting my description turns up missing. Would you say a lady, such as myself, would be safe in his company, alone?"

"With him?" Steve pointed a finger at Waylon and grinned. "No one safer you could pick in this bar, lady."

Waylon tipped his head to the bartender for such a strong endorsement.

"Thank you," she said, and Steve went to help another customer. "You're not a convicted felon are you, Waylon?"

Chuckling, he choked on his beer. "No, ma'am."

"Don't 'ma'am' me unless you're looking to kill the vibe. My name is Melanie. Are you involved with anyone, romantically, sexually, emotionally?"

That was *very* specific. "If this is only a one-night-at-a-time sort of thing, does it really matter to you?" He picked up the burger and bit into it.

"It does. I don't want to step on any toes and I'm not fond of cheaters."

She had amazing skin. Radiant. Smooth. All natural besides a bit of lip gloss. Hands down the sexiest thing about her was that bold, distinctive style of hers.

Waylon swallowed his food. "Lucky for you, I'm free and clear," he said and she studied him with keen interest as though she could detect a lie. "No entanglements on any of those counts." But he was interested in having one with her. "I hope it's the same with you."

He didn't mess with women who weren't available. Not even for a night.

She gave a little nod. "The same."

This was his lucky night. "Hey, how do you know I'm not lying?"

For all she knew, he could be a married cheater not wearing his wedding ring, or even a serial killer. There was that phenomenon where friends and relatives claimed the murderer was such a nice guy that they never suspected.

"I can tell," she said and, for some reason, he believed her. "Besides, you've got an honest vibe to you. Something about the way you carry yourself drew me to you."

"So, it wasn't my good looks that caught your attention." He chuckled again. From a distance, some women probably found him attractive, but up close, when they got a good look at the faint scars he still had from an accident as a teenager, he was aware his lack of a pretty-boy face wasn't for everyone.

"It was also your big hands." She winked at him.

Another chuckle rolled from his mouth despite trying to play it cool. He couldn't remember the last time or any time a woman had made him smile much less laugh.

She started to stand. "Let's go."

"Mind if I finish eating first, darling?"

"But I'm ready. Now." Her tone indicated she didn't apologize for what she wanted when she wanted it. "You understand I'm offering a night of fun, no-strings attached?"

"I do." He squirted ketchup all over his French fries. "But it's been a long day and I'm starving." He stuffed a few fries in his mouth.

Looking surprised, she plopped her behind back down on the stool.

This woman was used to getting her way. He had the feeling that after one night, he'd be wrapped around her little finger, but he couldn't make it too easy for her.

First impressions counted, lasted. She struck him as the type that enjoyed a bit of a challenge.

"They have takeout containers." She rested her elbow on the bar. "You could eat on the way."

"I don't like to get the inside of my truck dirty. Pet peeve."

"I suppose that's that a good thing. You know what they say about cleanliness." She sighed and even the sound of her irritation was hot. "If you're going to make me wait, you had better be worth my time."

"I've never had any complaints." He took another bite of the burger.

"Just because you haven't had any complaints doesn't mean the women were pleased with your performance. Maybe they didn't want to hurt your feelings or were afraid to speak the truth."

No danger of that with this one. Direct Mel wouldn't hesitate to hurt him in an effort to be honest. Of that, he was certain.

"Let me clarify. I always get rave reviews." He crammed some more fries in his mouth, chewed and swallowed. "But I can tell you're not easy to please, so I'll do my extra best." He definitely wanted to leave her craving more so he could see her again.

"Would you mind hurrying up?" she asked with a hint of a scowl.

He put a hand on her knee, stroked up her thigh to her hip. "I hope you don't aim to rush me in the bedroom, darling." He took a massive bite of his burger, practically inhaling his dinner. As much as he wanted to pique her interest by not appearing overly eager, he sensed a fine line with this one and was just as enthusiastic about getting her back to his place.

She leaned in close. Her soft floral scent curled around him in odd contrast to her sharp appeal. She picked up a napkin and wiped his mouth. "In the bedroom, I expect you to take your time. Make the most of the entire night. Bonus points if you can get me to scream your name."

Oh yeah, she was going to be fun. "I do like extra credit." To heck with finishing his meal. He pulled money from his wallet, dropped it on the bar, and put his hat on her head. She looked good wearing his Stetson. He couldn't wait to see it on her with those sexy heels and nothing else. "I'm definitely the right cowboy for you."

Looking back on it, after she had discovered he was a detective with the LPD, which meant they'd have to work together from time to time, and she'd still wanted to see him, he should have set down some of his own ground rules.

Instead, he'd made the mistake of doing it her way, on her terms, for almost three years.

The shower stopped and he waited for her in the hall.

She opened the door and stepped out, wearing one of his T-shirts that fell to her knees. A surge of awareness jump-started parts of him that needed to stay idle. Warm eyes centered on him and the world dropped out from under him. Her golden-brown complexion spoke of her Indian heritage and the bruises on her face were prominent. He ached to hold her.

A shuddering breath left her. "I understand why staying at the bed-and-breakfast in town wasn't a wise idea." Pushing her damp hair back behind her ears with trembling hands, she looked so delicate. "But I don't want to make things awkward between us."

Her distress was palpable. Understandable. What she'd experienced left survivors traumatized. PTSD as a result of an assault was common.

Looking at her, he'd forgotten just how fragile a strong woman could be.

"You need to be someplace familiar. Somewhere you feel safe. And definitely not alone." He crossed the space between them in two long strides, drew her up against him, and held her close.

Mel stiffened and a tremble racked her body.

At five-five, with no heels on, the top of her head only came to his chest. She was so small, so slender in his arms. But warm and soft, vibrant and *alive.*

Thank God, she'd gotten away from her assailant.

"No matter what, I'm here for you. As a friend, if that's all you want." Though he wanted to be so much more. "You don't have to be the strong, impervious ADA. Not with me. Whatever you need, M&M, I've got you. Always."

Going pliant, she melted into his embrace, gripped the back of his shirt, and buried her face in his chest. With her head tucked snugly under his chin, everything inside him quieted. She held him tight, her fingers curling into the fabric.

They stayed like that, silent, still, with him holding her for a long time until her breath came in ragged spurts. Her chest heaved against him and she cried. Gut-wrenching, muffled sobs. Tears rolled down her cheeks, leaving damp trails on his shirt in their wake. A barrier had come down. Something so elementary as him offering a warm hug had unraveled her.

The simple gesture of trust resonated through him—the act more powerful than any words. Mel's acceptance of his protection and comfort lit a spark of warmth in his chest. The one hopeful spot in this otherwise dreadful night.

She burrowed closer, her warmth seeping through his clothes.

Every inch of him thrummed with desire. It took all his willpower to keep the contact to only an embrace. He drew a deep breath, inhaling the scent of her damp hair. The tightness in his chest loosened. He'd missed her so much. The indulgence of this hug brought him some small measure of solace.

She raised her head from his chest and stared up at him.

He nearly flinched at the raw pain and vulnerability in her eyes, but he forced himself not to react because it would only cause her to retreat.

Bringing his hand to cup her face, he brushed his thumb over her cheek, repeating the slow motion not only to console her but because he needed this contact. Although he wanted to be her rock, her anchor, during this storm, she soothed something restless deep inside him. Brightened the darkest parts of his life, just by being near him.

"I didn't want you to bring me to your house, but… Thank you. I'm glad I'm here with you now." Her breath flowed warm across his chin, a soft caress. "Tomorrow, I need to go to Florence, Colorado. To the prison and see him face-to-face. Drake Colter," she said, referring to the Sand Angel Killer. The supermax prison was more than a five-hour drive, two hours south of Denver. "Find out if he might know anything about a possible copycat who could be after me. I can do it by myself, but I'd rather not. Colorado is a difficult place for me to go back to. Would you take me? If you can't," she added quickly, without giving him a chance to respond, "I understand. It'd be a last-minute day off for you. I'm sure you have better things to do with your time. Or there's a case you're working on. I'll be fine on my own."

The woman of steel who never asked for help wanted his. "Of course. I wouldn't let you go by yourself."

"*Let* me? At a later date, we should discuss this antiquated and ridiculous notion that you have the power to allow or disallow anything I do."

No need to ever have that chat.

"I misspoke. I can't stop you, but I would've pushed to go with you." He was pleased he didn't have to, and that she'd asked. "I'll call the chief." He needed to talk to her about assigning a detective to the case anyway. "Take a few personal days." He had a ton saved. His intent had been to spend a week with her on the beach somewhere on vacation. The romantic suggestion had sent her scrambling for the hills like he'd invited her to get shipwrecked on a deserted island with no hope of a rescue. "It won't be a problem. I just wrapped up a case."

"I appreciate you doing this." She gave him a sad smile, her eyes still glistening with tears.

His gaze fell to her mouth. The perfect, defined bow of her upper lip. The luscious fullness of her lower lip. He loved the way she chewed on it when she was concentrating and didn't think anyone was looking. Even bruised, she was the most beautiful woman he'd ever seen.

Sensations swept through him, battering his control. It'd been too long since he'd been this close to her, held her, kissed her, but he didn't dare overstep. Not when she was scared and vulnerable and needed to feel safe.

Releasing her, he stepped back and took a deep breath to clear his head.

"I made up the guest room for you." After Melanie had complained about the presence of the gun safe in the corner of his bedroom dampening the mood, he'd moved it to the guest room. He worried the sight of the safe, looming in the corner, might make her uneasy, but it was a small house with limited options. "I didn't want to assume you'd be comfortable in my bedroom. With me. Even though I'd be on my best behavior. You've got my word as a cowboy. No line will be crossed tonight. Not even if you begged." The vow brought a smile to her face that reached her eyes and filled him with warmth.

A tough promise to keep, but he would. "You wouldn't need to worry."

"I've known that about you since the first night I met you. That I wouldn't need to worry. It's the reason I risked going home with a perfect stranger. I'd prefer to be in your room."

Didn't mean she wanted to be in there with him. "I can take the guest room if you want."

"No need." She pressed her palms to his chest. "Could I ask another favor, as just a friend, since you've given me such solid assurances as a cowboy?"

"Name it."

"Would you mind holding me? Just until I fall asleep."

It would be his pleasure. She needed more comfort than a hug in a hallway could give.

"I think I can muster the strength to endure such a hardship." He kissed her forehead, loving the small moments when she lowered the wall, didn't pretend to be invincible and let him see her vulnerability. *His M&M.* Hard and lovely on the outside, but under that picture-perfect exterior, soft and sweet on the inside. First, she'd asked for his help and now for affection. He'd never deny her anything, especially not this. "Like I said, whatever you need."

Chapter Five

The next afternoon, sitting in the passenger's seat of Waylon's truck, Melanie was fuming as they drove through downtown Denver.

"I can't believe Colter was released ten days ago," she said for the hundredth time. Driving to the supermax in Florence had been a complete waste.

"The prison said it was on a technicality, but what kind of colossal error gets a convicted killer, sentenced to life behind bars, suddenly released?" Waylon asked.

"That's what I want to know." She tried calling the Denver district attorney, Brent Becker, the biggest jerk in the world, on his cell phone yet again. "It went straight to voicemail this time." Gritting her teeth, she wanted to punch something or someone but took a deep breath instead. Her cell phone rang. A spark of hope that Brent was finally returning her six calls withered when she looked at the caller ID. "It's my mom. I wonder why she's calling. It's almost one in the morning in Mumbai." Her parents were in India to visit her mother's family and to attend a wedding. "Hi, Mom. What's wrong?"

"You tell me, Mellie. I've had a bad feeling about you all day. Your father keeps saying it's nothing and that you're fine, but I haven't been able to fall asleep."

Causing her parents to worry while they were eight thousand miles away wouldn't do anyone any good, but she didn't want to lie either. "I'm okay. Please don't worry about me."

"It's my job to worry about you. I'm your mother," she said in Marathi, which Melanie had grown up speaking at home.

Her mother was adamant that Mel learned her native tongue, as well as Hindi and English. In college, she'd also picked up French, Italian and Farsi.

"Did anything happen?" Mom asked, segueing back into English.

Melanie weighed her words. "There's always something. You know that."

"What happened?"

If she told her parents the full story, they'd drop everything and fly out to see her. Only for a day or two, where they'd fret endlessly, pressuring her to leave Wyoming, and she'd worry she might be endangering them. The way they took care of her wasn't always in the way she needed. As a teen, they'd sent her to Phillips Exeter Academy, a boarding school that was a top feeder for Harvard, because they'd wanted the freedom to travel. To live unencumbered. Despite how much they'd loved her, how much she'd needed to stay near them as a young teenager, they'd still sent her away. Since then, she'd learned not to be an inconvenience and wouldn't become one now.

"Someone flattened the tires on my car last night at work, but the sheriff's department is involved and investigating the situation."

"Oh no."

"It's fine. That's what triple A is for."

"Vandalism is better than the horrible things I was imagining. I thought you might've been mugged or hurt or worse."

Melanie cringed on the inside. Her mother had some weird sixth sense when it came to her.

"Are you still using the AirTags I gave you?"

"Yes. I sewed an AirTag inside the lining of all my expensive purses and I have one on my keychain." After her mother had been mugged in New York City and the police had never found her beloved Hermès bag, she used extreme caution. "This isn't a good time for me to talk, Mom. I'm in the middle of doing research regarding a prior case." She slid a glance at Waylon, whose gaze was trained on the road, but she was aware he was listening to every word. "I'm with a detective who's been kind enough to help me on his personal time. Please, put your mind at ease. Give Dad and Grandma a hug. Okay."

"If you're sure everything is all right, I'll let you go. Your father is staring at me, giving me that look. You know the one," her mother said, and Melanie could visualize her father's expression. He was British and dispassionately sensible, choosing to make decisions based on hard facts not a bad feeling, which was one thing about him that Melanie loved. "Yes, Freddy, you were right. Mellie is fine. Happy now." Mom sighed. "Dad says hi and that I should be happy, too, but I still have that bad feeling. Like a wriggling knot in my chest." Another sigh. "No, Freddy, it's not indigestion."

Melanie smiled, suddenly missing her parents. She didn't see them often enough. "Love you both. Get some sleep. Enjoy the festivities. I've got to go." She waited for a reply and disconnected. "I hate being dishonest with them."

"You did your parents a kindness. Once we get to the bottom of this and get it resolved, then you can tell them everything." Waylon patted her hand.

The gesture was a comfort that alleviated an inkling of her guilt over her parents while boosting it in equal measure over doing something she'd never expected to do. Ask for help from the man whose heart she'd broken.

The depths of Waylon's kindness, one of the things she loved most about him, never ceased to surprise her.

Last night, he'd been extraordinary. A patient, perfect gentleman. He'd held her close, stroking her hair and back. She'd practically been cocooned by his large frame. Waylon was a big man, the size of a football player. His strong, hard body had been warm against hers, a reassuring haven in the sudden storm that had swept into her world. She'd wanted to kiss him, to lose herself for a moment in his arms, letting him make love to her, but the mixed messages wouldn't have been fair to him. He was a great guy. The best. Not a yo-yo she could yank back and forth on a whim when it suited her.

"Thank you for coming with me today." Not only had he been there for her in a way she didn't deserve after she'd called it quits with him, but he hadn't forced conversation on the long drive and hadn't brought up their relationship. Or rather, the end of it.

Waylon was a fighter. Went after what he wanted, and he'd made it clear he wanted her. It was the reason she stopped returning his calls. The man was persuasive and had filthy pillow talk she missed. Along with his touch and his kisses. And his cuddles.

But she couldn't help savoring this new layer between them, one of comfort, support. It felt tenuous, and oddly special, and she was reluctant to ruin it.

He flashed her a grin. "Not like I was going to let you, I mean," he said, catching himself, "I wouldn't want you to go alone to see a serial killer, and I'd rather it be me than someone else." His attention turned back to the road.

For the briefest moment, she wondered what her parents would think of Waylon. He was not only handsome and gentle, despite being the intimidating size of a bear, but also polite to the point where he could drive her nuts. They'd appreciate his character—honest and humble—and his work ethic. A natural leader who put in almost as many hours as she did and never stopped until the bad guy was behind bars.

There was so much about him to admire.

To love.

"We're here." He passed a line of news vans parked out front, pulled into the garage of the courthouse and had to go up to the top floor to find a parking spot. "Full house today."

Some days were busier than others but…

"This is unusual," she said. "Something must be going on."

Melanie flipped down the sun visor and checked her face in the vanity mirror. The concealer under her eye was starting to fade and purple bruising peeked through, but the makeup on her cheeks still looked okay. She pulled out the pair of oversized sunglasses she had tucked inside her purse and slipped them on.

Wearing shades indoors wasn't something she'd normally do, but today was one for exceptions.

They got out of the truck, cleared security, and made their way to the district attorney's office. She waved hello to familiar faces, avoided answering any questions, and tried to ignore the curious stares that were as much for her as Waylon.

Everyone checked out the man next to her. Not that she blamed them. Waylon was huge. Not only tall, but also burly. A solid two-forty, and not the doughy kind. The first night she'd seen him in Crazy Eddie's, he'd snagged her full attention right away. His size was intimidating and appealing in equal measures. He'd flashed the bartender an easy grin. Radiated calm affability. His eyes were warm, honest. Kind. She'd figured if he was interested and single, then he'd be the one.

At least for a night.

Melanie stopped in front of the desk of the DA's receptionist and clasped her hands.

Susan's eyes grew wide as saucers. "Melanie. I didn't expect you to show up here."

"Why not? You've given me the runaround for the last two hours. What was I supposed to do? Sit and wait for Brent to call me back like a good little girl?"

Susan opened her mouth, but no words came out.

"Is he in there?" Melanie pointed to the DA's office.

"No. He's preparing to give a statement to the media." The middle-aged woman had bags under her eyes and looked ten years older than the last time she'd seen her. "That's why he's been unavailable, and his cell is turned off."

"Why is Drake Colter free?" she demanded.

Susan grimaced. "It's a disaster. That's what the press conference is about." The older woman looked at her watch. "It'll start in twenty minutes, at three o'clock, if you care to stay for it."

"I don't want to listen to whatever garbage he's going to feed the press. I want to talk to him. Now."

"Where is he?" Waylon asked.

Susan looked at him, her gaze raking him from his cowboy hat, past his business-casual attire—a blazer, gray T-shirt that stretched taut across his muscular chest and jeans that hung on him in just the right way—down to his boots. "And you are?"

"Detective Waylon Wright." Pulling back his jacket, he flashed the badge that was hooked to his waistband beside his holstered gun. "Please, don't make me ask again, ma'am."

"He's smoking. Running through his speech. Trying to shake his nerves," Susan said, and Melanie should have guessed. "He's having a rough week. This might be the worst day of his life. Wait until after he speaks to the media, will you?"

Oh, poor Brent.

"No," Melanie said with an indignant shake of her head. "I won't wait."

"Still pushy, heartless and selfish as ever, I see." Susan narrowed her eyes and pursed her lips. "They have a name for women like you, but I'm too dignified to use such vulgarity."

Melanie pressed both palms down on her desk and leaned in. "Someone tried to kill me last night, Susan. You'll have to excuse me if I don't have enough sympathy for Brent because he's having a tough week. And whatever vulgar word you're thinking of, I've been called a lot worse by better people and I didn't lose a wink of sleep over it."

Susan reeled back in her chair aghast. "I didn't realize he'd go after you next."

"He who?" Waylon asked.

"The killer," Susan whispered.

"Drake Colter?" The irritation in Waylon's voice only echoed Melanie's. "And what do you mean by 'next'?"

"Everything is such a mess," Susan said. "Judge Babcock, who presided over the Colter case, the witness who testified that his alibi was a lie, Georgia Jenkins, and the one juror—the holdout who caved in the final hour, making the vote unanimous, and gave that primetime interview—Regina Sweeney, were all murdered after Colter was released."

Ice water ran through Melanie's veins, freezing her heart. Three women.

"Why wasn't she notified?" Waylon asked.

Susan shrugged. "I don't know. That's not my area."

Light-headed, Melanie was speechless for the first time in her adult life.

"Why was he released in the first place?" Waylon demanded. "And why hasn't he been arrested again after these new murders?"

"It's complicated." Bewilderment twisted Susan's features, emphasizing her wrinkles. "You have to ask Brent."

"I intend to," Melanie said, finding her voice.

They turned and stalked out of the office space. She led the way to the stairwell, which was the fastest way to a little-known spot where employees could smoke.

"Is it always a circus around this place?" he asked.

"It wasn't when I worked here." Because she had more or less been in charge and hadn't tolerated cluelessness. She hurried down the steps, patting herself on the back for forsaking her typical suit and heels in lieu of jeans and wedge shoes.

"Why did you leave Denver?"

The question blindsided her. "Multiple factors." She glanced at him. "I'm not trying to be evasive. Ask me again, another time, and I'll tell you."

"I'll hold you to that."

No doubt in her mind that he would.

On the first floor, she led him through a maze of hallways to the small courtyard. She spotted Brent. He was pacing back and forth, speaking to himself, smoking.

He usually enjoyed press conferences, a big public platform where he got to take all the credit, but it was evident from the way he waved his hands and his brow furrowed that he dreaded this one.

She shoved through the door and walked outside with Waylon beside her. "Brent."

His head whipped toward her, his eyes widening in surprise. "Melanie? What on earth are you doing here?"

"I was attacked at work last night."

"Not you, too." Brent hung his head and took a drag on his cigarette. "Did the assault make the news?" His green eyes flashed up at them. "Where are you living these days? Wyoming, right?"

The guy hadn't changed. Still despicable.

Waylon stepped toward him. "You should be asking her if she's all right."

"Clearly she is." Brent waved a nonchalant hand at her. "Walking, talking, alive." His tone was glacial, devoid of any hint of past affection.

Melanie couldn't believe she had almost slept with him. She took off her sunglasses and stared at him in disbelief. "A man tried to kill me and nearly succeeded."

He leaned toward her, taking a good look at her face. "I guess he did do a number on you. I can see a black eye poking through your makeup, and bruises on your neck, too. *Sheesh.* Did he choke you?" He reached for her.

She jerked away from his touch. The bruising on her face and neck was horrible, but at least it looked worse than it felt today. She'd done her best to hide it. Only so much makeup could do.

Waylon put up his palm, close to Brent's chest. "Watch your hands and keep them to yourself." His voice was calm, perfectly civilized, but something dangerous flickered in his eyes.

"And your name, buddy?"

"Detective Waylon Wright."

"Why is Drake Colter free?" she asked, trying to get the discussion back on track. "And don't brush it off by telling me it's complicated."

"But it is. And it isn't." Brent took a long drag on his cigarette and blew the smoke out off to the side.

She'd never been a fan of the smell of cigarettes, but after the assault last night, the scent of menthol turned her stomach.

"No lawyer doublespeak," Waylon said. "Just answer the question."

"Where to begin?" Brent asked, his tone flippant.

Waylon nudged his cowboy hat up with his knuckle. "Try the beginning."

"We believe the Sand Angel Killer first started taking victims in New Mexico, though we couldn't prove that," Brent said, "and suspected he worked his way up here to Denver."

"That's where he made his mistake and left behind DNA," Melanie said, filling in the blanks for Waylon. "When we finally tracked him down, turns out he was already in prison in Las Cruces for vandalizing the White Sands National Park, serving a one-year sentence. And we did eventually find a body out there, too, but we couldn't tie him to the murder. His incarceration made the process easy. We brought him to Denver, had him arraigned on murder charges, and he was returned to New Mexico on a court order until the trial started, where we got a conviction."

"Exactly." Brent put the cigarette in the smoking receptacle and took out another one. "There's the crux of the problem," he said as though that had explained anything.

"Yeah, that's clear as mud." Waylon waved at the air in front of him. "Would you mind?" he asked, indicating the cigarette. "Secondhand smoke kills."

"I didn't invite you to come out here and interrupt the one moment of peace that I've had today. Leave for all I care." Brent lit the cigarette. "I'm in crisis mode here."

"Focus, Brent." She snapped her fingers. "Why is that murderer on the loose?"

"Colter's appellate lawyer filed a motion to vacate the murder conviction based on a violation of the interstate agreement law approved by Congress back in 1970. The judge stated in her decision that county officials here violated the federal Interstate Agreement on Detainer's Law, or IAD, when we sent him back to prison in New Mexico as he awaited trial in the Denver murder case. The harsh reality is that the administrative decision to send him back unequivocally entitled the defendant to dismissal of the murder in the first-degree indictments with prejudice under the exacting requirements of the anti-shuttling provisions of the IAD."

A dismissal with prejudice meant that Drake Colter could not be retried in the murder case. "But there was a court order to transfer him," she said.

Brent rubbed the back of his neck. "Did you ever see one?"

"No." She shook her head. "I took your word for it."

"According to a document we received, created by the sheriff's department, it indicated a court order, but turns out that it doesn't exist." Brent blew out more smoke. "The sheriff needed Colter transferred. An administrative decision based on jail population and timing. It's a traditional practice to return prisoners to their 'home' correctional facility. Apparently, this loophole has been used before, recently by a defendant in New York, to get released. Over the next few years, I'm sure others will use it, too."

Waylon swore.

"Yeah," Brent said, smoothing a hand over his slicked-back hair, "tell me about it, buddy."

The gleam of his wedding band caught her eye and the burn of old embarrassment flared in her cheeks. For years, he'd flirted with her after hours, pretending he had feelings, constantly trying to sleep with her while he had a girlfriend unbeknownst to her the entire time. Not only had he taken credit for her work, being the face of many high-profile, career-making cases that she'd built, he had also tried to turn her into the other woman.

"Look," Waylon said, "I'm not your buddy or your pal. It's Detective."

Rolling his eyes, Brent shook his head. "I don't have time for this. Since we can't keep it quiet any longer, I have a press conference in a few minutes, where I have to explain this debacle to the media and apologize alongside the sheriff. People are going to get fired over this. I'm going to lose my job."

"Melanie almost lost her life last night." Disgust tightened Waylon's voice.

"Speaking of which, did it make the local news?" Brent asked, once again with flagrant disregard for her well-being. "I just need to know if I should include you in my statement when I talk about the recent victims."

She swallowed around the lump in her throat.

Curling his fingers into a fist, Waylon stepped toward Brent, making the DA flinch. Power emanated from him. A raw, lethal kind of strength. Every time she was near Waylon, that strength enveloped her in the comfort of a warm security blanket.

Maybe it was the sheer size of him. Maybe it was the badge and gun, although she knew and worked with plenty of other cops. None of whom ever had this effect on her.

She reminded herself that security went hand in hand with dependence, and dependence on any man wasn't something she could afford.

Melanie slid between them and put a hand on Waylon's chest. "He isn't worth it." Pivoting, she looked at Mr. Despicable. "I don't want to be mentioned. But I do want to know why Colter hasn't been arrested for the recent murders."

"There's no proof he's guilty."

"The judge, the witness and the juror…" she said, "were the bodies found in the same manner as the others?"

"They were missing for about twenty-four hours before they were found. Based on time of death, they weren't killed immediately. He kept them alive for roughly twelve to sixteen hours. But the bodies were left in exactly the same manner," Brent said. "In dunes. Impressions of sand angels."

"With the word 'sinner' written beside them?"

Blowing out smoke, Brent nodded. "Yep."

"Were any of them violated?" she asked, wondering if there had been any deviation or escalation from the other murders.

"No signs of sexual assault. Blunt force trauma to the head. Cause of death asphyxia due to ligature strangulation."

They'd all been strangled, like the previous victims. "Was sand poured in their mouths and found on their eyelids?" Those details had never been released to the press during the investigation but had come out over the course of the trial.

"Yep. The murders were all the same," Brent said.

"But why isn't Colter—"

Brent threw his hands up in the air, cutting her off. "Colter has an airtight alibi for the three."

"Which is what?" Waylon asked.

"He's at a residential community corrections facility because he didn't have any place to live and requested it, claiming he was worried he'd start doing drugs and drink again. They're helping him reintegrate and transition into society."

"A halfway house?" Waylon clenched his jaw.

Anger tangled with her frustration. "He's never tested positive for drugs," she said. Despite his claims that was the reason he couldn't remember what had happened during the timeframe when one victim, where his DNA was found, had been murdered.

"I know." Brent sighed. "But the claim is working to his benefit now."

"Which facility is he in?" Waylon asked.

"Fair Chance Treatment Center. Colter was considered present and accounted for either when the victims went missing or at the time of death. Regarding Judge Babcock, his alibi covered him when she was abducted and murdered. There was no DNA found at the crime scenes to contradict that. Our hands are tied where he's concerned. This is the greatest embarrassment of my career," Brent said, reducing the murder of three innocent women to the impact on his job. He looked around them at someone.

Melanie glanced over her shoulder to see who it was.

Susan beckoned to him with an urgent wave of her hand and pointed at her watch.

"Sorry you were attacked. Glad you're fine." The words were hurried and hollow. "Even better that I don't have to mention you." Brent stamped out his cigarette. "I've got to go. Showtime." He smoothed the front of his suit, checked his reflection in the glass and made a beeline for the door. "Wish me luck."

She wished him a speedy delivery of all the karma he deserved.

"I hope the reporters tear him to pieces," Waylon said to her.

"Ditto. But that weasel has a way of slithering out of tight, tiny corners." A remarkable survival skill.

"Come on," Waylon said, putting a hand on her back.

"Where to?" She hoped he didn't want to watch the madness of the press conference.

"Fair Chance Treatment Center. To ask Colter some questions. I'd prefer it if you hung back here or at least waited in the truck and let me do it without you, but I know you're going to insist."

Melanie had confronted plenty of criminals—thieves, arsonists, gang members, mafia bosses and murderers included—but something about Drake Colter, the darkness in his eyes, always made her blood run cold.

"I need to face him, look him in the eyes." In court, she showed no mercy when she prosecuted someone, especially a murderer. Melanie had gone after him with every tool in her arsenal, showed the world what kind of monster he really was, gotten a conviction, and the highest sentence possible: life imprisonment. Now this vicious killer was free. To do it again. She was relieved she wouldn't have to see Drake Colter on her own and that Waylon would be at her side. "I can't let him think I'm afraid of him."

Even though a part of her was terrified.

Chapter Six

At the front door of the Fair Chance Treatment Center, Waylon found it locked. He pressed the bell.

"FCTC," a bright male voice said through the speaker mounted on the outside. "How can I help you?"

"I'm Detective Wright and I'm here with ADA Merritt. We have some questions for Drake Colter."

"One moment please."

Waylon took in their surroundings again. An underprivileged neighborhood in a shady part of town. The *center* was little more than a glorified house. He didn't like that the rear was adjacent to an alley that was the perfect security blind spot for someone interested in sneaking in and out with a lower risk of detection.

A white nondescript passenger van was parked in the driveway. The glimpse of her assailant's vehicle on the surveillance footage only showed a partial side profile of the front. It could've been a passenger van or cargo.

He glanced at Melanie. Pushing her sunglasses higher on the bridge of her nose, she stood rigid, her head bowed, and appeared lost in thought. That jerk, Brent Becker, had given her plenty to contemplate.

The IAD law was a gaping hole in the justice system the size of the Grand Canyon if it allowed a convicted serial killer to be free on the streets after serving only three years of a life sentence.

The front door swung open as a chime sounded. A Black man in his late fifties, possibly early sixties, with a weathered face and receding hairline greeted them. "I'm Hershel. The lead counselor." He stepped aside, letting them in. They entered a small foyer that had a rudimentary desk, a laptop that was chained to it, and a chair. "The police have already been here several times this week to speak with Mr. Colter. I'll tell you the same thing I told them, he was present and accounted for during the times they specified."

"You saw him personally?" Melanie asked, keeping her sunglasses on inside the center.

"No. The night shift counselor does a room check at ten and another one randomly in the night and then a last one at six in the morning."

Depending on when the random check occurred, there could have been plenty of time to sneak out, commit murder, and make it back for the final inspection.

Waylon took out a pad and pen. "What's the name and number of the other counselor?"

"Kurt Parrish was on duty those three nights." Hershel rattled off his cell phone number. "He works from eight at night to eight in the morning."

"Is it possible for someone to sneak out during the night?" Melanie asked.

"Not without us knowing it." Hershel shoved his hands in the front pockets of his jeans. "When the security system isn't fully activated, like it is now, it's set to chime whenever any exterior door or window is opened. There's an electronic record. After 10:00 p.m., the security system is set. At that point, if a door or window is opened, it triggers the alarm."

"Could someone open a window at the same time a door is opened, so there's only one chime?" Mel asked.

"Sure, I suppose so." Hershel nodded. "But the security system won't fully activate if a door or window is left open. We'd get an error."

Waylon eyed the outdated panel near the door. "Ever have any problems with the system?"

"On occasion, sure we do." Hershel gave a one-shoulder shrug. "The system is old. When a battery needs to be changed in a sensor, it doesn't work properly until the security company can come out to fix it, which can take a few days, and sometimes the plug to the hub comes loose. Takes a good five minutes to reboot."

All weaknesses in the security system that could be exploited to tamper with the electronic record.

"Any of those issues occur recently, say over the past ten days since Colter has been here?" Waylon asked.

"As a matter of fact, yes. Kurt has mentioned a few things, but nothing out of the ordinary. I'm sure it's just a coincidence. Like I said, the system is old."

The security system was ancient, but Waylon didn't believe in coincidence. Gritting his teeth, he exchanged a frustrated glance with Mel. "Do you happen to know where Mr. Colter was last night," he said, "between seven and ten?"

"Last night?" Hershel tilted his head to the side. "Was someone else killed?"

Melanie's lips flattened into a grim line. "No, sir, but I was attacked."

"Brutally," Waylon added.

"Oh my goodness. I'm so sorry to hear that." Hershel looked and sounded sincere, unlike Brent, whose callousness had been mindboggling for a human with a beating heart.

"Such a shame what happened to you, but it couldn't have been Drake."

"How are you so sure?" Melanie asked.

"We usually have an hour of group therapy at six on Thursday nights, but I left early."

"How early?" Waylon interrupted. "And why did you leave?"

"It was around five or five thirty. That's when Kurt showed up early to cover the shift. Something I ate didn't agree with me or it was a twenty-four-hour bug. A few guys weren't feeling well. This morning, Kurt told me that everything was quiet. Some went to bed sick while everyone else gathered in the living room and watched the *Real Housewives* at nine, like always. A lot of the guys get into it in prison. No one ever misses an episode in this house. Unless they're feeling under the weather. The guys were all in their bedrooms at ten."

Melanie folded her arms. "Was Colter unwell last night?"

"Yes, he was. Turned into bed long before I left. Maybe around four."

"Does he share a room?" Waylon asked.

"The guys are lucky. They each have their own room. But Kurt logged them all present and accounted for at ten, at three, and again at six. I checked the logs as soon as I got in like usual. Drake was here last night."

What if the night shift guy, Kurt, had grown complacent with his job and only done a rudimentary check from the doorway? Someone claiming to be sick, or wanting to give the perception they're asleep, could stuff a few pillows in the bed to make it look like a person was there. Pretend to go to sleep early. Sneak out before the security system was fully activated.

If Colter went to his room at four, that would've given him

time to drive up to Laramie, wait two hours, attack her, then return to Denver and slip back inside FCTC.

Also, within the realm of possibility that Kurt was incentivized to look the other way through bribery or intimidation.

None of this gave Waylon a warm and fuzzy feeling that Drake Colter's alibi was airtight or that the convicted killer was innocent of these recent murders and the attack on Melanie.

"You heard Hersh. I didn't do whatever you're here to ask about," another man said, waltzing into the foyer.

Drake Colter.

An average-looking guy, both in height and girth. Waylon guessed him to be around his own age, midthirties. Wearing a wife-beater, arms covered in tattoos, with rattlesnake-mean eyes and greasy blond hair, he could come across as menacing.

Dangerous. Going up against the right person.

But Waylon was *waaaay* the hell more dangerous if it came to protecting Melanie.

Colter eyed him up and down, measuring his worth. His mouth twitched, his eyes shifting away. The evil scumbag didn't want a piece of him, but the guy dared to turn his attention to Melanie.

"Hey, you look at me and speak to me," Waylon said. "Not her."

"Or else what?" Colter asked, jutting his chin up in the air.

Waylon stepped in front of her, positioning himself as a barrier and smiled. "You *do not* want to test me."

Colter took a tentative step back. "I didn't catch your name."

"Detective Waylon Wright."

"I was here last night, Detective. Hersh confirmed it and so will Kurt Parrish. Because it's the truth. So, I didn't do whatever you came here to grill me about." Colter spoke while waving his hands around in an animated manner. "I'm sick of this harassment. My sentence was vacated. Not my fault you bozos messed up, but I know my rights and I don't have to talk to you." The wretch pointed a finger in Waylon's face. "Not without my lawyer present."

Waylon glanced down at the index finger inches from his nose and resisted the urge to snatch it and snap it. But his gaze fell to the underside of Colter's forearm.

To a list tattooed on his skin in black ink.

Waylon took the man's wrist and turned it so he could read the words clearly:

Alicia Babcock
Regina Sweeney
Georgia Jenkins
Kristin Loeb
Emilio Vasquez
Melanie Merritt

"What is this?" Waylon asked. "Some kind of hit list?" Anger simmered and smoldered in his chest.

Mel stepped around to see it, along with Hershel, who peered over her shoulder.

Colter jerked his arm away from Waylon's grip and proudly held it out for them to all see. "No, it's not a hit list," he said with a maniacal grin. "Just a permanent reminder of the people responsible for trying to lock me away forever." He clasped his hands together and rubbed his palms. "But no hard feelings anymore. I'm free while you all have egg on your face. At least, the ones still breathing." His gaze cut to Melanie. "For now."

Waylon stepped in his line of sight, barely containing his fury over the not-so-veiled threat. "What do you mean by *for now*? Do you have plans for the other three on your list of targets?"

"Targets?" Colter feigned a baffled expression. "I don't have any targets, Detective. I'm not some murderous mastermind. My only plan is to abide by the house rules and focus on my reintegration into the community so that I can be a productive member of society." A smile spread on his face, a sick gleam in his eyes. "Now, if you'll excuse me. We recorded the DA's press conference earlier. I think I'll watch it again. Hope the DA and sheriff are fired before they have a chance to quit." Colter turned and walked away.

"You don't blame DA Becker for your indictment and incarceration?" Waylon asked, the question stopping the serial killer in his tracks.

"No, I don't," Colter said with his back to them. "He wasn't the one who hired that intrusive investigator, Vasquez. Encouraged the podcaster, Loeb, to have me tried in the court of public opinion. He wasn't the one who prosecuted me. Picked the jury. Gave such a heartrending closing argument. Persuaded the families of the victims to speak at my sentencing." Colter looked over his shoulder at Melanie. "I told you I was innocent. Maybe you should've listened to me. How else can you explain what's happening now?" His grin deepened, turning sinister. "Hope to see you again ADA Merritt. Next time, come back without the big fella. Maybe I'll help you before it's too late."

"Where she goes, I go." Waylon stepped over, blocking Colter's view of her again. "Look at me. Speak to me."

"Aww, is ADA Merritt someone special to you, Detective Wright? Is it true love or true lust?"

"I'll be the one asking the questions."

"Well, I still have a couple more for you. Are you a tough guy, huh? Think you're an immovable object?" Colter chuckled. "When an unstoppable force with infinite torque meets a so-called immovable object, like yourself, there's only one outcome. That object gets moved. You see, the flaw for the object is that it lacks any force holding it in place. Maybe what's coming for her can't be stopped. Not even by you."

"We'll see about that," Waylon said, anger bleeding into his voice. "I'm not going to let anything happen to her."

"You can try. Give it your best shot. But I'm willing to venture a guess that you'll fail." A smug grin tugged at his ugly mouth. He turned around, putting his back to them, and started to walk away as he whistled a tune. The melody of a nursery rhyme. "There Was An Old Lady Who Swallowed A Fly." Right before he disappeared down the hall, he said, "You better hurry back to see me. Tick tock, Ms. Melanie Merritt."

Chapter Seven

Behind the wheel of his truck, Waylon looked over at Melanie as she hung up her cell. “Emilio isn’t picking up. His phone goes straight to voicemail.”

“Do you still have any friends over at the Denver PD?”

“I might have a couple left.”

“Good. Reach out to them. Tell them about Colter’s list, your attack, and the danger that Vasquez and Loeb are in. They also need to put a cop on the halfway house at night. We need to know for certain if Colter is sneaking out.”

“You don’t believe Hershel? Seemed trustworthy to me.”

“Maybe he doesn’t have all the facts and believes what he’s been told by the night shift guy. We need to question Kurt Parrish. Face-to-face. If he doesn’t return my call, we’ll have to swing back by the Fair Chance Treatment Center while he’s on duty.”

Melanie’s phone chimed. “It’s a text from Kristin Loeb. She’s meeting with the Sand Angelites right now and can’t talk. She feels like she’s on the verge of getting some kind of a lead.”

“Angelites? Care to elaborate?”

She took a deep breath. “We tried to label Colter the Sand Dune Killer. One of the detectives working on the case mentioned the impression of an angel the murderer made with the victims. The media dubbed him the Sand Angel Killer instead and it stuck. Guess it sold more papers and got more clicks online. The Angelites are a bunch of Colter's groupies. They formed a cult. Idolize him. They all wear gypsum around their necks. A soft, pale blue crystal that's supposed to symbolize soothing and peaceful energy. Another name for the stone happens to be Angelite."

"A cult for a serial murderer?"

"Happened with Manson. A lot of sick people out there. But the Sand Angelites claim that he's different because he only went after *sinners*," she said, using air quotes. "They believe he is cleansing the world of evil. How is that for twisted logic?" She sighed. "Though I can't fathom what any of his victims were guilty of besides the fact they were women. Vulnerable at the right place and right time for him to strike."

"What else does her text say?"

Melanie looked back at the phone. "Kristin is here in Denver up from Pagosa Springs. She's staying at the Mile-High City Motel and will be back to her room later tonight. She's willing to meet and share what she learns if we want to hang around."

"Yeah. We can stay the night at the same place. Chat with her and make sure she stays safe."

"You need to make a U-turn. The motel is in the opposite direction." Staring at the phone, Mel smiled. "She recommends the tavern across the street for dinner."

"Sounds like a plan. Tell me more about her."

"Kristin is an investigative journalist and true crime podcaster. One of the victims of the Sand Angel Killer was a student at her alma mater, the University of Denver. That's when she took an interest. She sheds light on unsolved murders, missing persons in settings that one might otherwise associate with a quaint getaway. The sand dune murders were perfect for her. Once we met, we clicked. She's warm and funny, has this way of disarming people."

"That's probably why she's so successful." His cell phone rang. "It's the night shift guy." He put the call on speaker through Bluetooth. "You've reached Detective Wright."

"Hi. This is Kurt Parrish. I got your messages. Sorry. I was sleeping. What's this about? I already spoke with some of your friends at the Denver Police Department."

"I'm from the Laramie PD."

"Oh, um, I didn't realize. You're a long way from home and I believe outside your jurisdiction."

Not easily sidetracked, Waylon said, "I had a few questions that I'd like to ask you in person if you don't mind."

Silence.

"Mr. Parrish? Are you still there?"

"Uh, actually, I do mind. I've been cooperative. You can get copies of my statements from the cops here."

"This is involving an assault that occurred last night," Waylon said, "while you were on duty. Do you have ten minutes for a face to face?"

A beat of hesitation. "Is this about Drake Colter?"

"It is."

"He was present and accounted for. In bed all night. He was sick. Ate something bad."

"Then it'll only take two minutes instead of ten, sir. We can stop by your home now if you'll give me the address."

"I don't have anything else to add," Kurt Parrish said. "Sorry I can't be more helpful. I, um, I hope that's enough for you. Got to go. I've got something important to do, an appointment I need to get to before work. I need to go." The call disconnected.

Mel raised an eyebrow. "Kurt Parrish sounded nervous."

"I agree. Cops tend to make suspects nervous. Not innocent people who are being asked rudimentary questions unless they have something to hide."

"That's not always true. A lot of people in the inner city are suspicious of the police. When I lived here, I was an advocate of the Denver PD community outreach program, to foster communication, address concerns, and build trust."

Back home, the cops were the good guys, pillars of the community, to be trusted. In most cases. The Laramie PD did have a problem with corrupt officers until the chief cleaned it up. Problems like that were probably more widespread in places like Denver. Not that he'd had much inner-city experience.

"We need to figure out what's making Parrish nervous," he said. "See if he knows more. Since we're spending the night, I say we go back to FCTC first thing in the morning when his guard is down and he thinks we've moved on."

"That strategy could work. I should call the office and check in with Darcy. She told me Gordon was out unexpectedly today. It's been happening a lot lately and I've had to pick up the slack. Since I'm not there, I just want to make sure everything is running smoothly."

While she spoke to the paralegal, Melanie finished giving him directions to the motel. Down the street on the corner was a large pharmacy store where they grabbed toiletries and a few essentials since they hadn't planned to stay the night.

He parked at the Mile-High City Motel and got them a room. First floor. Room 120—dingy carpet, outdated décor, musty smell. Typical low-budget place.

Across the street, the hostess at the tavern seated them at a booth in a secluded area, at Melanie's request, so they could speak privately. They ordered, got their drinks and waited for their meals.

"I'm sure today was a shock for you," he said. "Finding out about the three latest murders."

"That's an understatement. I'm on a hit list." She took a sip of her margarita on the rocks, no salt on the rim. "I think what's more disconcerting is that the DA's office here neglected to notify me. If they'd only given me the commonsense courtesy of a heads-up, I never would've left work late on my own."

Brent's carelessness made Waylon want to rearrange the DA's face. One phone call from Brent and Mel would've had a sheriff's deputy escort her to her vehicle.

But maybe it would have been worse if her assailant had seen the deputy and altered his plans. Decided to wait until she was home. Alone. Asleep. Even more vulnerable.

They needed to determine if Colter was behind this latest string of murders or if it was someone else, and stop him. Fast. "Colter claims he wasn't the Sand Angel Killer. Is it possible you got the wrong guy?"

"His DNA was found on two victims. We confirmed he was in Colorado on the dates of the murders, which contradicted the statement of his alibi. Georgia Jenkins, his girlfriend. Her statement fell apart under scrutiny. She claimed Colter threatened her, forced her to lie to the authorities."

"Any evidence to suggest that it might have been two perps working together?"

"None."

Their food was brought to the table. He cut into his steak while Melanie picked at her pasta. She'd barely eaten all day, though he understood her loss of appetite. After the last twenty-two hours, no wonder food held little appeal for her.

"Any differences between the murders in New Mexico and Colorado?" he asked.

"In New Mexico, it looked like he was just getting started.

The same blunt force trauma to the head and strangulation, with the bodies found in sand dunes." She tossed back a swallow of her margarita. "But the ones in Colorado had more flourish to them. The impressions of the sand angels with the bodies of the victims carefully placed in the center. *Sinner* scrolled in the sand. Evolution and escalation are typical in serial killers."

"Do you think Colter attacked you? Snuck out somehow? Or that it was someone else working on his behalf?" Either way, he felt certain that sick murderer was responsible.

"I wish I knew for sure. My gut tells me that he's getting help of some kind, if only we could pin down to what degree. Maybe it's from Kurt Parrish. The alibi is strong and apparently enough to dissuade the police from digging too much deeper into Colter."

"Did you hear back from your friends in the Denver PD?"

"I did. There's already a request to have Drake Colter officially monitored. One detective I know well has been watching the house at night after the second murder, but they need additional personnel because the back of the center abuts an alley. They don't have eyes on it. If he did sneak out last night, he used the alley and wasn't seen." She ran distressed fingers through her hair.

For a moment, he was mesmerized by the way the strands moved like a shimmery curtain of dark water, rich black and so thick. She was the most beautiful thing on the face of the planet.

He lowered his head. "You got a speedy response." Meant she still had a good working relationship with law enforcement. "So, tell me, what were your reasons for leaving Denver? Did one of them have something to do with Brent? I take it that he was the ex who was happy you left?"

She finished her margarita and caught the attention of the waiter. "I'm going to need another."

With a nod, the server took the empty glass.

"You asked if the relationship ended badly," she continued, "but you didn't ask the nature of that relationship. He was my boss. There was heavy flirtation on his part. Only after business hours when we worked late. Outside of the office at conferences, work dinners, that sort of thing."

"Did you ever sleep with him?" He hoped the answer was no. A slimeball such as Brent didn't deserve to be with a woman like Mel.

"I considered it."

His gut clenched. "Why?"

She hesitated. "I get lonely and I have needs."

Easy enough to find someone to scratch an itch. No need for her to settle for the likes of Becker.

"But I only entertained the thought," she said. "The flirting was one-sided on his part."

"You're beautiful. You could have any guy you want." She was the woman he should not have been able to get. Only by luck, or fate, that she'd gone to Crazy Eddie's that night, where she'd had her choice of cowboys, and picked him.

Smiling, she shook her head. "I'm also direct, blunt and assertive," she said, forgetting to list unapologetic about what she wanted—an admirable trait. "Plenty of guys find that off-putting."

Their server delivered her drink and hurried off to another table.

"When I lived here in Denver," she continued, "I worked long hours. Brent was interested and convenient."

"But he's such a—"

"I know," she cut him off, stopping the crass word from leaving his lips. "Nothing about him spelled *good guy*. That was part of his limited appeal. It meant I'd never fall in love with him." Mel stabbed a piece of penne with her fork. "The upside of his cold personality was that everything would've stayed all business at work. Outside of the office, things would've been casual. But it also would've been a human resources disaster waiting to happen. When I make DA, I don't want anyone to think I slept my way to the top."

Relief seeped through him, but one thing niggled at him. "Brent's appeal was that you'd never fall in love. You don't want that? Love. Marriage."

Her brow crinkled, caution darkening her eyes. "Sex is simple. Love is complicated. Difficult to balance with a demanding job. You know how many detectives end up getting divorced?"

"A lot." The divorce rate for cops was like seventy-five percent. "But you didn't answer my question about love and marriage."

She flicked a glance at her drink and then back at him. "Only a fool would want to fall in love with their boss. Besides, any distraction would hinder me from making DA. Not help me."

Carefully chosen words. Still not an answer. "Or it could be nice to have someone in your corner, no matter what."

Not meeting his eyes, she pushed pasta around on her plate with her fork.

A chime had her grabbing her phone. "It's Kristin. The text says she's onto something big. Will be back after eleven tonight. Room 204. She'll call once she gets in and compiles her notes about the Savior connection."

"Savior?"

"Savior with a capital S." She held up her phone, turning the screen toward him.

That gave them several hours until they could learn more from Loeb.

"Hey," he said. "Your career aside, I'm glad you didn't sleep with Brent. I don't like thinking about you with him." Or any other man for that matter.

"Is that why you wanted to hit him earlier?"

"Partly. But mostly the callous narcissist just had it coming," he said, and she grinned at him—a slow, devastating smile that sent a ripple of heat through him. "If you two didn't hook up, then why did the work relationship end badly?" He wondered.

"Four years of overtures, including the night before my last day. He stopped by my house and laid it on thick, but I had zero interest. He said rude things. Called me an iceberg. Assumed sex with me would've been like sleeping with a dead fish."

Ouch. Little did Becker know that though Mel was tough and remained levelheaded at work, she was passionate about everything. Once you got past her defenses, she was affectionate and open, the warmest, most vivacious person.

"The next day at the office, when I was saying my goodbyes, he announced that he was engaged."

Waylon set his fork down. "I take it you didn't know he was seeing anyone."

"Didn't have a clue. His girlfriend never attended work functions. I later learned because she travels a lot. He never mentioned he was involved with anyone, but I hadn't asked either," she said, her voice low, and the interrogation she had put him through when they'd met in the honky-tonk suddenly made sense. "One thing for him to take credit for my work. Quite another to try to use me as a side piece. Cheating is the worst kind of deception. Robs a person of their pride. Violates trust. I wasn't his girlfriend, but it was still humiliating." She shook her head and he wanted to erase the hurt look from her eyes and punch Brent in the face. "My dad cheated on my mother."

"I'm surprised, based on the way you talk about them. They seem like soulmates."

"They are. I meant my biological father, Aadesh. Not Frederick, who raised me as his own. I consider him my dad. My mom's first husband hurt her deeply. She couldn't forgive him. He left, remarried, and never looked back. He's a lawyer, too. Coincidentally." Her voice lowered. "Sometimes when I disconnect and put messy emotions in neat boxes, she says I'm like him. Aadesh. A chip off the old block." Her pained expression made him reach for her hand, but she pulled it away into her lap. "I may be like him in some ways, but I wouldn't cheat. Not ever."

"I know you wouldn't." He let Melanie absorb that, his trust and faith in her.

"Thank you."

"For the record, I would never cheat either. Who we are isn't all about genetics. I told you my father was mean-spirited."

"Disrespectful to your mom. I figured that's why you go out of your way to be so polite."

"It was more than that. He was abusive. Until I got big enough to stop him. That's when we moved from Wayward Bluffs to Bison Ridge." Later his mother remarried and moved his siblings farther north in Wyoming while he joined the army. After serving, he'd missed Wayward Bluffs and bought a house there. "My father is the reason I'm so careful with the way I deal with people, how I present myself. I never want to scare a woman, kids, hurt anyone, because I lose control. My worst fear is becoming my father."

"You never would. Never could."

He appreciated hearing that. Needed to know she believed

in him. "I used to be afraid of my anger when I was younger. Shoved all that rage and confusion behind a door. Bolted it firmly. But the army taught me I had to let it out. To be a good ranger. To live." Also, to love. "Anger isn't bad if you control it, learn how to channel it to achieve an objective." The six years he'd served, becoming a ranger, had helped make him the man he was today.

"You're one of the good ones. Like my dad, Frederick. The opposite of your father and the Brent Beckers of the world." She sipped her second margarita. "Can you believe Brent had the nerve to email me an informal invitation to his wedding?"

"After meeting that pompous jerk, I can. But the way he treated you back then and earlier today says a lot more about him and his character than it does about you." Melanie was exceptional in so many ways and it was Brent's loss for not seeing it. Waylon restrained a sigh, wishing it was at least his gain. "Besides the bonehead Brent, what was the other reason that made you leave Denver?" He finished his cola.

"In a nutshell, I was being stalked."

He nearly choked on the soda sliding down his throat. "What? Why didn't you tell me?"

"Once I left Colorado, it stopped." Her tone was casual, her demeanor nonchalant. "There was no reason to mention it to you or anyone else when we met."

"You should've told me and Holden last night. It might be relevant. Couldn't you have gotten a restraining order against the guy?"

"If it had only been one person, sure, but it was tough to get a restraining order against multiple people. Just when I thought I knew who they all were, more emerged, like cockroaches from the dark. Easier to simply leave."

An ex or a rebuffed admirer sure, but… "Multiple people?" This was starting to sound like the strangest stalking case he'd ever heard of.

"The Sand Angelites. They made me their pet project. Everywhere I went, one or more of them followed. They would pour a circle of sand around my car, sometimes leaving a bag of it near my front door. At night, they would pop up at the grocery store, in the parking garage, if I went to a restaurant, outside my house but across the street, always holding lit blue candles. Standing there, silent, staring, pointing at me. It would creep me out. But since it was in public and they never threatened me—"

"The cops couldn't do anything about those incidents," he said, finishing her sentence.

She nodded. "The last straw was when one of them broke into my home, cut himself, smeared his blood on the walls and threw sand everywhere. Isaac Meacham. I found him sitting in my living room, cross-legged, holding one of those damn blue candles. That was it for me. I gave notice at my job, sold my place, packed my bags and got out of there."

Not like Melanie to tuck her tail and run. She was a fighter. Especially when angered. Those Colter groupies must've really gotten to her.

Under the table, Waylon clenched his hand against the urge to touch her, comfort her. He hated how those people had terrorized her. "I take it you had him arrested."

"Of course. But I stopped sleeping and eating, and started wondering what would happen next." She chuckled, the sound cheerless, her face grim. "Out of all the big cases Brent stole and took to trial himself, I don't know why he didn't take that one off my hands. The one favor he could've done for me and didn't. Those Angelites made my life a living hell for months."

"Maybe the Sand Angelites are the ones who have evolved

and are escalating things. And if they are, then Kristin isn't safe around them."

"They've proven themselves to be creeps. Not killers. And Kristin is used to poking the bear, so to speak. No warning is going to stop her from taking risks."

"Poke enough bears and eventually you get mauled." He'd done enough poking as a detective to know.

Their server stopped at the table. "Can I get you two anything else?"

Melanie tapped her half-full glass. "Another margarita."

"Also, the bill and a to-go box for her," Waylon said.

Melanie didn't consume alcohol often, but when she did, she could hold her own for a woman with such a small frame. Still, he figured three margaritas should be her max since he wanted her to be lucid and able to think clearly when they got back to the room.

"No problem," the waiter said and left.

"The odds are someone is helping Colter," Waylon said. "Makes sense for it to be his groupies."

Tipping her head to the side, she pursed her lips. "Let's say it is them, doing his bidding in regard to the murders. One thing I can't wrap my head around is why would they wait until Drake Colter is released? Why not go after the people responsible for putting him in jail a year ago, two, three, when he was first convicted? Why would they deliberately implicate a man they idolize and potentially jeopardize his newfound freedom?"

Those were big questions they needed to answer.

Once they did, they'd be one step closer to catching a killer.

Chapter Eight

Three margaritas later, with Melanie putting most of her food in a to-go container, they paid the bill and left the tavern. The day had been long, draining, riddled with disastrous surprises. She needed to decompress and reset.

The only problem was her preferred method involved Waylon.

Naked. In bed.

With him, she'd made the mistake of breaking all her rules. No last names. No spending the night. No getting personal. No emotional investment.

Months of strictly sex between them had blurred together and soon she had been spending more nights with him than apart. Disentangling from him in the morning with nothing but coffee in her belly and an ache in her chest. After a year or two that had blossomed into weekends. Meals in bed. Dancing in that honky-tonk, Crazy Eddie's. Deep conversations after making love where she found it hard *not* to share. He'd not only slipped into her bed but also past her defenses, carving his way into her heart without her realizing until it was too late.

As they crossed the tavern's parking lot, she glanced over at him. Strong. Ruggedly handsome. Unequivocally hot.

Melanie wanted to feel him, skin to skin, that fierce pleasure only he could give her. But the idea of crossing the newly established line would be selfish and needy.

They walked to the corner and waited for the traffic light to change. He took her hand in his as they crossed the street. Smooth. Natural. Holding his hand was unexpectedly nice. His calluses rubbed against her skin and she liked the feel of his fingers, of him touching her, even in this small way.

Everything about Waylon, from the strength of his body to his work-worn hands, to the knife in his boot, to his protective instincts, and that compelling confidence, made it evident he was as fundamental as a cowboy could get.

And every bit as appealing.

Outside their room, Waylon wrapped a powerful arm around her waist and, spinning her back to the door, pressed his body to hers.

She put a palm to his cheek. Traced the line of the scar under his eye. Raked her gaze over the others—one bisecting his left eyebrow, a ridge on his forehead, another near his right cheekbone and on his chin. Wounds he'd gotten in a fight with Montgomery Powell when they'd been hotheaded teens. Waylon had been pushed into a trophy case and the broken glass had sliced up his face.

Now, the scars were faint, not grisly, giving him a rugged allure. Proof of his strength and good character. No matter the pain he'd suffered, the teasing he'd endured with mean kids calling him Scarface, despite the violence of his father, going to war in the army, he was a gentle, beautiful soul.

And sexy as sin.

Without a word of warning, he leaned in and captured her mouth in a hard, quick kiss that left her lips tingling and her thoughts scattered. The thrill of it shot straight down to her core. He tasted so good, the scent of him so *masculine*.

Her heart thundered, beating like a drum, and she wondered if he felt it against his chest.

She met his gaze, his warm eyes slowly softening her body and her resolve. "We talked about this." Months ago. On Christmas morning no less. After he'd shocked her with tickets for a romantic getaway. Instead of saying *yes* or giving him a gift wrapped with a red bow in return, she'd broken his heart.

"Did we?" His voice was husky and full of gravelly heat.

"Yes, and we already said everything we needed to." The boundaries had been clearly redrawn and now she wanted to erase them. But she didn't want to toy with his heart.

"As I recall, we didn't even come close." A hint of a grin danced on his lips. "You talked and I listened. To a lawyer, that might seem like a conversation. But to a cowboy, that's called a speech." The corners of his mouth hitched higher into an enigmatic smile, like he was hiding something, tempting her to peel off his clothes and figure out what it was. He gently slid the rough pads of his fingers over her cheek, his thumb stroking her bottom lip, sending a visceral ache that punched low and heavy, expanding fast and deep through muscle and bone and blood.

His gaze dropped to her mouth.

Her breath caught in her throat as the air around them stilled. A flash fire started low in her belly, but in the center of her chest was a corkscrew twist of emotion.

This here, with him, was something more. Stronger. Deeper. Scarier.

"I don't want to hurt you." When she'd told him she'd wanted space, that they needed to take an indefinite break, it had gutted her. She couldn't bear to put either of them through that again. "I don't want to cause you any more pain."

"Then don't." Leaning down, he breathed into her ear, "I can help you relax for a little bit. Give you what you need."

A shiver ran through her from her scalp to the space between her toes. If anybody could give her what she needed, this man could. He knew how to touch her, kiss her, hold her, when to talk dirty, when to be sweet. When to be rough and when to be tender.

Her thighs tingled, and she moistened her lips, debating. "You'd regret it."

"Never. I'll never regret a single moment with you." The glint of certainty in his eyes sucker-punched her heart. "Not even the ones that wound me."

It was suddenly hard for her to breathe. Where was his survival instinct when it came to her? "Why not when you should?"

"This isn't about me. It's about you. I can take your mind off things," he drawled, his voice all silky and rough at the same time. "Let me."

Melanie sure needed the escape, but as tempting as his offer was, this wasn't just one night for Waylon. He wanted more. A commitment. To go public. Marriage. A family. He wanted everything.

And she couldn't give him that. "It wouldn't be fair."

One of his big hands cupped her bottom and squeezed playfully. "Says who?"

"Me."

"All right. If it's not fair, then it's only because I have feelings you don't share." He studied her like this was some kind of test.

Her chest tightened. That couldn't be further from the truth. Her feelings for him ran deeper than he knew. She wanted him to be the one she turned to for everything, celebrate wins together, console each other through losses. Go to sleep with him, wake up beside him. She wanted to be his emergency contact, to be *his person.*

But wanting something and having it were two different things.

"It wouldn't be fair because, for me, it would only be sex." She was excellent at compartmentalization. "But for you—"

"Hold on," he said, cutting her off. "You can't speak for me, darling. Tonight, the deal is no rules. No boundaries. Forget about fair. When we make love, that kind of exchange between us doesn't get any more honest. All you have to do is take what you want." Stroking her back, his fingers playing over her spine, he looked at her, making her believe he understood everything about her.

"Waylon."

He gave her a sly grin that held way too much of a tiger's edge. Like he was on the prowl and not the one about to be used for sex.

"How about I do the taking until you tell me to stop." He claimed her mouth before she could respond, his tongue thrusting in, his other palm sliding from her waist, clasping her bottom in a two-handed grip, and grinding her closer.

Heat flamed through her body. The buzz from the margaritas mixed with the natural high Waylon always gave her had her swooning.

Maybe she could indulge and blame it on too many margaritas later.

His kiss deepened, his touch growing more urgent. Demanding.

Desire built low in her belly, coiling like a spring.

The room key jangled as he pulled it from his pocket, unlocked the door. He hauled her inside, both stumbling across the carpet.

He toed the door shut. Flipped the lock. Dropped the key.

Kissed her again, clasping the back of her neck, his fingers diving in her hair. "Need you." He angled his head for a deeper fit, long sweeps of his tongue sliding over hers. Torrid, hot, edging toward desperate. Familiar heat burned between them as his other hand tunneled under her shirt to stroke a hot path over her bare skin. "Need to be inside you."

That did it, muddling her brain and melting the last of her resistance.

Kissing him, touching him, she kept waiting for a sense of self-preservation, of warning, to kick in. For her body to stiffen, reminding her she should absolutely not do this again. Instead, her body betrayed her, arching toward Waylon like being pulled by some magnetic force.

She tossed his hat and peeled off his blazer. The T-shirt hugged well-defined muscles and well-worn jeans molded the rest of him. Clutching his sleek, sculpted biceps, she gave a low groan.

Mine.

The terrible stray thought made her heart stutter for all it implied. Possessiveness. Weakness. But she wanted him to be hers, if only for one more night. Needed every part of him. Intended to take it, yet her mind wouldn't shut down. "This is probably a mistake—"

Silencing her with a kiss, he tossed her shirt to the floor and unhooked her lace bra. "I am not a mistake."

She cringed on the inside, her eyes widening, mouth going dry. Being careful with her words, cautious with the hearts of previous lovers, had never been a concern. But Waylon was different.

"I didn't mean you," she said, putting her hand to his cheek.

"Good." He scooped her up like she weighed nothing at all, carried her to the bed and laid her crossways.

Then he climbed on top of her, the solid steel of his powerful arms braced on either side of her shoulders. All that warm muscle and delicious strength pressed against her much smaller figure. Waylon made her feel tiny, dainty. She loved the sexy contrast.

His gaze sharpened. "Stop thinking and relax." Smiling, he palmed her B-cup breast, his large hand almost enveloping her.

She shivered beneath his touch, giddy with anticipation. "Is that an order?" She ran her fingers through his thick hair, bringing his face closer until their lips were a hairsbreadth apart.

"Considering the only time that you follow them is in bed, yes." He nipped her bottom lip and kissed her, this time harder, slower. Deeper. Longer. "The first of many more tonight."

He was strong, insistent. Not the kind of man who'd treat her delicately, like she was made of porcelain. He expected and gave an uninhibited physicality. Melanie didn't have to think her way through intimacy with him. Didn't have to think at all.

Only feel. Enjoy.

She unfastened his belt buckle and lowered his zipper. "I'm all yours. Ready to please. Ready to be pleased."

He chuckled, a rich, melodic rumble that sent a bolt of wet heat between her thighs. Lifting up, he peeled her pants and underwear off. "Spread your legs." He spoke with that commanding tone she loved in the bedroom, and she did as he demanded, gladly, eagerly.

He settled between her thighs and every nerve ending in her body sparked to life.

There was lust and then there was *this*.

Need and desire and…*love*, inextricably tied together.

She slipped her hand into his boxer briefs, closing her palm around him. He gave a ragged groan, his hips flexing so that his hardness moved against her. The heady masculine scent of him sank deep into her pores. He nibbled her earlobe and trailed his mouth along the side of her neck, his warm breath making her toes curl with want.

"I've missed this," he said, capturing her wrists in one hand and pinning them above her head. His other hand slid from her breast, across her stomach, to the apex of her thighs, and she sighed at the blazing contact of his fingers, at the liquid pleasure that ran through her, arching beneath him. "Missed you."

Me, too. During their time apart, she'd grown numb, doing her best to deny the ache of loneliness.

He slid down her body until his head was between her legs and then his mouth on her, his palms on her thighs, anchoring her in place.

She gasped, now at his mercy. "Oh... *Waylon*." The chokehold of desire tightening into unbearable need made her catch back a sob. The craving for him was primal. She no longer cared about the consequences. Only wanted this. That rush from the feel of him. Waylon's mouth. His hands. His hips rolling against hers, taking her to the edge.

She whimpered, trying to hold on, not wanting to lose herself completely yet. "Wait."

"Done waiting."

Smiling, she cupped his face and tugged him up. "I want you with me."

He crawled over her again, grabbed his wallet and pulled out a condom. "This thing is ancient. Do I need it?"

They hadn't used one in two years when they'd decided unofficially to be exclusive. She hadn't been with anyone else and since he was still carrying around the same old one, she figured neither had he.

"No, you don't." She shoved the rest of his clothes down off him.

Closing her eyes, she arched her hips up to meet him as he glided in. She gasped at the sweet force of it. Her body clenched, nerves thrumming with the searing pleasure of being joined.

She and Waylon had right now.

And now had to be enough. So, she did the only thing she could. Kissed him. Held him. Laid herself bare.

For tonight.

Chapter Nine

Waylon held Melanie in his arms. Here with him, he could keep her safe.

Her head was on his chest, her arm draped across his stomach. They were sweaty and sated. Curled close around one another.

The only thing that had mattered when he made love to her was *her* pleasure, *her* well-being.

Not that it hadn't been easy for him to enjoy himself, too. Everything about Melanie spiked his hunger. Outside of bed, her bossiness was an odd kind of turn-on. In bed, her submission, her eagerness, even hotter.

Making love to her after so long undid him. Stripped him down to the marrow. Being with her again reinforced everything he felt for her. He'd do whatever it took to protect her.

This wasn't just a job, and she was more than someone he had to protect. She was everything to him, the one person on the planet who mattered most.

Waylon trailed a finger over the rise of her shoulder, down the deep dip of her waist and over the delicate curve of her hip. "I want you," he whispered, his lips against her hair.

She nuzzled her nose along the side of his neck, sliding her leg between his thighs. "You just had me, cowboy."

"From the second you walked into Crazy Eddie's, and I saw

you, it's only been you." Since their breakup, he'd managed a few dates. Nothing had made him want a second. Never any desire to sleep with other women. None had compared to Melanie. Deep down, he'd held out hope she'd come back to him. Waylon rolled on top of her, caging her with his body, because the next words out of his mouth would make her want to bolt from the bed. "When I say I want you, I mean I want us again. A real *us*."

Mel stiffened and then pushed his arm to get up.

But he didn't budge. "Don't run from me." His voice was gentle. "Or this discussion."

"You're no longer giving me orders I'm willing to follow. Get off me. I want to shower." She pushed his chest, urging him to move away, all the while writhing naked underneath him.

A confusing contrast.

He settled more of his weight on her lower body to keep her from arousing him further. "You owe me a conversation. Please, Mel."

Squeezing her eyes shut, she threw her head back against the pillow and sighed. Seconds ticked by where the sound of her uneven breathing filled the space between them. "Okay. Fine. Let's get it over with."

He gathered his thoughts. This might be his one chance to get answers. To convince her they should be together. "When you found out I was a detective with the LPD, why didn't you end things then? Why did you continue to see me?" He'd learned she was the new ADA much earlier but hadn't mentioned it or that he was a cop. Too afraid of what might happen.

Nothing scared him, except the prospect of losing her.

"When I moved to Wyoming, I figured I'd find a lover on my terms. Picking random guys up in a bar wasn't my style. You were the first and, for nine months, what I had with you was incredible. Until one of your cases landed on my desk. I should've ended it before both our hearts got any deeper entangled. I'm sorry I didn't. All right?"

A lot of words, none of which answered his question. "Not good enough."

"Just find yourself someone normal and easy. Someone to give you babies, who'll have dinner on the table for you when you get home."

Melanie was complicated, but beautiful and brilliant. One of the toughest people he knew. Getting her to see how special she was, to fight for him rather than against him, would be an uphill battle. But he wasn't a quitter.

Not when he wanted something, and he wanted Mel in his life.

"What is normal? What would I do with a woman who's easy?" Waylon had tried to move on, to forget about her, but the love he had for her never faded. "Maybe I can be the one who has supper waiting for you. Might not be home-cooked, but I can make sure it's hot." He heaved a sigh of exasperation, realizing what she was doing. "Stop trying to sidetrack me. You thought about breaking up with me sooner, but you didn't." He'd already been a goner at that point, totally hooked, craving her when they were apart. But letting their relationship bloom for three years, only to ice him out, had devastated him. "Why not? I wasn't important to you. It was only a dalliance, right?" Waylon waited for a response. "Was it a game? The forbidden fruit tasted better, huh?" He wanted to know. Needed a straight answer. "Mel."

"I didn't mean it. I only said those things to keep Holden from looking any deeper into the mystery man who'd given me flowers. Into you." She slung her forearm over her eyes like an added layer of protection. "I didn't end things with you because...because I had already fallen for you. I liked what we had. The way you made me feel. Trust is hard for me. But I trust you, completely. I care for you. I know it was selfish and reckless and risky, but I didn't want to lose you."

Shock rocketed through him, her admission echoing in his head.

But she'd thrown away their relationship so easily, so abruptly, that it had made his head spin. Her actions made even less sense now.

Then again, caring about someone didn't mean you loved them. "Look at me."

She hesitated.

"Look. At. Me."

Slowly, she slid her arm from her face and her gaze lifted to his. Tears welled in her eyes.

"I love you," he said, and she swallowed convulsively, going rigid underneath him. "I would've sworn you felt the same. That's why I bought those airline tickets to the Caribbean." Surprising her with them for Christmas had been a risk. One he'd been willing to take. They had spent three straight days together, making love, talking, eating, watching TV, all mostly in bed. Tim McGraw's "Shotgun Rider" had come on the radio. He'd taken it as a sign the time was right. Serenaded her, belting out the lyrics from his heart. The way she'd smiled, the light in her eyes, had made him certain they were meant to be. "I wanted to take things to the next level. Why did you push me away? And don't give me any garbage about your job."

Tears leaked from her eyes but her brow furrowed. "You thought I was lying?"

"I wanted a real relationship, for things to get serious, and it scared you. So, you ran from me." *Like a coward.* But he swallowed those words, sensing the insult would only derail them when he wanted their relationship back on track.

"Yes, it scared me. You were pushing me for everything. I

didn't know how to make it work and keep it a secret. We were doomed to fail eventually anyway. But I didn't lie to you. I've never been dishonest with you about anything."

"The Wyoming Rules of Professional Conduct for attorneys prohibit sex with clients but doesn't directly address whether prosecutors may have relationships with police officers working on their cases. I looked it up."

Narrowing her eyes, she punched him in the gut, hard, and shoved his chest. "Move. Let me up right this instant, Waylon Wright."

He eased off her, crawling away.

Sitting up, she scooted back until she hit the headboard. She wiped the moisture from her eyes and glared at him. "Since I started seeing you, that very issue was raised in two different cases. One in Kentucky and the other in Illinois, in sensational fashion I might add. Both with *female* prosecutors who were romantically involved with lead detectives working on cases they took to trial. One prosecutor was suspended by her office and publicly humiliated until she quit. In the other case, a judge vacated a sentence in a notorious murder and local officials called for the prosecutor's resignation. It was stated that defendants have a right to trial by a disinterested prosecutor whose vision is not clouded and an intimate relationship between a prosecuting attorney and a lead investigator is considered anything but disinterested. An emotional entanglement could keep a prosecutor from disclosing problems in a case that might embarrass the investigator, among other things." She brought her knees into her chest and wrapped her arms around her legs. "If we continued, the way you wanted, I'd have to disclose my relationship with you and ensure all the cases you're a detective on are assigned to someone else."

Perfect. There was a way for them to be together. "That's our solution. Do that."

"How about, *I'm sorry I called you a liar, Mel*?" She hopped out of the bed and folded her arms, covering her breasts. "Or try apologizing for using sex to emotionally manipulate me."

"I'm sorry I thought you lied, but what happened between us was honest. We agreed on no rules, no boundaries tonight. I'm not sorry you open up after sex, and I'm not sorry you had three margaritas." In the afterglow, with her walls lowered, when shades of vulnerability surfaced, he felt closest to her.

Her chin tucked toward her chest. "You admit it? You hatched this plan in the restaurant."

"This is the only way you talk to me." He stood and gently clasped her shoulders. Leaning in, he put his mouth to hers in a firm, quick press of his lips. She tasted warm, but her sweetness had a bite. "You're trying to sidetrack me by picking a fight." He lowered his forehead to hers. "You just told me we can be together. No more hiding, if that's what you want. Is it?"

"There is a way, but it comes at a cost. To me. One that impacts my career and not yours." She jerked loose from his grip. "One that limits me and not you. One that exposes me to public scrutiny, as a woman, in a manner that you will never experience. Those women had their sex lives dissected in the media, with former lovers, who weren't even relevant to those cases, giving comments about them. The worst you'd endure is a bunch of high-fives from some of the guys on the force for sleeping with the ADA." She shook her head, her features twisted in misery, as though he had asked the unthinkable. "I want to be the district attorney someday. I've worked incredibly hard for it. But that won't happen if I declare to the world we've been sleeping together and have to recuse myself from your future cases. All your previous cases that I've prosecuted could be looked at and reopened. Criminals could walk free."

"You're picking your career over us?" This spark, this connection, didn't happen every day. Hell, he wanted to marry her. Spend the rest of his days with her.

"Don't you get it? I'm the one who has to choose. The one who has to sacrifice something. Not you."

"I'm not asking you to sacrifice. But I am asking, how do you feel about me? Do you love me?"

"This isn't helpful." Melanie lowered her head. "I don't want to do this."

Maybe that was his answer. Or the only one he'd get from her.

"You're a selfish coward." He spoke the words without thinking, but she needed to hear it. "I've done everything in my power to get you to fall in love with me, to fight for us. In an alternate universe, perhaps, you would." He wished she would simply tell him that she didn't love him and put him out of his misery. "But we're not in that multiverse timeline. We're in this one, where you make the rules and I just have to live with them."

Her gaze lifted to his. "That's not fair."

"Yeah, well, it's the truth."

Turning away from him, she grabbed her things. "I'm going to shower and get dressed. It's late. Kristin should be back at her room by now or sometime soon."

Melanie marched to the bathroom and slammed the door.

Dropping to the bed, Waylon scrubbed his hands over his face. Frustration welled in his chest. That conversation had not gone as he had hoped.

What bothered him the most was he'd told her he loved her. Not just tonight but also on Christmas. Flat-out asked her how she felt this time and she never said those three little words back.

He snatched his boxer briefs from the floor, put them on, grabbed his jeans and shoved his legs in. By the time the shower stopped, he was fully dressed, cowboy hat on his head. He sat on the bed, waiting for her.

The lump of his wallet in his back pocket reminded him of a conversation he'd had with Chance Reyes, a lawyer who had been involved in a high-profile case he'd worked on in December that had centered around Monty Powell as the prime suspect. The situation had taken a deadly twist and Waylon had ended up helping rescue Chance's sister, who had been kidnapped.

Waylon took out his wallet, removed the embossed business card on textured card stock, and stared at the printed words: Ironside Protection Services.

On the back, handwritten, was the direct personal line of the owner. The company had offices from the Rocky Mountains to the Great Plains. Chance had told the founder of the company, Rip Lockwood, about him, sang his praises, and extended an offer of employment if Waylon was ever interested. He had dismissed it. Recently, he'd been promoted to the rank of lieutenant. His reputation was unimpeachable. He had a home at the LPD.

Not being a law enforcement officer, starting over from the bottom, working his way up, proving himself to new people, hadn't been something he wanted.

Still wasn't.

But Melanie was right. Why did she have to be the one to sacrifice?

He needed to figure out what he wanted more. His home with the LPD. Or to be with Melanie. A woman determined to push him away. He didn't even know whether she loved him, and if she did, would it be enough? Would she ever put him first in her life, ahead of her ambition? Would she ever find balance between her job and having a family?

Did she even want to when she thought they were *doomed to fail*?

The bathroom door opened. Steam wafted out, followed by Melanie. "Ready to go?" Her tone strictly business.

He slipped the card in his wallet, shoved it in his pocket and opened the door for her as his answer.

As they walked to the outdoor staircase, she pointed to a beat-up old pickup truck parked between the ice machine and the stairs. "That's Kristin's truck. Wonder how long she's been back. I hope she wasn't afraid to call, thinking we fell asleep."

He put his hand on the hood. "It's cool. She's been back for a while. Maybe she was tired and decided to wait until the morning."

"Only one way to find out."

They made their way to the second floor and headed down the walkway.

The door to Room 204 was ajar. He put his hand out, stopping Melanie and putting her behind him. "Wait here." Drawing his weapon, he nudged the door wide open with his boot. "Kristin Loeb? It's Detective Wright and ADA Merritt. Are you in here?"

He stepped inside. The curtains were drawn. Moonlight cascading in from the open door provided the only light. Scanning the room, he took in the signs of a struggle. Broken lamp. Bedspread askew. One sandal on the carpet beside a cell phone. He crept around to the other side of the bed.

His gaze fell to a circle of sand. Two feet in diameter with an impression of an angel in the center. He ran to check the bathroom, only to confirm what he already knew.

Cursing, he hung his head as anger stabbed his chest. He stepped out of the bathroom and glanced at Melanie. "I think he's taken her. Call 9-1-1."

Chapter Ten

The Mile-High City Motel buzzed with activity, swarming with the police.

Melanie stood beside Waylon, along with Detective Stoltz from the Denver PD, who she wasn't familiar with, and watched the replay of the surveillance footage outside the motel.

Kristin pulled into the lot at ten forty. A white cargo van followed close behind. The driver parked two spots down from her truck and watched her walk to her room, then repositioned in front of the staircase. The license plate had been removed, but at least they could tell that it wasn't the same type of vehicle as the passenger van used by the FCTC.

A man dressed in black, wearing a motorcycle helmet, climbed out. He had on a backpack, probably containing the sand and doll he'd used to make the angel impression. Taking the steps two at a time, he hurried up to the second floor. He put his gloved left hand up to the peephole, blocking the view, and knocked with his right hand.

Kristin opened the door, almost without delay. He hit her, knocking her backward, deeper into the room, and stalked inside, shutting the door behind him.

"Wonder why she just let him in like that?" the detective

said. "Without verifying who it was, especially since it was so late."

"She probably thought it was us knocking on the door." Melanie wrapped her arms around herself. Guilt gnawed at her. She and Waylon had been making love and arguing, distracted, when they should've been focused, on the lookout for Kristin. "We were supposed to meet up to discuss a lead she was following. Share information."

Now the killer had her. Because Melanie had indulged herself with Waylon.

On the playback, minutes later, the man carried Kristin out of the room, along with her messenger bag.

"All her notes, her digital voice recorder, her laptop was in that bag," Melanie said. "Kristin carried that stuff with her everywhere." Inside the room, they hadn't found any of her tapes or notebooks. Kristin only used a particular kind, leather hardcover in sky-blue, with an elastic band. She always had them on her.

"The last people to see Kristin Loeb were the Sand Angelites," Waylon said. "Either one of them followed her to the motel or they told whoever did where to find her."

"I'm not so sure." Melanie looked between the two detectives. "Kristin went to the press conference. The killer could have been there. He could've been following her since she left Pagosa Springs for all we know, if it's not Drake Colter."

The Denver detective stared at her with pity in his eyes, making her self-conscious of her black eye and the other disturbing marks on her face and neck. She wished she had purchased makeup from the drugstore to cover her bruises, but she hadn't been thinking of it at the time.

"We need to speak with the Angelites," Waylon said. "Do you know where to find them?"

"I have an address that was good three years ago." Melanie

gave it to them. "Isaac Meacham owns the house. He inherited it from his father, along with a lot of money."

"Let's go talk to them. Find out what they discussed with Kristin," Waylon said. "On the way, can you give your Denver PD friend a call and see if Colter is at the FCTC?"

Javier Jimenez was a dedicated cop, currently watching the house.

"Hold your horses." Detective Stoltz raised a palm. "This is outside your jurisdiction, Wright, but you're welcome to accompany me to question the Angelites."

"I'm not going with you," Melanie said, and Waylon narrowed his eyes, probably sensing she was up to something. He knew her better than she liked at times. "I don't want to be anywhere near the Meacham house or the Angelites." Those people, with their gypsum necklaces, blue candles and spooky stares terrorized her, had driven her out of Denver. Their actions hadn't been violent, but they had been insidious and sinister. "I'll call JJ so he can make sure Colter's at the center, but then I'll head over to the FCTC so the two of us can question Kurt Parrish while I'm there."

She also needed to speak with Drake Colter. Alone.

That wasn't something Waylon was going to allow. As much as she tried to educate him about how he couldn't stop her from doing anything, the truth was, when he set his mind to a goal, including restricting her actions, nothing could deter him.

He had an iron will as formidable as hers.

Colter knew a lot more and had gone so far as to taunt them with the fact. If Waylon wasn't with her, that madman would think he had the upper hand and might let something vital slip.

She had to do this. For Kristin's sake.

"I don't like it." Waylon's voice was firm, his gaze drilling into hers. "Better if we stick together."

"Kristin is running out of time. Based on the last three victims, he'll keep her alive for twelve, maybe fourteen, hours before he kills her. It'll be faster if we split up. You know I'm right."

Waylon took her arm by the elbow and steered her across the room to a corner. "He's got Kristin," he said in a harsh whisper. "I can't let him get you, too." The affection in his voice tore at her heart.

After they'd found Kristin's empty motel room where the sand angel had been left on the floor as a message, Waylon hadn't hesitated to hold her, console her, as they'd waited for the police. Now, he was determined as ever to still protect her.

People often said a lot of things in the heat of an argument like the one they'd had earlier. But what a person did after was what really mattered. And when they did something meant to help someone else, without thinking about how it could benefit them, it resonated.

Waylon's actions, despite how she'd pushed him away touched her.

He was different than other men she had been involved with. What they shared was different, too. A far contrast from any of the carefully structured failed relationships she'd experienced.

"Kristin is alive," she said. "We have to do everything we can to save her. There are ten officers outside. I'm sure two of them can give me a ride to the FCTC. I'll stay with my friend until you pick me up or they take me to you. I won't be alone. I'll be fine."

His gaze hardened. "I still don't like it. A couple of beat cops playing chauffeur is one thing, but protecting you is something else, and I don't know this JJ."

"He's a competent, seasoned detective in a dangerous city

with one of the highest homicide rates," she pointed out, willing to go so far as to list his commendations.

"That may be, but how do I know he isn't going to roll over for you, following any order you give him, no matter how reckless?" Waylon asked, raising an eyebrow like he sensed her plan. "Where you go, I go, remember."

Another tug on her heart. "We need to find Kristin before it's too late. If we don't, I'll never forgive myself." She put her hands on his chest. An affectionate gesture she never would've dared to risk doing in front of an officer back at home, but in Colorado the same scrutiny didn't apply. She needed Waylon not to fight her on this. "The clock is ticking. We don't have time to waste. It'll be faster if we separate. Divide and conquer," she said, pleading with her eyes. "This isn't about JJ. This is about you trusting me."

He considered her for a moment and finally nodded, albeit reluctantly. "We check in with each other. Every twenty minutes. Text, phone call, something."

"Okay."

His brow still creased with worry. "Do you have one of your AirTags in this purse?"

"No." She'd opted for a Kate Spade leather bag, simple with a strap long enough for her to wear cross-body. It only cost two hundred dollars. Not thousands like some of her others. "But I've got my key chain that has one."

"Mind if I link it to my phone?"

She was willing to do whatever he wanted to put his mind at ease. "Not at all." She took it out of her purse to make pairing easier. After opening the Find My app on her own phone, she tapped the items tab, selected the AirTag located on her key chain and, under the share section, clicked on Add Person.

The rest was relatively straightforward and the process

only took a couple of minutes. Now, he'd be able to track her in the event of a worst-case scenario.

Waylon turned to the other detective. "I need two officers to give her a ride to the Fair Chance Treatment Center. They need to stay with her until I get there, or they bring her to me."

Detective Stoltz nodded. "For the former ADA, I can make that happen. You put away a lot of bad guys, ma'am. At great personal risk, I might add. I remember hearing about what those Sand Angelites did to you. Horrible the way they harassed you. The least the Denver PD can do is keep you safe while you're back."

"Thank you," she said. It was nice to have her efforts recognized.

"Also, the perpetrator likes to leave his victims in sand dunes," Waylon said. "We need to have local authorities patrolling all of them throughout the state for the next twenty-four hours."

"That's a good idea." If the murderer couldn't access the dunes, it might buy Kristin more time.

Waylon bent down, pulled a revolver from the ankle holster hidden in his boot. "Take my BUG," he said, using the acronym for his backup gun, and handed it to her.

Melanie tucked the Smith & Wesson in her purse. She'd never been comfortable with guns until Waylon had insisted that she knew how to handle one properly and learn to shoot in case of an emergency.

With everything going on, being attacked at her job, the sand left on her doorstep and now Kristin kidnapped, this counted as an emergency. She was glad for the knowledge and the gun.

"Every twenty minutes," he said, reminding her.

"I'll be sure to check in. You do the same."

When Waylon had gotten overly protective of her in front

of Colter, he had not only exposed himself but also the fact they were in a relationship or, at the bare minimum, that he had feelings for her. No telling who that killer had contacted and what details he had shared.

For all they knew, Colter considered Waylon a threat.

If he did, it would now make them both targets.

TWENTY MINUTES LATER, she was at the Fair Chance Treatment Center. She'd already fired off a text to Waylon and was speaking with Detective Javier Jimenez when she got a response.

Waylon: We're pulling up to the Sand Angelites house now. It's dark. They're either asleep, want to give that impression or aren't in there.

Waylon had taken his truck and followed behind Detective Stoltz. They'd wanted to get on the road and head back home once finished since they wouldn't be able to speak with Kristin.

Another chime.

Waylon: Be safe. Stay with the detective.

Melanie considered a reply but couldn't come up with an honest one that wouldn't raise his suspicion. Waylon had sharp instincts and a keen insight into her. Lying to him wasn't feasible. She'd only take the chance if she was willing to deal with his ire.

She chose no response as the best one and put her phone in her purse, leaving the handbag unzipped to give her easy access to the gun inside.

"No one has left the house since eight," Detective Javier Jimenez said as they spoke in front of FCTC. "At least, not from where I could see. Using the back alley is a possibility. As soon as I got your text about Kristin Loeb disappearing from her motel room, I checked. Drake Colter was in there. The motel is less than fifteen minutes away from here, with no traffic. It's possible he stashed her somewhere and made it back inside before I could verify that he was in the house."

They hadn't discovered Kristin was missing until eleven twenty. More than enough time for Colter to be the culprit.

"Of course, Drake Colter denies having any knowledge of what happened to Loeb," he said.

"Of course." Melanie shook her head, disgusted with the fact that a convicted murderer was on the loose and very well taking more innocent lives. "JJ, I hope they're paying you overtime for this."

"I wish." A half smile highlighted the wrinkles in his tan face. "My bigger concern is my wife. She's not happy with the extra hours on this now that we have two little ones."

Melanie patted his shoulder. She had no idea how he managed to juggle it all. Marriage, kids and this job. This work sucked away a small piece of one's soul. Took up most of their time and exposed them to the depths of darkness many civilians couldn't fathom.

Her thoughts careened back to Waylon. He understood her, accepted her in a way few ever had, including her parents. Unlike a lot of men she'd dealt with, he wasn't threatened by her confidence or blunt style. What they had was rare, but how could they ever make it work? Something would have to give for them to be together. Or more like *someone*. The prospect of her being the one to do the giving made her heart hurt. But the last several months without Waylon had been awful.

"What's the key to success? Is your wife a stay-at-home mom?"

"Nope. She's an ER nurse. The key is flexibility. Recognizing that we're not superheroes and getting lots of help. Her mom fills in when she can. Our siblings pitch in, too. The kids are with her sister tonight since my wife has a shift. It takes a village, right?"

"I suppose it does."

Melanie was an only child. Her parents were wealthy enough to bounce between the United States, Great Britain and India. Even if they lived closer, they weren't the pitch-in sort. She'd practically grown up in a boarding school, getting the best education their money could buy.

Waylon's family sounded warm and tight-knit, but no longer lived nearby.

Not that any of it mattered. She was the ADA and he was a top detective with the LPD. No point going down this rabbit hole. Some things weren't meant to be.

"Any updates in getting more eyes on the FCTC and Drake Colter," she said, refocusing the conversation to the business at hand.

"Since Kristin Loeb is now missing, the request to have more bodies on the FCTC will be fast-tracked. We should have four officers posted around the clock within forty-eight hours."

That was a spot of good news. If only it took less time. "I'm going to go in. Talk to Parrish and Colter."

"I'll go with you. I told them to expect more questions tonight."

Having a detective at her side hadn't worked out earlier. She needed to do things differently. "I'd prefer it if you hung back out here."

JJ frowned. "Drake Colter is only out of prison because of a technicality. The man is dangerous."

"He is." Two simple irrefutable facts. "But he also likes his freedom. He's not going to lay a finger on me inside with you waiting for me out here." If for some reason she was wrong, then she had the revolver in her purse. "I think I can get more information out of him this way."

"Sure?" His skeptical tone indicated he was unconvinced her strategy was worth the risk.

"I'm sure." Even though she was aware Waylon would hate the idea. But he wasn't there to stop her.

"Have it your way, but I'll be right by the door, where I can hear every single word in case you need backup."

"All right." She went up to the front door with JJ. "When you questioned Parrish tonight, did you do it inside the house?"

"Yeah, why?"

"If he's helping Colter sneak out, I doubt he'd be likely to confess where Colter could be eavesdropping. I'll talk to him again down on the sidewalk. You hang by the door then. Okay?"

"Sure." JJ shrugged. "Let's try it."

Waylon was right. She pushed for what she wanted and everyone fell into line. The only one to ever push back and stand his ground was him.

Smiling at the realization, she rang the bell.

The door opened and she came face-to-face with a man. Casually dressed in an open button-down plaid shirt over a cotton tee. Neatly trimmed dark hair and a mustache.

"Kurt Parrish, this is former Denver ADA Melanie Merritt," JJ said.

The man looked to be in his early forties, stood about five-ten or close to it, and was on the heavier side. His gaze roamed over her face. "What happened to you? Are you okay?"

"I was attacked. Possibly by Drake Colter, but most certainly by someone he knows."

Parrish's mouth twisted, his brow furrowing. "How can I help you?"

"I'd like to ask you a few questions. Would you mind stepping outside?" Without waiting for him to answer, she turned around and headed down the stairs.

The door creaked behind her and footsteps followed.

She waited for Parrish to join her on the sidewalk.

"I already told the detective over there that Drake Colter has been here all night," he said quickly.

"Yeah, I know. For all your shifts, Colter has been here. Present and accounted for."

"Exactly. That's right. I don't know what else I could tell you." He folded his arms across his chest and rubbed his chin.

"The truth. For starters." She eyed him, and Parrish opened his mouth to protest, but she continued. "Colter isn't finished with his hit list. The woman who was kidnapped tonight is on it. Along with myself. It's a matter of time before there'll be plenty of eyes on this house. Now is the time to come clean. To tell us the truth while we can still help you find a way out of this. Because detectives are going to start investigating you next."

"Me?" Parrish rocked back on his heels, his eyes growing wide as saucers. "But why? I haven't done anything wrong."

"Maybe. Right now, you're not the one in trouble. But I'm not sure it's going to stay that way."

Parrish raked a hand through his dark hair and flicked an uneasy glance back at the house.

JJ stood on the porch, keeping an eye on her as well as the foyer inside the FCTC.

"If Drake Colter has been leaving this house at night," she said, "and you've been covering it up for him, we're going to find out. It won't take much to get a search warrant and have a techie examine the digital record of your security system."

"We've had some problems with the system." He licked his lips and rubbed his chin again. "It's an old system that needs to be replaced. Everything that's happened with it lately is typical stuff. No one's fault. You can ask Hershel. He'll tell you the same thing."

Rambling, saying too much, was a key sign someone was lying. Either Kurt Parrish had tampered with the security system or he'd let Drake Colter meddle with it to hide his comings and goings.

"So I've heard. I bet those problems occurred on the same nights that women disappeared and were murdered. I'll go so far as to predict that it even happened tonight. If I'm right, it won't look good for you," she said, and his gaze dropped, bouncing around, like a man with something to hide, one trying to figure out what to do and say next. "This is a matter of life and death, Mr. Parrish. Time is running out for Kristin Loeb, who was taken tonight, and for you if you're helping Colter. Once we have evidence that you're lying, that you're aiding and abetting a serial killer, then you become an accomplice to murder. Then the DA's office will bring you up on charges, throw the book at you, and ensure you're doing time behind bars along with your close buddy, Drake Colter. You won't be shown any leniency."

Biting his bottom lip, Parrish blanched and looked almost sick. Glancing up at her, he folded his button-down shirt around himself. In the next breath, he smoothed it out again.

The movements were born of nerves, a way of stalling, giving himself time to think.

Melanie didn't rush him. She stayed still and quiet, studying him.

This was the moment where impatient cops and ADAs messed up by talking. Better to let him fill in the uneasy silence. Hopefully, with a confession.

"You're right, this is a matter of life and death, but I've got nothing else to say." Parrish's voice was shaky, his gaze refusing to focus. “I wish I could help you but…” Grimacing, he shook his head. “I can’t. I’m sorry.”

Parrish wasn’t simply nervous. He was scared.

“We can protect you from him.” She gestured toward the house with her head. “Keep you safe if you’re worried telling us the truth will endanger you.”

Parrish hesitated. Then he closed his eyes, squeezed his hands together and shook his head.

“Just talk to me,” she said. “I can help get you immunity, but you’ve got to give me something to work with. Now, before Kristin Loeb is murdered.”

“You can’t help me.” Opening his eyes, Parrish looked at her. Fear etched across his pale face. “I didn’t do anything wrong. Drake Colter was here tonight and every night I’ve been on shift. Please leave me alone.” He spun around and hurried up the steps, disappearing into the house.

Melanie released the breath she’d been holding along with her hope that Kurt Parrish would’ve caved so easily. She swore under her breath, berating herself for not pushing him harder. Kurt Parrish had cracked a little, letting his vulnerability show, but she’d needed him to break.

Looking at the Fair Chance Treatment Center, she couldn’t afford to make the same mistake with Drake Colter.

Chapter Eleven

A Sand Angelite had finally opened the door, letting them into a surprisingly spacious entryway in the two-story Tudor-style house. The woman was young. Appeared to be no older than twenty-six, maybe twenty-seven. Probably still got carded in a bar. Blonde. Green eyes. Tall. Pretty. A shapely figure on display in a formfitting tank top, sans bra, and a tiny pair of shorts that left little to the imagination. She would've been his type before meeting Melanie.

Her name was Luna Tuttle. The woman showed them into the living room. She turned on a lamp and lit several blue candles, bending over seductively to do so, hoisting her bottom up in the air to draw their attention. Stoltz was captivated by her while Waylon chose to take in the modest décor of the room instead. She lit incense, a mix of patchouli and something cloyingly sweet. Then she left them and went to wake the others.

Stoltz and Waylon waited, his thoughts revolving around Mel. He reassured himself that she was with three officers, one of whom was a detective that she considered to be a friend. A pro and a con on that point. Whether or not JJ would roll over to her demands wasn't the issue. Trust was, and he needed to have some in her.

Melanie was competent, capable and armed.

She'll be fine.

Still, he was anxious to get through this and get back to her. Seeing her, touching her, being in her presence, was the only thing that would truly ease his nerves.

Finally, all the Angelites had gathered in the living room and they could speak with them.

"This is Isaac Meacham," Luna said, introducing the last one to enter.

The deranged man who had broken into Mel's home and stripped away her peace of mind. He was around Drake Colter's age, mid to late thirties. With long curly hair and wearing a sky-blue tunic that matched the stone the entire group had either dangling around their necks or affixed to a bracelet, flowy linen pants and barefoot, he looked like his picture should be in a dictionary beside the definition of a cult leader.

Bringing his hands into a Namaste position in front of his chest, Isaac said, "What can we do for you at this late hour, Officers?"

"Detectives," Stoltz said, clarifying. He took out something to jot down notes. "Is this everyone?" Using his pen, he pointed around the room at the seven individuals huddled together. "Your entire group?"

"Our entire family is not present this evening," Isaac said. His voice gentle, his tone almost welcoming.

"How many of you are there?" Waylon asked, eyeing him.

Isaac smiled. "We are legion for we are many."

"Oh, brother," Stoltz said, taking the words from Waylon's lips. "So, would you say that's what...about ten? Twenty?"

Isaac shrugged. "It's hard to quantify legion."

Rolling his eyes, Waylon sighed. "Mr. Meacham, was Kristin Loeb here this evening?"

"She was."

Stoltz clicked the top button on his retractable ballpoint pen. "What did you discuss?"

"She asked questions and I answered them."

"What questions specifically?" Waylon pressed.

"There were so many, I don't recall." Isaac appeared bored or utterly serene, not a care in the world. "Perhaps you should ask Ms. Loeb."

"Unfortunately, we can't," Waylon said. "She was kidnapped earlier." He let that dangle, taking in their reactions. Bland. Unsurprised. Not a single one of them so much as batted a lash at the news. "You wouldn't happen to know anything about that, would you?"

"Why would I?" Isaac said, answering the question with another. "Or any of us, for that matter."

Stoltz cleared his throat. "Did you or any of your Angelites," the detective said, waving his pen around at the group, "have anything to do with her kidnapping?"

"We did not. My family, here before you, are peaceful. We do not inflict harm on others. We pride ourselves on being pacifists."

The specificity of the way he spoke struck Waylon as odd.

"Any idea why someone would want to kidnap her?" Stoltz asked.

Isaac clasped the blue stone sitting on his sternum between his thumb and index finger. "Ms. Loeb was an investigative journalist sticking her nose in all sorts of troubling things. Perhaps she was onto a story that angered the wrong person. Perhaps she was a sinner in need of redemption. Perhaps it was fate. I do not know. I suppose the only person who can say with any real certainty is the one who took her."

Shaking his head, Stoltz gave Waylon a look that screamed, *Can you believe this BS?*

The other Angelites either stood with their hands clasped or sat cross-legged on the carpet, all with unaffected expressions.

Stoltz jotted down the response from Isaac that didn't answer any of their questions. "What time did Kristin Loeb leave your house?"

"I'm not certain." Isaac eyed the little spiral notepad with a wary look. "We invited her to break bread with us. She left sometime after she was finished eating dinner." Isaac glanced around at the others. "Does anyone remember?"

"Eight thirty," Luna said quickly and Stoltz made a note.

Waylon studied her. "How can you be sure of the time?"

"She wanted to be somewhere before nine. I remember thinking she only had thirty minutes and needed to hurry."

If that was true, then the Sand Angelites might not have been the last ones to see and speak with Loeb. "She was pursuing something regarding a Savior. Or a Savior connection. Does that mean anything to any of you?"

The gaze of every Angelite swung to Isaac and they waited. It was the first time they'd done that. After the other questions, their attention had stayed focused on either Waylon or Stoltz.

This Savior thing meant something.

Isaac shook his head. "We have no idea what was going through her head. I wish we could be of more assistance."

Waylon seriously doubted that. "Have you or anyone in your *family* been in contact with Drake Colter?"

"Drake is with us at all times. In here," Isaac said, touching his forehead, "and here." He put a hand over his heart.

Waylon restrained a sigh. Frustration nipped at his nerves. "Did you visit him in prison?"

"The only true prison is that of the human body. A cage that falls to the wayside, turning to dust when we transcend from this world into the next."

Stoltz scratched his head. "What about since his release?"

he asked, sounding equally as exasperated as Waylon felt. “Have you seen him in person, spoken to him on the phone?”

“His release was cause for celebration.” Isaac held his hands out, palms up, a soft smile on his face. “We’ve all seen him to rejoice.”

“When?” A hint of excitement made Stoltz’s voice rise in pitch as he turned the page in his notebook. “And where?” The detective waited with his pen poised above the paper.

“In the sacred space where the sands of time flow,” Isaac said. “There we can see him, speak to him, connect with his spirit whenever we choose.”

The other detective’s shoulders sagged and he muttered something under his breath.

This was going nowhere. “Let’s try this another way.” Waylon tamped down his frustration and turned to Stoltz. “I’ll take one outside. You grab another to question in the kitchen. Yeah?”

“Yeah. Otherwise this will take all night.” Stoltz pointed to a frail-looking young man. “You, kid, what’s your name?”

“Jovian.”

“Show me to the kitchen. The rest of you stay here.” The two headed off.

Before Waylon had a chance to single someone out, Luna Tuttle tapped his forearm, drawing his attention. “I wish to be of service. This way.” She gestured for him to follow her and led him from the room, down the main hall in the opposite direction of the front door.

“Where are we going?”

Wide-eyed, she lifted a finger to her mouth and cast a wary glance back at the living room. Once they were further down the hall, she whispered, “There’s something I need to show you. Away from the others." Her serene expression was gone. The young woman now looked spooked.

With groups like the Angelites, separating them and speaking confidentially tended to produce better results. Sometimes there was a weak link in the chain that could be broken; someone disgruntled, afraid, willing to talk once free of the scrutiny of the group.

Luna turned down a side hall, leading him to the first door on the left. "It's in here. In my room." Opening a door, not too far from the entryway, she waved him inside with urgency.

The bedroom was bathed in candlelight. More cloying incense smacked him in the face, making him gag.

"This is an old house," she said. "The walls are thick. No one will overhear us in here." She hurriedly closed the door behind him.

"What did you need to show me?"

She padded over to a dresser near the door, opened the top drawer and took something out.

A small, sky-blue notebook. Leather-bound. Elastic band around it.

"It's Miss Loeb's."

Waylon took the notebook and thumbed through it. Lots of notes about the legal technicality that had resulted in Colter's release. Details from the press conference DA Jerk had given. Kristin had either watched it or had been there in person, which would've made sense since she'd driven up from Pagosa Springs. Notes on Isaac Meacham. The Angelites. The last thing written in the notebook was Meacham circled twice with an arrow drawn to Drake Colter. After that, several pages had been ripped out.

"Where did you get this?" he asked.

"Isaac gave it to me for safekeeping."

"Why give it to you?"

She shrugged, blank-eyed, a docile look on her face. "He often asks us to do things that require trust with no explanation."

"Did you tear out any pages from the notebook?"

"No. That's how I received it."

Slipping the notebook in his pocket, he moved to the other side of the room near the window, taking in her room. "Do you have any idea what this Savior connection that Ms. Loeb was interested in could be?"

"Drake Colter is a savior of sorts. Freeing sinners from this wicked world." She sashayed toward him slowly. "And Isaac is a different kind of savior. He found me living on the streets, addicted to drugs. He cleaned me up and gave me a home. A family. Saved me from the darkness inside myself. From the darkness in the world," Luna said, reinforcing the reasons for her to be loyal to the Angelites, making him wonder why she would betray Meacham's trust. "Maybe that's what she meant."

Doubtful. Whatever the connection, it wouldn't be straightforward and irrelevant. Loeb had stumbled onto something important. "Did Meacham ever visit Colter in prison?"

She eased closer, her beguiling manner, the candlelight and the bed making him uneasy. "I don't know. Isaac doesn't report to us."

"Did he ever give any of you orders that he said were directly from Drake Colter, on his behalf, or to help him in any way?"

"Isaac does not command us." Closing the distance between them, Luna invaded his personal space and he staggered backward into a corner. "He shepherds. Guides us to our purpose. Humbly asks for our service." Two more steps and she brought her body flush against his, her breasts brushing his chest.

"Whoa." He raised his hands, avoiding any inadvertent physical contact on his part, and scooted around her, putting several feet between them. "No touching, miss."

"What's wrong, Detective?" A guileful smile played on her lips. "I saw the way you looked at me after I let you in." Her innocent demeanor evaporated like smoke clearing. The woman was a chameleon, going from acolyte, to scared cultist, and now flirty minx. "Your spirit called mine. I was listening and I heard."

"There was no calling of anything to anyone." He'd been taken off guard by her skimpy attire, but he hadn't ogled, had kept his gaze above her neck and his focus solely on the job. "This is a misunderstanding."

"I don't think so. You're a man and I'm a woman. I can tell you're attracted to me. Your body is calling to mine. I'm an open vessel, willing to receive you. Rather than chase your tail in the darkness, why don't we commune without words instead." She pulled her tank top over her head and tossed it to the bed.

Waylon's pulse spiked as he averted his gaze. "We're done here. Go back to the living room." Spinning on his heel, he opened the door and hustled down the hall, looking for the other detective. "Stoltz!"

"In here."

Waylon followed his voice and the bright light to the kitchen, where he found the detective and the frail guy, thankfully, still clothed.

"You are the instrument of true violence," Jovian said, rubbing the stone attached to the bracelet on his right wrist. "Only when a sinner is released from the prison of their vessel can they begin to atone on a higher plane and find redemption. I cannot help you because you are lost in darkness. Destined to run in circles, blindly chasing your tail. Go in peace." Putting his hands in Namaste, he gave a slight bow and left the kitchen.

Stoltz turned to Waylon with a perplexed look. "Did you do any better?"

"The girl took off her top and asked to commune with me. Without words."

The detective's eyebrows shot up. "Why doesn't that kind of thing ever happen to me?"

"Consider yourself lucky." The detective would have to include that in a report whereas Waylon didn't have to worry about paperwork since this was technically on his personal time. He scrubbed a hand over his face, the ick factor about the incident with Luna Tuttle still bothering him, making him feel dirty, even though he hadn't done anything inappropriate. "I did get this from her," he said, handing over the notebook, "but I want to take pictures of the pages that are left."

"Left?"

"Several were ripped out." His guess was those pages contained the link they were looking for. "These Colter cultists aren't going to cooperate."

He took out his phone to check in with Melanie. They'd exceeded the twenty-minute mark. Easy for them both to get caught up and sidetracked while investigating. He refused to worry prematurely. It'd only anger her. He'd send a text and wait no longer than two minutes for a response. Then he'd worry.

"You're probably right," Stoltz said, "but we've got to question the rest of them."

True, but precious time would be wasted. They had to go about this in a different way.

Starting with getting a list of Drake Colter's visitors at the prison in Florence and copies of all the mail he received.

Chapter Twelve

Melanie finished collecting her thoughts and composed herself before heading to meet JJ at the front door. Another text came in.

Waylon: Only getting cultish drivel from these crackpots. Hope you're having better luck.

Taking a breath, she messaged him back. Let you know in a few minutes.

"Colter is waiting for you in the foyer," JJ said. "I'll be right here, and we're keeping the door open."

A tingle along the back of her neck urged her to use caution. She slipped the strap of her purse over her head, wearing it cross-body, and ensured the handle of the gun was within easy reach. She needed to push Colter as hard as possible. Regardless of the personal risk. It might be the only way to save Kristin.

Steeling herself, she stepped inside, closing the door enough to obscure JJ from Colter's sight, but cracked open so that the detective could overhear the conversation.

"ADA Melanie Merritt, you're back sooner than I expected." He stood leaning against the back wall, dressed in dark slim-cut jeans, a black long-sleeved Henley, with his hands in his pockets. His eyes narrowed. "Your face looks like it's been through a meat grinder. Your neck, too. Does it hurt?"

She noticed he didn't ask what happened. "Looks worse than it feels, but pain is fleeting," she said, wishing again that she'd purchased makeup.

"Perhaps that of the body, but what about the soul? It must hurt you, deep down, to keep losing people you collaborated with. People I can only presume are being killed because you tried my case with such vehemence. Not that I would know the perpetrator's true motives."

"Just a guess on your part, huh?"

A smug look crossed his face. "I see you took my advice and didn't bring the big fella, Detective Waylon Wright. Not that it isn't possible to bring a big guy such as him to heel. By the way, where is he?"

"Busy following a lead."

"I bet he's busy all right. Maybe he's found a pretty young thing, a lot warmer than you, to keep him occupied," he said and she tensed—an unexpected reflex. "But how is he supposed to keep you safe if he isn't here?"

Colter had shaved and showered since the last time she'd seen him. His hair no longer looked greasy, but clean. He had deceptive surfer-boy good looks. In the simple attire that could've come off the rack of Banana Republic or any upscale clothing store, he looked like a nice guy. The friendly next-door neighbor.

But she knew better. A monster lurked behind that cleaned-up veneer.

"I can take care of myself," she said, her tone conversational, and put a steady hand on her purse.

"Bet plenty of dead women said the same thing before they underestimated the wrong person. I wonder how many."

The words rattled her, making her wonder, too, for a second. "Tell me, do you often sleep in jeans and long sleeves in the summer?" she asked, needing to regain control of the line of questioning.

"I'm flattered you want to know what I sleep in, ADA Merritt. Would you like to come back to my bedroom, take a private peek at my pajama drawer, and get to know one another better on a first-name basis?"

"I'll pass, but I'm sure Detective Jimenez would be interested in having a look."

A half grin tugged at his mouth. "I changed my clothes and put this on after Kurt woke me from a *deep sleep* to let me know the cops were here. I heard Kristin Loeb is missing. Wish I could say it's such a shame, but I didn't particularly care for her."

"Did you take her?"

"I don't understand how that would be possible." His devilish eyes gleamed with amusement. "I've been here all night."

"Then you know who did, don't you?"

That grin spread into a vile smile. "I'm under no obligation to answer your questions."

"Don't you want to cooperate?"

He pushed off the wall and stalked toward her. The stench of menthol cigarettes wafted from him, and a chill slithered down her spine. "Why would I? I've already admitted that I didn't care for her."

"Was that her sin? Upsetting you? Getting under your skin? Was that the sin of your first victims, too?"

"Weakness is a sin in my book. But a necessary one in the circle of life."

Only someone sick and evil could rationalize cold-blooded murder. "There isn't a drop of remorse in you, is there?" she asked, stricken by his twisted mind.

"Hard to feel bad about a rabbit being prey for a wolf. It's in a predator's nature to hunt, to kill the weak and vulnerable. Those bunnies with their bushy tails are so cute, so soft, their bones so fragile. They frighten easily, and I think it's that fear that a wolf enjoys most. Or maybe it's the hunt. How that craving builds and builds during the chase, expanding with every breath, the excess seeping from the pores, making his mouth water with anticipation of the kill."

Melanie's nerves tightened and she did everything in her power not to let it show. "Kristin isn't a rabbit, and she isn't weak."

"Wasn't she?"

Melanie's stomach clenched. *Wasn't.* He was talking about her in the past tense. Not a good sign. Was she already dead?

Colter pushed up his shirtsleeve and turned his arm so the list of names was upright for her to see. "Six people stole something from me. Three years of my life. A cardinal sin that demands the sweetest kind of retribution. Not that I would dream of seeking it."

She kept her expression sterile. "You're a serial killer. Kristin didn't steal anything from you any more than I did. It's called justice." Melanie raised her chin, not letting her gaze waver from him for a second despite the fear prickling her. "She's a brave woman. Had the courage to show the world who you really are."

"You think you know me. You don't." Eyes narrowing, he shook his head in a slow eerie manner and tipped his head to the side, reminding her of the man wearing the helmet who had attacked her. "Not yet. But you will. Soon." He took a step closer, keeping his hands in his pockets. "Very soon and then you'll learn you're not in control of this situation. No matter how much you mistakenly think you are."

Her chest constricted with fear and anger, but she couldn't let him dare think he was getting to her. "I know exactly who you are. What you are. A murderer. A liar. A coward." Melanie watched him, noting the slight twitch of his mouth, the hard set of his jaw. She was getting to him. *Good.* She just needed to push a bit harder. "And when this is over, you're going to be back where you belong. Rotting behind bars in a supermax prison for the rest of your life."

"For a dead woman walking, you've got a lot to say."

She fought back a shudder just as JJ stormed inside the house. He shoved the front door so hard it banged against the wall. She grimaced at him. He was too soon.

Two more minutes alone with this animal was what she needed.

"All right, Colter, that sounded like a threat to me," the detective said. "Maybe we should take a ride down to the station and continue this chat in an interrogation room."

Colter smirked. "I assure you that was not a threat, Detective Jimenez. Now a real threat would've been something more forceful," he said and shifted his gaze from the cop to her. "I don't know, maybe something like, 'I'm going to wrap my hands around your throat and choke the life out of you, and when it's over I'm going to fill that smart mouth of yours with sand and walk away scot-free.'"

A ball of dread dropped into her stomach.

JJ grabbed Colter and threw him up against the wall, smashing the side of his face against the plaster.

"Hang on, Detective, that was just for instance," Colter said, raising his hands in submission. "I was giving you an example of a threat to show you the difference. That's all. No harm done. I would never dare threaten her seriously. And certainly not with witnesses in earshot. I was well aware you were on the other side of that door the entire time, listening. Are you sure you want to do the paperwork of hauling me in? 'Cause my lawyer is going to bring a few news cameras with him when he shows up to have me released. He's got them on speed dial, and I gave him a heads-up after you knocked on the door earlier."

JJ looked over his shoulder back at her. His silent question hung in the air.

Melanie wanted Drake Colter in jail and for a lot longer than three days. Patience was hard, but key. She shook her head.

With a frown, JJ let him go.

"I'm glad to see reason prevail." Colter brushed off his clothes. "I think I'm going to head back to bed." He stretched and yawned as if tired. "Next time, if you have any more questions for me, I'll consider answering them with my lawyer present. Or maybe I won't. Let you *keep chasing your bushy tail*. So much more fun. You have a good night, ADA Merritt. Sleep tight and watch out for those sand bugs because they bite." Colter sneered at her before turning around and stalking off down the hall.

Seething, Melanie tramped out the door and marched down the stairs.

JJ was right behind her. "Why didn't you want me to haul him in?"

She bristled at him questioning her decision as she headed over to his car. "I'd rather give him enough rope to hang himself." Colter was too cocky, too damn sure of himself and whatever plan he'd cooked up. It was only a matter of time before he made a huge mistake. She only hoped it would be sooner rather than later and that they'd be able to save Kristin. The podcaster had hours, not days. "You should've given me two more minutes with him."

"Rather than you provoke a murderer, I should take him in. We could hold him for up to seventy-two hours," he said, telling her what she already knew. "Plenty of time to see if Kristin Loeb's DNA is on his clothes."

"If he took Kristin, he didn't do it wearing that outfit." Surely he would've disposed of the clothes he'd worn while committing a crime. That was how they'd got him last time. His DNA on the victim and that of the victim's found in his apartment.

"How do you know?"

"Because he's smarter than that. Learned from his past mistakes." Colter could play the part of the fool when he wanted, come across as uncouth, the way he had earlier today, wearing the wife-beater, probably to fit in better with the other men in the house. She'd seen him do it before in front of a jury, acting meek and docile, as though he wouldn't hurt a fly. But that animal had an IQ of 120. Only fifteen points shy of hers. Underestimating him would be a mistake. "He expected us to come here tonight. Just like he expected a visit from the police after the other three women turned up dead. This is a game to him. Every single move he's made, including requesting to be placed in a halfway house to give himself an alibi, is a part of it." She drew a cleansing breath. "He's behind this and he's getting help. We need the police on the front and back of the house, day and night. Wherever he goes, we need eyes on him."

"That's already in the works. There has to be something else. Another angle to pursue. Another way to nail that scumbag. How do we beat him at his own game?"

This *was* a game to him, but other pieces were on the board. They needed to focus on those. The most vulnerable ones. "Kurt Parrish. He's scared. He's also lying and covering for Colter for some reason. We need to know what it is." Then a thought occurred to her. "Before a prisoner is released, how far in advance are they notified of what halfway house they're going to be placed in?"

"I'm not sure," JJ said with a shrug. "In regular circumstances, a year's notice, but with Colter's odd situation, much less. Maybe a month or two beforehand."

Released prisoners assigned to a halfway house could also request a specific area, to be closer to friends, family, a support system, which would narrow down the options to one or two places before he knew for certain.

"Long enough for him to have someone figure out the best person to exploit over here at the FCTC. Look into Parrish's financials, question his family and friends to see if anything has changed in his life recently. Whatever leverage Colter is using, whatever hold he has on Parrish, we need to find it. Use pressure to make Parrish crack. He came close tonight." So close, she could taste it. She rubbed her temple, trying to figure it out. "I need you to speak to the other men that live in there. But away from the center, without Colter knowing. If Colter is sneaking out with Parrish's help, someone inside knows about it. We need to get them to talk."

"Too bad your investigator, Vasquez, isn't available."

He was the best at what he did. "Have you heard anything about Emilio?"

"Yeah, he's alive and well. On a cruise with his wife. According to the sister-in-law, they get back early tomorrow."

Knowing Emilio, and how driven he had been on the Sand Angel Killer case, he would be eager to investigate, putting himself in harm's way.

"After what happened to Kristin," she said, "he and his family will need police protection." Despite not letting Colter see how much this weighed on her, it did. She couldn't help but feel somewhat responsible for the three deaths and

Kristin's disappearance. Vasquez and his loved ones could still be safeguarded.

"He's not the only one who needs protection," JJ pointed out. "You're not safe here, or in Wyoming, by the looks of your face. Maybe you should take some time off, lay low somewhere far away until we can get to the bottom of this."

"I ran once. I won't do it again." Instead of running scared, she should be used as bait, to lure Colter or the copycat killing innocent people for him. Not that Waylon would ever agree to such a plan. "I need to see this through. Besides, I have a job back home that I have to do."

"Some things never change." JJ exhaled a heavy breath. "Then you need protection, too. Around the clock."

"Kristin is the one we need to worry about right now. Not me." If anything happened to the investigative journalist because she'd let her guard down in a moment of weakness with Waylon, she'd never forgive herself. "I'm covered. I've got strict instructions to either stay with you or have those guys," she said, gesturing to the patrol officers who had given her a ride over to the FCTC, "take me to my bodyguard."

She understood the need to be protected, but all the forced proximity with Waylon made it impossible for her to compartmentalize her messy emotions where he was concerned.

Confronting how she felt about Waylon, taking on the pressure of his feelings for her, and coping with this nightmare of Drake Colter at the same time was pushing her limits of what she could handle.

Her personal drama had to be set aside.

Stopping Colter and finding Kristin needed to be her sole focus.

"Why isn't this bodyguard with you?" JJ asked. "Where is he now?"

"Questioning the Sand Angelites." Something she was

happy not to do. They were a bunch of fanatics who made her skin crawl. Those weirdos were willing to go to great lengths for Drake Colter, including stalking her and breaking into her home.

Yet they had never harmed her physically.

Isaac Meacham could've tried to kill her that night in her house instead of sitting like a passive yogi, holding a blue candle. Aside from freaking her out and making a ghastly mess, he hadn't even done any real damage to her property. The sand and walls had been cleaned up and, after a fresh coat of paint, no one could tell what had happened. That night, Isaac hadn't uttered a single word. Not one threat. Hadn't resisted arrest.

But could she be wrong about the Angelites? Were they more than creepy cultists?

Were the Sand Angelites killers, puppets, working under Drake Colter's influence?

She had to puzzle it out, find the answers before Kristin Loeb ran out of time.

Chapter Thirteen

The clock on the dash read four ten. Two hours before dawn broke. It was still dark outside.

Waylon exited off Interstate 25 rather than take it farther north to I-80, which would have nighttime roadwork until six. He'd decided to take the shortcut instead that would save them close to an hour of driving and get them home that much sooner. It had been a long, draining night and they were both in dire need of rest.

He hit the ramp on to the smaller US Route 287 headed north. They hadn't gotten any sleep, but the good thing about the early hour, no traffic was on the road. The lane in front was clear and there was no one behind them.

Sweet darkness.

The lack of traffic and the roadwork on I-80 were the only reasons he'd chosen the shortcut that he didn't dare use during rush-hour congestion. US 287 was known for accidents at peak hours due to tired truckers, students going between Colorado State University and Southeastern Wyoming University, and a lack of passing lanes, but now they practically had it to themselves.

He preferred the route for expediency and, when the sun was up, for the breathtaking scenery.

They were still in Colorado but had already passed Fort

Collins and were less than an hour from home, drawing closer to the Wyoming border every second.

With all the time they'd spent on the road in the past twenty-four hours, he wished they had been in Melanie's luxury crossover with plush leather seats and fully functional A/C instead of his old GMC that had more than a hundred and seventy-five thousand miles on it. She would've been far more comfortable.

Not that she had complained.

Despite the fact she preferred the finer things in life, she was always at ease with the simple way he lived. Never a snide remark or backhanded compliment. He'd gotten that from other women on occasion. Mel might be sophisticated, and he'd wondered if they'd get along outside of bed in the early days because of it, but she wasn't snooty.

He'd never put up with a snob, or anyone who thought the rules didn't apply to them because of money, much less consider rearranging his world for someone like that.

Waylon glanced over at her. She was still awake. The tension that had been in her shoulders had faded away and her features were relaxed.

But they were both restless.

For him, it wasn't simply that he was driving or worried about her safety. He hadn't shared every detail of how things had gone with Stoltz at Isaac Meacham's house. Keeping secrets from someone he cared about wasn't his style. He was more of an open book, making him wonder why he hadn't spit it out already.

"I need to tell you something that happened at the house when we were interviewing the Sand Angelites. It's nothing really." Though it felt like a big icky something. "It might upset you, but it shouldn't." Honestly, he didn't have a clue whether it would bother her. Their status was still in limbo and a big question mark remained regarding how she felt about him.

Head resting against the seat, Mel turned, looking at him. "What is it?"

"One of the Angelites, a young woman named Luna Tuttle, kind of, sort of, cornered me."

"Cornered you?" she asked. "I don't understand. Was she a big woman who felt like she could take you on? That doesn't sound like them. I've never known them to be violent or physically aggressive."

He needed to be concise, matter-of-fact. "Cornered me in a bedroom."

One brow raised, head slightly inclined, Mel looked as aloof as royalty. "Go on."

"She took off her top, with nothing underneath. Basically, offered to have sex with me."

Melanie's gaze fell.

"It made me uncomfortable, and I got out of there."

She squirmed in her seat, fidgeting with her hands, and glanced out the passenger's-side window.

He waited for her to say something. Anything. When she didn't, he thought it best to move on, "There's one thing about the Sand Angelites that keeps bugging me."

"Don't you mean one *more* thing? Luna Tuttle making a pass at you in a bedroom that you never should've been in, I take it with the door closed, would be one thing." Her tone sounded more annoyed than accusatory. Then she said, "It figures. Only a matter of time."

"What is that supposed to mean?"

"Nothing."

That was very much something. "What's only a matter of time?"

"You disappointing me." She shook her head. "Not that

I have any right to be upset that some pretty young thing scrambled your brain. Even though we just had sex a couple of hours beforehand."

Being this upset meant she cared deeply. "You heard the part where I didn't do anything and left the room?"

"I heard you." She folded her arms. "How many women have you slept with since we met?" She took a quick breath and waved a hand. "Never mind. I don't want to know. We were never officially exclusive anyway."

Weren't they? Isn't that the reason they'd stopped using condoms while she stayed on the pill. "I haven't been with anyone else since that night you came home with me from Crazy Eddie's. Not even while we were on a break." He thought about that, how important details and transparency were to her. "Well, I did have dinner with a couple of women after you stopped returning my calls, but that was the extent of it. I never even kissed them."

"You're free to do what you want," she said flippantly.

"What I want is you, Mel. Have you been with other guys?"

Silence descended for too many painful heartbeats.

"No," she finally said. "I've been too busy working and I know better than to get cornered in a bedroom."

She was right. He should've been smarter.

The moment the Tuttle woman led him to her room, a red flag should've flashed in front of him. But he'd honestly thought she was going to break ranks from the Angelites, betray them, and give him some information that might save Kristin Loeb. His guard had been down around her. She was demure. Clearly not a threat, at least not in the typical way. And, well, pretty. Silly that attractiveness could be weaponized, used against his defenses, but it had been.

"I can understand questioning the Angelites separately, isolating them from the group, which makes sense, but did you choose this Luna Tuttle to speak to, or did she volunteer?" Melanie asked, still not looking at him.

He replayed it in his head. "Tuttle volunteered."

"She targeted you, Detective. You were a sucker for an attractive woman and acted against your better judgment, which is what bothers me." She kept staring out the window at the dark landscape, trees lining the highway, and the approaching mountains. "Like I said, Tuttle is one thing. Now you've got something else. Are you sure there aren't more than two things? We are talking about the Angelites."

"Okay, there is a lot, but at the top of the list is something a couple of them said."

"Let me guess. Was it about sinners and redemption? Or maybe something to do with how we're lost in darkness and only they can see clearly?"

"They both made remarks about us *chasing our tails*. Odd, right, that they would both use the same turn of phrase, in separate rooms, at different times? Can't be a coincidence."

Stiffening, Melanie finally looked at him. "Since we're sharing things that might upset the other, it's my turn." Something in her tone made him brace himself. "Drake Colter used similar words about me chasing my tail when I spoke to him at FCTC. Alone."

Anger flared hot and Waylon clenched the steering wheel. "You did what?"

"Before you blow a gasket, hear me out. I don't think it's a coincidence that Colter and the Angelites used the same words. I think it was deliberate. To send us a message that he's the one in control. I also think he spoke to the Angelites. Told them to anticipate a visit from you. Had this Tuttle woman make a sexual overture toward you to mess with me."

The last part drew his gaze. "Why do you think that?"

"Because he flat-out said that you weren't with me because

you were busy with a pretty young woman who was warmer and more open than me."

He'd been lured to the room as part of a ruse, set up to be seduced. But why?

Melanie huffed a breath. "It prickled me when he suggested the idea and stung to hear you confirm it. I don't know why I'm letting that evil monster push my buttons," she said and Waylon wondered if it had been done simply to hurt Mel. "Colter must've spoken to Isaac Meacham or someone else at their house after we saw him this afternoon. Orchestrated the whole thing. That's the only explanation for..."

High-beam headlights popped on behind them. Waylon put a hand up to his eyes against the harsh glare of sudden bright light that had materialized out of nowhere. He would've sworn nobody had been behind them, and he'd been checking, but if the person had been driving without their headlights on after the turn onto US 287, he wouldn't have seen them.

"What the heck?" Melanie turned, looking out the back window.

Waylon's focus shot to the rearview mirror.

The vehicle accelerated fast, getting a lot closer, too close, in a span of a few seconds. The driver must've floored it.

This was a two-lane highway, with only one for each direction that didn't widen until after they had gotten beyond the mountains. There were lots of bends on the road. With the straightaway looming ahead, maybe the other driver wanted to pass them now, but it didn't appear he or she was moving into the other lane.

Waylon put on his hazard lights, hoping it would encourage them to go around. Instead, the other vehicle zoomed up, coming right at them, and rammed the back of his truck.

His GMC jolted violently, jostling them forward in their seats.

Melanie gasped. "They're trying to run us off the road!"

"Or kill us," he said tightly.

Either was bad news that didn't bode well for them. He pressed down on the gas, going past the speed limit of sixty-five. The engine strained at eighty. With no oncoming traffic, he dared to cut across the yellow line into the adjacent lane, and the other vehicle followed.

The van, possibly another truck—hard to tell with the blinding glare of the high beams—exceeded their speed, eating the distance between them, catching up quickly.

An edge caught in his throat. The vehicle plowed into them again, rocking his truck harder than the last time they'd been hit and forcing him to swerve.

Gripping the seat and bracing a hand on the dash, Mel glanced over at him. "Can you outrun them?"

His old GMC Sonoma was reliable, compact, useful for hauling large objects that weren't too heavy, like appliances and lumber. Small enough to maneuver through tight spaces, but his truck was tiny and light compared to heftier ones. The vehicle behind them was larger, heavier and more powerful than his.

No way he could outrun the other driver.

Waylon wrestled the wheel as they veered back over the yellow line into the correct lane and he managed to bring the truck back under control. "Not in this thing."

"How long do you think they've been following us?" she asked.

"I don't know." Waylon cursed and shook his head. "My guess is since I left Meacham's house."

"But the Angelites aren't violent."

He pressed down on the accelerator, trying to avoid another hit. The chassis rattled and the engine whined when he pushed it to ninety. Waylon glanced at the dashboard just as the oil pressure icon started blinking. The truck wouldn't take much more of that.

"They could've easily followed me after we finished talking to them at Meacham's house."

"And they could've also told someone else where you were when you questioned them separately. Or it could've been Colter. Maybe he called his friend who's helping him kill people. You picked me up right in front of the FCTC. I was outside for a while with JJ before you showed up."

The vehicle was closing the distance once more.

Waylon was ready or did his best to be. The big vehicle slammed into them. He jerked the wheel hard, using the weight of his GMC Sonoma to hold his ground. The other automobile backed off, falling behind a couple of yards.

But he knew it wouldn't last.

The pavement offered no shoulder and they neared a particularly treacherous curve in the winding road. He'd have to slow down to a safe speed. No other choice. On the west side of the highway was a towering mountain wall of solid rock. On the east was a sheer drop-off. He couldn't remember how far down and, in the dark, he couldn't tell. Why had he taken the chance with the shortcut?

This section of Route 287, cutting around the mountain, was perilous, dubbed the "highway of death." The driver had timed the attack on them perfectly. Waiting until they'd reached the most dangerous point.

Who the heck was behind the wheel?

Drake Colter was no doubt responsible, but he wasn't so foolhardy as to be driving with attention laser-focused on him after Kristin Loeb had been taken last night. Had he sent Isaac Meacham, another Sand Angelite, or someone else after them?

The driver switched off the high beams and Waylon swore.

They wouldn't be able to see the next hit coming until it was too late.

An engine roared up behind them. The growling sound grew louder as it closed in.

Waylon slowed for the curve but cut the wheel hard, veering back over into the oncoming lane, toward the side of the mountain. He came within inches of skimming the driver's side against the rock.

He didn't know which would be worse, colliding into the jagged wall of rock, smashing into an oncoming vehicle, or crashing into old guardrails that might be weakened by corrosion or destabilized by the highway shoulder beneath it.

Grimly, he decided the guardrail with a looming cliff-side drop might be worse.

Melanie leaned toward him, her face tense, her eyes filled with fear. He had to get her out of this in one piece, unharmed.

The vehicle rammed into their rear bumper. It was all Waylon could do to keep from wiping out on the rock wall. Rather than crash into the side of the mountain, he cranked the wheel, taking them back over into his lane just as they came out of the deadly curve of the road, clearing the peak of the drop-off, and hit a straightaway.

Up ahead, the highway was dark and clear of other cars.

While Waylon focused on keeping his GMC on the road, the vehicle behind them pulled around and raced up along the back of the driver's side. In the side mirror, Waylon caught a glimpse of the outline. A behemoth truck that outmatched his in every way—size, weight, engine, horsepower.

The dark-colored truck crashed into them as Waylon whipped the wheel to the left, turning into the hit. The vehicles locked, clashing like steel beasts. He struggled to maintain control. Metal screeched against metal, the mechanical screams grating like fingernails on chalkboard.

Swearing under his breath but otherwise maintaining his composure, Waylon eased his foot down on the brake pedal, hoping to unlock them. He didn't dare jam it to the floor and risk sending the GMC into a deadly spin.

The tires grinded against asphalt, the smell of burning rubber filled the air. His truck shuddered. Finally, the other driver jerked them apart, but Waylon's GMC fishtailed.

He sped up, desperate to try and make it to the next exit before they were hit again.

Too late.

The other vehicle sideswiped them. This time sending his truck into a skid. He tried to steer into it, but he couldn't recover. In spite of Waylon's best efforts, the skid became a sickening spin.

"Waylon!"

"Brace yourself," he said, turning the wheel in the direction the vehicle wanted to go, which was his only hope of regaining control.

As if the truck had a mind of its own, the GMC rotated three hundred and sixty degrees, careening toward the edge. Instinctively, he reached out, putting an arm across Melanie, doing anything he could to protect her while keeping his other hand on the steering wheel.

They smashed into the guardrail and steel shrieked.

Chapter Fourteen

Melanie's teeth clattered together hard enough to ignite sparks of pain in her jaw, shooting all the way into her temples. The seat belt, which stretched diagonally across her chest from right shoulder to left hip, instantly cinched so tight that her breath was wrenched from her.

Their truck rebounded from the guardrail, not with enough momentum to cause them to collide with the other vehicle but with so much torque that they spun in a full circle again.

Waylon jerked the steering wheel back and forth erratically, fighting for control. Melanie struggled to orient herself.

As they came out of the second three-hundred-and-sixty-degree rotation, the other vehicle struck them, plowing into the driver's side. She didn't see it coming, only felt the blow that knocked the breath from her lips and sent them crashing into the guardrail once more.

She turned toward Waylon. Past his window, she looked through the windshield of the other vehicle and saw the driver.

The man wearing a black helmet revved the engine of the full-sized truck. The front fender of the massive vehicle didn't lose contact with Waylon's door, directing all that horsepower, forcing their vehicle deeper into the guardrail. The larger truck shoved them five or maybe ten feet.

A grinding-scraping of metal on metal. A flurry of golden

sparks bursting up like a swarm of summer fireflies against the dark sky.

Their truck began to pitch to the right. The guardrail was giving way.

No. No!

She glanced below, out her window, her heart in her throat. Through the darkness, she could make out a steep slope and trees, but had no way of knowing how far down the drop was or what was at the bottom.

Steel buckled, and with a rending screech the guardrail cracked apart. In a jangle of detached posts and railings, the truck slipped sideways along the embankment.

Melanie's stomach twisted with nausea. Even though she was restrained by the seat belt and Waylon had thrown his arm across her body instinctively, she pressed her right hand against the door and her left against the dashboard, bracing herself.

Gravel and dirt spewed into the air. Their truck continued in a bumpy, jarring slide down the slope. As it was happening, she couldn't believe it. Her brain registered the tumble toward death while her heart stubbornly clung to hope.

Then the embankment grew steeper and the truck flipped over.

A scream tore from Melanie's lips. Her belt jerked painfully against her chest. Their descent was fast and hard. Gasping for breath, pulse pounding like a drum in her ears, she wrenched painfully from side to side in the harness of the seat belt.

She prayed for a sturdy tree, a spur of rock, something to stop their fall.

The headlights sliced the darkness. She wasn't sure how many times the truck rolled—maybe only three times—because up and down had lost all meaning.

Her head banged into the cab ceiling so hard it nearly

knocked her out. She couldn't tell if she'd been thrown upward or if the roof had dented inward. Trying to slump in her seat, terrified the ceiling might crumple further on the next roll, she worried for Waylon, who was so much bigger than she, that his skull might be crushed.

The windshield shattered, showering the safety glass. The headlights blinked off.

His truck rolled onto its roof again but slipped farther into the seemingly bottomless ravine with a thunderous, clattering roar. Her life flashed before her eyes, full of emptiness, regrets, fears, despite her fearless façade. All the things she'd never said and should have.

The GMC whooshed to the bottom, bounced, landing upright on its wheels, the back end crashing into something, bringing them to a merciful halt.

Thank you.

Her head spun. The sound of rushing water filled her ears.

The river. They'd stopped inches from it.

She turned to Waylon. The dashboard lights were still on, reflecting his sweat-slicked face and closed eyes.

"Waylon?" Her voice was hoarse.

He was slumped over in his seat, only held up by the seat belt, head bent toward her, resting against his shoulder.

She touched his face. "Waylon."

He didn't move. Something warm and sticky covered his right temple and cheek.

Blood.

Her heart squeezed. Dread thrummed in her veins.

Please, be alive. I don't want to lose you.

With trembling fingers, she touched him just under his nose. A sob of relief punched out of her when she felt the warm exhalation of his breath.

Waylon was unconscious. Not dead.

Fumbling with the release mechanism on her seat belt, she had to get him out of there. Head injuries were dangerous. He needed medical attention as soon as possible.

The safety harness disengaged and she freed herself from the entangling straps. She groped around for her purse. Found it and called for help.

Once finished explaining to the 9-1-1 operator, she put the phone on the dash.

"A highway patrol officer will be to your location momentarily, ma'am, and an ambulance has been dispatched. I'll remain on the line with you."

"Thank you," she said, her voice shaky. "But he's still not conscious. I don't know what to do." Her throat constricted.

"Help is on the way, ma'am. Stay calm."

Melanie pressed her hands to Waylon's cheeks, cradling his face. "Don't die," she whispered in his ear. "I love you. Please stay with me." Tears welled in her eyes. "Wake up. Please, wake up. I can't lose you." Panic fluttered in her chest. What if he never regained consciousness? What if she did lose him? He'd been out too long. How were emergency services going to reach them once they arrived? "Waylon! I order you to wake up. Right now."

As if on command, he roused with a grunt. His head lolled. Then he opened his eyes, his gaze taking in their surroundings before finding hers. "Are you all right?" he asked, reaching for her.

He was alive and awake. She was going to be fine.

Hot tears rolled down her cheeks. "Yes, I'm okay." She wrapped her arms around his neck and held him tight.

They'd come so close to dying. Too close.

No matter how hard she tried to ignore her feelings for him, to keep some semblance of emotional detachment, she just couldn't do it any longer.

She couldn't walk away from him again. Couldn't spend the rest of her life aching to be near him.

But could she give up the one thing in her life that gave her a sense of purpose for him?

WAYLON OPENED HIS EYES, reorienting himself to the ER room. Dim fluorescent lights. Hospital gown. Scratchy sheets. Thin blanket. IV in his hand. Too many machines.

He longed for the comfort of his own bed.

"Did you have a good nap?" Melanie yawned from the chair she was seated in at his bedside and took hold of his hand.

"Yeah, I did." Between sheer exhaustion and getting his head knocked around in the accident, he'd needed the shut-eye much more than he had realized. "How long was I out?"

"You fell asleep about thirty minutes after they brought you back from getting the CT scan. So, that would be..." She glanced at the clock on the wall. "About four hours."

It was already past noon.

The truck that ran them off the road had fled the scene after they'd broken through the guardrail. The slide down the slope had been terrifying in the dark with no way to tell how far they'd had to fall.

Fortunately, it had only been a few hundred feet down the embankment when they'd slammed into the trunk of one of Colorado's venerable old ponderosa pines. It had taken a lot of time to get them out of the ravine, to fill out a police report and to have a battery of tests run on him. Melanie had whiplash but was otherwise okay.

So far, the police had nothing on the other driver or the exact make and model of the truck that had driven them off the road.

His GMC was now an old hunk of metal. Totaled in the accident that had nearly killed them both.

They were lucky to be alive.

"Is the cop they assigned still here?" He'd refused to leave her alone for a CT scan or to even sleep until the police had agreed to post an officer by the room, protecting Melanie.

"Yes. We have not one, but two. A second officer arrived a little bit after you fell asleep."

He was relieved the local authorities were taking the threat seriously. "Did I miss anything important while I was sleeping?"

"I updated Holden and JJ about the accident and asked the two to keep each other in the loop. Also, I finally spoke to Emilio Vasquez. The investigator I used to work with in Denver."

"And? Is he okay?"

"He's fine." She nodded. "So is his family, but he's angry about the situation, the recent string of victims, what's happened to Kristin. They became friends during the Colter case." Lowering her head, she bit her lip. "We're all so worried about her. She's been missing for more than thirteen hours," she said, her voice choked with emotion.

The implication hung in the air between them. The odds of finding Kristin Loeb alive at this point were slim and plummeted further with each passing minute.

She looked up at him, her eyes glistening with tears. "This is all my fault. Once we found out what room Kristin was in, we should've changed ours to be as close to hers as possible. I should have texted her our room number. Set chairs out on the walkway and waited for her outside. There were so many things I should've done differently instead of allowing myself to get distracted with you."

The blow hit him hard and deep. He squeezed his eyes closed against the sudden jab of pain in his chest. Melanie regretted sleeping with him. Blamed herself for what had happened to Kristin.

Opening his eyes, he met hers. "This isn't your burden to carry. The fault is mine. More mine than yours. I've underestimated who we're up against at every turn. At the motel, the Sand Angelite house, on Route 287." Making mistakes wasn't like him. They were being outmaneuvered. Without a full understanding of the enemy, who was operating two steps ahead, they were blindly chasing their tails. "Don't blame yourself." He didn't want her to put that unbearable weight on her shoulders. "Blame me instead."

"I can't. It wouldn't be fair to you."

"Guilt and blame aren't going to solve anything. Those are the real distractions. That's what Colter wants."

Her gaze fell, like she was thinking. "You're right. That is precisely what he wants. He told me as much when I questioned him."

"Colter is determined to get under your skin. Don't let him. Kristin might still be alive. We have to believe that until we have a concrete reason not to." If Colter was going to kill her, or have someone else do it, he'd want Melanie to know she was dead. They had to treat this as a missing person case until her body was found. "You're alive. So is Vasquez. Let's not waste time beating ourselves up. Okay?"

She hesitated. "I'll try."

"What about Vasquez's family? Are they in protective custody or being watched?"

"He left his family behind in Florida with relatives for their safety and came back alone. Emilio is determined to investigate. Using his big gun, a hacker he's relied on from time to time. Orson. The guy has a genius-level IQ. Hacked into some government agency when he was only fourteen. Also, Stoltz and JJ are working the case together and are going to keep a close eye on Emilio, and make sure nothing happens to him. Since Emilio and I are both protected, JJ is going to use his time focusing on the case instead of playing watchdog at the FCTC. He plans to put pressure on Kurt Parrish and question the other men staying at the center, like I suggested. The Denver PD will have eyes on the front and back of the FCTC at night. JJ hopes that additional manpower will be approved to follow Colter during the day, too."

"Any idea what the holdup is?"

"JJ thought Kristin's kidnapping would ensure things were fast-tracked, and to some extent it was, regarding eyes on the FCTC, but his captain is reluctant to authorize more manpower."

"Why?" One convicted killer was free and people he had a vendetta against were turning up dead or kidnapped.

"All the evidence points to a copycat and Kurt Parrish is supplying an airtight alibi for Colter. JJ is going to try to go over his captain's head for approval."

Waylon winced. "That's not going to go over well."

"JJ is aware and willing to take the risk. Hopefully, they can get Parrish or one of the other men at the center to give them something. Stoltz submitted a request for Colter's list of visitors and copies of his mail to the supermax in Florence, and Emilio will be helping investigate. I'm sure we'll get something to go on."

"There's a lot for Vasquez to dive into. Any idea where he's going to begin?"

"Finding Kristin is his priority. We're hoping she's still alive." Melanie shoved her hair behind her ear. "I forwarded him my texts from her and he has the notebook that you got at Meacham's. He's going to get the detectives to check her home computer. Emilio said all her notes on her laptop should've synced automatically to the cloud. I hope there's something for him to go on. That it wasn't all in her notebooks."

"He'll find something." He tightened his fingers on hers, wishing they weren't stuck in a hospital when they should be investigating themselves. "Don't worry."

"I hope that's not just wishful thinking or you trying to make me feel better."

"Emilio must be excellent at his job because you chose him as your go-to investigator. Speaks volumes about him. And he's using a topnotch hacker. Emilio has skin in the game. You were attacked, Kristin was taken, and his name is on Colter's hit list. If there's something to go on, any lead, Emilio Vasquez will find it."

She took a deep breath. "You make a good point. I do tend to choose individuals who are not only adept but also relentless." She flashed him a smile that made his chest ache for an entirely different reason.

A question he had for her had been niggling at him since the doctor had examined her and deemed her okay aside from whiplash. "Earlier, between the tests, with the doctors and nurses coming in and out, it didn't seem the right time to ask." He'd had bloodwork, a neurological exam, cognitive testing and brain imaging. "The thing with Luna Tuttle, are we okay?"

Her brow furrowed. She shook her head and his heart sank.

"I'm sorry," he said. For falling for Tuttle's ploy and for asking about their status when she was worried about her friend Kristin.

But their relationship was important, too.

For nearly three years, he'd put his feelings and their situation on the back burner. If they couldn't face this together, after almost dying, then maybe they never would.

"I didn't mean to upset you," he added.

"Don't be sorry. I let Colter get into my head. I shouldn't have. All that matters is we survived."

That wasn't all that mattered. He wanted more than just to survive. "You matter, how you feel, what you think. In the motel room, when we argued, you thought we were doomed to fail and in the car, you said, *it figures*, like you expected me—"

She pressed her fingers to his lips, silencing him. "The doctor said you're supposed to rest."

Waiting, avoiding, stonewalling only squandered precious time. He was done with that. Waylon lowered her hand from his mouth. "What did you mean by 'it figures'?"

"It's just…" She glanced away from him, her expression turning inscrutable. "Nothing important. I shouldn't have said it."

Dealing with messy emotions wasn't her strength, and he could see she was bleeding, on the inside. A deep wound he needed to expose. "You don't say things you don't mean. I need you to tell me. Even if you think it'll hurt me."

Taking a breath, she rested a hand on his chest and looked at him. "Every person I've ever been close to, every guy I've dated, has let me down, disappointed me in some way. Even my parents. It's taught me that it's a mistake to depend on others, to need them."

"The guys you dated were probably jerks. Like Brent. Guys you chose because you never wanted to get close to them. Never wanted to love them. As for your parents, when you've talked to me about your years at boarding school, I could see it bothered you. The loneliness. What it was like being a minority there." Exeter, Harvard undergrad, Yale law school. How she'd felt different and struggled to fit in until she'd embraced who she was and decided to stand out. "It's like this sore spot for you with your parents. But they love you."

During their time together, she'd taken a few calls on speaker at her place or his. Her mother's voice had radiated warmth. Her dad, Frederick, always had supportive words, praised her, told her she was the brightest and could achieve anything. How they'd both uplifted her, encouraging her to be the best version of herself without tearing her down.

It was also clear that they had hardwired ambition into her and, along with that, came high standards she'd felt pressure to meet.

"I know they do." Looking unconvinced, Mel pulled on her trademark work smile that he'd learned was one hundred percent phony.

"They just don't show it the way you want. Every time they paid for school, bought you an expensive gift, that was them saying they love you. That they want to take care of you. They're not perfect. Neither am I. They make mistakes. So will I. So will you. But I want to be there for you. No matter what, I'll show up for you, big things, little things. When you need me most, I won't let you down. I promise."

Fresh tears sprang to her eyes. "I'm scared."

Melanie was a warrior with a chink in the armor. A wound of some kind. Before coming to Colorado with her, he'd figured it was heartbreak over a guy in her past. But now he realized she'd never invested enough emotionally to get her heart broken.

"Scared of what, darling?"

"That it won't work. *Us.* Our jobs, the conflict of interest. Our lifestyles, the long work hours. How to juggle a family and be there for children. I won't abandon mine, exiling them to boarding schools. I'm afraid that I'll disappoint you. Break your heart again. That you'll break mine and I won't know how to go on without you. Waylon, you almost died. What if you had?"

The long list of her worries made his head throb, but now he saw her clearly. She was sharing the part of herself that she kept hidden in darkness. This was progress.

During the fall over the side of the embankment, terror had had a chokehold on his heart. He hadn't been worried about his own safety. Only Melanie's.

His last thoughts before he'd blacked out had been about her; how much he loved her, how he regretted not fighting harder for her.

Tears fell from her eyes and rolled down her cheeks. "That's my greatest fear. Loving you, committing to you, sacrificing for you, only to lose you."

He tightened his grip on her hand. "You can't have a rainbow without a little rain."

Her brow crinkled. "Is that a lyric from a country song?"

Honestly, he didn't know. Maybe it was. Those tended to blur together in his mind. "What I'm trying to say is everything that came before us was the rain. I want to be your rainbow, M&M. I would sooner hurt myself than hurt you. I want to make you happy. I know how you need to be loved. That you need someone to show up for you. To be present in your life. To listen to you. To hold you. To be your soft place to fall. Your safety net." They both needed that. "Let me be your huckleberry."

"Waylon." She got up out of the chair and sat on the edge of the bed. Leaning close, she caressed his cheek. "You make it sound so simple. So beautiful."

That's what taking a leap of faith was—a simple, beautiful act of courage. And he believed Melanie had the guts to do this with him. For him.

"I'm asking you to love me," he said. "To trust me."

"I do love you." She took a shuddering breath. "I love you and I trust you. More than anyone else in the world."

He wiped away her tears, cupped her face in his hand and kissed her softly, tenderly, full of every emotion in his heart. "You have no idea how long I've waited to hear that."

Through a hiccupping sob, she smiled. "I wanted to tell you last year. After we first went dancing. Then I lost the nerve. Started thinking about all the reasons not to say it. But the biggest obstacle to telling you, was…well, you."

Not the explanation he'd expected. "How so?"

"If I told you how deeply I felt about you, that I loved you, Waylon, you never would have stopped fighting for us. You would've been even more determined."

He couldn't fault her there. "That's true." He kissed her again.

"Our jobs, the problem that the conflict poses for me professionally, is still a big issue."

"Don't worry about our jobs. We're going to work it out." He had yet to reach out to Rip Lockwood, the owner of Ironside Protection Services. They had plenty of offices, but he wasn't aware of any close to where they lived. Taking a position with IPS might require him to relocate or travel a lot. Going from a secret relationship to a long-distance one wouldn't be ideal. Maybe he'd have to do that for a while until a detective position opened in Cheyenne, a city within easy driving distance in the next county over. He was willing to go through any inconvenience if it meant they'd be together, out in the open. "You won't have to sacrifice."

"I don't want you to either."

They deserved a real chance at happiness together. He was willing to do whatever necessary to give that to them.

"You said you trusted me, so I'm going to hold you to it." He gave her a small grin, not wanting her to worry. "Everything is going to be okay. Believe me?"

She pressed her lips to his and his chest swelled with affection for her. "I believe you, Waylon Wright. Because a cowboy is only as good as his word." A smile spread across her face, brighter, warmer, sweeter than sunshine.

He made a vow then and there to coax those out of her as often as he could and leaned in for another kiss.

A throat cleared, drawing their attention to the doctor who had slipped inside the room around the curtain. "I don't mean to interrupt, but your test results came back. I'm happy to tell you that everything looks good. Considering what you've been through. You have a grade II concussion and should recover with no problems. I want you to get plenty of rest. Don't overexert yourself. For the first forty-eight hours, try to limit activities that require a lot of concentration. Light exercise and physical activity as tolerated thereafter. It's best to have someone stay with you and check on you for at least twenty-four hours to ensure that your symptoms aren't getting worse."

"I'll be with him," Melanie said.

"Good. Glad to hear that. Any questions for me?"

"When can we get out of here?" he quipped.

"I can start your discharge paperwork. Should take a couple of hours to get it processed. Sorry that we're not faster around here."

Seemed typical for an emergency room in his experience.

"I heard your vehicle was totaled and that you two are from out of town," the doctor said. "Are you going to need a ride to the bus station?"

"We're covered," Waylon said. Before his CT scan, he had called his brother, Gunner. Told him what had happened and asked him to give them a lift home. "My brother will be here no later than three o'clock."

"The timing sounds perfect. I'll go get your paperwork finalized."

As the doctor left the room, pulling back the curtain,

he glimpsed the uniformed arm of one of the officers stationed outside.

"Are you sure it isn't too inconvenient for your brother to give us a lift?" Melanie asked.

He was close with Gunner, with all his siblings. Except his sister. "Yeah, it's no problem. He wasn't doing anything at his ranch that couldn't wait a day. Besides, we haven't seen each other since New Year's." After Mel had dumped him, he'd gone to visit his family and ring in the new year with them. It had been good to see everyone, to catch up, but it hadn't eased his pain or his loneliness. "And once he learned we nearly died, he was willing to do somersaults through a hundred flaming hoops if I'd asked him to."

Melanie chuckled. "I can't wait to meet him."

This was new territory for them. Admitting their feelings. Taking a chance on a real relationship. Meeting relatives.

They could work through the logistics and politics of their jobs, through the juggling act of having a family. They could have everything they wanted. Be happy together.

Provided they lived long enough.

He had to stop Drake Colter and find whoever his accomplice was before he tried to kill Melanie again.

Chapter Fifteen

Melanie was grateful to be back at Waylon's house. Tucked in his bed.

Safe and sound.

Early morning light poked through the curtains. The sound of a pan clattering pulled her fully from sleep. She rolled over in the bed to find Waylon gone.

Last night, they'd made love. They'd tried to resist since he wasn't supposed to overexert himself. She'd decided for the sake of his health to take full control. They'd taken it slow, spent the time memorizing each other's bodies all over again, escaping fear and frustration, savoring a second chance at life. At love.

Goodness, she'd wanted him. That feeling. The burning, insatiable hunger that made her euphoric and enraptured and emotional all at the same time.

Throwing on one of his T-shirts, she padded to the kitchen. Her entire body ached, muscles she rarely used protesting with every step she took. Although she had been given a clean bill of health at the hospital, aside from the whiplash, which was also pronounced, the doctor had warned her that she might feel this way and it was entirely natural after the accident.

She found Waylon standing at the kitchen sink in his underwear, washing dishes. He had made coffee and breakfast. A pile of hot blueberry pancakes waited on the kitchen island.

"I'm supposed to be the one taking care of you." She plopped down on a stool.

The kitchen resembled the rest of the house; rustic, warm, comfortable. She loved the details like the dark wood beams on the ceiling that were the same color as the hardwood floors, the stone-textured backsplash with German smear that he'd installed himself behind the stove.

Her place looked like a model house from the pages of a magazine while his felt like a cozy home.

"Figured we could take care of each other." He poured coffee in a mug and set it down in front of her. "You went more than a day and a half with no rest. I don't know how you were able to stay up, watching over me in the hospital. I wanted you to sleep in this morning and to wake up to a hot breakfast."

His mention of the time had her glancing at the clock on the wall. A little after nine on Sunday morning. Kristin had been taken two days ago but not yet forty-eight hours. Last night, it hadn't been easy for Melanie to fall asleep. She'd been racked with worry and guilt.

No news, no new leads, had only made it worse.

The cold pit opened in her stomach once more, the fear that Kristin was dead, the fear that Colter was unstoppable. The fear of not having a future with Waylon.

Would they get to have one together?

Melanie smiled nervously, not wanting Waylon to pick up on her worries. She'd promised not to get bogged down with guilt and blame.

They had to catch Colter and his accomplice. All his victims deserved justice.

She'd focus on getting it for them.

Melanie put her feet on the pegs of the stool and rose, bending over the counter to give him a kiss. "You really are the sweetest. And a good cook, too." Much better than her.

"My mother raised seven of us, six boys. She made certain we all knew how to cook, clean, sew and didn't subscribe to notions of household chores being delegated based on sex. Plenty of times one of us boys were stuck in the kitchen or doing laundry while my sister worked the ranch."

"I'm happy to hear about the equality in the Wright household and plan to take full advantage of your cooking skills." Melanie gave him another kiss before grabbing her purse and sitting back down. Two messages had come in while she was sleeping. She scrolled through both.

JJ: ADX Florence info in. See emails. Loads to process. Wright cc'd.

Darcy: Let me know if you need me to come in to work today. Happy to help. Already cleared my schedule since you were out Friday.

Darcy really was the best, anticipating that Melanie might need her.

"Were there any updates while I was asleep? JJ mentioned emails from the prison." She figured it would be quicker to ask him.

"As a matter of fact, I was going to tell you about that." He gestured with his head toward the hall and left the kitchen.

Shoving her phone back in her purse, she swiveled on her stool, hopped off and followed him down the hallway, past the bedrooms and bathroom. In the front of the house, his living room and dining room were one large open space only separated by the walkway running between them.

"The visitor list and copies of Colter's mail came in. I spent the morning downloading and printing the emails." He waved his hand at the dining room table long enough to comfortably seat eight.

A printer sat beside three stacks of printed visitor logs and copied correspondence covering three years.

"How long have you been awake?"

"Awhile."

"Printing all this must've taken an hour, give or take."

"Give or take. I was lucky I had enough copy paper. Good thing I buy it by the case instead of the ream." He tapped the box on the floor with his foot. "I volunteered us to go through everything. According to Stoltz, Kurt Parrish is definitely afraid and hiding something. They're going to interview his friends and family, and Vasquez will have access to Kristin's computer today. Also, there are finally officers assigned to watch Drake Colter around the clock. If he leaves the FCTC, there'll be eyes on him."

"I call that progress." She turned back to the overwhelming stacks of paper on the dining room table.

"I propose we get started after we eat."

"You'll get no argument from me."

He slung an arm over her shoulder and they traipsed back toward the kitchen.

"That stack is going to take all day to sort through, analyze, and connect the dots on our own." Maybe longer. "How do you feel about me asking Darcy to come over and help? She's willing to work today and she's the best researcher in the office."

"I don't mind. I'll just have to do my best to keep my hands off you while she's around. The last thing I want is to complicate things for you by having someone in your office think that there's more to you staying here besides me trying to protect you."

"She already knows I was attacked at the office. Not as though I could hide it from her with the shattered door and crime scene tape. Also, she's aware that you're the one protecting me and drove me to Colorado. I don't think it'll be a problem."

Provided they didn't slip up in front of her.

The idea of their relationship no longer being a secret was welcomed. The specifics on how that would happen were still unknown to her, but she trusted Waylon to come up with a solution they could both accept.

"Eat first." Waylon shoved the stack of pancakes closer to her. "Then reach out to Darcy." He slid her purse down the kitchen island to the other side of him. "Boyfriend's orders."

She smiled at him. "Boyfriend" was too small a word for what Waylon was to her. Significant other. Partner. Her person. Stronger terms. Better suited to what he meant to her.

The yummy smell of the breakfast made her stomach grumble with hunger. She'd skipped dinner last night, unable to eat, anxious over Kristin. The more time that passed, the bleaker the outlook.

Her hope of them finding Kristin alive was waning, but she refused to give up until she had no other choice.

Another grumble from her stomach. Starving herself wasn't going to help.

She stabbed a couple of pancakes with a fork and put them on her plate. "Tell your mother I appreciate her modern parenting style."

His brother, Gunner, had been so much like him in personality and looks. Not quite as broad or tall. In football terms, if Waylon was the size of a tight end, then Gunner was built more like a quarterback. Handsome, too, in that rugged Wright way. Super polite to the point that he had called Melanie “ma’am” so many times it grated on her nerves until she had insisted that he call her by her first name.

Not only had he given them a ride back to Wayward Bluffs, he’d also coordinated with his other siblings and arranged to have a loaner car waiting at the house.

An old SUV. Beat up but dependable.

She respected their frugality of driving a vehicle as long as possible rather than always chasing the newest model. That admirable value had certainly crossed over into other areas of Waylon’s life.

Once he committed to something or someone, he stayed committed.

“Tell her yourself,” he said, sitting beside her. “Gunner pulled me to the side and told me she wants to come down sometime soon. Stay a night or two. Meet you.”

“Meet me?” She grabbed the syrup and poured it on her pancakes. “Why?”

“Well, I may have talked about you when I visited at New Year’s. She could tell I wasn’t over you. Then Gunner told her that I had been in the accident with *my Melanie*.”

“Hmm.” She shoved a forkful of food into her mouth, stalling for time, and nearly melted at how good the pancakes tasted. Fluffy, moist, fresh blueberries bursting on her tongue. And he had heated the syrup.

“I can always tell my mom it’s not a good time to visit,” he said, “if you’re not ready for that.”

“It isn’t a good time and I’ll never be ready, so you may as well let her come. But our current problem may still be an issue for the foreseeable future.” She prayed that wouldn’t be the case. “Will it be safe for her to visit?”

“She wouldn’t be alone. One or more of my brothers will be with her.”

Melanie tensed. Not a mom visit, but a family visit.

"It'll be fine." Waylon put a hand on her lower back. "We'll do fajitas and serve strong margaritas."

She chuckled. "Is that going to be your beverage of choice to get me to loosen up?"

"You betcha. That or wine. Either seems effective."

A cell phone rang.

Waylon grabbed her purse from the counter and took the phone out. "It's your boss's wife. Mrs. Weisman."

"I wonder why she's calling." They were scheduled to have brunch in a couple of weeks. Maybe it was to cancel. Gloria was big on etiquette and didn't leave such notifications for the last minute if she could help it. Melanie took the phone from him and answered. "Hello?"

"Hi, Melanie, it's me, Gloria." Her tone was restrained, not as jubilant as usual. "I hate to disturb you so early on a Sunday morning."

It was after nine. Not early at all for her. "How are you? How's Gordon?" Her boss had been out of the office unexpectedly. "Darcy told me that he's feeling under the weather."

"Do you have a minute?" Something in Gloria's voice made Melanie stiffen with concern.

"For you, I have more than a minute. What can I do for you?"

"It's Gordon. He's going to be in the hospital a few more days."

"The hospital?" Melanie dropped her fork on the plate. "I didn't realize it was something serious." She'd been under the impression he'd had a cold or the flu.

"Yes, unfortunately, it is," Gloria said gravely. "Once he's released from the hospital, we've agreed that he's going to be at the house and won't be back to work."

Melanie reeled with surprise. "For how long?"

"Indefinitely."

Shock hit her like a physical blow. "Oh no." If Gordon wasn't planning to come back, then it would have been because of something awful. Her mind spun with the possibilities. None of them anything she could bring herself to say. "What's wrong with him?" she asked, hoping it wasn't what she imagined.

Waylon put a comforting hand on her shoulder and she was glad to have him there, beside her, her safety net.

My person.

"Cancer," Gloria said, her voice cracking with emotion. "He's had it for a long time and didn't want anyone to know. He was in remission for a while, but it's come back. We've talked about it and it's time to tell people. When you get a chance, he'd like you to stop by the hospital and see him."

"Of course. I'll make it a priority." She glanced at Waylon. The concern in his eyes almost made her tear up. Going through Colter's mail and list of visitors could wait a couple of hours. Actually, it didn't have to wait, she could have Darcy get started while she went to see Gordon. "I can come by the hospital today, within the hour, if that's okay."

"He'd like that," Gloria said. "He's in Room 311. Thank you, Melanie. I know how busy you are. I appreciate you making the time."

Gordon was her boss, the best kind, who had put the office's full resources at her disposal without question. He gave her a great deal of leeway and she appreciated having him as a sounding board. But he and Gloria were also her friends. Her move to the Cowboy State had been a rushed one and difficult, under less-than-ideal circumstances. She'd been a fish out of water. They'd welcomed her into their home and lives when she'd known no one. Introduced her to people, helped her build bridges and make connections. Paved the way for her to succeed in town, professionally and personally, when they hadn't had to. She'd never experienced such generosity at any other office.

They were the closest thing she had to family outside of her parents.

"I'll always make time for you two," Melanie said. "See you soon."

AS THEY STRODE into the hospital, Waylon ached to wrap his arm around Melanie, the way he would've done if they were out in the open with their relationship. But they still had some big things to work out before that could happen. So, he kept his hands at his sides.

Waylon hit the call button for the elevator. The doors opened right away, they got on and rode it up to the third floor.

Melanie had been quiet since the phone call from Mrs. Weisman. Waylon had learned Gordon had cancer, but after that, Mel had retreated. She tended to get that way when processing something important, whether it was a case or something that hit closer to home.

When she got quiet like this, pushing never worked. He decided to give her space until she was ready to talk. Then he'd be there, a shoulder to lean on, a patient ear to listen.

The elevator chimed and the doors opened. They made their way down the hall, passed the nurses' station to Room 311.

"Mel, my dear." Gordon held out his hand when they entered.

He looked frail, older than the last time Waylon had seen him in person. Maybe the knowledge of his condition colored his perception or the last couple of days, with his illness worsening, had taken a toll on him.

Removing her sunglasses, she took his hand and sat in the chair at his bedside.

Gordon already looked sickly but paled further. “What happened to your face?” he asked, sounding aghast.

Melanie grimaced as she reached for her cheek.

She’d taken the time to put on a little makeup, to mask the severity of her bruises, but she’d kept the application light, not bothering to try to hide them entirely since the marks seemed determined to poke through.

“I don’t want to trouble you with the specifics,” she said. “You have enough to worry about.”

The office probably hadn’t told him because he’d been unreachable in the hospital, no doubt with his wife as the gatekeeper of communication to keep his stress low.

“At least tell me if that’s the reason Detective Wright is with you.”

“It is,” Waylon said. “Circumstances require ADA Merritt to have police protection.”

Gordon’s brow creased with worry. “What happened? Are you all right?”

“I’m okay. Thanks to Detective Wright.” She pulled on a smile. “Where’s Gloria?”

“Since you were coming to the hospital, I told her to take a break. To go home. Eat a proper meal. Take a nap in our bed instead of in one of these uncomfortable chairs.”

That was love. The only time Melanie hadn’t been with Waylon in the hospital was when he’d had to be taken for his CT scan, but he had ensured that an officer had stayed with her.

The Weismans had been together a long time. Thirty-five or forty devoted years. They were the gold standard of marriage in town.

“I wish you had told me,” Melanie said. “That you were sick.”

“Once people find out, they treat you differently. I wanted

to keep it quiet until…" He took a deep breath. "Until I couldn't any longer and, so, here we are."

"How much time do you have?" She shook her head, like she'd caught herself, hearing the words. "I'm sorry. Is it rude to ask?"

He smiled. "That's what I love about you. Your honesty. The lack of pretense with you."

That was also one of the things Waylon loved about her as well. "I'm going to step out in the hall," he said. "Give you two some privacy."

She glanced back at him over her shoulder. "Thanks."

"I won't go far."

Mel smiled. "I know you won't."

Waylon left the room and leaned against the wall near the threshold of the open door.

"I might have a couple of years left," Gordon said. "If I'm lucky. Time that I want to spend with Gloria. Not in the office, hastening my demise with work."

"I don't know how we're going to manage without you," Melanie said.

"You don't need me." Gordon gave a light chuckle. "You're going to do great as the acting DA."

"Me?" The surprise in her voice was genuine.

For years, she'd wanted that promotion, but Waylon was certain that she didn't want it like this.

"It was always going to be you, Melanie. I didn't hire you to be the assistant district attorney. I hired you with the intention of you replacing me."

Waylon was thunderstruck by his endorsement, his confidence in her. Not that he should've been. Mel was extraordinary.

"I-I had no idea," she said, sounding as astonished as he felt.

"I wouldn't have lasted as long as I did without you taking on so much work. So many tough cases. Without complaint. You're not simply a rising star. You're an unstoppable rocket ship. You're going to go far. I could even see you as the state attorney general someday," Gordon said, taking Waylon's breath away.

State attorney general.

A huge job.

A huge deal.

Melanie had only ever talked about making DA, but for a person like her, someone so driven, once she achieved one goal, a new one would have to replace it.

In some circles he was familiar with, it was a shameful thing for a woman to have too much ambition. Waylon had heard both men and women speak on it. Antiquated, old-school thinking, in his opinion.

He wasn't sexist, but he had been guilty of assuming that Mel was a highly competitive and determined female willing to step over anybody who got in her way. That she might have burned bridges in Denver doing so.

The truth was the Brents of the world had taken advantage of her while she'd been busy building bridges. She'd had to work twice as hard to get to where she was today.

Waylon admired her for not giving up, not settling for less than she deserved. The level of her ambition shouldn't be the measure of her value or success or something she should ever be ashamed of having.

Melanie *was* a rocket ship and he wanted to help her blast through the stratosphere.

"That's so kind of you, Gordon," she said.

"Not kind. It's just the simple truth. You've got a bright future ahead of you. I've reached out to some folks, some powerful people in this great state. Called in all my favors on your behalf. Asked them to transfer that goodwill to you. To help you rise. To ensure your success. Even the best rocket ship needs fuel, propulsion, and an excellent guidance system. Great things are in store for you. I've been assured."

Waylon wished he could've seen Melanie's face. She was going to get everything she'd ever wanted.

"I don't mean to sound ungrateful," she said, "but why would you do such a thing for me?"

"Gloria and I never had children. We weren't able to conceive, and I didn't want to adopt. Shortsighted on my part, looking back on everything. I regret denying her the opportunity to be a mother. Since you came into our lives, you've been like a daughter to us. I don't need those favors anymore. Let me do this for you."

"Thank you. Mind if I hug you?"

"Bring it in."

Waylon peeked around into the room. Melanie leaned over and hugged Gordon.

"I don't know what to say."

"Say, you'll still call Gloria after I'm gone," Gordon said, patting her back "and have lunch with her on occasion."

As Melanie sat back down, Waylon drew back out of sight.

"It would be my pleasure," Mel said. "You know how much I love Gloria."

"There. Nothing else needs to be said on that matter. Now, you're going to tell me exactly what happened to your face and why you need police protection."

Waylon strode down the hall toward the elevator. Once certain there was no danger of him being overheard while keeping an eye on anyone going in or out of Gordon's room, he pulled out his phone and the business card from his wallet.

Hard to believe that Rip Lockwood, the one-time leader of the Iron Warriors Motorcycle Club, was an illustrious business owner who had built a small empire in security and protection services. The last he'd heard about Lockwood, from Melanie unofficially, was that he had helped bring down a notorious bad guy in town they had all been after for years.

The achievement had come at a great personal cost. Lockwood and a former sheriff's deputy he'd ended up marrying had gone into hiding from a drug cartel. The very same cartel that Waylon had helped the Powells deal with.

Waylon dialed the private number on the back of the card. The phone rang three times and he worried that it would go to voicemail.

His phone vibrated. A text came through, flashing on the top of his screen.

Holden: Kristin Loeb's body was found. Call me for details.

A thread of ice slithered through Waylon's gut and twisted. He was just about to hang up and call the chief deputy.

But, finally, on the sixth ring, someone picked up. "This is Rip Lockwood."

"Hello." His mind blanked. It took him a beat to gather his thoughts. "This is Detective Waylon Wright." He considered asking Lockwood if they could schedule a chat for a later time. But he had no idea when that would be, whether they'd get another break in the storm. Maybe it was better to take a few minutes to get his questions answered while Melanie finished her visit with Gordon. "Chance Reyes gave me your number. He told me that you might have a position available for me in Ironside Protection Services."

"First, let me thank you for going to war against the Sandoval Cartel. My family and I no longer have to keep a low profile in no small part because of you."

"Lives were at stake. Action needed to be taken. Without

delay. I took it. Simple as that." The situation had been more complicated, but his explanation didn't need to be. He'd only done what was right. Necessary.

"Chance told me I was going to like you," Lockwood said. "He was right. I understand we have something in common."

News to him. Waylon didn't have any earthly idea what he could have in common with a former motorcycle club president. "Oh really. What's that?"

"Chance did a deep dive into you and gave me a very detailed dossier."

Another news flash. Waylon felt at a disadvantage.

"We're both veterans with a unique skill set," Lockwood said. "I was a Marine Raider."

"Army ranger," Waylon said, a reflex and unnecessary since this guy already knew everything about him.

The interesting part was not only had they served their country, but they had done so in Special Operations. They were both force multipliers. Deadly weapons.

"You were highly decorated," Lockwood said.

"The military likes giving out medals."

"True, but you also received plenty of commendations as a detective as well. Those can be rare on the force."

"The goal was never about recognition but rather seeking to make a real difference in the world." In the fight against evil and for those who couldn't fight for themselves.

His thoughts veered back to Kristin Loeb. To the devastation that was about to hit Melanie.

To the monster named Drake Colter.

His gut burned with the need for justice.

"You're modest, too," Lockwood said.

Waylon's phone vibrated again. A text from Stoltz. Holden must've updated the Denver PD.

"Um, I don't mean to be rude," Waylon said, "and I know

I called you, but there's a case I'm working on and I just received some information that requires my attention. Can we do this another time?"

"It's taken you six months to dial my number. Now that I've got you on the line, I don't want to let this opportunity pass. Give me two minutes. Hear out the proposition I have for you. Then you can take as much time as you want to think it over or reach out again at your convenience with any follow-up questions. What do you say?"

Waylon stared down the hall at Gordon's room. How was he going to break the news to Melanie?

The thought made his heart sink.

Everything good—their decision to commit to a real relationship, the door opening to her professional dreams—was tied up with the bad—Gordon's illness, the latest SAK murders, Kristin Loeb's body being found.

This wasn't just a simple storm to weather. It was a tsunami. One catastrophic wave after another, all triggered by a major earthquake.

Melanie was taking a breather, a moment to connect with Gordon.

Waylon had to believe they'd have a future together and needed to plan for it during this brief lull between the waves. He could give Lockwood two minutes. "I'm listening."

Chapter Sixteen

Emptiness yawned through Melanie. She wrung her hands in the passenger's seat of Waylon's loaner vehicle. A tense silence filled the SUV on their way to the crime scene.

Ice cold. Shut it down.

Be ice cold.

She repeated the mantra over and over, needing the emotional distance between herself and what she was about to face.

The sand dune came into view, and Melanie's pulse picked up. Three, *four* emergency vehicles, plus a KLBR news van, were parked off to the side of the road near mile marker 15. No proper lot to be seen.

This wasn't like any of the other sand dunes SAK had used, which had been state parks, complete with a visitor's center.

Then again, none of those had been in the wilds of Wyoming. Melanie hadn't even realized the Cowboy State had sand dunes. Much less within a forty-five-minute drive of where she lived. As close to leaving the victim in her backyard as he could get.

She tamped down the hot rush of anger. The sharp pang of guilt.

Be ice cold. Ice. Cold.

"The sand dunes out here, do they only cover a small area?"

she asked, her voice having a tinny sound that grated on her ears. “Is that why there’s no parking lot?”

“The Red Desert is massive. The largest desert unfenced landscape in the lower forty-eight with over half a million acres of contiguous wild country that spans five states.”

The emptiness inside her spread. “That’s a staggering size.” The number of acres he’d spouted off rattled in her brain. “I had no idea.”

“But I did. I just didn’t think that homicidal monster would follow us back up here to leave her body. It should’ve occurred to me after the accident.”

Bad enough she was beating herself up, she didn’t want Waylon torturing himself, too. “You mean the accident that almost killed us and left you with a concussion. Even if it had occurred to you, little good it would’ve done. This is no state park where entrances can be monitored and patrolled. Out here, he has free rein.” A chill skittered down her spine and she scrubbed her hands on her thighs.

Waylon placed one of his large warm palms on top of hers. “We can take as long as you need. There’s no hurry to get to the crime scene.”

At least he hadn’t once asked the predictable *Are you all right?*

She’d been prepared for it, but it hadn’t come.

I’m alive. Kristin isn’t. She was not all right. Would never again be all right until she brought her killer to justice. She guessed Waylon suspected as much.

“Waiting any longer won’t make this any easier,” she said. “We should go.”

Her phone chimed with a text.

Darcy: Hank came over to help go through the documents since you’re busy with other things. He also brought lunch, sandwiches, for everyone. Hope that’s okay.

Busy with other things.

Such a simple phrase for one of the hardest things in her life that she was about to do.

"What's up?" Waylon asked.

"Darcy's boyfriend is also at the house, helping to comb through the documents." She started typing a reply. "He's a nice kid." Hank was Darcy's age, only seven years younger than Melanie, but they both had a youthful, starry-eyed quality. "A paralegal, too, with a firm in Bison Ridge."

Mel: No problem. Thanks.

"If he's anything like Darcy, the way she showed up armed with a variety of highlighters and different-colored sticky notes, then I'm all for the extra assistance today," Waylon said. "It's been one thing after another."

"Kristin is dead. This isn't another thing to do or manage."

He stilled. "I know. She was smart and dedicated. Warm and funny. And she was your friend." He took her hand and held it.

Melanie glanced at him. Her throat tightened at the look of love on his face. Tears stung her eyes.

She pulled her hand free before her emotions started spilling out and she unraveled into a sobbing mess. "I'm ready."

Waylon grabbed his windbreaker that had LPD printed across the back in bright yellow. He opened the door and a warm gust of air washed over them. They climbed out. She walked around to him while he pulled the jacket on over his T-shirt. Not that he needed the windbreaker.

Even at a glance, she could see they knew everyone out there. In addition to the sheriff's department, there was also a Laramie PD detective. Brian Bradshaw.

Melanie did her best to appear unaffected, in control, which worked until she hit the sand. Trudging through the uneven, shifting terrain tested her composure, threatening to break the dam holding back raw emotion.

Erica Egan, KLBR reporter and unofficial town nuisance, spotted them and descended like a vulture ready to pick their bones clean of any tidbits of information.

A bubble of panic rose in Melanie's chest.

Waylon guided her past the reporter, positioning himself between her and the camera.

"ADA Merritt, is it true that you were close friends with the victim, Kristin Loeb?" Egan asked, maneuvering to the opposite side.

Melanie lowered her head, tilting it away from the news camera trained on them. "No comment."

Raising his hand at the camera, Waylon cut across in front of her, blocking them from getting a clear shot of her.

The relentless reporter refused to give up. "I was told that you provoked this latest murder because you don't know when to accept defeat," Egan said, and Melanie tripped, nearly face-planting in the sand, but Waylon caught her arm, keeping her from falling. "Would you care to comment on that?" She thrust the mic toward them.

"No," Waylon barked the single word.

They crossed the perimeter the sheriff's department had established. Two deputies prevented Egan and her camera-person from following them.

"Where does she get that kind of stuff from?" Melanie asked Waylon.

"Who knows? She may work for KLBR, but Egan is nothing more than a tabloid journalist."

Melanie was inclined to agree. Egan was drawn to sensationalized stories and controversial subject matter, always using a deplorable sound bite as a hook to draw viewers.

They approached the cluster of deputies.

Brian Bradshaw and Holden Powell spotted them and headed over to meet them.

“Glad you were assigned,” Waylon said, shaking Brian’s hand. “What in the hell is Egan doing here?”

“We couldn’t stop her from coming,” Brian said.

“Why not?” Melanie glanced over her shoulder at Erica Egan, who was making the cameraperson point the lens in their direction. “How did she even find out about the body or the location?”

Holden put his hands on his hips. “She’s the one who informed us. An anonymous tip came in from the killer. Called the news station.”

“The voice was digitally disguised,” Brian said. “I’ve got the recording. I’ll let you hear it, but I figured you’d want to see the body first.”

They strode across the sand to the group of men milling near the body. A perimeter had been cordoned off. The only person inside the yellow-tape circle appeared to be the sheriff’s deputy, who was also their current crime scene tech. He wore white Tyvek coveralls and a blue face mask and held a camera.

Kristin lay in the center of a sand angel. Her head tilted back, her face pale, blond hair fanned out like a halo, purple markings on her neck. Sand on her eyes. In her mouth.

Inches below her feet, a word was scrolled in the sand with stones.

Sinner.

The sight of Kristin and the rapid sound of the camera snapping pictures, click-click-click, made Melanie’s stomach heave. Spinning around, she thought she might be sick and covered her mouth.

Waylon put a hand on her shoulder and squeezed.

“My best guess is that she’s been dead for more than

twenty-four hours. Maybe closer to thirty-six," the CSI said. "But so many different factors can severely impact the onset and timeline of rigor mortis. Temperature. Activity before death. Physical conditions where the body is found. The ME will be able to give a more definitive time."

"Why don't we step over here?" Holden suggested. "We'll play the recording the killer left at the news station."

They walked off to the side. Melanie kept her back to the crime scene. Part of her felt like a coward for not being able to look longer at Kristin. The other part was filled with rage.

Brian took out his phone. "You're going to need to brace yourself." He threw a cautious glance at Waylon and then back at her. "We can go back to your vehicle and let you sit down first."

Melanie shook her head and folded her arms across her abdomen. "We'll listen to it here." She'd rather do it standing. Less likelihood that she'd fall apart.

"Okay." Brian played it for them.

This statement is for Erica Egan. I am the Sand Angel Killer. I have chosen you, Ms. Egan, to spread my message. I want the world to know the truth. I want them to know my wrath, said the creepy, electronically altered voice. The cadence was sickeningly familiar. *To know that my most recent cleansing, of Kristin Loeb, the sinner, was provoked. ADA Melanie Merritt dragged her good friend into my crosshairs. She doesn't know when to accept defeat. Instead of the Denver DA and the sheriff giving a press conference, Merritt should have been the one standing behind the podium, on live television, begging for my forgiveness. She should have admitted that her judgment was impaired and biased while working at the Denver DA's office. That she made a heinous mistake, falsely charging and persecuting the wrong man for my crimes.*

The tone was whispery and raspy and cold and eerily insistent. *I'm willing to give her a chance to atone. She must show contrition, on the air, on her knees, begging me, by nine o'clock tonight, or I will claim another sinner before the sun rises and their blood, along with that of Kristin Loeb's, will be on her hands. Tick tock, Ms. Melanie Merritt.*

Melanie's chest constricted. Her heart started racing, palms sweating.

"You've got to be kidding me," Waylon said.

She squeezed her eyes shut, but saw the image of Kristin, dead, splayed out in the sand. Melanie had missed her at the motel by minutes. *Minutes.* The thought was agonizing.

If she hadn't gotten distracted, focused on Waylon, decompressing, making love to him, fighting with him, they would've been watching out for Kristin's arrival. What if they had spotted the tail on her? And what if they had put out an APB on him? What if they had caught him in the act, had gone up to the room to check on her sooner during the attack and intervened?

What if, what if, what if...

"Mel?"

She glanced up. Waylon was watching her closely. Again, he had the sense not to ask whether she was okay.

"Are you all right?" Holden stared at her. "Do you need a drink of water or to sit down?"

"What I need is to have Drake Colter back behind bars." She clenched her hands. "There's no limit to the depths of his depravity," she muttered under her breath.

A cold lump lodged in her throat and swelled. She felt like she was choking on it. Forcing herself to take a few deep breaths, she strained to stay steady on her feet.

Waylon watched her eyes, as if gauging her reaction.

She was used to seeing photos of crime scenes. Not being

at them in person, forced to face the ugliness and senseless brutality up close and personal. For him, and the other two men, they had been to plenty of crime scenes and dealt with some horrid number of victims—the ones who had survived and the ones who hadn't been so lucky.

Waylon rubbed her arm, as though he understood her emotions pinged around like pinballs beneath the surface layer of ice she needed to get through this.

"Is it possible you got the wrong guy in Denver?" Brian asked. "Maybe the person who murdered Ms. Loeb is the real Sand Angel Killer."

Melanie opened her eyes and stared at him. "Drake Colter is a murderer. I'm one hundred percent positive. Not a doubt in my mind. The only thing that I might be wrong about is that he didn't do it alone."

Holden scratched his chin. "I take it, then, that you won't be making a statement of contrition tonight on the air."

"Down on her knees? Begging?" Waylon snapped. "There's no way that's ever going to happen. I won't let it."

Bristling, Melanie glared at him, annoyed that he knew what she was thinking. Except for the last bit. "I can speak for myself." She turned to the chief deputy. "Exactly what he said. I'm not making any such statement about impaired and biased judgment, that would only invite every criminal I prosecuted in the Denver office to have their attorney file an appeal on that basis." It would be a legal disaster. "I will never accept defeat. Or ask the forgiveness of a cruel, sadistic killer who gets off on taking human life."

Holden grimaced. "We've got ourselves a moral dilemma. I understand why you want to take a stand against this guy, but there'll be a consequence." He let that dangle for a moment. "Someone else will die. And that woman," Holden said, pointing to Egan, who was still filming them, "is going to tell the world that it's your fault. That you had a chance to save someone and chose not to. Can you live with the fact that by not doing what this sicko wants, someone else will pay for it?"

Bile rose in the back of Melanie's throat, making the tender flesh burn. Her thoughts whirled and gnawed at her. She didn't care if the world condemned her, but she didn't want anyone else to die because of her.

"Still time to think it through," Brian said. "Almost nine hours before you have to make a decision, either way, that you might regret."

Melanie glanced over her shoulder at Kristin's body again. The woman had been a good person. A whip-smart investigative journalist, passionate, caring, who hadn't deserved to die at the age of forty. At the hands of a monster. "I don't want anyone else's blood on my hands."

"No one's blood is on your hands," Waylon said, drawing her gaze. "This isn't your fault. You can't consider it. The criminals you prosecuted in Denver could walk free. Not only that, but you also have to think of your career. The long-term implications of making a statement like that."

Her career was important but preventing the death of another innocent person was far more important. "If I can save someone, then I have to, don't I?"

"You might not have any other choice," Holden said grimly.

"There's always a choice. Step aside," Waylon thundered, staring daggers at the chief deputy until Holden raised a hand in submission and walked away, Brian leaving alongside him. Then he looked back at her. "You don't have to do this." His voice lowered. "Mel, you can't negotiate with a terrorist. A known murderer. Listen to me. The way Drake Colter spoke about you haunts me. That sadistic killer blames you. Mostly you. And that's what this deadly game of cat and mouse that he's playing is all about. Hurting you *before* he kills you.

That's the reason he had Luna Tuttle try to seduce me, because he picked up on our relationship. Now he wants to take away your career."

Waylon's jaw twitched with suppressed emotion. "Even if you do go on national television, begging some heartless animal for forgiveness that he doesn't deserve, there's no guarantee that he'll spare whatever victim he's chosen. And make no mistake about it, he has already chosen her. Trust me, you'll regret making a deal with this devil."

Waylon was right.

In her heart, she knew what he was saying to be true.

But she also couldn't live with the choice to do nothing, to not try. The consequence of another innocent person dying was too much for her to bear.

Chapter Seventeen

The summer rain shower only added to the heaviness Waylon and surely Melanie felt, making the air outside dense and muggy.

By the time they made it back to his house, the rain had stopped. Inside, Waylon couldn't believe the amount of work Darcy and her boyfriend had accomplished.

"Here's the log of people who visited Drake Colter over the three years he was incarcerated." Darcy handed them the sheets of paper she had stapled together. Her red hair was pulled into a high ponytail that swayed when she spoke in an animated way, like she'd had too much coffee. "Highlighted in pink are regular, routine visitors. There were six. I wrote their names on a bright pink sticky note."

Stephen Wolpert
Isaac Meacham
Luna Tuttle
Jovian Tuttle
Aimee Frazer
Nancy Colter

Waylon and Mel exchanged glances at the two names on the list they recognized. Isaac, cult leader supreme, was a no-brainer, and another name he knew too well.

Based on what had happened at the Sand Angelite house, it shouldn't have surprised him that the Tuttles were also on the list. The skinny kid Stoltz had questioned in the kitchen turned out to be Luna's brother, Jovian.

"Any idea who Stephen Wolpert, Nancy Colter and Aimee Frazer are?" Melanie asked.

"Wolpert is his attorney. Nancy Colter is his mother. She stopped visiting last year because neuropathy in her feet became too much for her, according to her Facebook page. Aimee Frazer is a convicted stalker. Instead of being obsessed with celebrities, her preference is for felons."

"We know that Luna Tuttle is a Sand Angelite," Melanie said, "who idolizes Drake Colter. You wouldn't happen to know her relation to Jovian, would you?"

Waylon hadn't given her a full rundown of the who's who Sand Angelite list. "Jovian is her brother."

"Both their Facebook pages went dark about four years ago," Darcy said, "following the tragic death of their parents. The father died of a heart attack sometime after the mother was murdered." The redhead grimaced. "It's so sad."

"Murdered? What happened to the mother?" Waylon asked.

"You're never going to believe this, but the mom was one of the victims of the Sand Angel Killer."

Melanie rocked back on her heels, stiffening. "What was her name?"

Darcy leafed through her notes. "Celestia something."

A gasp escaped Melanie's lips. "Celestia de la Fuente." Her voice was low, her eyes haunted. "She went by her maiden name. Her husband declined to speak in court to influence the judge regarding sentencing."

"Yeah, that's right," Darcy said, looking at her notes. "His name was Rob Tuttle."

"Celestia had two kids, but I didn't know their names."

Melanie appeared lost in thought. "I didn't make the Tuttle connection," she said, looking rattled.

Waylon folded his arms across his chest to keep from holding her or touching her in any way that would make it known they were romantically involved.

"Would you like me to make you a cup of tea?" Hank asked, like this was his house. Seated at the dining table in front of a pile of papers, the young man sported a trendy hairstyle cropped low at the back and on the sides, with the curly front hanging long across his eyebrows. He sipped from a mug that had come from one of the kitchen cabinets.

Waylon slid an annoyed look his way.

"I'm sorry. Darcy and I like to have tea while we work instead of coffee. I brought my own." Hank patted his messenger bag. "Chamomile. Lapsang souchong. Earl Grey. Spiced chai."

"No, thank you." Melanie dismissed the offer with a wave of her hand.

"Do you need a minute?" Waylon looked at her. "In the kitchen? Or outside?" Anywhere they could have a moment alone for him to comfort her.

"I'm fine."

That's what a warrior would say, but it was clear she wasn't fine.

Melanie took off her purse and set it on the table. "What else did you find?"

"For the rest of the visitor's list, if someone saw Drake Colter three times or more, but without any kind of routine, I highlighted them in blue," Darcy said. "And anyone who only paid a visit once or twice is marked in yellow. Green, I reserved for individuals who not only visited him but also sent him correspondence. They're written on the—"

"Green sticky note," Waylon said, completing her sentence.

With a bright smile, Darcy gave an enthusiastic nod, making the ponytail bob.

There were only three names on that list.

Stephen Wolpert
Nancy Colter
Owen Udall ➔ OHU

"What's with the arrow pointing to OHU?" Waylon asked.

Hank raked his curls from his eyes. "Only one person wrote to Drake Colter with any consistency."

"That's an understatement," Darcy said. "Try once a week for three years. I made the connection between the initials on the letters and the name listed in the visitor's log."

"OHU. Those are the initials in the return address and how every letter was signed." The young guy handed them each a sheet of paper. One letter was from OHU and the other from Drake Colter.

"What was the return address?" Waylon queried.

Hank grabbed another sheet from the table. "A PO box in Denver." He handed it to them. "Nothing overt stands out in any of the letters that I've read so far. Talk of how things are going in prison, what Drake had to eat. The other one mentions taking long walks, what OHU is watching on television. All innocuous stuff. But I think they may have been writing in code."

Waylon raised an eyebrow. "Why?"

Hank came around the table and pointed out something on each letter. "A passage in the Bible is referenced in every single letter. One hundred fifty-five from OHU and one hundred forty-two from Drake. At first, I thought it might be a way to share inspiration. You know, something hopeful. But then I started thinking about it. There's nothing religious about the tone. Nothing inspirational actually written. In fact, they both went out of their way to be as boring and under the radar as possible. Also take a look at the paragraphs, the way they're broken up. It's kind of odd. Like they wanted certain sentences, certain words, in a specific place."

Now that it had been pointed out, the oddity struck Waylon clear as day.

"He wasn't sure," Darcy said, "but once I took a look, I had to agree. They were probably using a code so they could communicate without being flagged by the prison when the letters were screened."

"Any idea what they were saying back and forth?" Melanie asked.

"No clue," Hank said, shaking his head. "We'd need an expert in code breaking. Even though we know they were using the Bible, the cipher can't be decoded without the key. Is it the numbers of the chapter and verse? Or something specific to the lines referenced in the Bible? It could take us weeks to figure out the true meaning of a single letter. Who knows how long it would take to decode almost three hundred of them?"

"Hopefully, Drake Colter and his accomplice will be behind bars in a matter of days," Waylon said. "Not weeks." He looked at Mel. Her gaze fell and she chewed on her lower lip. "What is it?"

"We don't have that kind of time." She glanced at the clock on the wall near the dining room table.

Two o'clock.

Her brow furrowed and she shoved her hair back behind her ears.

Waylon could practically read her mind. "You can't still be considering it," he said.

"I'm not considering it." But she gave him a baleful look. "I've already decided to do it."

Waylon set his jaw.

"Do what?" Darcy asked, staring at Mel.

"Nothing," Waylon said to the paralegal and turned to Melanie. "Please. Don't do this." The last thing he wanted was to start a debate with her that he wouldn't win. Especially when they didn't have any privacy.

"I have to," Melanie said, a determined look in her eyes. "Otherwise, I won't be able to live with myself."

Hank raised a tentative hand. "Excuse me. What are we talking about?"

Waylon groaned and, before Melanie could respond, her cell phone rang.

She unzipped her purse. As she removed her phone, the handbag tipped over on the table and the handle of his BUG slipped out.

Both Darcy and Hank noticed it.

Waylon tucked the handle back inside and zipped her purse closed.

"It's Emilio."

"Put it on speaker," Waylon said.

Melanie nodded and tapped the icon. "Hi. I've got you on speaker with Detective Wright and a couple of paralegals are with us."

"I'm here with Stoltz and Jimenez, but they're both on their phones. Melanie, I'm sorry to hear about Kristin."

"She was your friend, too. It's a blow for both of us."

"I have lots to update you on," Emilio said. "We were able to access Kristin's cloud. There weren't any recent notes from her. I guess they were in her notebooks."

Waylon swore under his breath and Melanie started chewing on her lower lip again.

"But she had her laptop, home computer and phone all synced. I was able to retrieve her browser history. The last thing she searched on the internet was Savio House. A non-profit organization that helps to place foster children in temporary and permanent homes."

"That's what the text Kristin sent me was about."

"Yeah, I think so," Emilio said. "Savio autocorrects to Savior."

"What was the Savio connection that she found?" Waylon asked.

"Turns out that Isaac Meacham's father took in foster kids. Specifically, Drake Colter, Aimee Frazer and Owen Henry Udall. The last two visited Colter in prison. Not only that, but Isaac Meacham's father died under suspicious circumstances. One of the executive leaders at Savio, Vonda Van Nolan, told me that shortly before Bill Meacham's death, they received an anonymous tip that he was abusing the kids and subjecting them to brainwashing. Something to do with a new religious movement that incorporated the principles of Darwinism."

"That would explain a lot," Waylon said.

"Ms. Van Nolan also met with Kristin the night she was kidnapped. They talked about Udall at length. Going through the rest of Kristin's browser history, she must've pieced together that Udall attended law school at the University of Denver during the same time the DU student was killed. I think the last lead she was following was about him."

"Maybe she found him," Melanie said.

"That's what we're thinking. The last address Kristin used in Google Maps matches the current known address for Udall. My hacker, Orson, has been digging into Isaac Meacham's finances. Guess whose name Udall's apartment is rented under and who's been footing the bill for the past twelve years?"

"Isaac Meacham," Waylon and Melanie said in unison.

"Bingo. Meacham even paid for Udall's bachelor's degree in criminal justice and for law school, though Udall didn't finish. Hey, look, things are moving fast on our end now," Emilio said. "The detectives have enough for an arrest warrant for Colter."

"Based on what?" Waylon asked. "You guys must've turned up something concrete."

"Detective Jimenez got Kurt Parrish to break. One of the guys living at the Fair Chance Treatment Center admitted to seeing Colter sneaking out and Parrish helping him cover it up. Parrish completely fell apart when confronted with an eyewitness account. He claims the Sand Angelites kidnapped his girlfriend, who he's been dating for a month. Love at first sight and he's completely devoted to her. Parrish stated that they're holding her hostage and unless he does everything Colter wants, they've threatened to kill her."

Something about it scratched at Waylon's nerves, had his cop instinct pinging.

Melanie shook her head. "That doesn't sound like the Angelites. They're disturbing, but I've never known them to threaten anyone with bodily harm, especially not murder."

"Any validity to it?" Waylon asked. "Who's the girlfriend?"

"Luna Tuttle."

Waylon swallowed a grumble as Mel sighed.

The whole thing had been a setup from the beginning. Luna Tuttle must have cozied up to Kurt Parrish, got him to care about her, only to use that infatuation against him. "She's one of the Sand Angelites."

"Yeah, I'm aware. Stoltz told me that you interviewed her," Vasquez said, and Waylon thought, way to bury the lead. "Colter's airtight alibi is gone, he has a hit list tattooed on his arm and his Sand Angelite buddy appears to have been helping him the entire time. All that gave the detectives enough to get a warrant for Colter and Meacham, who's been aiding and abetting him."

"Meacham is a planner, a cult leader and the money guy." Waylon raked a hand through his hair. "He's been aiding and abetting, but he's not the one kidnapping and possibly killing people."

"Hang on a second. Detective Jimenez wants to talk to you."

"Hey, Melanie," Jimenez said, coming on the line.

"You're on speaker with my bodyguard and a couple of others."

"There's been a development." Jimenez's voice was grave. "I hate to be the one to tell you this." A pause on the other end.

"JJ? What's wrong?" Melanie asked.

Another beat of silence and Waylon's chest filled with dread. "Whatever it is, spit it out."

"The arrest warrant came in for Drake Colter. We reached out to the officers who were following him, but they lost him."

"What?" Rage leaked into Waylon's voice. "How in the hell did that happen?"

Mel's gaze was dark, ominous. She looked like a dam about to burst.

"Colter has supposedly been looking for a job. They lost him in the Park Meadows Shopping Mall. The place is pretty big."

Waylon clenched his hand. "How long has Colter been running around today with no one watching him?"

"Since nine thirty."

"How is that possible?" Melanie asked. "The mall doesn't open until ten."

"Mall entrances are open an hour before the mall stores do and walkers are welcome."

Waylon swore. "He could be anywhere by now. Why didn't the officers report in that they'd lost him?"

"They were embarrassed. Hoped they'd be able to find him before it was an issue.

"Listen, Colter knows he has to be back at the FCTC no later than ten tonight for check-in. He has no idea about the arrest warrant. We'll pick him up then."

"We think he might be working with a third person," Waylon said. "This Udall fellow. A man left a message for Melanie at the KLBR news station. Threatened to punish her for prosecuting the wrong man as the Sand Angel Killer. You need to find Udall and bring him in for questioning."

"Already working on it. Don't worry. This son of a gun is going down. Once we have him in custody, we'll let you know."

"Thanks," Waylon said.

Melanie disconnected. The worry on her face mirrored the same concern that had his pulse pounding.

"Are we safe here?" Hank asked.

"Yes." Waylon nodded. "Colter doesn't know where she is."

"But what about his other accomplice?" Melanie stared at him. "The one who left the message at KLBR. He might know I'm here."

"He's got his sights set on another victim. Someone else he plans to use to hurt you before he comes after you again."

"I've been thinking," Melanie said, "what if he targets someone I care about? Gloria Weisman." Her gaze shifted to the paralegal. "Darcy."

The young woman cringed. Her boyfriend hurried to wrap a protective arm around her.

If the killer's intent was to inflict the most pain, then those targets would be high on his list. "I'll text Holden now about Mrs. Weisman." With her husband in the hospital, she was alone and an easy unaware target. "Call her and make sure she's safe. Tell her to stay at the hospital until a deputy gets there and to notify security now."

As Melanie strode off to the side and made the call, he whipped out his phone and quickly fired off the message to Holden.

He received a reply in less than a minute that Mrs. Weisman would be protected.

Melanie hurriedly explained over the phone. "I'm sorry to endanger you, Gloria." A pause. "Thank you for understanding." She hung up.

"What about me?" Darcy asked, pressing her forehead against her boyfriend's shoulder.

Hank rubbed her back. "Do you want me to stay at your place, babe?"

"Why don't we ever go to your house?" The redhead looked up at him, her mouth in a slight pout. "Can't I stay with you?"

Her boyfriend tensed for a second then smiled. "Of course you can."

"Sure you don't mind?" Darcy sniffled.

"Positive."

"Are you armed?" Waylon asked him.

The guy shook his head. "I don't care for guns."

Waylon stepped toward him. "Do you know how to use one properly?"

"Yeah, I do."

"I can lend you one until this is resolved and Darcy isn't in any more danger." Waylon had plenty.

"Please." Darcy stared at the younger man with wide pleading eyes. "It'd make me feel better."

"Okay." Hank nodded. "Just temporarily."

"I'll get you one from my safe."

"No need. I can give him the one in my purse." Melanie reached for her handbag.

Hank raised a palm. "It can wait until we're ready to leave."

"Thank you so much," Darcy said.

"Well, I definitely need a cup of chamomile tea now. Does anyone else want one?" Hank looked around.

"Maybe I'll try the chamomile, also," Melanie said. "To settle my nerves."

"Make that three." Darcy kissed her boyfriend on the cheek and then the guy looked at Waylon expectantly.

"None for me, thanks, but since you already know where everything is…" Waylon gestured for him to go to the kitchen.

"Three chamomile teas coming up." Hank strode down the hall to the kitchen.

"What did Holden say?" Melanie asked.

"He's going to send a deputy to the hospital. Only one problem. They don't have the manpower to watch over her for more than a day or two with everything else going on."

"Hopefully, that's all she'll need. I'll reach out to Erica Egan about making a statement on air tonight, before nine, since she already knows why I need to."

Waylon glanced at Darcy, who sat at the table, her attention turned to the letters. "Are you sure I can't convince you not to do this?" he asked Mel.

"This is something I have to do."

Porcelain shattered in the kitchen. "Is everything all right?" Waylon asked.

Hank tore down the hall and into the dining room. "There was someone outside in the back. A man, I think. But I can't be sure because they were wearing a black helmet."

Waylon's pulse quickened. The location of the crime scene in the desert and the roads they had to take to reach it, made it easy for someone to watch the area from a distance. What if Colter's accomplice, the one who'd left the message at the news station, had been staking out the Red Desert crime scene? What if he had waited to see if Melanie would show up, only to follow her back to Waylon's house?

"Stay here." Waylon drew the service sidearm holstered on his hip. "Put the chain on the door, call 9-1-1 and then Holden." Without waiting for acknowledgment, he raced off along the hall.

In the kitchen, he rushed to the sink, made sure the window overlooking the back was locked, and peeked through the curtains, darting his gaze around. Grass and trees as far as he could see. No one lurking about. But if it was the same man who had attacked Mel, no telling where he could be by now. Hiding behind a tree. Or a shrub. Or looking to enter through a window.

Slipping the chain on the back door, he wished, for the first time, that he didn't live in such a remote location and had neighbors close by who'd spot a prowler.

An obvious prowler dressed in all black, wearing a helmet, skulking around his property in broad daylight.

Something about that was off. Felt wrong. Still, best for him to check the rest of the windows in the house to be sure everything was secure. Then he'd have the others hunker down in the living room while he searched outside.

Spinning around, Waylon froze as his gaze fell to the bottom of his stove, snagging on a tiny, red-blinking light—one that shouldn't have been there under the kitchen range. Razor-sharp coldness zipped down his spine. Wires surrounded the LED light that started flashing faster in warning.

He'd seen enough improvised explosive devices in the army for his brain to register what he was staring at. A bomb had been planted.

Inside his house!

Melanie.

Waylon made it two steps when there was a hollow *whomp.*

Heat and debris slammed into him. The propulsive force of the blast lifted him off his feet, hurling him through the air. The back of his skull smacked something hard. Breath exploded from his lungs with an *oomph!*

Black spots danced in front of his eyes. Bile scored his throat. Pain lanced through his body. Heaviness pulled his eyes shut and darkness swallowed him.

Chapter Eighteen

An explosion came from the kitchen with a giant crack of fire and deafening sound, fragments of rubble spitting from the doorway. The punch of the concussion shook the house.

Her ears rang from the jarring noise. Smoke billowed from the hall.

Paralyzed with horror, Melanie was crouched, cell phone clutched in her hand, cringing in shock. Then realization set in. The blood drained from her face.

Waylon. He'd been in the kitchen when the detonation went off.

Was he injured? Alive?

"Waylon," she cried out, praying he would respond. No answer. "Waylon!"

She lunged toward the smoke, but a strong hand snatched her arm, holding her back.

Hank.

Metal glinted in the light. The gun from her purse was in his raised hand. He swung the weapon, hitting her across the face with it.

The blow sent her whirling around, her hand opening on reflex, dropping the phone and sending it clattering across the hardwood. She slammed into the dining room table. Her knees buckled. Reaching out to steady herself, she fumbled for something to latch onto, knocking her purse to the floor as she fell.

Darcy screamed.

Gut-wrenching pain mixed with blinding fear rattled Melanie to the core. She saw stars. Blinked through the agony in her head. Her vision blurred. Her stomach heaved.

"Shut up!" Hank yelled at Darcy, who was still screaming hysterically. "I told you to be quiet!"

"Oh my God! Babe, what are you doing?"

Hank pointed the gun at Darcy. "Sit down and be quiet."

"But we have to call for help."

Melanie's head cleared. She searched the floor, her gaze flying over her purse, her keys, to her phone. *There.* On the other side of the walkway, near the living room.

She had started texting Holden, before the explosion, but had never had a chance to hit Send. She prayed that a neighbor had heard the blast and called 9-1-1, but she couldn't rely on that. Couldn't wait for first responders who might not yet be on the way.

Climbing to her hands and knees, she prepared to make a dash for the cell phone.

"Help isn't coming." Hank kicked Melanie in the stomach, sending a nauseating bolt of pain through her abdomen.

Then he turned to the living room and shot her phone. The cell bounced from the floor, landing in scattered pieces.

Darcy screamed again, the shrill shriek at the top of her lungs.

Hank raised the gun at her and fired.

Silence.

A dark red spot bloomed on Darcy's stomach. Stunned or in shock, the young woman glanced down at the gunshot wound and looked back up at Hank. "Why?"

"Because this was always meant to happen. You were a

means to an end. *Babe.*" He stalked toward Darcy. "Don't get me wrong. I enjoyed my time with you and you're great in the sack. If I thought Isaac had a chance at converting you into a believer, things might've worked out differently, but you're too loyal to that woman," he said, pointing the barrel at Melanie, "to see the truth about her. That she's a sinner."

Darcy clutched her bleeding abdomen. "Sinner?"

"Her transgression is the worst. Our number-one sin. She messed with the wrong pack of wolves."

Hank fired again—the sound making Melanie jump—pumping a second bullet into Darcy. The young woman collapsed. Hiccupping gasps of air came from her.

On a burst of panic, Melanie scrambled up from the floor.

Hank lunged, ramming her from behind with a foot to her back. She flew forward, her head smacking against the hardwood. Pain roared through her skull.

A weight crushed down on her, centered on her spine, and he yanked her head back by the hair. "Time for us to take a little ride."

If he took her to a second location, her chances of survival were nil. Here, in this house, she had some chance to fight, to stay alive.

Melanie screamed and flailed. She groped for her purse, for anything to use as a weapon. Her fingers closed around her keys.

For an instant, she considered trying to stab him with the car key, but he had a gun. He could blow a hole in her with a simple pull of the trigger. Just as he'd done to Darcy.

The AirTag.

There might not be a way to stop him from forcing her to leave the house, but if she took the key, maybe it'd help the authorities locate her.

Waylon.

Was he dead?

She would've given anything to run to the kitchen. To see if he was still breathing.

She had hope that he might be alive and injured, and clung to it.

"Come on." Hank pulled her up to her feet by her hair and shoved her forward. "Walk. We'll be taking my vehicle and you'll be driving."

Melanie pretended to double over in pain and clutch her stomach as she slid the key into the pocket of her jeans.

Hank jammed the muzzle of the gun to the back of her head. "Don't make me tell you again. Move."

WAYLON STRUGGLED TO open his eyes. An acrid ether odor filled his nostrils. A sharp burning sensation seared the back of his skull.

Swallowing the harsh rush of acid, he lifted his hand—the Glock still gripped tightly in his fingers—and tried to focus. Get his bearings.

A wave of nausea made his stomach roll and quake as he forced his way to his knees, gasped from the pain in the back of his head, and then got to his feet. His mind reeled.

Smoke and dust worked down into his lungs, making him cough. He glanced around. Fire. Rubble. His kitchen was in pieces.

Shards of shrapnel from the stove had stabbed his right thigh and pierced his abdomen. Both fragments were large enough for him to remove without tools but small enough not to have caused serious injury as long as they hadn't hit a femoral artery.

A wood beam fell from the ceiling, crashing onto what was left of his kitchen island. Dust clung to his clothing and face. His gaze fell over the wreckage of his kitchen, landing on what remained of his stove.

A bomb. In his house.

Had it been Hank? Darcy?

Or had they been working together?

"Mel!" He gagged at the smoke. Waving a hand in front of his face, he coughed.

Limping, he hurried from the kitchen, down the hall. He had his gun up at the ready. His pulse throbbed in his temples.

How long had he been knocked out?

Pressure welled in his chest behind his sternum. She had to be alive. She had to be okay. If anything happened to her…

"Melanie!"

His already pounding heart slammed into his ribs at the sight of Darcy on the floor. Blood. A lot of it. Melanie and Hank were nowhere to be seen, and the front door was wide open.

Darcy gasped for air and reached for him with a trembling hand covered in blood.

Holstering his gun, he raced back to the hallway bathroom. Grabbed the med kit and a towel. Hustled back to the young woman. Wincing through the pain as he knelt beside her, he pressed the towel to her wounds. "We've got to apply pressure."

Two gunshots. Centered close in her abdomen. One bullet had definitely hit her stomach. He suspected the second had struck her liver. The blood was nearly black.

She didn't have long to live.

"Cold." The word came out from her lips as a raspy whisper. "Numb." She coughed, spitting up dark red blood.

Not good signs. She was fading fast.

Even if an ambulance was on the way, they wouldn't be able to save her.

She reached out to him again and he took her hand in his, still keeping pressure on her wound.

"Darcy, do you have any idea where Hank might've taken Melanie?" *Hank.* Owen Henry Udall.

She shook her head. "No," she said like it hurt to speak, to breathe.

"Please, think." His gut tightened with panic. *Hang on, Darcy. Don't die.* "Do you know where he lives?"

A small nod. More blood sputtered from her mouth. "Followed. Him." She took a choppy breath. "Once." More blood sputtered from her mouth. "So c-c-cold."

"I know you're cold. I'm so sorry." He tightened his grip on her hand. This young woman had done nothing wrong other than falling for the wrong guy. One more innocent person whose life was cut short by evil. "Where did you follow Hank to? Where does he live?"

"Followed. To. Blossom..." Another ragged inhalation. A tear leaked from the corner of her eye and her last breath left her in a sigh as her head lolled to the side.

Waylon roared, angry, desperate, sickened at this senseless loss of life. He'd lowered his guard. Let the enemy inside his home. Gave that animal the chance to take what he loved most in the world.

"Blossom what?" he muttered to himself now that Darcy could no longer answer.

Street. Road. Drive. Way.

And where? Wayward Bluffs? Bison Ridge? Laramie?

What was the house number?

Molten fury flooded Waylon's system and he wanted to explode in vengeance.

But that wouldn't do anything to save Melanie. Not until he got his hands on Hank and used that rage to beat the life from him.

He whipped his phone out of his pocket. The cell shook in his hand.

Think, damn it. Think.

Isaac Meacham had paid for Udall's apartment for twelve years. Maybe he was still paying.

Waylon dialed Stoltz. When the detective answered, Waylon didn't wait for a greeting. "Melanie has been taken. By a man named Hank. I think it's Owen Henry Udall. It's the only explanation."

The detective swore.

"Is Emilio still with you?" Waylon asked.

"Yeah."

"Have him reach out to his hacker friend. See if Isaac Meacham is paying for a rented house or apartment anywhere in Wyoming." He spouted off the most likely towns. "Possibly on a street or road named Blossom. I need this. ASAP. We don't have a minute to spare." Every second counted. Melanie might not have much time.

"We're on it," Stoltz said.

He disconnected.

Climbing to his feet with a groan, he dialed Brian Bradshaw. His gaze fell to the cell phone that had been shot to pieces on his floor. He limped past it and over to one of the front windows. Pulled back the curtain. Looked outside.

Hank's SUV was gone. At least Waylon knew what vehicle they were in.

"Bradshaw here."

Waylon quickly explained what had happened, the explosion, Darcy's murder, and gave a physical description of the man who took Mel. "Put an APB out on him. Hank…" He realized he didn't know what fake surname the man was using. "I believe his real name is Owen Henry Udall. He's driving a late-model Chevy Tahoe. Black." Thank goodness he recalled the plate number and passed that along, too.

But that wasn't enough.

Waylon needed to find Melanie. Now. He couldn't even go after them, not knowing which way they'd gone on the road at the main intersection. East toward Bison Ridge? North, deeper into Wayward Bluffs? South toward Laramie?

Or someplace else entirely?

A string of curses flew from his lips and he pounded a fist on the window frame.

"We're going to find her," Brian said. "I'll have Holden send a deputy out to your place right now." They hung up.

Waylon stared at his cell, wishing it to ring with a call from Emilio.

Limping back over near Darcy, he grabbed the medical kit and sat at the table. He flipped it open. Dumped out the things he needed. Saline. Two types of gauze, the regular kind and QuikClot Combat to control bleeding fast.

Gritting his teeth through the pain, he pulled out the pieces of shrapnel from his thigh and abdomen. He flushed the wounds with saline. The burning flare of pain made him gasp. He dabbed at the injuries, checking that the sites were free of metal and debris. Quickly, he applied the hemostatic dressing then wrapped a bandage around his leg and torso. He popped a couple of painkillers into his mouth and swallowed them dry.

Waylon had been lucky. If he had been standing closer to the kitchen range or if the payload of the explosive had been larger, he'd be dead.

But that still left Mel alone with a killer.

He shoved the med kit away and glanced at what was left of her cell on the floor. Melanie didn't have her phone. No way to call for help. To let anyone know where she was.

But what if…what if she had her purse?

Pushing up from the dining room table, he looked around. Her handbag was on the floor.

His heart sank.

Then he remembered, the AirTag synced to his phone wasn't in the lining of her purse but on her keys.

Snatching the leather bag from the floor, he dumped out the contents. Wallet. Lipstick. Sunglasses.

No keys.

Hope was a fragile bubble in his chest, but he didn't dare give it oxygen yet. On his phone, he swiped over to the Find My app icon and tapped, opening it.

Keys popped up as active. Two miles away. And moving. The app brought up directions on how to get to the AirTag.

He could track them.

Based on their current heading, it looked like they were on the way to Bison Ridge. That delicate bubble of hope ballooned.

Waylon was on his feet, hustling to his guest room without thinking about it. At the Barska biometric safe, he pressed his index finger to the fingerprint reader. The LED light blinked green, unlocking it. He swung the handle and opened the safe that stood less than a foot shorter than him.

For a second, he glanced at the black-velvet box on the top shelf next to his pistol rack. The diamond engagement ring inside had cost him three months of his salary. When he had planned to take their relationship to the next level, to him that meant a proposal on the beach. Asking Melanie to risk more had to come with the promise of more.

A lot more. Like a commitment for life.

One he still intended to make to Melanie.

Waylon grabbed the shotgun from the adjustable gun rack, slinging the strap on his shoulder, took two boxes of ammo, shells and 9mm bullets, and his bulletproof vest. He double-checked that his knife was still in his boot.

Armed and ready to wage war in hell, if need be, he rushed out the front door and ran to his SUV.

Hold on, Melanie. I'm coming for you.

MELANIE SLID A terrified glance at Hank. He was staring at her. The gun was pointed at her side.

Poor Darcy.

And Waylon.

Were they alive? Both dead?

Was she next?

Her hands trembled on the steering wheel. "You said you don't like to use guns."

"Not my favorite weapon of choice. I prefer to use my hands. More personal."

"You don't have to do this Hank. Or should I call you Owen?"

"To my friends, I'm Hank. But you're not a friend. You," he said, poking her in the side with the barrel. "Are." Another forceful jab that had her cringing away from him. "Prey." Harder this time.

She winced from the pain. "Where are we going?"

They were driving down a rural road that was the fastest way to get to Bison Ridge from Wayward Bluffs. This route had dissuaded her from living out this far when she'd first moved to Wyoming. At night, with the lack of lampposts, the darkness had given the road an eerie feeling. Quiet. Isolated.

Like it was the perfect spot for aliens to land.

In the afternoon, it was still quiet and isolated, farmland stretching for miles on either side and not a house in sight.

The perfect spot for a serial killer's hideout.

"You have a date," Hank said in a jovial tone. "With destiny."

Was he taking her somewhere to kill her? Or to toy with her first?

"I don't believe in destiny." Everything she'd achieved, she'd worked for and earned. But she couldn't deny that the way she'd met Waylon, the timing of them both in the right place at the right time, the instant chemistry, had indeed seemed like fate. "It's an excuse to wait for things to happen instead of making them happen."

"I made this happen. You and me together in this car, on this road." He laughed. "Doesn't really matter what you believe. But your destiny is named Drake Colter. My brother, for all intents and purposes, was on the way up here from Colorado when I first came over to Detective Wright's house to lend a helping hand. He should be waiting for us at the house by now." A chime sounded. "Maybe that's him, wondering about the timing of the festivities." Hank pulled out his phone. His brow creased. His face twisted in anger. "Pull over and stop the car."

"Why?" Her mind spun with possible reasons. Something was wrong. A glitch of some sort in his plan. Whatever it was, he didn't like it.

He lifted the gun and pressed the muzzle to her temple. "Stop the car."

Jerking the wheel to the right, she veered off onto the muddy shoulder. She wished there had been a streetlight pole for her to crash the car into. Or another vehicle. A large tree near the side of the road. Any distraction, even a reckless one such as a deliberate collision, had to be seized if she was going to get out of this alive.

But there were no houses for her to run to, no pedestrians to flag down, no one to call the authorities for her. Unless she managed to wrestle the gun away from him, or knocked him out, she wouldn't make it far.

She slammed on the brakes. "What are we doing?"

"You think you're so clever. Don't you? But you're not." Raising his phone, he turned the screen to face her.

Melanie's heart nosedived to her toes. The small glimmer of hope she'd had turned into bitter ash on her tongue.

A time-sensitive alert had popped up on his iPhone. It read:

AirTag Found Moving With You
The location of this AirTag can be seen by the owner.

"Where is it?" he yelled.

"I don't know what you're talking about."

"You've got an AirTag on you." Hank swore, calling her a foul name. "Give it to me."

"Please." She raised a shaky hand. "I don't have one."

"Drake wants you whole and unspoiled so he can damage you himself. But if you don't give me that AirTag, I'm going to put a bullet in you. Somewhere painful that won't kill you." He redirected the aim of the gun lower. "I'll start with one knee and then move on to the next. Where is it?"

Beyond the pain of taking a bullet, it would take away her ability to run. A small window of opportunity might open where she'd need to be able to make a break for it. But she'd never escape if he shot her in the knee.

He pressed the muzzle to her kneecap and put his finger on the trigger.

Shaking, Melanie shoved her hand in her pocket and pulled out the AirTag.

Hank snatched the small device from her palm, rolled down the window and tossed it outside. "Drive."

Melanie stared out the window to where he'd thrown her one lifeline.

How would anyone be able to find her?

She pressed down on the accelerator. The tires spun for a few seconds and she hoped they were stuck in the mud.

"Give it more gas," Hank said, and she did as he ordered.

The engine revved, the tires spinning, spewing mud, and then they were free.

She cursed her luck as she pulled back onto the road.

No cars behind them or in front. They were in the middle of nowhere and she was trapped with the devil at gunpoint.

"Like I told you," Hank said. "Help isn't coming. There's no rescue in your future. Only your penitence before my brother kills you. That detective, your bodyguard, the one Drake thinks you're sleeping with, is dead. And so is my fake girlfriend, Darcy. When the authorities find you, it'll be in the desert. Where you belong. Laid to rest as a sand angel."

Chapter Nineteen

Stomping on the brake, Waylon brought the SUV to a screeching halt. He glanced at the Find My app on the phone. According to the GPS locator, Melanie should be right here.

But there was nothing and no one around. His heart skittered.

Maybe the accuracy of the position was off. He threw the vehicle into Park, his gut tightening.

Wearing his bulletproof vest, Glock drawn, he jumped out of the SUV and followed the arrow on the app off the road into the tall grass.

A horrible thought struck him. What if she was dead? Her body hidden behind a shrub or a tree or in the grass.

No, no. He shoved the grim, grisly idea away and tried to focus. A lot of time and planning, probably three years' worth, had gone into this diabolical scheme to insert someone close to Melanie and murder everyone on the hit list. Hank would want to leave her body in the desert, in a sand dune. Not off on the side of the road, rushed.

And then there was Drake Colter. Who was MIA. Could he be here in the local area? Had he lost his tail just to come here and kill Melanie himself?

Waylon trudged through the grass, swiping at the brush,

and his gut tightened more because he found the AirTag attached to Melanie's key chain. He picked it up and stared at it—his only way to track her. Gone.

Heart in his throat, he curled his fingers into his palm, battling against the fear and desperation threatening to break him.

No. He refused to let evil win. Not on his watch. Not with his woman's life on the line. He wasn't going to lose her. Couldn't.

He turned back toward his vehicle and spotted something that might help.

Fresh tire tracks. Starting from the muddy shoulder at this very spot, heading back onto the road. It must've been theirs.

He could follow the muddy trail for a bit, until it ran out, but without more to go on, it wouldn't get him far.

His cell phone rang. "Wright here."

"This is Orson. Emilio's friend. I was told to call you directly to save time if I found something."

"Please tell me you did."

"Isaac Meacham is paying for a short-term lease on a house in Bison Ridge rented under the name of Hank Ludal. I've got an address on Blossom Trail."

Waylon ran to his vehicle as Orson gave him the exact house number. "Thank you."

"I'm letting the local authorities know that an officer is en route and requests backup as we speak. I've also given them your badge number for authentication."

Waylon threw the gear in Drive and sped off. "How are you able to do that?"

"Don't ask. You're welcome." The line went dead.

Flooring it down the road, he prayed he'd get to Melanie before any harm came to her. He'd made her a promise that when she needed him most, he'd be there for her.

A promise he had to keep come hell or high water.

HANK HIT A button on the visor and one door to the three-bay garage attached to a newly constructed house on Blossom Trail lifted.

The area was remote. The house sat on plenty of acres. No neighbors within shouting distance.

"Pull in," he said, waving the gun.

Melanie drove inside the garage and parked beside a plain white van. The same van that had been captured on her home security footage and that had been used in multiple crimes, including the abduction of Kristin. On the far end was a banged-up dark gray truck. Most likely the one he'd used to run them off the road.

"Drake is here waiting for you." Hank opened the center console and pulled out zip ties.

Oh, God, no. He was going to restrain her. How was she going to fight? Run?

Survive?

"Hands behind your back."

She shifted away in the car seat, putting her hands toward him. "Tell me, were you the one who found out about the legal precedent to get Colter released?"

"Sure did. A professor brought up the case in class. I didn't think there'd be any way to get him freed. Then that convicted murderer in New York was released. Sweet loophole, huh?"

Nausea washed over her in waves.

Warm plastic wrapped around her wrists and he cinched the zip ties tight until they cut into her skin.

He got out, keeping the gun trained on her, walked around the vehicle and opened the door. "Get out."

She did.

After he closed the door, he nudged her forward with the gun. "Go on. Destiny has waited a long time for this moment."

Walking toward the door that led inside the house, she

searched for a weapon. There were lots on and around the workbench. Shovels. A hammer. Four-by-fours. A drill. Screwdrivers.

None of which she could use with her hands restrained. Hank was practically right on top of her, watching her closely.

He opened the door and pushed her inside the house, into the kitchen.

A television was on somewhere deeper in the house. Sounded like a rerun episode of one of the *Real Housewives* playing.

Hank shoved her down into a chair. Then he zip-tied her wrists to one of the slats in the back of the wooden chair. Putting two fingers in his mouth, he gave a piercing whistle. "Drake! I've got a bushy-tailed, bright-eyed rabbit for you to slaughter."

The television turned off.

Silence. Followed by heavy, slow footsteps approaching.

Then singing. The lyrics to a nursery rhyme. "There Was An Old Lady Who Swallowed A Fly."

"Perhaps she'll die," Drake crooned as he waltzed into the kitchen, dancing. "But in your case, ADA Melanie Merritt, there's no question about it. Today will be your last."

A greasy ball of dread dropped into her stomach and churned.

"I hate to ruin this special moment you've dreamed of for so long," Hank said, "but the cops are on to us. They've issued arrest warrants for you and Isaac."

"Does he know?" Colter asked.

"By now, I'm sure he does. He's probably sitting in a holding cell. There's nothing we can do for him. At least he won't spend much time behind bars."

The sick joy in Drake Colter's eyes dimmed as he swore.

"This might be a good thing in disguise," Hank said.

"Oh really. How so? Our brother is going to be arrested."

"In jail, he can recruit full-time. Look at what he did with the Tuttles. Even after their mother was murdered, Isaac still turned those two into believers. All because the mother had been having an affair. Just think of how many hopeless, angry prisoners he can convert into loyal Sand Angelites. When he gets out, we'll have an army on our side. We'll be unstoppable. But first, we have to make it across the border into Canada once you're done with this one." Hank tipped his head at Melanie.

Drake's evil gaze swung back onto her. "This all could've been avoided if you had only listened when I told you that I was innocent."

"I think we have very different definitions of innocent."

"I didn't kill those women in Colorado several years ago. My brother over here is the real Sand Angel Killer."

Smiling, Hank put a hand over his heart, the other behind his back, and bowed. "Those were my victims. That's why I was so determined to get my brother out of jail and why you needed to be taught a lesson."

"But your DNA was found on two of the victims," she said to Colter. "You had to have been involved in their deaths." Not only was she curious, but she needed to buy herself as much time as possible. The only way to do that was to keep them talking. She didn't know if she could get out of this. Every minute she stalled gave her another minute of breathing. "You were with them on the day they died. Weren't you?"

"I picked them out," Drake said, "had a little fun with them and held them for safekeeping until Hank was ready to finish them off."

That made him an accomplice to murder. "What about the women murdered around Santa Fe found in the sand dunes?"

Drake shrugged. "Those bunnies were mine. I hunted them. Killed them."

"Then you're not innocent, you sick, twisted monster!"

"But you didn't catch me for that. I was arrested, prosecuted by you and convicted for murders I didn't commit."

Hank knelt in front of her. "I saw the fine work my older brother was doing in New Mexico. Our foster father had encouraged spirited competition before we killed him, and Drake became the new alpha of our family. I saw how I could improve on his work. Elevate it to an art form."

"The sand angel idea," Drake said, patting him on the back, "was very impressive. I wish I could've taken credit for it, but unfortunately, I couldn't. And being blamed for it, how you got my girlfriend to lie under oath, ticked me off."

"I'd never allow a witness to perjure themselves. Maybe she knew what you really were and decided to stop you."

"Maybe." Drake stepped closer to her. "But that act of defiance got Georgia killed."

"Did you do it? Were you the one who killed them?"

"Every single one of them." Colter pulled up his shirtsleeve and pointed to the list tattooed on his arm. "Babcock. Sweeney. That backstabbing ex-girlfriend. Nosy Loeb sniffing around where she didn't belong."

"I snatched them," Hank said. "Held them until Drake could sneak out of that Fair Chance Treatment Center."

"Except for Kristin." Drake grinned. "I took her and killed her in the motel room and then handed her body off to my brother," he said, and her stomach roiled as fresh guilt washed over Melanie. "I even came for you personally, ADA Merritt." His smile turned menacing. "First, I had to poison the chili at FCTC that made everyone sick. Get Hershel to go home early. I needed extra time for the trek to Laramie. Thanks to Hank, I knew exactly where the cameras in the parking garage would be and I almost had you, too. Could taste your fear. Your pain.

"I even followed you after you were done with the police. But leaving the sand angel on your doorstep had been a mistake. Intended to be my calling card for the cops, but that clued you in and scared you off from staying at your house. I tracked you to the detective's place with my headlights off. You two looked cozy, pretty familiar, with his arm around you, guiding you inside. I wasn't sure how we were going to get past him, but it was only a matter of finding the right unstoppable force to take care of that immovable object."

"The bomb was my idea." Hank took a half bow this time. "I just had to keep suggesting to Darcy to volunteer her time to help you. To offer to come over to make your life easier."

"Now that your detective is out of the way, my wait is over." A malevolent gleam sparked in Colter's eyes. "It's your turn to suffer and die."

Her heart punched into her throat. "Wait. Wait. Don't you want to see me on live television, admitting that I was wrong. Down on my knees, begging your forgiveness? You could record it, watch it again and again."

Colter frowned. "I was really looking forward to that. But once I realized the cops were following me, it complicated things. Easier to kill you sooner rather than later." He dug into his pocket and pulled out a plastic bag. "First, let's have some fun. Remember what I told you the wolf loves most about the hunt. The fear in the prey. Nothing brings that out more than giving the prey a preview of what it'll be like to die." Holding the bag open, he stepped toward her, ready to put the plastic over her head.

Terror gripped her. Melanie screamed and kicked Drake Colter in the knee and kept throwing the heel of her foot into flesh and bone, determined to fight until her last breath.

WAYLON CREPT AROUND the side of the house. The loaded shotgun was slung on his shoulder and his Glock was drawn, at the ready in a two-handed grip. He peeked into one of the garage windows. Hank's Tahoe was parked inside along with a white van and big gray truck.

This was definitely the correct house. He had to get this right. Had to control the scene and his entry. If he messed this up, then Melanie might die.

He couldn't let that happen.

He snuck around the house, hugging the walls and crouching low. The curtains were drawn. The house was a good size. Lots of rooms. She could be in any of them.

Gripping his gun more firmly, he crept up to the back window. The curtains were parted. But he didn't rush to take a look. Instead, he listened.

One man laughed—a gut-deep, creepy cackle.

Another shouted, "Woo-eee! Look at her thrashing like a fish out of water."

"That's what it's going to feel like when I choke the life out of you." The voice was Drake Colter's. "The only thing missing is my hands around your throat."

Adrenaline drop-loaded into Waylon's system as he snuck a peek inside the room.

Melanie restrained to a chair, struggling to get free. A plastic bag wrapped tightly over her head. She couldn't breathe.

Drake Colter and Hank stood around her, mocking her suffering, enjoying her pain.

Rage lit a fire in him and he knew precisely how to control the burn.

He needed to breach quickly. Had to get that bag off Melanie's head as soon as possible.

Inspecting the door, he didn't think he could bust it open with the swift thrust of his bootheel alone. He holstered the

Glock. Aimed the shotgun at the lock at close range. Steadied his breathing. Directed the heat of the fire blazing inside him and pulled the trigger.

Boom!

Waylon kicked in the door with all the force he could muster in his good leg and swept inside. "Police! Get on the floor!"

Both men froze in temporary shock, their mouths open, their eyes wide.

"Facedown. Hands on the back of your heads," Waylon finished yelling the order.

Hank lunged for the gun on the kitchen counter. The Smith & Wesson.

The SOB was going to try to shoot him with his own weapon.

Pumping the shotgun, ejecting the empty shell and loading a new one, Waylon redirected the aim to the man standing closest. He opened fire, blasting a hole in Hank, sending his body flying across the kitchen.

Melanie was kicking, thrashing with her legs, wriggling her whole body, desperate for air.

As Waylon pumped the shotgun again, Drake Colter charged at him, howling like a rabid animal, and tackled him backward.

The shotgun went off.

Boom!

The blast hit the ceiling as they stumbled out of the house and hit the ground. On impact, pain radiated through Waylon and he lost his grip on the shotgun.

Swinging wild and hard, Drake Colter punched him in the face. Once. Twice. The blows kept coming.

Waylon took it. Didn't fight him. Used the heat of that white-hot anger to absorb the punches. To sublimate the pain. Focused through it. Reached for the holster on his hip. Curled his fingers around the handle of his Glock. Aimed precisely where he wanted the bullet to go.

He fired, putting a slug straight into Drake Colter's cold-blooded heart.

The dead man collapsed on top of him.

Waylon shoved him off over to the side.

Jumping to his feet, he groaned through the pain. He sprinted into the house and bolted to Melanie.

Waylon tore a hole in the bag, letting in precious air. Melanie raked in a desperate breath. He ripped the rest of the plastic from her face and around her throat.

Throwing a glance at Hank, he checked to make sure he was dead. His lifeless body was slumped on the floor. Blood gushed from a wound in his chest. The Smith & Wesson had fallen from his hand.

Melanie was hyperventilating, shaking all over.

Reaching into his boot, he pulled out his knife and cut the zip ties from her wrists. She leaped out of the chair and into his arms.

Waylon hugged Melanie tight, never wanting to let her go. "Let's get you out of here. Away from this." The death. The terror.

"Thank God you came." She started crying, clinging to him, sobbing so hard, as if the only thing holding her together was his embrace. "I thought he might've killed you."

"You're not getting rid of me that easily."

She wept harder and chuckled, all mixed together in a tearful jumble.

Keeping his arms around her, he guided her out the back door, past Colter, around the house, to his SUV. Sirens wailed in the distance, drawing closer but still minutes from arriving.

He sat Melanie in the passenger's seat and caressed her

face. “I’ve never been so scared in my life.” He’d been terrified to lose her.

“I couldn’t tell. You were so fast. So controlled. You were amazing.”

“That was just training. What they don’t prepare you for is this. Coming so close to losing the one person who means everything.”

She threw her arms around his neck and hugged him again. “But you didn’t lose me. And I didn’t lose you. We’re alive. Despite the odds. I think that means Hank or Owen Henry Udall was right about one thing.”

He pulled back and looked into her beautiful eyes. “What’s that?”

“Destiny. It’s real. And you’re mine.”

Five days later...

DUSK SETTLED OVER the Atlantic, but the temperature didn’t drop with the sun. Melanie nestled up against Waylon on the two-person chaise longue the Saint Lucian resort had set up for them on the beach under a wide umbrella.

Listening to the waves break on shore and watching the sun set on the horizon, she was filled with gratitude to have this moment with him. “I’m sorry we didn’t do this at Christmas.”

He tucked her closer and rubbed her arm. “We weren’t ready.”

“Still, it shouldn’t have taken both of us nearly dying for us to decide to be together and go on vacation. You know, when we get back, we’re going to have to figure out how to handle things with our jobs.”

“Already done.”

She pulled away, leaned up on her forearm and stared at him. “What do you mean? What’s done?”

“I quit.”

Whipping off her sunglasses, Melanie's jaw unhinged. "But we were supposed to come up with a fair solution. I didn't want you to quit."

"Forget about fair. I didn't want you to compromise on your dreams. Why should you?"

"Because one of us had to and I didn't want it to be you." A life with Waylon was worth any sacrifice. She saw that now.

"There's no rule that states either of us had to lose something." He slid his shades down the bridge of his nose and looked at her. "Do you really want to get into this now? I was hoping we could wait until our candlelight dinner."

"I'd rather hear that you're unemployed and what the plan is without candlelight."

"Okay. First, I'm not unemployed. I accepted a position with Ironside Protection Services. I spoke with the owner, Rip Lockwood."

Melanie was well acquainted with Rip and his wife, Ashley. Last she'd heard, they were expecting their first child. "Doing what?"

"Turns out that he has an informal office in our local area. Gigs that the Iron Warriors handle, mostly protection and security details. Anyway, with him gone, he was looking for someone to run the office. Not only to deal with the Iron Warriors, but also recruit, expand the scope of work into more investigative stuff. As a detective and veteran, he thought I'd be perfect, especially when it comes to liaising with the local authorities."

"Wow. So, you'd go from a one-or two-person show with the Laramie PD to being a boss."

"Team leader. Making double what I earn now. Plus recruitment bonuses. I'd only have to report to Rip, but would be given the leeway to run things as I see fit."

"That's..." She was at a loss for words. "Perfect."

"I thought so. That's why I accepted and quit."

Leaning close, she slid her leg between his thighs and ran her hand up his beautiful, hunky, bare chest. "We have to celebrate."

"I agree." He slid his palm along her thigh over her bikini cover-up. "I was thinking we should have a party."

She reeled back. "A party? With people?"

"Yeah. With our families. Maybe a couple of others like the Powells." He moved his hand from her leg, dipped into their beach tote bag, and took out a black-velvet box. "An engagement party."

Melanie's heart skipped a beat.

His eyes were warm and serious. The tender expression on his face made her legs so weak they might've given out on her if she were standing.

"I was going to do this at dinner." Looking nervous, he opened the box and took out a stunning pear-shaped diamond ring.

"Waylon." She sucked in a breath.

He took her hand, his fingers big and callused, and slid the ring on her finger. "I love you, M&M. More than anything in this world. I want to be there for you, no matter what life throws at us, now and forever. Will you do me the honor of marrying me, darling?"

"Oh my gosh!" she squealed, not realizing excitement would fill her to bursting at this moment. She wrapped her arms around him and squeezed him tightly. "I love you, too."

"Is that a *yes*?"

"Yes." Feeling a giant sigh of relief from him, she pulled back and smiled. "Yes, Waylon. I'll be your huckleberry."

* * * * *

afterglow
BOOKS

SCAN ME

Pray Now
2005

Daily Devotions for the Year 2005

Published on behalf of the
PANEL ON WORSHIP
OF THE CHURCH OF SCOTLAND

SAINT ANDREW PRESS
EDINBURGH

First published in 2005 by
SAINT ANDREW PRESS
121 George Street, Edinburgh EH2 4YN

ISBN 0 86153 360 7

British Library Cataloguing in Publication Data
A catalogue record for this book is available from the British Library

Text illustrations by Colleen Pugh
Typeset by Waverley Typesetters, Galashiels
Printed and bound in Great Britain by Mackay & Inglis Ltd, Glasgow

Contents

Preface

'Give thanks in all circumstances' (1 Thessalonians 5:18). From our own experience and from the treasury of prayer from biblical times onwards we know that an honest life of prayer will contain moments of penitence, pain and protest as well as praise. However, these words from the letter to the Thessalonians contain a deep truth. The truth is that a sense of gratitude, thankfulness, provides the most fertile soil for the nourishing and flourishing of the life of faith. Faith grows when it is rooted in a continually remembered awareness of all that God has given us and all that God has done for us.

This year's *Pray Now* will encourage the growing and deepening of our awareness of the richness and variety of God's gifts to us. First, we are invited to reflect on the gifts of a good Creator, gifts built into the fabric of our own lives and the life of the world. Faith sees the extraordinary in the ordinary; our most treasured symbols are breath, water, bread and wine.

The middle section draws us into the rich variety of gifts we share with one another in community. It invites reflection on how profoundly we are shaped, moulded, challenged and encouraged by one another and how we are fed by the whole range of the human story. Finally, *Pray Now* focuses on the special gifts encompassed by that precious, beautiful word, 'grace'. As you use this year's guide, may the grace of our Lord Jesus Christ go with you, to deepen your sense of grace abounding, and of being held within that love which will never, never let us go.

LEITH FISHER
Convener of the Panel on Worship

Introduction

Jesus said: No one has greater love than this, to lay down one's life for one's friends. You are my friends if you do what I command you (John 15:13–14).

In a consumer culture and society of takers, often we find it hard to comprehend what it means to really give and really receive. However, God through Christ and the Spirit continually reaches out to us in generosity and grace and there are many good gifts for us to discover and experience.

This year, the members of the Prayer and Devotion committee worked on the theme of 'gifts', beginning with Life on Day 1. Whether people believe in God or not, we all have a sense that 'life is a gift' – life is given and is taken away. Day 2 and beyond quite naturally took the committee into a progression of how we understand and receive gifts – in nature, in community and through grace – and we hope that as readers use the book month by month, the spiritual journey will be deepened.

Pray Now 2005 was written by the committee in the year 2004 and during our writing session, as a group, we have shared some good news with each other, we have eaten together and have prayed, talked and laughed together. I would like to think that the mix of ages and backgrounds on the committee, as well as the friendship and support we have shared, has brought a balance and well-rounded feel to this year's publication.

2004, of course, also marked the sixtieth anniversary of the D-Day landings. In preparation for worship to mark this event we were enriched in our reflections on 'gifts' as we remembered and gave thanks to those who gave their lives to give others freedom. Sixty years on, thinking of how the world could have been and bracing ourselves for the present and future challenges to peace and justice, *Pray Now* 2005 should help us in our devotions to focus on: ways to live peacefully together; how not to take things for granted but give expression to our faith; hopes and dreams; and, above all things, ways to continue to follow Christ to the cross and beyond for the glory of the Kingdom.

As this year's book was put together, we were struck once again by the simple truth that God's gifts are unconditional but our response and acceptance of them are hindered by many things. A central focus for us has been the cross and the gift of Christ and we pray that as you move from 'Life' to 'Everlasting Life', from days 1–31, you will grow, as we have, in an understanding of how truly to be friends of Christ.

GAYLE TAYLOR
Convener of the Prayer and Devotion Committee

Using this Book

This book provides material for prayer, meditation, and study for each day of the month. In each new month, then, the cycle begins again. It is hoped that the material is so written that it is possible to return several times in this way and discover something new. The newness will not necessarily be from the material but from ourselves.

However, some features will help users to 'move on' rather than simply go over old ground. For one thing, a variety of readings are offered. It is not intended that all of these are used at any one time but that, perhaps, one only is read. This year, titles given to each passage help us to choose what we will read that day.

Again, the prayer activity is designed so that, on returning again to one that has been used the previous month, we may find ourselves with an entirely new experience of prayer, even though beginning from the same starting point.

The illustrations are also meant to provide food for thought, and for prayer.

During the period of this edition, a new hymn book, the *Church Hymnary: Fourth Edition*, is to be published and will increasingly be used. To celebrate this, many of the 'blessings' are taken from hymns from this book, referred to throughout as *CH4*.

There are two points at which members of the Church of Scotland may include material particularly relevant to their Church. Each day, there is prayer for some aspect of the work of the Church universal. The example given in *italics* refers to that area of work as it is carried forward in the Church of Scotland, but it is expected that those from other branches of the Church will substitute their own material. Again, at the end of the book there is a list of Church of Scotland Mission Partners, each with the day given for which they are to be prayed for. Members of other branches of the Church may wish to substitute similar persons or topics for prayer at that point.

The material should not be used slavishly but in the way that is most helpful. You may, for example, wish to substitute other prayers or readings, including the Lord's Prayer.

We also include a separate list of daily Bible readings, based on the Scripture passages used in Church on Sunday by congregations that follow the lectionary in *Common Order* (the Revised Common Lectionary). It is taken from a Uniting Church in Australia publication, *With Love to the World*, which also includes notes on the readings. Information about obtaining this publication is included with the list of readings.

Audio tapes from previous years are still available. Proposals are in place to provide material on CD to accompany future editions of *Pray Now*. Further information from the Office for Worship, Church of Scotland, 121 George Street, Edinburgh EH2 4YN; swilson@cofscotland.org.uk; 0131–225 5722, ext 359.

Days of the Month

Gifts in Nature

Day 1

LIFE

In God's hand is the life of every living thing.

~ Job 12:10 ~

Lord God, in whom we live and move and have our being,
understanding that life is not our right but your gift,
realising that we are not owners but stewards of creation,
appreciative that you temper the wind to the shorn lamb,
that you feed the ravens,
that you mark the fall of a sparrow,
that your fatherly care is over all things and people,
help us also to care –
for all creatures,
for the well-being of others,
and for ourselves: our bodies ... our minds ... our souls.

Lord God, source of truth and life,
enable all who help to create life:
men and women in procreation,
obstetricians and midwives,
researchers into matters of fertility,
to act wisely and responsibly.
Direct the work of all who seek to unravel the mysteries of life:
biologists and psychologists,
and all who enhance human life.
Help farmers and shepherds and vets,
all who deal with your creatures,
to be considerate –
and help each and all to know the Good Shepherd
in whom is abundant life ...
and ever to choose him and his way. AMEN.

Readings

Genesis 1:24–31	*The creation of life*
Deuteronomy 30:15–20	*The call to choose life*
Job 10:8–13	*Acknowledging God as creator and preserver*

Luke 12:22–30	*Life more than food*
John 10:10–15	*The Good Shepherd who gives abundant life*
Acts 17:22–8	*The God who gives life and breath*

Prayer Activity

> Try to get a time of silence and then: listen to your breathing ... your heart beating ... sense your eyes blinking ... your blood flowing – and wonder and give thanks for the marvel that you have been given life.

Prayer for the Church

Those who bring care and encouragement to people in any kind of need and who work for a healthier society in which all may find fulfilment

especially the Board of Social Responsibility.

Blessing

O Lord of life, bless this little life of mine.
Tell me that I matter so much
that you came to earth for me,
that you died for me,
that you rose and live for me.
So, blessed, may I be a blessing. AMEN.

Day 2

THE SENSES

I praise you, for I am fearfully and wonderfully made.
~ Psalm 139:14 ~

Creator God, continually you renew the gift of life
in giving us senses with which to savour it to the full,
and through their power you deal graciously with us.

When you looked at the new-created world and *saw* that it was good,
you showed that you meant us to see beauty in all things and all people;
and when Jesus singled out Bartimaeus the beggar and made him see again
he was calling us to look upon others and see the real person underneath.

Because you are a God who *heard* the cry of your people
so we are to hear not just those who please but those also who disturb us;
and when Jesus said to the deaf man, 'Ephphatha',
he opened our ears not just to hear sounds but also the silence beyond.

As you *smelled* the incense burned by a grateful people
so our bodies are given to worship you and not for seeking sensation;
and when the house was filled with the aroma of precious ointment
Jesus called us to a life of generosity rather than self-gratification.

As God wrestled with Jacob till dawn and *touched* his thigh,
so you bless us as much during the struggle as when at peace;
and when the woman touched the hem of Jesus' garment,
so we learn that we do not touch for taking but for healing.

As God *tasted* the offering of Elijah and exposed the false gods,
so we relish the life offered by the one true bountiful God;
and when Jesus shared the bread and wine with his disciples,
he offered us a foretaste of life when all are reconciled in his kingdom.

Remove from this earth, Lord, senseless slaughter
which does not savour the riches given to us in others.
Curb the appetite which craves fulfilment
and turns the globe into a supermarket for the rich.
Silence the pulsing air which surrounds us with noise,
preventing us hearing the voice of need,
even our own need. AMEN.

Readings

Genesis 1:26–31, Mark 10:46–52 (sight)
Psalm 34:1–10, Mark 7:31–7 (hearing)
Exodus 30:22–38, John 12:1–8 (smell)
Genesis 32:22–32, Matthew 9:20–2 (touch)
1 Kings 18:36–40, Luke 22:14–19 (taste)

Prayer Activity

Choose one of the senses. Think back on the day, or back to the previous day, and try to remember incidents when you were conscious that this sense was being employed. Reflect on whether they were good, bad, productive or unproductive, enjoyable or disturbing. Then try to recall one incident where the sense in question must have been in use but you were not conscious of it. What were you missing, as experience, or as spiritual insight?

Prayer for the Church

Those who speak for the Church and show the relevance of the Gospel for our life in society

especially the Church and Nation Committee; the Scottish Churches' Parliamentary Office.

Blessing

Creation's broad display
proclaims the work of grandeur,
the boundless love of one
who blesses us with beauty.

(Carlos Rosas, in hymn 'Let's sing unto the Lord',
from *CH4*, by permission)

HARVEST

For everything there is a season, and a time for every matter under heaven.

~ Ecclesiastes 3:1 ~

Constant God,
spring, summer, autumn, winter –
this is the pattern of our lives.
Easter, Pentecost, Harvest, Christmas –
these are the seasons of our Church.

Today, I think of spring
– fresh starts, green shoots, hope, new life.
I give thanks for summer
– bright sun, fresh air, rest and recreation.
And I remember now autumn
– glorious colours, cleansing breezes, hands gathering crops.
For the winter will come and there will be frost, bitter winds, bare trees;
times will be hard,
life will show signs of death.

Tomorrow – when life begins, all over again,
help me, God.
When work seems futile, when time feels short, when relationships are lost –
show me the new thing, push me forward, love me back to reality –
for you really are the same
– yesterday, today and forever.

Readings

Genesis 8:13–22	*Seed time and harvest*
Isaiah 43:18–21	*A way in the wilderness*
Mark 4:26–32	*The harvest has come*
John 4:31–8	*The fields are ripe for harvesting*
Revelation 14:14–16	*The hour to reap has come*

Prayer Activity

Life today is often full of electronic communication, convenience food and ready made products to consume. Notice the intricacy of things made for you and by you – plant some seeds, bake or cook food to eat – use your hands to create, mend or decorate something today – and as you do, praise God for the sheer detail of his provision and care.

Prayer for the Church

Those who study Christian teachings and explore the meaning of the faith

especially the Panel on Doctrine.

Blessing

Praise God for the harvest of mercy and love
for leaders and people who struggle and serve
with patience and kindness, that all may be led
to freedom and justice, and all may be fed.

(Brian Wren, in hymn 'Praise God for the harvest of orchard and field' in *CH4*, by permission.)

Day 4

SLEEP

I will both lie down and sleep in peace;
for you alone, O Lord, make me lie down in safety.

~ Psalm 4:8 ~

O Lord God, who neither slumbers nor sleeps,
we thank you for sleep –
for a good night's rest,
for a blessed forty winks,
for sweet dreams.

O God, we thank you for Jesus
who knew weariness and tiredness,
who could sleep in the storm –
for his heart was stayed on you,
who can raise us from the sleep of death.

Forgive us for
taking sleep for granted,
not giving time to sleep,
sleeping when we should be awake,
and for any sleep of faith.

Be with those who cannot sleep:
because of illness and pain,
because of worry and anxiety,
because of a bad conscience.
Grant them healing, balm,
and the serenity that is there in Christ for all. AMEN.

Readings

Genesis 28:10–17	*Jacob's dream at Bethel*
Judges 16:18–22	*Samson's sleep*
Mark 4:35–41	*Jesus asleep in the storm*
Mark 14:32–42	*The disciples sleep in Gethsemane*
1 Thessalonians 4:13–18	*Concerning those who are asleep*
1 Thessalonians 5:1–11	*Whether we wake or sleep*

Prayer Activity

> Sit in a comfortable chair – perhaps before a good fire and after a pleasant drink. With no pressing engagements, no phone liable to ring – relax, and with Christ's balm, enjoy, enjoy …

Prayer for the Church

Those who at all levels encourage and enable different branches of the Church to relate to and to learn from each other about the Gospel they share

especially the Committee on Ecumenical Relations; Action of Churches Together in Scotland (ACTS); Churches Together in Britain and Ireland; Churches Together in England; the Conference of European Churches; the World Council of Churches.

Blessing

O may my soul on thee repose,
and may sweet sleep mine eyelids close,
sleep that shall me more vigorous make
to serve my God when I awake.

(Thomas Ken, in hymn 'Glory to thee, my God, this night', from *CH4*.)

Day 5

LIGHT AND DARKNESS

Consider whether the light in you is not darkness.

~ Luke 11:35 ~

Lord,
my world is flooded with bright lights,
offering me entertainment,
persuading me to buy,
putting a shine on bad news,
claiming to show me 'reality'.
Why does it all seem so staged?

And what of the light within me?
Does it not glow and fade
as the dark silhouettes of greed or envy,
bitterness, arrogance or self hatred
chase across its surface?

Help me to recognise when things seem clear
only because of my driving ambition,
when things seem so obvious
only because I am not taking others into account,
when my light is merely darkness dressed up.
Illuminate me from within with your Word.
Make me a lantern that shows others the way:
with a generosity which spills into darkest corners,
with a level of understanding which reveals what is true,
with a strength of love which glows mid distrust and fear.

Readings

2 Samuel 22:26–30	*You are my lamp, O Lord*
Proverbs 4:18–19	*The path of the righteous is like the light of dawn*
Luke 11:33–6	*Putting the lamp on the lampstand*
John 3:18–21	*People loved darkness rather than light*
Colossians 1:11–14	*He has rescued us from the power of darkness*
2 Peter 1:19	*A lamp shining in a dark place*

Prayer Activity

Darkness does not possess the ability to remove light, but light forces darkness to scatter. Find a dark place and sit for a spell. Feel for the match and light the candle. Watch the flame grow in strength. Follow the light out to the periphery, and see how far that little light can stretch. Now kindle Christ's light in you. Imagine it permeating your whole body and mind, and watch it reaching out to the people and community among whom you live.

Prayer for the Church

Those who take the church to the places where people spend their lives, and bring back insights to be shared in the church

especially chaplains to hospitals, industry, prisons, universities, colleges, schools and residential homes.

Blessing

They sing because thou art their Sun:
Lord, send a beam on me;
for where heaven is but once begun,
there alleluias be.

(John Mason in hymn
'How shall I sing that majesty? from *CH4*.)

Day 6

UNDERSTANDING AND REASON

For now we see in a mirror dimly, but then we will see face to face.

~ 1 Corinthians 13:11 ~

Eternal God, whom no one has ever seen nor can see,
we admit that you are beyond our highest thought of you:
our best language often mere babble,
our understanding only partial,
our very reasoning sometimes unreasonable.
But we bless you that we can reason and understand.
We rejoice that limited though we are,
we can yet appreciate that you make sense,
and often the only sense.
We rejoice that you reveal yourself in many ways:
in nature, in Scripture, and supremely in Jesus your Son
who bids us call you 'Father' – a god, the God,
to be reached and realised in humble love,
as we respond to that down-to-earth love that first loved us.

As we thank you for your unreasonable mercy and love
that can pardon and empower us,
that can spare and save us,
deliver us from futile reasoning and the closed mind.
By the Holy Spirit,
open our eyes to see wonders in your world and in your law,
unstop our ears to hear your word in scripture and in Christ,
quicken our intellects to appreciate life and better to understand it.

Father of lights,
we remember those who grapple with problems and perplexities:
seeking a way through political dilemmas,
seeking beneficial scientific solutions,
seeking to unravel the secrets of the universe.
Give them, and give us, that wisdom
that has its beginning in you. AMEN.

Readings

Job 32:6–10	*The Almighty gives the understanding spirit*
Matthew 13:10–17	*The reason for the parables*
Luke 2:41–7	*The boy Jesus in the Temple*
Romans 1:19–25	*No excuse for not honouring God*
Ephesians 1:15–23	*A prayer for wisdom, understanding, and appreciation*
Hebrews 5:11–14	*The immature reproved*

Prayer Activity

Look into a clear night sky and, like the Psalmist, ask the question: 'What is man that thou art mindful of him …?' Move from wondering enquiry to real thought and some understanding and appreciation of the universe and your place within it – and give thanks.

Prayer for the Church

The local councils of the Church where support is given and policies made

especially the Presbyteries, their Moderators and Clerks; Kirk Sessions and Session Clerks; Congregational Boards, Deacons' Courts and their Clerks.

Blessing

The peace of God which passes all understanding,
keep your hearts and minds in Christ Jesus. AMEN.

(Philippians 4:7.)

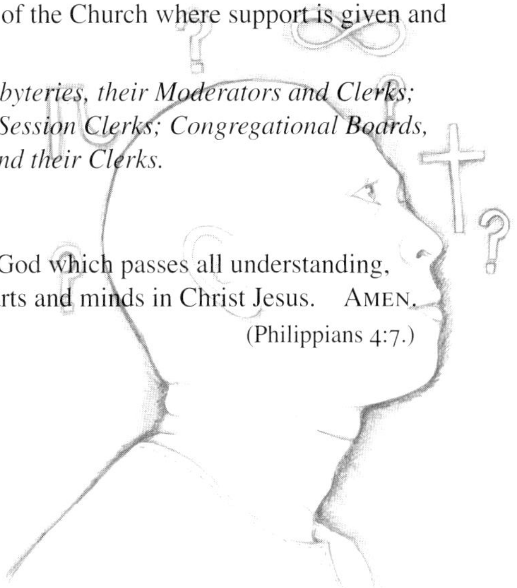

Day 7

TALENTS AND ABILITIES

For it is as if a man, going on a journey, summoned his slaves and entrusted his property to them; to one he gave five talents, to another two, to another one, to each according to his ability. Then he went away.

~ Matthew 25:14–15 ~

Lord, where was I when you gave out the talents?
It sometimes feels that I have no talents at all,
that I am not worthy to have even one talent.
Lord, have mercy on me.

I live in a world that praises talented people,
that raises them up and puts them on a pedestal;
often they forget that their talent is a gift from you.
Lord, have mercy on them.

We crave to be talented and to have great abilities.
Children long to be the next Beckham or Madonna.
Adults hanker after success and the fame it brings.
Lord, have mercy on us.

Lord, give us talents and abilities that we can use for others,
the ability to love our neighbour unconditionally,
the talents to care for our neighbours' needs.
Lord, have mercy on us. Amen.

Readings

Exodus 35	*Sabbath regulations*
Deuteronomy 8	*People are given the land*
Matthew 25:14–30	*Parable of the talents*
2 Corinthians 1:3–11	*Paul gives thanks to God*

Prayer Activity

> We all have talents and abilities, some we are aware of and some we use often. Sit quietly for a few moments and think of a time when you used a talent or ability that you may not have been aware of, and ask God to help you develop and use it.

Prayer for the Church

Those involved in the building up of new churches in new communities

especially those working in New Charge Development and those carrying forward the implementation of the Church Without Walls *report.*

Blessing

All that I am, all that I do,
all that I'll ever have I offer now to you.
Take and sanctify these gifts
for your honour, Lord.
Knowing that I love and serve you is enough reward.

(Sebastian Temple, part of verse 1 of hymn from *CH4*, by permission.)

Day 8

HEALING

He said to her, 'Daughter, your faith has made you well: go in peace'.

~ Luke 8:48 ~

Lord, teach me how to experience your healing Love.
Flow in me and through me and around me
in a way that feeds me,
strengthens me,
reassures me,
transforms me, lets me grow.
Allow your healing Love to flow through me to others
in quiet ripples of gentle love,
in waves whose force
I do not know or understand.

Enable me to trust that a phone call made at
an appropriate moment,
a chance meeting in the street,
a word spoken in the passing,
can be a miracle.

Let me listen to your Word
knowing that some Bible stories
will change my life,
bring healing in me –
healing which also means wholeness, an integration
in me:
heart speaking to mind,
body teaching me intuitive skills,
a readiness to allow your creative Spirit to mould me
anew.

Readings

1 Samuel 16:14–23	*Music bringing healing*
Mark 2:1–12	*From paralysis to walking*
Luke 8:40–56	*Your faith has cured you*
Luke 13:10–17	*You are rid of your trouble*
2 Corinthians 5:11–17	*You are a new creation*

Prayer Activity

Stories can change our lives. Hold in your heart an area of your life in need of healing and bring alongside that one of the healing stories of the Gospels. Say to God, 'Help me to know you speak directly, specifically, to me and, like a child having a story and wanting to hear it again and again, let me keep listening to your whisper of love in a story I love, without understanding why my heart wants it, loves it, needs the story like I need air and food. Help me trust you will keep speaking to me through it, bringing meaning, healing, purpose and growth.'

Prayer for the Church

Those who encourage and assist congregations explore and develop patterns of life and mission appropriate to their own context

especially the Scottish Churches' Community Trust and the Parish Development Fund.

Blessing

The healing God who is changing you
goes before you
with whispers and shouts:
do not be afraid;
listen and love.

CHILDREN

And he took them up in his arms, laid his hands on them, and blessed them.

~ Mark 10:16 ~

O God our Father, after whom all fatherhood is named,
and in whose heart is the love of a mother,
we give thanks for children –
    for the pleasure in begetting them,
    for the joy in their safe delivery,
    for their trusting expectant nature,
    for the delight they so often bring.

O God the Son, who came as a little child,
we give thanks for your example and teaching –
    taking children into your arms,
    putting a child right in the centre,
    warning us against harming a little one,
    telling us in them of our need for humble trust.

O God the Spirit, by whom Mary conceived,
we thank you for your continuous activity –
    encouraging parents to love and care,
    teaching those who would teach,
    leading those who would lead,
    inspiring all concerned for the young.

O God, Father, Son, and Holy Spirit,
bless all children everywhere. AMEN.

Readings

Isaiah 9:6–7	*To us a child is born*
Zechariah 8:1–8	*A vision of the New Jerusalem*
Luke 2:1–7	*The birth of Jesus Christ*
Mark 10:13–16	*Jesus blesses little children*
Matthew 18:1–6	*On humility and not harming children*
Matthew 21:14–17	*The children's praise in the Temple*

Prayer Activity

> Think back to your own childhood. Remember adults who were kind and supportive to you. Think of one or two children you know now: your own, some in your street, some you know and meet. How might you show you care about them? Give them perhaps some of your time or a word of encouragement or a smile?

Prayer for the Church

Those who steward the Church's financial resources and recall its members to the meaning of Christian giving

especially the Board of Stewardship and Finance.

Blessing

'Look to the child, here in your midst,
who has so much and more to say
of what it means to follow me,
to come and walk my way.'

(Leith Fisher, in hymn 'Says Jesus, "Come and gather round"',
from hymn in *CH4*, by permission.)

Gifts Given in Community

Day 10 *Community*

Day 11 *Hospitality*

Day 12 *Music*

Day 13 *Encouragement*

Day 14 *Writing, poetry, art*

Day 15 *Dance*

Day 16 *Teaching, enabling*

Day 17 *Stewardship*

Day 18 *Patience*

Day 19 *Vision*

Day 20 *Love*

Day 10

COMMUNITY

Now the whole group of those who believed were of one heart and soul, and no one claimed private ownership of any possessions, but everything they owned was held in common … There was not a needy person among them …

~ Acts 4:32, 34 ~

Gracious God,
through Father, Son and Holy Spirit you demonstrate relationship.
in your creation – you display harmony and union,
in Christ – you nurture love and human connection,
in the Holy Spirit – you move us towards each other.

But our actions demonstrate: 'look out for number one', 'do your own thing', 'every man for himself'.

God, so many things move us away from each other, into ourselves alone.
Life is often so self-gratifying, communication is often so faceless and nameless, relationships often a source of stress and grief.

And so we eat alone, we keep our feelings to ourselves, we watch others suffer and do nothing.

Loving God, direct us in our being together today.
Christ, forgive us and remind us of love's worth.
Holy Spirit, open our eyes to see beyond ourselves.

Readings

Numbers 11:16–17	*'Gather the elders of Israel'*
Deuteronomy 26:12–15	*Remembering the outsiders*
Matthew 5:1–11	*The Beatitudes*
Romans 12:3–16	*One body, many members*
1 Corinthians 12:12–20	*If one member suffers, all suffer*

Prayer Activity

> The community of God (Father, Son and Holy Spirit) is often called the Trinity. Think of three parts of your life – perhaps work, friendships and leisure. Are these three things totally separate? How do they relate to each other? Offer in silence some thoughts about how these areas of your life help you to be together with others and with God.

Prayer for the Church

Those who explore the things of the spirit and share what they find with others

especially the newly established joint Spirituality Group in its work for the renewal of the Church.

Blessing

Love is the light in the tunnel of pain;
love is the will to be whole once again;
love is the trust of a friend on the road:
God is where love is, for love is of God.

(Alison Robertson, in hymn 'Love is the touch', from *CH4*, by permission.)

Day 11

HOSPITALITY

Do not neglect to show hospitality to strangers, for by doing that some have entertained angels without knowing it

~ Hebrews 13:2 ~

Lord, you only ask
that I welcome the stranger
as you have welcomed me.

For in Christ
you have brought *me*, the wanderer,
the exile, back home from the far country
into the warmth of your house,
and into the household of your people.
You have welcomed me to your table
and spread bread and wine before me.

Such welcoming grace
is the very essence of all that you are
and of all that I am called to become.

Lord, I pray for my church,
and for my part in its life.
May we be a people of warmth,
of gracious welcome,
a homely house for the exile,
a table spread in the wilderness
for the stranger and the wanderer.

Readings

Genesis 18:1–8	*A warm welcome for three strangers*
Luke 15:18–24	*Time to go home*
Isaiah 55:1–5	*Come to the feast!*
Matthew 25:34–40	*The Christ who goes in disguise*
Luke 10:38–42	*Too busy to listen to your guest?*

Prayer Activity

Construct a prayer place for yourself. This might be a corner in a room, an attic, or wherever. In this special corner put photographs or other reminders of people for whom you pray. When you go there, imagine that you are welcoming them into the circle of your prayer.

Prayer for the Church

Centres to which people may withdraw to renew body and mind and to engage more deeply in worship and study, seeking the relevance of the Gospel for the modern world

especially Scottish Churches' House, Carberry, the Badenoch Christian Centre, the Abbey and MacLeod Centres on Iona, Key House (Falkland) and other retreat centres.

Blessing

For everyone born, a place at the table,
for everyone born, clean water and bread,
a shelter, a space, a safe place for growing,
for everyone born, a star overhead.

(Author sought, verse 1 of hymn from *CH4*.)

Day 12

MUSIC

Let all who take refuge in you rejoice; let them ever sing for joy.

~ Psalm 5:11 ~

What music makes my heart sing?
What rhythm and melody sets my heart on fire
with love and desire for life?

What music brings me relief,
lets my pain flow and grow into new form?

What music opens me up inside,
leading me on pathways familiar and unfamiliar,
rhythm bringing security, melody inspiring spontaneity?

What music enables friendship for me
– with people – with the Spirit,
creating a community, an orchestra of companionship
    that arises from I know not where?
Yet I recognise when it is there … and here.

May music be prayer for me,
gateway to joy for me,
doorway to reassurance for me,
touching place of love for me,
release of tension and suffering for me,
harbinger of balance and healing for me.

Lord, help me to use the gift of music
to allow your life to sing within me,
to enable me to live my life in harmony with you,
vibrating to the music of your Love.

Readings

1 Chronicles 15:1, 16–28	*Music for the Ark*
Psalm 5	*Shouts of joy*
Psalm 49:1–4	*Music revealing meaning*
Ephesians 5:15–21	*Make music in your hearts*
Revelation 5:6–10	*Singing a new song*

Prayer Activity

> Make your own music. Here is a way to do that. Take a word or text that is meaningful for you at present. Repeat it to yourself, chanting it first on one note only. Continue. Then let a melody arise out of that.

Prayer for the Church

Those who ensure that the fabric of church buildings is maintained and that the Church's heritage in buildings be conserved for the good of the Church and the nation

especially the General Trustees.

Blessing

The peace of Christ makes fresh my heart,
A fountain ever springing.
All things are mine since I am his!
How can I keep from singing?

(Robert Lowry and Doris Plenn, in hymn 'My life flows on', from *CH4*.)

Day 13

ENCOURAGEMENT

For whatever was written in former days was written for our instruction, so that by steadfastness and by encouragement of the scriptures we might have hope.

~ Romans 15:4 ~

Sometimes we get so discouraged;
life is an ever-constant struggle,
even our faith fades and falters.
In the midst of this remind us
that you encourage us still.

Triune God, Parent, Son and Spirit,
refresh us daily
with words of encouragement.

We are week and feeble,
constantly needing and seeking
your attention and approval.

Yet why do we find it easier to put others down
and look for the negative in every situation
instead of giving a word of encouragement
or even a smile to people we meet?

Lord, as you encourage us by your presence and your word,
may we seek to find ways of encouraging
all those we meet today and every day.

Readings

Acts 4:32–7	*Believers share their possessions*
Acts 20	*Part of Paul's travels*
Romans 15:1–13	*Paul gives encouragement*
Philemon	*The story of the runaway slave*

Prayer Activity

> Reflect on any chance meetings or activities you have taken part in during the last twenty-four hours. Were there times when you chose to criticise rather than encourage? Think ahead to encounters you are to have today, tomorrow. What difference could your encouragement make?

Prayer for the Church

Those involved with Christian counselling and healing

especially the Christian Fellowship of Healing, and any local group in your church or area.

Blessing

When I'm feeling down and sad,
nothing much to make me glad,
help me to remember,
you are there for me.

(Joy Webb, verse 1 of hymn from *CH4*, by permission.)

WRITING, POETRY, ART

When I look at your heavens, the work of your fingers,
the moon and the stars that you have established …

~ Psalm 8:3 ~

Living God,
you are the Creator,
indeed you are the primal artist.
For human art in its glorious diversity,
in all its multi-faceted wonder,
is at best a reflection of your beauty,
an echo of the music of your singing,
an accent of the Word by which
you brought worlds into being.

You, Lord, are the potter, the craftsman, the Makar,[2]
and from the crude raw material
of this my life,
from the crude raw material
of this your Church,
you would shape something of eternal beauty.

Today I pray for your Church:
that the community of faith
might truly be a welcoming place for artists,
that in word, in music and song, in dance,
in form of clay or stone, wood or paint,
your glory might truly be reflected,
your Gospel celebrated.

Readings

Exodus 39:1–7	*Beauty in the finest details*
Psalm 8	*Reflections on being human*
Psalm 19	*Symmetry and pattern in creation*
John 1:1–5	*Thoughts on design and the Designer*
Romans 1:18–23	*No excuse for idolatry*
Revelation 4:1–11	*A vision of worship*

[2] Makar = poet (Lowland Scots).

Prayer Activity

> Bring into your prayer-corner a 'work of art'. This could be a photograph, a postcard, a woodcarving, a piece of pottery … Let God speak to you through this object and make this a focus of prayer for five minutes or so.

Prayer for the Church

Those who ensure that the local church is well supported and staffed and who take initiatives in mission and outreach where people live, work and take leisure

especially the Board of National Mission.

Blessing

So give thanks for the life and give love to the maker,
and rejoice in the gift of the bright risen Son,
and walk in the peace and the power of the Spirit
till the days of our living are done.

(Kathy Galloway, in hymn 'Oh the life of the world', from *CH4*, by permission.)

Day 15

DANCE

… then the Lord God formed man from the dust of the ground, and breathed into his nostrils the breath of life; and the man became a living being.

~ Genesis 2:7 ~

In the beginning was the Word …
sound, vibration, movement, the essence of Life.
Without movement of breath,
without movement of heartbeat,
we would not be alive.

Thank you, Lord, that my breath and heartbeat dance together
although I do not understand and can but slightly control their rhythm and interaction.
Help me to trust in the dances of life within me.

May my breath make love to your Spirit within me;
may my passion reel with your Passion;
may I 'Strip the Willow' in reality or imagination;
and may I know you have given me this joy.

May each of us value the forms of dance that have enlivened us.
Whether we physically dance or not,
help us recognise the Dance of life.
Help us look for patterns in our relationships –
people with whom we tango,
others with whom we waltz.

Help us recognise you in movement and feelings
that evoke love and joy, fullness of well-being.
Enable us to be people who find you in our bodies.
May we experience our bodies as living text for us,
your Living Word dancing us into vibrant existence
from the dance of our breath and heartbeat.

Readings

Genesis 2:4–7	*Breath of Life*
Job 12:7–13	*Learning of God in nature*
2 Samuel 6	*David dances before the Lord*
1 Kings 1:38–40	*Processional dance for King Solomon*
John 16:19–24	*Dance of life*

Prayer Activity

Ponder – and dance? – this extract from a poem:

For this is my message, the message of a dancer.
Within your being, within your mind and living body,
lies a world of joy and power.
Within you lies a kingdom you know little of,
the kingdom of fearless living, of sharing love and
unfolding glory.
All this and more is yours.

from 'How beautiful the mountains' by Ruth St Denis; in *Wisdom Comes Dancing: Selected Writings of Ruth St Denis on Dance, Spirituality, and the Body*, ed. Kamae A. Miller, p. 138.

Prayer for the Church

Those who are in my own congregation, helping it to be part of the living, witnessing Church.

Blessing

Let all creation dance
in energies sublime,
as order turns with chance,
unfolding space and time;
for nature's art
in glory grows,
and newly shows
God's mind and heart.

(Brian Wren, verse 1 of hymn in *CH4*, by permission.)

Day 16

TEACHING, ENABLING

For it is God who is at work in you, enabling you
both to will
and to work for his good pleasure.

~ Philippians 2:13 ~

Lord God, where would we be
if there were no teachers or enablers –
those who play an important part
in shaping the people we are today
and will be tomorrow?

As Christ lived and taught,
people realised and recognised
God among them,
so today we thank you for all
whose patience and tireless efforts
help us to learn new things
in a way that is easy for us to understand.

As Christ inspired and healed,
people found they were capable
of things they never dreamt of,
so today we thank you for those who enable,
for their ability to see something in us
which they are able to help us to shape
and hone into a special gift.

Lord, it is no easy task to teach or be an enabler for others
and we give you thanks for this wonderful gift
and for the many people in our world who are blessed with it.
May they be aware of their gift and use it to inspire
all the people you lead them to, for your glory. AMEN.

Readings

Proverbs 8:1–21	*The gifts of wisdom*
Acts 7:1–53	*Stephen speaks to the council*
Acts 14:1–20	*Paul and Barnabas in Iconium and Lystra*

Prayer Activity

> Look back and think of someone who taught or enabled you to do something. Give thanks to God for that person. Are you still in touch with them? Why not contact them and tell them how much what they did meant to you?

Prayer for the Church

Those who are concerned that the physical surroundings of the local church assist towards deeper worship, warmer hospitality and stronger witness

especially the Committee on Artistic Matters.

Blessing

God who is love,
Jesus who teaches love,
the Holy Spirit who enables us to love,
guide us and lead us, this day and every day.

STEWARDSHIP

God saw everything that he had made and indeed, it was very good.

~ Genesis 1:31 ~

From this beautiful creation
to the diversity of our living,
we are your stewards of love, O God.
From the spoils of this planet
to the offerings of our lives,
we are your stewards of love, O God.
From the abundance of Nature
to the giving of our being,
we are your stewards of love, O God.

✓ May we live life fairly,
hold it lightly,
love it gently,
so that balance is encouraged
and justice revealed
in all we say and do –
from our possessions
to our talents,
from our politics
to our religion.

So we pray for those who flaunt their pride and those who offer humility,
those who desire more and those who long for the least,
those who hoard everything for themselves and those who long for equity. AMEN.

Readings

Psalm 85	*Righteousness and peace will join hands*
Proverbs 15:16–17	*Rich and poor*
Jeremiah 22:1–9	*A message to the king*
Matthew 5:1–12	*The Beatitudes*
Luke 15:11–32	*The Lost Son*
Acts 4:32–3	*Sharing possessions*

Prayer Activity

Focus on some part of your body (head, heart, back, face, etc.). Feel it, become aware of it. Think of what it does and what you do with it. Do you care for it, push it too hard, take it for granted? Think of how you use it in your life and how it is used in your care for others: supporting, encouraging and strengthening. Focus on this part of your body throughout the day and reflect on that experience.

Prayer for the Church

Those who care for members of the armed forces as they seek to preserve peace in the world

especially the Committee on Chaplains to Her Majesty's Forces.

Blessing

✓ Today journey simply.
Today love well.
Today may each step you take
sketch the shape of heaven.

Day 18

PATIENCE

I waited patiently for the Lord; he inclined to me and heard my cry.

~ Psalm 40:1 ~

Lord,
we find it so hard to be patient in our world.
We want everything immediately:
instant credit, instant meals, instant entertainment,
instant relationships, even.

No, we don't want to wait;
we want it NOW!

Yet the Scriptures are full of people waiting –
in stillness, in hope, in longing,
waiting for your promises to become reality,
waiting for the dawn of your Kingdom,
waiting for you to act …

You would remind us that the waiting time,
the time of 'Yes … but not yet …'
is the learning and growing time.

You would call us to action in waiting,
being active in your service,
being busy about our Father's business
as we await your Kingdom's dawning …

Today I remember all who wait –
the oppressed, the exploited, the anxious, the grieving.
May they find you in their waiting time.

Readings

Psalm 40	*A song of patient hope*
Psalm 130	*Waiting for the morning*
Isaiah 40:1–5	*Words of consolation and encouragement*
Luke 2:22–32	*Patience rewarded*
Romans 5:1–5	*The forging of Christian character*
Galatians 5:22–6	*Spiritual fruits, not religious nuts!*

Prayer Activity

Mental relaxation in God's presence can be a form of patient prayer. The discipline is one of relaxing the mind and waiting. Practise this kind of praying. Allow yourself to relax and to enter into the experience. Taking time simply 'to be' can sometimes help us to become more aware of the wonder and vitality of life's gifts.

Prayer for the Church

The Church as it meets in council and assembly and those who plan for and resource its meetings

especially the Board of Practice and Procedure; the Moderator of the General Assembly; the Principal Clerk and the Depute Clerk.

Blessing

I waited patiently for God,
For God to hear my prayer;
and God bent down to where I sank
and listened to me there.

(Psalm 40, para. John L. Bell, from *CH4*, by permission.)

Day 19

VISION

The man looked up and said, 'I can see people, but they look like trees, walking'.

~ Mark 8:24 ~

Lord,
to us you say, 'Can you see *anything*?'
For too often we stumble around
as those who have but little vision.

We live as in a world of fuzzy shapes
and muddy greys
compared with the clarity of vision
and concentrated focus which you would give us.
Truly, in your light we see light.

Yet perhaps we prefer the grey to the glory.
Too much light hurts our eyes
and we are cosier in the shadows.

Yet, Lord, we need vision,
for without it we perish;
we need visionaries,
those who would initiate us
into a new way of seeing.

Today I pray for preachers and poets,
potters and painters,
prophets and playwrights,
for all disturb us, who shake us, who say to us,
'Can you see *anything*?'

Readings

Exodus 3:1–6	*When the extraordinary breaks into the ordinary*
Jeremiah 1:11–19	*The prophet as one who sees*
John 9:1–12	*From blindness to sight*
2 Corinthians 3:12–18	*Reflecting the glory of the Lord*
Revelation 1:12–16	*A vision of Christ*

Prayer Activity

> Build a collection of photographs cut from magazines/ newspapers. Look for disturbing/ challenging/inspiring images. Give attention to one of these images. Let it speak to you and flow into prayer.

Prayer for the Church

The organisations of women and men who worship, study, and reach out to others

especially the Church of Scotland Guild.

Blessing

The peace of Christ enfold me,
the strength of Christ uphold me,
and the light of Christ surround me,
as I journey on. AMEN.

Day 20

LOVE

I led them with cords of human kindness, with bands of love …
I bent down to them and fed them.

~ Hosea 11:4 ~

You can't help yourself, God,
you can't help but love us:
in our hurt, you hold us;
in our turnings, you call us;
in our sinfulness, you understand us;
in our straying, you challenge us;
in our hesitation, you persuade us;
in our anger, you listen to us;
in our silence, you wait for us;
in our reluctance, you bide with us;
in our fear, you stay with us;
in our loneliness, you speak to us;
in all of life, you love us;
and you can't help yourself.

And finding no reason to do so
(other than the want, the desire, and the instinct)
you give of yourself to us and the world.
May our communities be this way,
our societies, our neighbourhoods, our families.
And may the love that cannot help itself
hold and shape this world,
cradled by, and drawn, to your Realm.

Readings

Deuteronomy 11	*The Love of God*
Psalm 23	*The Lord our Shepherd*
Hosea 11:8–9	*I cannot give you up*
John 13:1–10	*Feet-washing*
1 Corinthians 13:1–8	*Love*
1 John 4:7–21	*God is Love*

Prayer Activity

Choose an everyday object, or a particular colour, or an image, photograph or memory and dwell on it, look at the intricacies of it, and consider what stories from the Scriptures it reminds you of, what promise it leads to, or how God's promise was opened up through those things. Hold that throughout the day, particularly whenever you see that colour, object or image.

Prayer for the Church

Those who seek to renew the life and mission of the Church and establish its priorities

especially the Council of Assembly and the new developing structures of the heart of its administration.

Blessing

May our souls stir the day with divine conspiracy,
and fill this place and every place we dream of
with rumours from the yet unmade journeys of love.

Gifts of Grace

Day 21

FAITH

Peter answered him, 'Lord, if it is you, command me to come to you on the water.'

~ Matthew 14:28 ~

Lord, I am just like Peter:

for I too am so often a turmoil of
believing and doubting,
of faith and denial.
Like Peter walking on the waves,
I step out in faith
but then I look down and panic;
I take my eyes from you
and begin to sink.

To me also you say,
'Why have you so little faith?'

Perhaps I need to learn the lesson
that Peter himself learned:
that you, Lord,
are on the inside of my believing
and that faith is not about having the strength
to hold on to you
but having the humility to be held.

Today I remember all who need to know
the strong grip of your hand upon theirs.

Readings

2 Kings 6:15–19	*The vision of faith*
Matthew 14:22–33	*The practice of faith*
Matthew 15:21–8	*The persistence of faith*
Hebrews 11:1–3	*The essence of faith*

Prayer Activity

> In the language which Jesus spoke, Aramaic, the sense of the word faith is captured in the colloquialism, 'Go for it'. In what area of your life are you seeking that sort of energy and courage? Reflect and make this into your own prayer in words that also express expectancy of some form of answer.

Prayer for the Church

Those who bring their creativity to bear on making known the Church and the Gospel, in print, film, news media, sound and website

especially the Board of Communication.

Blessing

Be upon each thing our eyes take in,
be upon each thing our ears take in,
be upon our bodies which come from earth,
be upon our souls which come from heaven,
evermore and evermore. AMEN.

(*Wee Worship Book*, Wild Goose Publications 1999, p. 35.)

Day 22

FORGIVENESS

'How often should I forgive? As many as seven times?'
Jesus said to him,
'Not seven times, but, I tell you, seventy-seven times'.

~ Matthew 18:21–2 ~

God, how many times do I have to despair and be depressed by the news?
What a terrible world!
People are abusive, aggressive, cruel and uncaring.
People spoil their surroundings, misuse things given to them,
make my life problematic and never the way I'd like it to be.

Do you ever feel like that?

Do you ever weep at the things we do to each other?
Do you ever raise your hands in disbelief at things we say and don't say?
And do you ever feel ashamed of us, despairing and depressed?

God, how many times have we failed to do your will
– seven times? Seventy-seven times?
How many times have we crucified you
with our apathy and selfishness and deliberate sin?

God, I know how hopeless many situations seem.
I know how it feels to see no way forward or out of the mess.
I know the weight of past regret and constant doubting
as to whether I am good enough for you and for the people in my life.
I know the sting of guilty tears and the discomfort of pride and greed.

Today, help us all to know you.
Help us all to find a way back to you –
a way with a future of hope and promise,
a way with new beginnings, apologies accepted and burdens laid down.

Help us all to find your peace that truly passes all understanding
and that leads to the possibility of life in all its fullness.

Readings

Psalm 25:16–22	*Relieve the troubles of my heart*
Matthew 6:7–15	*Teach us how to pray*
Luke 6:32–6	*Be merciful*
2 Corinthians 2:1–11	*Anyone whom you forgive*
James 5:13–18	*Confess your sins to one another*

Prayer Activity

Gather a few medium-sized stones or pebbles. Place them in a heap. Let them represent the weight of grievances that hold you back, grievances arising from 'unforgivable' wrongs that have been done to you. Today, take one of these in your hand; think of the incident that it represents. Consider how God has forgiven the person(s) concerned. Try to do the same as you lay the stone aside.

Prayer for the Church

Those who monitor developments in human knowledge and bring the insights of the Gospel to bear so that new discoveries might be used wisely

especially the Society, Religion and Technology Project.

Blessing

Forgiveness is your gift,
both cleansing and renewing,
to catch us when we drift,
our base desires pursuing;
and hug us back to life
and bring us to a feast
where all will celebrate
the life your love released.

(Ian Fraser, verse 1 of hymn in *CH4*, by permission.)

Day 23

HOPE

For in hope we were saved. Now hope that is seen is not hope … But if we hope for what we do not see, we wait for it with patience.

~ Romans 8:24–5 ~

Lord,
as we look around at our world today
we see people everywhere who have lost hope.

Lord, restore our hope;
remind us that our hope is in Jesus,
in his death and resurrection.

Lord, we are blind;
in every town and city
people are groping around in darkness.

Lord, help us to see the light.
May the light of hope shine out from us
that others may see and desire it for themselves.

Lord, we are impatient.
We live in a world of quick fixes;
people want it now – '24/7'.

Lord, give us patience.
Grant us excited anticipation
as we wait for the fulfilment of our hope.

Readings

Psalm 33	*The greatness and goodness of God*
Psalm 62	*Song of trust in God alone*
Matthew 12:15–21	*God's chosen servant*
Romans 5:1–11	*Results of justification*
Romans 8:18–31	*Future glory*

Prayer Activity

Sit quietly and reflect for a few moments on the deepest hopes and desires of your heart; as you think of each, share it with God and ask him to show you how to bring it to fulfilment, if it be his will.

Prayer for the Church

Those who bring Christian principles to bear on the educational curriculum and who prepare courses to help young people understand the excitement of a living faith

especially the Department of Education.

Blessing

Let there be greening,
birth from the burning,
water that blesses and air that is sweet,
health in God's garden,
hope in God's children,
regeneration that peace will complete.

(Shirley Erena Murray, from hymn 'Touch the earth lightly' from *CH4*, by permission.)

Day 24

THE CHURCH

Now you are the body of Christ and individually members of it.

~ 1 Corinthians 12:27 ~

Lord – your church a gift?
Sometimes I look round and cannot believe I'm here!
Can this really be what you meant?
My fellow Christians are so different from me.
They are full of awkward edges.
They don't always seem to have got it quite right.
Must I love them all and carry their burdens?

And what of the wider church?
Sometimes tradition seems to overtake compassion,
bigotry and intolerance take the place of acceptance,
divisions give the lie to the message of reconciliation.

Yet you have called us to be a *sign*
of the true community that God plans for the world;
and as the word of God is preached, believed and obeyed,
we are shaped into an *instrument* for bringing it to pass;
and as we share in communion at the table of Jesus Christ
we become a *foretaste* of the reconciled life in God's kingdom.

Grant that as Christ's body we may see diversity as a gift,
and so challenge a world where differences are taken as cue for conflict.
Grant that our awkward shapes may fit together
to build strong walls of a temple to your glory.
Grant that we may live in our traditions and customs in such a way
that we are continually open to the renewing of your Holy Spirit.

Readings [images of the church]

Jeremiah 31:31–3, 1 Peter 2:9–10 [people of God]; 1 Corinthians 12:12–13, Romans 12:4–8 (body of Christ); 2 Corinthians 6:14–18 (temple) Philippians 1:3–11 (koinonia, communion); John 15:1–11 (vine); Acts 20:28–35 (flock); Matthew 22:1–14 (wedding party); John 3:25–30 (bride)

Prayer Activity

Call to mind your local church. What is your immediate image of it? Rows of people in pews? A solid stone building? Re-imagine your church using some of the images above. Choose one of them, e.g. vine, bride, body, wedding party, and think of the way your church would link together, move, react, pray if that were the only possible picture of how things should be.

Prayer for the Church

Those who help us take our place in, and be enriched by, the experience and witness of the Church throughout the world

especially the Board of World Mission, Scottish Churches' World Exchange, St Colm's International House, Edinburgh, and including the special project on HIV/AIDS.

Blessing

Our faith a channel make
to give us grace. Our judging hearts now take,
and lead us into oneness for your sake.

(William Rutherford, in hymn 'Lord, can this really be?', from *CH4*, by permission.)

Day 25

JOY and LAUGHTER

Then our mouth was filled with laughter, and our tongue with shouts of joy; then it was said among the nations, 'The Lord has done great things for them'.

~ Psalm 126:2 ~

What kind of laughter have you made, God?

People laugh in disgust, to scoff,
we laugh when the tension is just too much.
Some laugh at their schemes and plans, excited by their cunning.
And we laugh in the face of criticism to show we don't take it seriously.

But it is the best medicine.

We enjoy a good laugh with family and friends.
Some things are so funny, we are amused, we can't help it.
We love to laugh after feeling low –
it lifts us up, we feel better.
Surely God, this is what you made laughter for
– excitement at good news,
– delight in company and shared experience,
– joy at the unexpected;
the kind of joy that Mary felt
as her world turned upside down that first Easter morning,
the kind of joy a baby can bring,
the kind of joy that love brings beyond pain
– joy that can't be contained, that just bursts out–
like laughter.

So today God,
may I not take myself too seriously,
may I see the funny side,
and may I make someone smile, even laugh, for your sake.
AMEN.

Readings

Genesis 18:1–15	*Abraham and Sarah*
Psalm 126	*Our mouth was filled with laughter*
Isaiah 61:1–4	*Oil of gladness instead of mourning*
John 20:1–18	*The disciples rejoiced*
2 Corinthians 7:5–16	*I am overjoyed in all our affliction*

Prayer Activity

Think about someone or something that makes you laugh or think of some good news you have recently heard. Smile to God as a prayer and give thanks for God's uplifting spirit.

Prayer for the Church

Those who enable the celebration of life and faith through the arts and help others by this means to discover their gifts and talents

especially the Netherbow Arts Centre.

Blessing

Sing to God with gladness, all creation,
sing to God the song of God's great love,
sing to God who made the heavens,
sing to God who made the loveliness of earth!
Sing to the Lord, sing Alleluia,
sing to the Lord, sing with joy!

(James Quinn, verse 1 of hymn from *CH4*, by permission.)

Day 26

THE SCRIPTURES

Thy word is a lamp to my feet and a light to my path.
~ Psalm 119:105 ~

O Lord God we thank you for the Scriptures –
its thrilling stories of high adventure,
its poetry that touches and lifts the heart,
its disturbing and challenging prophecy,
its letters of encouragement and exhortation,
its strange and wonderful visions,
and above all its telling of Jesus: the Word made flesh.
We bless you that in the Scriptures
all human life is there, and your life is there for us
to comfort and chastise and console us,
to direct us to Christ and the everlasting way.

O God, who inspired people to record
your royal law, your lively oracles,
help us not only to read our Bible
but to discern its imperishable truth,
to hear your word in its words and to be enriched in every way.

O God, we remember
all who translate the Good Book,
all who publish the Scriptures,
all who disseminate the Bible,
all who study and interpret it,
all who proclaim your Word in it.
We pray for ourselves
as we try to live by its precepts
and trust and follow the Word that is Christ. AMEN.

Readings

Isaiah 40:6–9	*The word of our God stands for ever*
Luke 24:13–27	*The risen Lord interprets the scriptures*
John 20:26–30	*Why John tells of the risen Jesus*
2 Timothy 3:14–17	*All scripture inspired by God*
Hebrews 4:12–13	*The word of God living and active*
2 Peter 1:16–21	*Men, by the Spirit, spoke from God*

Prayer Activity

Read one of the suggested passages, preferably aloud. Which verse specially touches your heart? Take it away with you today!

Prayer for the Church

Those who today, in the name of Christ's Church, will share their faith through word or action

especially in some local initiative for outreach or evangelism.

Blessing

Vine of truth, in you we flourish;
by your grace we learn and grow.
May the word of Christ among us
shape our life, your will to know.

(Ruth Duck, in hymn 'Holy wisdom, lamp of learning', from *CH4*, by permission.)

Day 27

WISDOM

The fear of the Lord is the beginning of knowledge;
fools despise wisdom and instruction.

~ Proverbs 1:7 ~

Lord, we live in a world of information:
of websites and databases,
of satellite television and video-conferencing.
Facts and figures are at our very finger tips.
Every kind of knowledge is but a moment away.

Yet, Lord, we who know so much
have so much to learn in the halls of wisdom.
The ancients, the sages and prophets
(though we might think them primitive)
are truly our masters and our mentors.
We who are overflowing with information
are summoned to that school which charges no fees
but from which we never graduate
this side of eternity.

I remember that reverence of you
is the beginning of wisdom.
I pray for all preachers, teachers, and evangelists
as they seek to introduce people
to the One who is the wellspring
and fountainhead of all wisdom and learning.

Readings

Psalm 1	*The way of life and the way of death*
Ecclesiastes 3:1–8	*A time for everything*
Matthew 7:24–9	*Hearing and doing*
1 Corinthians 2:6–10	*Wisdom is more than knowledge*
Proverbs 8:22–31	*Wisdom and creation*
Matthew 25:1–13	*The wise and the foolish*

Prayer Activity

Try this ancient way of prayer called Lectio Divina (literally 'divine reading' or 'reading with the heart'). Select a portion of scripture (a psalm is ideal) or a short extract from a devotional book. Read it slowly and meditatively. When a word or phrase strikes you, pause and go over it several times. When you have taken all you can from that word or phrase, move on. Do this again and again.

Prayer for the Church

Those who witness to the living Christ in the midst of his people, in Word and Sacrament, those who as deacons lead the Church in living out the Gospel, and those who recruit, train and support them

especially the Board of Ministry.

Blessing

Praise the Spirit, who enlightened
priests and prophets with the word;
hidden truth behind the wisdoms
which as yet know not their Lord;
by whose love and power in Jesus
God himself is seen and heard.

(David Hurd, in hymn 'Praise the Spirit in creation', in *CH4*, by permission.)

Day 28

THE SACRAMENTS

... and when he had given thanks, he broke it and said, 'This is my body ...'

~ 1 Corinthians 11:24 ~

God who reaches out for us,
how can we know you better?

There are the Scripture stories, a great read,
convincing, often moving,
making us want to believe and to follow.
There are the doctrines,
often, it's true, read from between the lines,
developed in dialogue and in prayer over centuries,
making sense of life in God,
giving us a faith we can discuss and share.

Yet, Lord, you give us more to go on.
For at times in your earthly life
you reached out and embraced us within your own life,
giving us a direct line that remains open even now.
Your very own waters of baptism drench us;
in cup and bread you put the taste of servanthood in our
    mouths.
You invite us, Take and eat;
you command us, Go and baptise.
Taking the ordinary things that sustain our lives –
word, water, wine and bread –
you renew us in mind, in body and in spirit,
and show in us before the whole world
what true community can mean.

We pray for our broken communities,
where sharing is fraught with danger;
for places of religious or ethnic conflict,
where the holy things only help determine who is the
    enemy;
when the ordinary things of life are squandered,
so that there is no water to bless,
no bread to pass, and the cup is empty.

Help us all to see the things and people around us
not as there for our disposal
but as bearers of messages from you,
sacraments to call us to abundant life.

Readings

Isaiah 25:6–10	*The feast for all peoples*
Matthew 26:26–30	*The Last Supper*
Mark 1:4–11	*The baptism of John*
John 21:9–14	*A meal with the Risen Christ*
Acts 16:11–15	*An early baptism*
1 Corinthians 11:23–34	*The words of institution of the Lord's Supper*

Prayer Activity

Take two ordinary objects, one a piece of bread or a container of water, the other quite different – a pebble, a carving, a picture, a household object. Reflect on how the bread or the water becomes sacramental, a sign taking us directly to the side of Christ. Then reflect on the other object, and ask yourself in what way it also speaks of God and conveys God's life to you.

Prayer for the Church

Those who guide and administer the details of the Church's life at national level

especially the Central Co-ordinating Committee; Personnel bodies; the Nomination Committee; committees concerned with Pensions, Investments, and Housing for those who have retired.

Blessing

Out of the open heavens
God's Spirit comes
down like a dove
in peace and power.

(Leith Fisher, in the hymn 'Out of the flowing river', from *CH4*, by permission.)

Day 29

INCARNATION

And the Word became flesh and lived among us …
full of grace and truth.

~ John 1:14 ~

When you put on flesh and we share breath,
when you put on flesh and we walk together,
when you put on flesh and we laugh and weep with you,
God,
may I recognise these as holy:
each a moment of incarnation,
where you have held me especially close,
knowing me and my needs,
giving yourself to my pain and joy,
loving me completely in my incompleteness.

God, may I linger in these moments,
touching the promise that is given
of an ever-present love
given fully and lavishly,
painstakingly,
and let that love shape my being,
holding the promise close to myself,
trusting it as fully and lavishly as it is given.

And may the world hold it too.
May my friends and family know of these moments,
my community and neighbourhood discover this promise,
and each person, no matter where they are,
know of a God who put on flesh for them.

Readings

Isaiah 53:1–9	*The Suffering Servant*
John 1:1–18	*In the beginning was the Word …*
John 14:9–14	*In the Father*
Colossians 1:15–20	*Christ the visible likeness of the invisible God*
Hebrews 1:4–14	*About the Son*
Revelation 22:12–13	*The First and the Last*

Prayer Activity

> Make a diary today of where you have discovered love present: people you have met, places you have been, conversations you have had, stories you have heard. Also consider the places and people you heard about today that seem to be without love. How can you bring God's love to them, through awareness, commitment, telling their story and putting flesh on the promises of incarnation?

Prayer for the Church

Those who guide the Church in temporal matters and see that in its dealings justice prevails

especially the Law Department.

Blessing

God bless you with careless handfuls of love.
God hold you and bend you towards the light.
God walk with you, folding love into each adventure,
and God meet you in each moment of incarnation.

THE HOLY SPIRIT

A wind from God swept over the face of the waters.

~ Genesis 1:2 ~

Spirit of God,
like a wind you swept over the earth
while it was still a formless void.
We can only imagine what it can have been like
to watch the earth take shape and form –
but you were there, before the beginning of time
you were with God and you were God.

Spirit of God,
you are our helper, enabler, comforter,
supporting us in times of trouble and distress.
In our world today, you interpret for us the Word
and inspire your people,
prompting us to pray for others
and leading us into community.

As at Pentecost, break down the barriers
in us and around us in the world.
We pray that you would continue to be with us
throughout our lifelong journey with Christ;
may we always be aware of you
and thankful for you.

Readings

Psalm 51	*A prayer of forgiveness*
Matthew 1:18–25	*A story of Jesus birth*
Luke 2:25–35	*Simeon blesses Jesus*
Luke 11:1–13	*The Lord's Prayer*
Acts 2:1–12	*Pentecost*
Acts 7:54–60; 8:1–2	*The stoning of Stephen*

Prayer Activity

Find a quiet space and sit down comfortably. As you sit become aware of your breathing, slowly in and out. The Holy Spirit is often called the Breath of God; imagine as you breathe in that you are breathing in God's Holy Spirit. As you breathe in and out allow the spirit/breath to flow through you and give you peace and comfort. Try to do this for several minutes, as you are able.

Prayer for the Church

Those who lead worship, those who seek new words and melodies, those who wrestle with the life of prayer, and those who prepare resources to help them

especially the Panel on Worship.

Blessing

Holy Spirit, gift bestower, breathe into our hearts today.
Flowing water, dove that hovers, Holy Spirit, guide our way.
Love inspirer, joy releaser, Spirit, take our fears away.
Reconciler, peace restorer, move among us while we pray.

(Verse 1 of hymn from *CH4*; author being sought.)

Day 31

ETERNAL LIFE

Even though our outer nature is wasting away, our inner nature is being renewed day by day.

~ 2 Corinthians 4:16 ~

We can't imagine a life without the body;
how can there be life without a body,
without senses, movement, people around us?
Yet how many of the really important things happen
when the body is still?
– having an imaginary, loving conversation
with someone who is absent, or who has died;
– taking a decision which changes your life
or the life of others around you;
– letting someone do something for you
that you are incapable of doing for yourself,
so that they grow in the service of God.

God beside us, God within us,
God before us, God beneath us,
God surrounding us,
do you need us to have hands before you can give us gifts?
a brow before you can bless us?
a stomach before you can nourish us?
Sometimes we feel so confined by our earthly tent.
We groan with frustration.
Painful limbs or painfilled memories stop our tracks,
and we long for the 'house not made with hands'.

For you, God, there is no frontier between life and death.
Christ is our passport, our courier, our border crossing.
For you the living and the dead are one,
the cloud of witnesses as real as the day,
waiting to welcome us to your side.

Readings

Psalm 103:8–18	*As for mortals, their days are like grass*
Ecclesiastes 3:9–15	*A sense of past and future*
John 14:1–7	*'I am the way, the truth, and the life'*
2 Corinthians 4:13–18	*Our outer and our inner nature*
2 Corinthians 5:1–11	*A house not made with hands*

Prayer Activity

Select one of the saints or others commemorated in the 'On this day' feature in the Church of Scotland's website or from another version of the Christian Calendar. Read what it says about the person and sit with them in your imagination until you feel he/she is as real to you as the next person you will meet. Reflect on how you and he/she are equally real to God.

Prayer for the Church

Readers, elders and local church leaders, and those who provide training for them and for all Christian people as they seek to grow in faith, prayer and service

especially the Board of Parish Education.

Blessing

Since I am coming to that holy room
where with the choir of saints for evermore
I shall be made thy music;
as I come I tune the instrument here at the door,
and what I must do then, think here before.

(George Herbert in *Common Order*, p. 5.)

DAILY BIBLE READINGS

The asterisk denotes the following Sunday's readings and psalm prescribed in the Revised Common Lectionary (and as in* Common Order*), or the readings set for special festivals.*

These readings come from the Australian publication, *With Love to the* World, a daily Bible reading guide used throughout Australia and increasingly world-wide. It contains short notes on each passage by writers who are knowledgeable about the biblical background. It is published quarterly. Copies can be ordered through the Church of Scotland's Office for Worship (see Acknowledgments page). The likely annual subscription would be under £10.

NOVEMBER 2004

Mon	22	Romans 13:11–14*
Tue	23	Amos 5:14–22
Wed	24	Matthew 24:1–14
Thu	25	Matthew 24:36–44*
Fri	26	Matthew 24:45–51
Sat	27	Isaiah 2:1–8*
Sun	28	Psalm 122*
Mon	29	Romans 15:4–13*
Tue	30	2 Kings 1:2–17

DECEMBER

Wed	1	Matthew 3:1–12*
Thu	2	John 8:31–47
Fri	3	John 8:48–58
Sat	4	Isaiah 11:1–10*
Sun	5	Psalm 72:1–19 (1–7, 18–19*)
Mon	6	Matthew 11:2–11*
Tue	7	1 Thessalonians 2:13–20
Wed	8	Job 1:6–28
Thu	9	James 5:7–11 (7–10*)
Fri	10	Revelation 2:8–11
Sat	11	Isaiah 35:1–10*
Sun	12	Psalm 146:5–10*

Mon	13	Matthew 1:1–17
Tue	14	Matthew 1:18–25*
Wed	15	Matthew 1:26–38
Thu	16	Romans 1:1–7*
Fri	17	Isaiah 7:1–9
Sat	18	Isaiah 7:10–16*
Sun	19	Psalm 80:1–7, 17–19*
Mon	20	Isaiah 63:7–9*
Tue	21	Psalm 148*
Wed	22	Titus 2:11–14 (*Christmas Eve)
Thu	23	Hebrews 2:10–18*
Fri	24	Luke 2:1–7
Sat	25	Luke 2:8–14 (1–20* Christmas Day)
Sun	26	Matthew 2:13–23*
Mon	27	Psalm 96 (*Christmas Day)
Tue	28	Luke 2:15–21
Wed	29	Jeremiah 31:7–14*
Thu	30	John 1:10–18*
Fri	31	Ephesians 1:3–14*

JANUARY 2005

Sat	1	Matthew 9:14–17 (*New Year)
Sun	2	Psalm 147:12–20*
Mon	3	Matthew 3:13–17*
Tue	4	Acts 10:34–43*
Wed	5	Colossians 1:24 – 2:5
Thu	6	Ephesians3:1–12 (*Epiphany)
Fri	7	Isaiah 49:8–16a
Sat	8	Isaiah 42:1–9*
Sun	9	Psalm 29*
Mon	10	Revelation 22:1–5
Tue	11	John 1:29–42*
Wed	12	1 John 2:18–25
Thu	13	1 Corinthians 1:1–9*
Fri	14	2 Peter 1:1–11
Sat	15	Isaiah 49:1–7*
Sun	16	Psalm 40:1–11*

Mon	17	Matthew 4:12–17
Tue	18	Matthew 4:18–25 (12–23*)
Wed	19	1 Corinthians 1:10–18*
Thu	20	Amos 3:1–8
Fri	21	Isaiah 8:18–22
Sat	22	Isaiah 9:1–4*
Sun	23	Psalm 27:1–9 (1, 4–9*)
Mon	24	Matthew 5:1–12*
Tue	25	1 Corinthians 1:18–31*
Wed	26	1 Corinthians 4:8–13
Thu	27	Zephaniah 2:3; 3:11–13
Fri	28	Psalm 37:1–11
Sat	29	Micah 6:1–8*
Sun	30	Psalm 15*
Mon	31	Isaiah 58:1–9a

FEBRUARY

Tue	1	1 Corinthians 2:1–12
Wed	2	Matthew 5:13–20
Thu	3	Matthew 17:1–9*
Fri	4	2 Peter 1:16–21*
Sat	5	Exodus 24:12–18*
Sun	6	Psalm 2*
Mon	7	Romans 5:12–19*
Tue	8	Matthew 6:1–6, 16–21 (*Ash Wed)
Wed	9	1 Corinthians 9:24–7
Thu	10	Matthew 4:1–11*
Fri	11	Genesis 2:4–7, 15–20a
Sat	12	Genesis 2:20b – 3:7 (2:15–17; 3:1–7*)
Sun	13	Psalm 32*
Mon	14	Matthew 20:17–28
Tue	15	John 3:1–17*
Wed	16	Acts 8:1–13
Thu	17	Romans 4:1–5, 13–17*
Fri	18	James 2:20–6
Sat	19	Genesis 12:1–9 (1–4a*)
Sun	20	Psalm 121*

Mon 21 Romans 5:1–11*
Tue 22 John 4:5–15 (5–42*)
Wed 23 John 4:16–26
Thu 24 John 4:27–42
Fri 25 Isaiah 42:14–21
Sat 26 Exodus 17:1–7*
Sun 27 Psalm 95*

Mon 28 John 9:1–12

MARCH

Tue 1 John 9:13–34 (1–41*)
Wed 2 John 9:35–41
Thu 3 Ephesians 5:8–14*
Fri 4 John 8:12–20
Sat 5 1 Samuel 16:1–13*
Sun 6 Psalm 23*

Mon 7 John 11:1–16 (1–45*)
Tue 8 John 11:17–32
Wed 9 John 11:33–45
Thu 10 Psalm 116:1–9
Fri 11 Romans 8:6–11*
Sat 12 Ezekiel 37:1–14*
Sun 13 Psalm 130*

Mon 14 Isaiah 50:4–9a*
Tue 15 Philippians 2:5–11*
Wed 16 Matthew 21:1–11 (*Palm Sunday)
Thu 17 Matthew 26:1–5, 14–16 (26:14–27:66*)
Fri 18 Matthew 26:31–46
Sat 19 Matthew 26:47–68
Sun 20 Psalm 31:9–16*

Mon 21 Colossians 3:1–4*
Tue 22 Matthew 26:69 – 27:10
Wed 23 Matthew 27:11–31
Thu 24 1 Corinthians 11:23–6 (*Maundy Thurs)
Fri 25 Matthew 27:32–54
Sat 26 Psalm 118:1–2, 14–24*
Sun 27 Matthew 28:1–10*

Mon	28	John 20:10–18
Tue	29	John 20:19–31*
Wed	30	Matthew 28:11–20
Thu	31	Isaiah 43:1–12

APRIL

Fri	1	1 Peter 1:3–9*
Sat	2	Acts 2:14a, 24–32*
Sun	3	Psalm 16*
Mon	4	Acts 2:14a, 36–41*
Tue	5	Ezekiel 12:21–8
Wed	6	1 Peter 1:17–23*
Thu	7	2 Peter 3:14–18
Fri	8	Daniel 3:13–35
Sat	9	Luke 24:13–35*
Sun	10	Psalm 116:1–4, 12–19*
Mon	11	Isaiah 33:10–16
Tue	12	Acts 2:42–47*
Wed	13	Nehemiah 9:6–15
Thu	14	1 Peter 2:19–25*
Fri	15	Hebrews 13:17–21
Sat	16	John 10:1–10*
Sun	17	Psalm 23
Mon	18	Acts 6:1–7
Tue	19	Acts 7:55–60*
Wed	20	1 Peter 2:2–10*
Thu	21	Isaiah 28:9–17
Fri	22	John 14:1–14*
Sat	23	Isaiah 8:11–20
Sun	24	Psalm 31:1–5, 15–16*
Mon	25	Jeremiah 29:1, 4–13
Tue	26	Acts 8:5–17
Wed	27	Acts 17:22–31*
Thu	28	1 Peter 3:13–22*
Fri	29	John 14:15–21*
Sat	30	Isaiah 41:17–20

MAY

Sun	1	Psalm 66:8–20*
Mon	2	John 17:1–11*
Tue	3	1 Peter 4:12–14, 5:6–11*
Wed	4	2 Corinthians 11:19–31
Thu	5	Luke 24:44–52 (*Ascension)
Fri	6	Acts 1:1–5
Sat	7	Acts 1:6–14*
Sun	8	Psalm 68:1–10, 32–5*
Mon	9	John 7:37–9 (*alternate)
Tue	10	John 20:19–23*
Wed	11	Acts 2:1–11 (1–21*)
Thu	12	Acts 2:12–21
Fri	13	1 Corinthians 12:3b–13*
Sat	14	Numbers 11:24–30 (*alternate)
Sun	15	Psalm 104:24–35 (24–34, 35b*)
Mon	16	Deuteronomy 4:32–40
Tue	17	Numbers 6:22–7
Wed	18	2 Corinthians 13:11–13*
Thu	19	Matthew 28:16–20*
Fri	20	Genesis 1:1–25 (1:1–2:4a*)
Sat	21	Genesis 1:26–2:4a
Sun	22	Psalm 8*
Mon	23	Genesis 6:9–7:1 (6:9–22, 7:24, 8:14–19*)
Tue	24	Genesis 7:24, 8:14–22
Wed	25	Psalm 46*
Thu	26	Romans 1:1–17 (1:16–17, 3:22b–28 (29–31)*)
Fri	27	Romans 3:21–31
Sat	28	Matthew 7:21–9*
Sun	29	Matthew 8:5–13
Mon	30	Matthew 9:1–13 (9–13, 18–26*)
Tue	31	Matthew 9:18–26

JUNE

Wed	1	Genesis 12:1–9*
Thu	2	Genesis 12:10–13:1

Fri	3	Romans 4:1–12
Sat	4	Romans 4:13–25*
Sun	5	Psalm 33 (1–12*)
Mon	6	Romans 5:1–11 (1–8*)
Tue	7	Romans 5:12–14, 18–21
Wed	8	Matthew 9:35–10:8*
Thu	9	Matthew 10:9–23
Fri	10	Genesis 16:1–15
Sat	11	Genesis 18:1–15*
Sun	12	Psalm 116:1–2, 12–19*
Mon	13	Genesis 21:1–7
Tue	14	Genesis 21:8–21*
Wed	15	Matthew 10:24–31 (24–39*)
Thu	16	Matthew 10:32–9
Fri	17	Romans 6:1– 4 (1b–11*)
Sat	18	Romans 6:5–11
Sun	19	Psalm 86:1–17 (1–10, 16–17*)
Mon	20	Genesis 22:1–19 (1–14*)
Tue	21	Genesis 23:1–20
Wed	22	Romans 6:12–19 (12–23*)
Thu	23	Romans 6:20–3
Fri	24	Matthew 10:40–2*
Sat	25	Matthew 11:1–15
Sun	26	Psalm 13*
Mon	27	Matthew 11:16–24 (16–19, 25–30*)
Tue	28	Matthew 11:25–30
Wed	29	Genesis 24:34–49 (34–8, 42–9, 58–67*)
Thu	30	Genesis 24:50–67

JULY

Fri	1	Song of Solomon 2:8–13* (or Psalm 45:10–17*)
Sat	2	Romans 7:1–13 (15–25a*)
Sun	3	Romans 7:14–25a
Mon	4	Romans 7:25b–8:8 (8:1–11*)
Tue	5	Romans 8:9–11
Wed	6	Matthew 13:1–9, 18–23*

Thu	7	Matthew 13:10–17
Fri	8	Genesis 25:19–34*
Sat	9	Genesis 26:34–5, 27:5–10, 30–8
Sun	10	Psalm 119:105–12* or Psalm 119:1–8*
Mon	11	Genesis 27:41–28:5
Tue	12	Genesis 28:10–22 (10–19a*)
Wed	13	Romans 8:12–17 (12–25*)
Thu	14	Romans 8:18–25
Fri	15	Matthew 13:24–30 (24–30, 36–43*)
Sat	16	Matthew 13:36–43
Sun	17	Psalm 139:1–12, 23–4*
Mon	18	Matthew 13:31–5, 44–52 (31–3, 44–52*)
Tue	19	Matthew 13:53–8
Wed	20	Genesis 29:1–14
Thu	21	Genesis 29:15–32, 30:22–4 (29:15–28*)
Fri	22	Romans 8:26–30 (26–39*)
Sat	23	Romans 8:31–9
Sun	24	Psalm 105:1–11, 45b* or Psalm 128*
Mon	25	Romans 9:1–13 (1–5*)
Tue	26	Romans 9:14–24, 30–2
Wed	27	Genesis 32:9–12, 22–31 (22–31*)
Thu	28	Genesis 33:1–4, 35:1, 5–15
Fri	29	Matthew 14:1–12
Sat	30	Matthew 14:13–21*
Sun	31	Psalm 17:1–15 (1–7, 15*)

AUGUST

Mon	1	Matthew 14:22–36 (22–33*)
Tue	2	Matthew 15:1–9
Wed	3	Genesis 37:1–4, 12–28*
Thu	4	Genesis 41:14–16, 29–30, 33–6, 39–43
Fri	5	Romans 10:1–13 (5–15*)
Sat	6	Romans 10:14–21
Sun	7	Psalm 105:1–6, 16–22, 45b*

Mon	8	Romans 11:1–2a, 11–24 (1–2a, 29–32*)
Tue	9	Romans 11:25–36
Wed	10	Genesis 41:46–9, 53–4; 42:1–8
Thu	11	Genesis 45:1–15*
Fri	12	Matthew 15:7–20 (10–20, 21–8*)
Sat	13	Matthew 15:21–31
Sun	14	Psalm 133*

Mon	15	Matthew 16:1–12
Tue	16	Matthew 16:13–20*
Wed	17	Genesis 45:16–46:5
Thu	18	Genesis 50:1–3, 15–26
Fri	19	Exodus 1:8–2:10*
Sat	20	Romans 12:1–8*
Sun	21	Psalm 124*

Mon	22	Romans 12:9–21*
Tue	23	Romans 13:1–7
Wed	24	Exodus 2:11–25
Thu	25	Exodus 3:1–15*
Fri	26	Matthew 16:21–8*
Sat	27	Matthew 17:1–2, 14–22
Sun	28	Psalm 105:1–6, 23–6, 45c*

Mon	29	Matthew 18:1–9
Tue	30	Matthew 18:10–20 (15–20*)
Wed	31	Romans 13:8–14*

SEPTEMBER

Thu	1	Exodus 4:1–5, 10–17, 27–31
Fri	2	Exodus 5:1–9
Sat	3	Exodus 11:10–12:14 (12:1–14*)
Sun	4	Psalm 149*

Mon	5	Exodus 13:17–14:14
Tue	6	Exodus 14:19–31*
Wed	7	Exodus 15:1b–11, 20–1
Thu	8	Romans 14:1–12*
Fri	9	Romans 15:1–13
Sat	10	Matthew 18:21–35*
Sun	11	Psalm 114*

Mon	12	Matthew 19:13–30
Tue	13	Matthew 20:1–16*
Wed	14	Matthew 20:17–34
Thu	15	Exodus 15:22–16:15 (16:2–15*)
Fri	16	Philippians 1:1–20
Sat	17	Philippians 1:21–30*
Sun	18	Psalm 107:1–9*
Mon	19	Philippians 2:1–11 (1–13*)
Tue	20	Philippians 2:12–3:1a
Wed	21	Matthew 21:12–22
Thu	22	Matthew 21:23–32*
Fri	23	Exodus 16:16–35
Sat	24	Exodus 17:1–13 (1–7*)
Sun	25	Psalm 78:1–4, 12–16*
Mon	26	Exodus 18:1, 10–27
Tue	27	Exodus 19:1–25
Wed	28	Exodus 20:1–4, 7–9, 12–20*
Thu	29	Matthew 21:33–46*
Fri	30	Philippians 3:1b–11 (4b–14*)

OCTOBER

Sat	1	Philippians 3:12–21
Sun	2	Psalm 19*
Mon	3	Philippians 4:1–9*
Tue	4	Philippians 4:10–23
Wed	5	Matthew 22:1–14*
Thu	6	Exodus 30:22–31:11
Fri	7	Exodus 32:1–14*
Sat	8	Exodus 32:15–35
Sun	9	Psalm 106:1–6, 19–23, 43–8 (1–6, 19–23*)
Mon	10	Exodus 33:1–11
Tue	11	Exodus 33:12–23*
Wed	12	Exodus 34:1–9, 29–35
Thu	13	1 Thessalonians 1:1–10*
Fri	14	Matthew 22:15–22*
Sat	15	Matthew 22:23–33
Sun	16	Psalm 99*

Mon	17	Matthew 22:34–46*
Tue	18	1 Thessalonians 2:1–8*
Wed	19	Exodus 40:1–16, 34–8
Thu	20	Deuteronomy 33:44–52
Fri	21	Deuteronomy 34:1–12*
Sat	22	Psalm 90:1–12 (1–6, 13–17*)
Sun	23	Psalm 90:13–17
Mon	24	Joshua 1:1–3, 2:1–14
Tue	25	Joshua 3:1–17 (7–17*)
Wed	26	1 Thessalonians 2:9–16 (9–13*)
Thu	27	Matthew 23:1–12*
Fri	28	Matthew 5:1–12 (*All Saints)
Sat	29	Revelation 7:9–17 (*All Saints)
Sun	30	Psalm 34:1–22 (1–10, 22* All Saints)
Mon	31	Matthew 24:32–45

NOVEMBER

Tue	1	Matthew 25:1–13*
Wed	2	1 Thessalonians 2:17–3:13
Thu	3	1 Thessalonians 4:1–18 (13–18*)
Fri	4	Joshua 6:1–5, 15–16, 20–5
Sat	5	Joshua 24:1–3a, 14–31 (1–3a, 14–25*)
Sun	6	Psalm 96*
Mon	7	Judges 2:7–23
Tue	8	Judges 4:1–9a, 14–23 (1–7*)
Wed	9	Psalm 123*
Thu	10	1 Thessalonians 5:1–11*
Fri	11	1 Thessalonians 5:12–28
Sat	12	Matthew 25:14–30*
Sun	13	Zephaniah 1:7, 12–18
Mon	14	Matthew 25:31–40 (31–46*)
Tue	15	Matthew 25:41–6
Wed	16	Ezekiel 34:1–16 (11–16, 20–4*)
Thu	17	Ezekiel 34:17–31
Fri	18	Psalm 98
Sat	19	Ephesians 1:15–23*
Sun	20	Psalm 100*

SERVING OVERSEAS WITH THE CHURCH OF SCOTLAND

Day 1 MALAWI: Andy and Felicity Gaston with Katy and Daniel

Day 2 MALAWI: Helen Scott, Bruce Ritchie

Day 3 ZAMBIA: Colin Johnston, Jane Petty, Georgina and Brian Payne, Marlene Wilkinson

Day 4 KENYA: Elaine McKinnon, Alison Wilkinson

Day 5 SOUTH AFRICA: Graham and Sandra Duncan

Day 6 NEPAL: Marianne Karsgaard, Christine Stone

Day 7 SRI LANKA: John and Patricia Purves

Day 8 TRINIDAD: new appointment awaited

Day 9 CENTRAL ASIA: Alastair and Mary Morrice

Day 10 LEBANON: David Kerry

Day 11 THAILAND: Mike and Jane Fucella with Rachel and Aylie

Day 12 ISRAEL AND PALESTINE: Clarence and Joan Musgrave

Day 13 ISRAEL AND PALESTINE: Chris and Sue Mottershead, Karen Anderson

Day 14 ISRAEL AND PALESTINE: Gwen and Mark Thompson; Fred and Diana Hibbert

Day 15 JAMAICA: Margaret Fowler

Day 16 JAMAICA: Roy and Jane Dodman

Day 17 BERMUDA: Alan and Elizabeth Garrity

Day 18 BAHAMAS: John and Jillian Fraser with Crystal and Natalie (Freeport); Alastair and Nina Gray (Nassau)

Day 19 TURIN: Rob and Anne Mackenzie with Alyssa

Day 20 ROTTERDAM: Robert and Lesley-Ann Calvert with Simeon, Zoe, Benjamin and Daniel

Day 21 ROME: William and Jean McCulloch with Jennifer

Day 22 AMSTERDAM: John and Gillian Cowie with Matthew, Sarah and Ruth

Day 23 BANGLADESH: Gillian Rose, Andrew and Rosemary Symonds, James Pender

Day 24 LAUSANNE: new appointment awaited

Day 25 GIBRALTAR: Stewart and Lara Lamont
COSTA DEL SOL: new appointment awaited

Day 26 GENEVA: Paraic Reamonn, Ian and Roberta Manson with Andrew, Robert and David

Day 27 BUDAPEST: Ken and Jayne MacKenzie with Mairi, Catriona, Ruaridh and Kirsty, Bertalan and Elizabeth Tamas

Day 28 BRUSSELS: Matthew Ross; Andrew Gardner

Day 29 MALTA: David and Jackie Morris

Day 30 PARIS: Bill and Esther Reid

Day 31 LISBON: new appointment awaited

RESOURCES

Several Boards and Committees of the Church of Scotland provide regular up-to-date information about their activities. See below for contact details.

The Board of World Mission

(See p. 81 for a list of those serving overseas with the Church of Scotland.) Information on World Mission matters is available in *Update* from info@world-mission.org, where details of personnel and locations are given. There is also *Insight*, a quarterly publication, subscription £3.50 per annum, which is available on application; tel. 0131 225 5722. The website address is www.world-mission.org.

The Board of Parish Education

The website address is www.parisheducation.org.uk. The Board's address is 21 Young Street, Edinburgh EH2 4HU and the telephone 0131–260 3110.

The Church of Scotland Guild

A Newsletter is produced three times per annum, available from the Guild Office, tel. 0131-225 5722. The Guild also has a website at www.cos-guild.org.uk.

The Board of National Mission

NM News, published regularly, can be ordered from the Board: 0131–225 5722.

The Board of Social Responsibility

See the *Circle of Care* newsletter available from the Board, tel. 0131–657 2000. There is also a prayer letter. The website is www.socialresponsibility.org.uk. The Board's address is Charis House, 47 Milton Road East, Edinburgh EH15 2SR and the email: info@charis.org.uk.

With the exception of the Boards of Parish Education and Social Responsibility, the address to use is Church of Scotland, 121 George Street, Edinburgh EH2 4YN.

ACKNOWLEDGEMENTS

Scriptural quotations, unless otherwise stated, are from the *New Revised Standard Version Bible*, © 1989 Division of Christian Education of the National Council of the Churches of Christ in the United States of America, published by Oxford University Press.

The blessings at the conclusion of each day, whose sources are given, are reproduced by permission. Those unsourced are original to this publication.

The list of Daily Bible Readings is from *With Love to the World* and is reproduced by kind permission of the *With Love to the World* Committee.

Pray Now 2005 was prepared by members of the Panel on Worship's Prayer and Devotion Committee: James Campbell, Douglas Galbraith, Roderick Hamilton, Douglas Lamb, Ian Murphy, Lyn Peden, Gayle Taylor (Convener) and Jenny Williams.

For further information about *Pray Now* and other publications from the Panel on Worship, contact:

PANEL ON WORSHIP
Church of Scotland
121 George Street
Edinburgh EH2 4YN
Tel: 0131 225 5722
Fax: 0131 220 3113
e-mail: swilson@cofscotland.org.uk